SIXTY STORIES

DONALD BARTHELME published seventeen books, including four novels and a prize-winning children's book. He was a longtime contributor to *The New Yorker*, winner of a National Book Award, a director of PEN and the Authors Guild, and a member of the American Academy and Institute of Arts and Letters. He died in July of 1989.

DAVID GATES is the author of three acclaimed works of fiction, *Jernigan*, *Preston Falls*, and *The Wonders of the Invisible World*. He is a book critic at *Newsweek*.

By Donald Barthelme

Come Back, Dr. Caligari
Snow White
Unspeakable Practices, Unnatural Acts
City Life
Sadness
Guilty Pleasures
The Dead Father
Amateurs
Great Days
Sixty Stories
Overnight to Many Distant Cities
Paradise
Forty Stories
The King
The Teachings of Don B.
Not-Knowing

FOR CHILDREN
The Slightly Irregular Fire Engine

Acclaim for *Sixty Stories*

"Donald Barthelme may have influenced the short story in his time as much as Hemingway and O'Hara did in theirs. *Sixty Stories* is a *Whole Earth Catalogue* of life in our time."

—Anatole Broyard, *The New York Times*

"Barthelme has probably done more than any other single American writer to redefine our notion of narrative arts." —*San Diego Union*

"His is an unerringly accurate reflection of what life was really like from 1960 to 1980. If any contemporary writing survives the next century, Barthelme's prickly, hilarious stories will be there." —*People*

"If you read straight through these stories you're bound to be struck by the volume's cohesiveness. Donald Barthelme's writing is from the outset firm and sure, entirely his own. He experiments as freely nowadays as he did when younger, and his experiments reveal a rare exuberance, an unfailingly joy in words and possibilities.

—Anne Tyler, *The Detroit News*

"Barthelme can focus our feeling into a bright point that can raise a blister. These sixty stories show him inventing at full pitch."

—Guy Davenport, *The Washington Post*

"This book reinforces our faith in what talent can do generally. For the man is one of those whose pioneering leaves others looking puny. . . . The last such city-lover to dabble in so many voices and points of view was no American but James Joyce, and to find such an ironic virtuoso in our own literature is a blessed discovery." —*The Boston Phoenix*

DONALD BARTHELME

Sixty Stories

Introduction by
DAVID GATES

PENGUIN BOOKS

PENGUIN BOOKS
Published by the Penguin Group
Penguin Group (USA) Inc., 375 Hudson Street, New York, New York 10014, U.S.A.
Penguin Group (Canada), 90 Eglinton Avenue East, Suite 700, Toronto,
Ontario, Canada M4P 2Y3 (a division of Pearson Penguin Canada Inc.)
Penguin Books Ltd, 80 Strand, London WC2R 0RL, England
Penguin Ireland, 25 St Stephen's Green, Dublin 2, Ireland (a division of Penguin Books Ltd)
Penguin Group (Australia), 250 Camberwell Road, Camberwell,
Victoria 3124, Australia (a division of Pearson Australia Group Pty Ltd)
Penguin Books India Pvt Ltd, 11 Community Centre, Panchsheel Park,
New Delhi - 110 017, India
Penguin Group (NZ), 67 Apollo Drive, Mairangi Bay,
Auckland 1311, New Zealand (a division of Pearson New Zealand Ltd)
Penguin Books (South Africa) (Pty) Ltd, 24 Sturdee Avenue,
Rosebank, Johannesburg 2196, South Africa

Penguin Books Ltd, Registered Offices: 80 Strand, London WC2R 0RL, England

First published in the United States of America by G. P. Putnam's Sons 1982
Published in Penguin Books 1993
This edition with an introduction by David Gates published 2003

The author is grateful to Little, Brown and Company for permission to reprint the stories from *Come Back, Dr. Caligari* and to Farrar, Straus & Giroux, Inc., for permission to reprint the stories from *Unspeakable Practices, Unnatural Acts; City Life; Sadness; Guilty Pleasures; The Dead Father; Amateurs;* and *Great Days.* "Aria," "How I Write My Songs," "The Emperor," "Thailand," "Heroes," "Bishop," and "Grandmother's House" appeared originally in *The New Yorker.* The author is grateful to *The New Yorker* for permission to reprint "The Farewell." The author also wishes to thank *Esquire* for permission to reprint "The Emerald" and *Fiction for* permission to reprint "The Farewell."

ISBN 978-0-14-243739-1
CIP data available

Printed in the United States of America
Set in Adobe Sabon

Contents

For explanatory notes on the text, please visit www.penguinclassics.com/sixtystories

Introduction

Donald Barthelme was still alive when this volume was first published back in 1981, and he himself signed off on its modest, no-spin title. I always wondered why, since title-giving was one of his great knacks. He'd called the original books in which these stories appeared *Sadness* or *Great Days* or *Come Back, Dr. Caligari* or *Unspeakable Practices, Unnatural Acts*, and the titles of individual stories practically raise an index finger and give you the kitchy-coo: "I Bought a Little City," "Our Work and Why We Do It," "The Falling Dog," "See the Moon." Even the one-worders—"Paraguay," "Margins," "Aria"—bristle (to use one of those words Bartheleme put his brand on) with strangeness. So why settle for *Sixty Stories*? Maybe he despaired of coming up with any one title that could overarch such a various landscape, though that had never stopped him before. Or maybe, like the narrator in "I Bought a Little City," he "didn't want to be too imaginative." He might have figured sixty was a good round number—it would have been like him to make a little game of caring about good round numbers—and then picked something unpretentious and reasonably euphonious to go with it. Sixty Texts? Sixty Fictions? Not just intolerable, but unpronounceable.

But about that word "stories." Obviously Barthelme's idea of a story subverts the still-standard Chekhovian template: modest deeds of modest people leading up to a modest epiphany. He wickedly characterized such pieces in a ready-to-rumble 1964 essay as "constructed mousetrap-like to supply, at the finish, a tiny insight typically having to do with innocence violated." The parables of Kafka, the pastiches of S.J. Perelman, the monologues of Samuel Beckett, the swashbuckling absurdities of Rafael Sabatini, fairy tales, films, comic books—all these contributed as much to his sense of what a story might be as the exquisite contraptions of *Dubliners* or *In Our Time*. In later years, he could better afford to praise traditional or neotraditional fiction: he admired Updike and Cheever, Ann Beattie and Raymond Carver. But his own work continued to skitter away from any genre that seemed to spread its arms in suffocating welcome—including so-called "metafiction," the genre to which critics most often accused him of belonging. He protested against this, and pointed out that only rarely—as in *Snow White*'s mid-novel questionnaire—did he explicitly make an issue of his fiction's very fictiveness. Still, especially in such knockoffs of nineteenth-century storytelling as "Views of My Father Weeping" and "The Dolt," he seems to savor conventional narrative for its quaintness rather than for any possibility that we might drift slackjawed into a state of suspended disbelief. For Barthelme, plots and characters aren't fiction's *raison d'etre*, but good old tropes it might be fun to trot out again. More than once he described his pieces as "slumgullions": another word with the Barthelme brand, not merely pleasurable to the ear and the eye, but dead accurate. His stories are rich, dense, flavorsome throwings-together of this, that, and the other thing, concocted for the inextricable purposes of pleasure and sustenance.

Still, once he'd discovered and perfected what we think of as the Barthelme Story—"The Indian Uprising," say, which slumgullionizes the Old West, 1960s urban alienation, *Death in Venice*, and God knows what-all—he got too restless to keep cranking out the product. As the narrator of "I Bought a Little City" says: "I thought, What a nice little city, it suits me fine. It suited me fine so I started to change it." He went on to devise stories that are all dialogue ("Morning"), stories that are quasi-essays ("On Angels"), quasi-parables ("A City of Churches"), quasi-parodies ("How I Write My Songs") or quasi-legends ("The Emperor"), stories that appropriate large chunks of "found" material ("Paraguay"), stories that revert for a change to straight old-school narrative ("Bishop"), stories within stories ("The Dolt"), stories that seem to be pure freestyle riffing ("Aria"). They suited him fine. There was just one problem: terminally well-read as he was, Barthelme knew that all these forms had already been done to death. This is part of their charm for us: knowing that he knows that we know he knows it. But a writer as ambitious as Barthelme couldn't stay in any of these outmoded modes for long. So then what?

Barthelme could probably have been happy among the High Modernists: marching shoulder-to-shoulder in the vanguard with Joyce and Woolf, Eliot and Pound, making it new. Kicking over the played-out paradigms, twisting linear narrative into a Möbius strip, making the haunt and main region of his song the consciousness of his consciousness of his consciousness, cutting up Baudelaire, Wagner, Jacobean drama, and contemporary pop songs and shoring the fragments against his ruins, building Homeric/Dantean epics out of blocks of text carved from Confucius and John Adams. From *The Waste Land* to Duchamp's ready-mades—and on through *Naked Lunch* and "The Adventures of Grandmaster Flash on the Wheels of Steel"—the twentieth century's characteristic artistic procedure was (pick your term) collage, appropriation, assemblage, bricolage, or sampling. (Here's an exchange from Barthelme's "The Genius," in this book's companion volume, *Forty Stories*: "Q: What do you consider the most important tool of genius today? A: Rubber cement.") This cut-and-paste, recombinatory method of making it new, of course, implied that there *was* nothing new, though the modernists didn't go out of their way to advertise that. The hell of it was, by the time Barthelme came along, even making it new was getting old. Among the works he samples—along with *Hamlet*, Wittgenstein's *Tractatus* and Muddy Waters's "Mannish Boy"—is *The Waste Land* itself.

For Barthelme, the question of what to do after modernism had already done it all wasn't mere intellectual-careerist handwringing; it was also a personal agon. His father was a party-line modern architect, an admirer of Mies van der Rohe, Frank

Lloyd Wright and Le Corbusier. "We were enveloped in Modernism," Barthelme said in a 1981 interview with J.D. O'Hara. "The house we lived in, which he'd designed, was Modern and the furniture was Modern and the pictures were Modern and the books were Modern." Since this house was in Houston, Texas, Barthelme also grew up enveloped in the energetically subversive Americana that such expatriate modernists as Pound and Eliot approved of on principle—think of Pound's persona as the Americodger Old Ez—and recoiled from on instinct. He told O'Hara about listening to the radio and hearing Bob Wills and his Texas Playboys, whose music was a high-spirited collage of country, jazz, blues, Mexican, and Bing Crosby pop. In the city's black jazz clubs, he heard such visiting musicians as Erskine Hawkins and Lionel Hampton rework pop songs into fresh, vernacular-modernist works by improvising on their underlying structures. "You'd hear some of these guys take a tired old tune like 'Who's Sorry Now?' and do the most incredible things with it, make it beautiful, literally make it new," he recalled. "The interest and the drama were in the formal manipulation of the rather slight material. And they were heroic figures, you know, very romantic." He may have witnessed such cutting contests as the one evoked in his story "The King of Jazz," in which the master trombonist Hokie Mokie (himself the successor to "Spicy MacLammermoor, the old king") tries to fend off a younger competitor.

So Barthelme's home and his community, as well as his reading and his writing, gave him a usefully acute case of the anxiety of influence—and the influence he seemed most anxious about was that of modernism itself. "Remember," he told O'Hara, "that I was exposed early to an almost religious crusade, the Modern movement in architecture, which, putting it as kindly as possible, has not turned out quite as expected." He was always interested in the way younger writers revere and then overthrow their forebears, sometimes by the process Harold Bloom calls "strong misreading": Blake's interpretation of Milton as a Satanic-prophetic visionary, to use one of Bloom's examples, or the high-modernist practice of willfully misappropriating and miscontextualizing fragments of canonical literature, which were threatening to the degree that they were revered. Barthelme, like Bloom, could hardly miss the Oedipal overtones: his best novel, after all, is *The Dead Father*, whose title character—a talking statue-carcass who reminds us of King Lear, Tolstoy, Jehovah, and Blake's Nobodaddy—gets dragged to his grave, protesting and orating all the way. Yet Barthelme, as he liked to remind us, was "a doubleminded man." The very baldness of that title suggests his bemusement at such an overfamiliar paradigm; no old-time modernist would have been so bathetically blunt.

Literary historians call Barthelme a postmodernist, and he didn't resist the designation as strongly as he resisted being called a metafictionist. "Critics . . . have been searching for a term that would describe fiction after the great period of modernism," he said in a 1980 interview with Larry McCaffery—" 'postmodernism,' 'metafiction,' 'surfiction,' 'superfiction.' The last two are terrible; I suppose 'postmodernism' is the least ugly, most descriptive." But in the 1987 essay "Not-Knowing," written two years before he died, he said he was "dubious" about the term and "not altogether clear as to who is supposed to be on the bus and who is not." Since the word gets applied both to works supposedly weirder-than-modern (weirder than *Finnegans Wake*?) and to works far more conservative (Raymond Carver's stories, Philip Johnson's buildings), "postmodern" is useful as a chronological marker, like "eighteenth-century," and worthless as a characterization of a particular esthetic, like "Baroque." It might be most sensible, then, simply to look at Barthelme as one more writer who came along after older writers had already done what he would like to have done—as Dante came along after Virgil who came along after Homer—and who had a hard time, as writers have always had, figuring out how to reconcile his admiration for his predecessors with his ambition to make something of his own.

Barthelme's particular Dead Father was Beckett—who had a Dead Father of his own. "I'm just overwhelmed by Beckett, as Beckett was by Joyce," he told interviewers Charles Ruas and Judith Sherman in 1975. "By the way, let me make clear that I am not proposing myself as successor or heir to Mr. Beckett, in any sense. I'm just telling you that he is a problem for me because of the enormous pull of his style. I am certainly not the only writer who has been enormously influenced by Beckett and thus wants to stay at arm's length . . . There are other lions in the path as well . . . It's just that Beckett is the largest problem for me." Here and there, Barthelme lets himself write in this or that Beckettian mode: the relentless comma-spliced monologue of "Traumerei" (cf. *The Unnamable*), the vaudevilleian-stichomythic banter of such late pieces as "The Leap" (cf. *Waiting for Godot*), or the comic pedantry of "Daumier" and "A Shower of Gold" (cf. *Murphy*). What's more radically Beckettian is Barthelme's compulsion to fly blind, to approach the unknowable as an area for exploration, and his sense of the mind's cubistic noisiness. "The confusing signals, the impurity of the signal, gives you verisimilitude," he told J.D. O'Hara. "As when you attend a funeral and notice, against your will, that it's being poorly done." (This, by the way, catches almost exactly Beckett's tone and cadence—except Beckett might have used the formal "one" construction instead of the colloquial "you.")

Like Beckett, Barthelme uses his well-nurtured taste and wide-ranging erudition to point up their ultimate uselessness. "Is it really important to know that this movie is fine, and that one terrible, and to talk intelligently about the difference?" his narrator asks at the end of "The Party." "Wonderful elegance! No good at all!" Like Beckett, he's a meticulous observer and compulsive cataloguer of the things of this world, knowing that they offer no certainty or security.

> Red men in waves . . . accumulated against the barriers we had made of window dummies, silk, thoughtfully planned job descriptions . . . I analyzed the composition of the barricade closest to me and found two ashtrays, ceramic, one dark brown and one dark brown with an orange blur at the lip . . . a red pillow and blue pillow, a woven straw wastebasket . . . a Yugoslavian carved flute, wood, dark brown, and other items. I decided I knew nothing.
>
> —"The Indian Uprising"

Like Beckett, he's God-haunted yet unbelieving.

> —We are but poor lapsarian futiles whose preen glands are all out of kilter and who but for the grace of God—
> —Do you think He wants us to grovel quite so much?
> —I don't think He gives a rap. But it's traditional.
>
> —"The Leap"

And like Beckett—or like Shakespeare, for that matter—he doesn't worry much about the distinction between the dark and the comic.

Yet Barthelme would never have written a line like Nell's speech in *Endgame*: "Nothing is funnier than unhappiness, I grant you that." His is both a sunnier and a more worldly spirit. "The world is waiting for the sunrise," his narrator says in "The Sandman." (Neither the narrator's own words nor Barthelme's, of course; he's quoting the old pop song.) And while we may well wait forever—in fact, isn't that Rule One?—its failure to arrive doesn't make the sunrise less real. Barthelme has a lively sense of the absurd, but no feel for the punishingly bleak; even if all *is* vanity, he doesn't hold a little thing like that against the world and the flesh. "Anathematization of the world," he writes in *Snow White*, "is not an adequate response to the world." Both as writer and citizen, Barthelme cherished acts of political decency, like the narrator's effort, in "The Sandman," to get help for some black kids who'd been arrested for sodomizing and suffocating a little boy. "Now while I admit it sounds callous to be talking about the degree of brutality being minimal, let me tell you that it was no small matter, in that time and place, to force the cops to show the kids to the press at all. It was an achievement, of sorts." That "of sorts" undercuts the "achievement" with a Beckettian sigh; still, the achievement remains. Similarly, though physical pleasure and human connection may be hard to come by and impossible to hang onto, Barthelme never seems to feel betrayed by their absence and never doubts their absolute value. In "The Zombies," the ultimate symptom of deadening at the hands of a "bad zombie" is to "walk by a beautiful breast and not even notice." So is Barthelme wiser and more humane than Beckett? Or just whistling in the dark, punking out on the ultimate implications of what he knew?

Beckett's skepticism extends even to language itself—to the very language, that is, with which he expresses his skepticism about language. "You would do better, at least no worse," his Molloy tells us, "to obliterate texts than to blacken margins, to fill in the holes of words until all is blank and flat and the whole ghastly business looks like what it is, senseless, speechless, issueless misery." Barthelme had no inclination to follow the old man to such an extremity; when it came to language, he was a believer—even a booster. "The combinatory agility of words," he wrote in "Not-Knowing," "the exponential generation of meaning once they're allowed to go to bed together, allows the writer to surprise himself, makes art possible, reveals how much of Being we haven't yet encountered." He makes the anti-Beckettian argument that art, with its ability to "imagine alternative realities," is "fundamentally meliorative," that "the artist's effort, always and everywhere, is to attain a fresh mode of cognition"—and that the writer's particular task is "restoring freshness to a much-handled language." Doesn't this emphasis on manner rather than matter put Barthelme among literature's marginal Crazy Uncles—Firbank, Edward Lear, John Lyly—instead of among its august Dead Fathers? Doesn't it show Barthelme as deficient in moral earnestness? When O'Hara pressed him on this point, Barthelme had the answer ready. "I believe that my every sentence trembles with morality in that each attempts to engage the problematic," he said. "The change of emphasis from the what to the how seems to me to be the major impulse in art since Flaubert, and it's not merely formalism, it's not at all superficial, it's an attempt to reach truth, and a very rigorous one."

Since a writer can no more invent a new vocabulary than a painter can invent a new spectrum, Barthelme's project of restoring freshness to language—"to purify the dialect of the tribe" is how Pound put it—led him to ragpick words, phrases, tones of voice, and modes of diction from the obscure and neglected past, from the demotic present and from the surreal specialized lexicons of technology, philosophy, even the military. "Mixing bits of this and that from various areas of life to make something that did not exist before is an oddly hopeful endeavor," he wrote in a short essay about his story "Paraguay." "The sentence 'Electrolytic jelly exhibiting a capture ratio far in excess of standard is used to fix the animals in place' made me very happy—perhaps in excess of its merit. But there is in the world such a thing as electrolytic jelly; the 'capture ratio' comes from the jargon of sound technology; and the animals themselves are a salad of the real and the invented." He had a good ear for bad writing: "I'm very interested in . . . sentences that are awkward in a particular way," he said in a 1970 interview with Jerome Klinkowitz. In such pieces as "How I Write My Songs," he elevated the ungainly—the passive voice, the ill-chosen word, the clunky cadence, the banal thought—to the poetic simply by putting a frame around it. "Another type of song which is a dear favorite of almost everyone," his fictive songwriter Bill B. White tells us, "is the song that has a message, some kind of thought that people can carry away with them and think about. Many songs of this type are written and gain great acceptance every day." He was even proud of the Orwellian "loudspeaker-like tone" he achieved in this sentence from "The Rise of Capitalism": "Cultural underdevelopment of the worker, as a technique of domination, is found everywhere under late capitalism." Why? In part, as he explained to O'Hara, because its "metallic drone" undercut the truth of its assertion with a dreary countertruth: nothing will ever be done about it. But also in part because, as the modernists knew long ago, ugliness has its weird beauty if you hold it up and look at it.

In his affectionate play with language, his erudition and his lurking earnestness about the redemptive force of art, Barthelme sounds less like Beckett than like Nabokov, that other man-mountain of late modernism. Nabokov, obviously, was the better linguist, but Barthelme read at least as widely and with a more open mind: not to reinforce a set of mandarin prejudices but to explode what few he ever had. (It's hard to imagine Nabokov studying up on the conquest of Mexico, taking notes on hoodoo charms or listening to Muddy Waters.) Barthelme paid him notably, perhaps suspiciously, scant attention. (In his 1964 essay "After Joyce," he kissed off Nabokov in a single sentence along with—for some reason—Henry Green; this was almost a decade after *Lolita.*) If Beckett was Barthelme's Dead Father, Nabokov might have been his dark Uncle Claudius: uncomfortably like him, yet radically opposed in spirit. Like Nabokov, Barthelme can be clever and allusive to the point of obscurity, but he never pulls chilly practical jokes on his readers and never seeks, as Nabokov did, to misdirect them. As the narrator of "The Sandman" says of his willful, depressive, and sexy girlfriend, distance is not Barthelme's thing—"not by a long chalk." Beneath his surface of corruscating omniscience beats a kindly heart. He seems to want you to be in on his jokes, to share the joyous agility of his conceptual and linguistic leaps, the abundance of his cornucopiously stocked memory, and not to sit gazing at him from the cheap seats in resentful admiration. In essays and interviews, he explained with as little mystification as possible how he put together his pieces—considering that the process of writing is essentially mysterious—and how we might go about appreciating them. Much of the pleasure in reading Barthelme comes from the way he makes you feel welcome even as he's subjecting you to a vertiginously high level of entertainment.

My comparing Barthelme with Beckett and Nabokov suggests that I think he, too, is a King of Jazz. Can he really hold his own in a cutting session with those cats setting the tempo, and Joyce and Woolf sitting at a table in the back listening for wrong notes? Who knows? He's been gone less than fifteen years; we might have a clearer view of what he accomplished in another fifty. Certainly he's become canonical: there he is, in every anthology and on the shelves of every bookstore, right after John Barth. But a lot of unread and unreadable people get to be canonical. Unlike such co-generationists as Harold Brodkey or Don DeLillo or John Gardner or Cormac McCarthy, he doesn't do the High Seriousness thing. Which is odd, because the contemporaries he read with pleasure were folks like Thomas Bernhard, Max Frisch, William Gass, Walker Percy,

García Márquez, Peter Handke—serious, some of them, to a fault. He's got all the political, sociological, literary, philosophical, and spiritual anxieties any writer could be blessed with, yet reading him never feels like a duty. That wouldn't bode well if you were bucking for King of Jazz, though it might keep you from going out of print. Neither would the shortcoming he confessed to J.D. O'Hara—"I don't offer enough emotion"—if it were really true. He never emoted, but that's a different thing. Any reader sophisticated enough to stick with Barthelme in the first place must sense the sadness he's at such pains to evade with all his funning, and feel the joy when a last line—see "Report," see "The Death of Edward Lear," see "Traumerei"—hits home.

Barthelme is a quintessential writer of the twentieth century, looking Janus-faced to both the past and future, and with a third eye turned inward. Yet he's also an anomaly. Nobody before him really reads much like him: neither Beckett or Nabokov, nor such minimalist realists as Hemingway, nor such fabulists as Kafka and Borges, nor such parodists and pasticheurs as Perelman and Firbank. Nor has he become anybody's particular Dead Father. Once in a while, George Saunders or Mark Leyner or Jim Shepherd will write something that reminds us of him. (Compare Saunders's "Pastoralia," in which faux cavepeople are trapped in a futuristic theme park, with Barthelme's "Game," whose characters are confined in the control room of a missile silo.) A few even newer jacks seem to have read him—or to have read people who've read him. The preemptively self-ironic title of Dave Eggers's *A Heartbreaking Work of Staggering Genius* sounds like Barthelme; so does the artfully broken English at the beginning of Jonathan Safran Foer's *Everything Is Illuminated*. But if there was ever a School of Barthelme, as there was a School of Carver, it's left scarcely a trace. He's too erudite, too intellectually nimble, and too many-minded. (That "double-minded man" business is an undercount—in this book, by a factor of thirty.) An aspiring Barthelme imitator would first have to choose which Barthelme to imitate.

In "Not-Knowing," Barthelme wrote that art is "a true account of the activity of mind." These stories are reports of his expeditions into mapless worlds of language and thought, perception and memory, undertaken with no preconceptions about what he might tell us and how the reports might read—he had to go there first. Not stories of W doing X to Y with the result that Z, but stories of what goes on in a vast, various, and noisy consciousness, each story taking its unique shape from its creator's intuition of what the piece itself demands. Each one singing its own tune in its own voice. So: *Sixty Stories*. Just what the man said. It's not a modest title at all.

Sixty Stories

Margins

Edward was explaining to Carl about margins. "The *width* of the margin shows culture, aestheticism and a sense of values or the lack of them," he said. "A very wide left margin shows an impractical person of culture and refinement with a deep appreciation for the best in art and music. Whereas," Edward said, quoting his handwriting analysis book, "whereas, narrow left margins show the opposite. No left margin at all shows a practical nature, a wholesome economy and a general lack of good taste in the arts. A very wide *right* margin shows a person afraid to face reality, oversensitive to the future and generally a poor mixer."

"I don't believe in it," Carl said.

"Now," Edward continued, "with reference to your sign there, you have an *all-around wide margin* which shows a person of extremely delicate sensibilities with love of color and form, one who holds aloof from the multitude and lives in his own dream world of beauty and good taste."

"Are you sure you got that right?"

"I'm communicating with you," Edward said, "across a vast gulf of ignorance and darkness."

"*I* brought the darkness, is that the idea?" Carl asked.

"You brought the darkness, you black mother," Edward said. "Funky, man."

"Edward," Carl said, "for God's sake."

"Why did you write all that jazz on your sign, Carl? Why? It's not true, is it? Is it?"

"It's kind of true," Carl said. He looked down at his brown sandwich boards, which said: *I Was Put In Jail in Selby County*

Alabama For Five Years For Stealing A Dollar and A Half Which I Did Not Do. While I Was In Jail My Brother Was Killed & My Mother Ran Away When I Was Little. In Jail I Began Preaching & I Preach to People Wherever I Can Bearing the Witness of Eschatological Love. I Have Filled Out Papers for Jobs But Nobody Will Give Me a Job Because I Have Been In Jail & The Whole Scene Is Very Dreary, Pepsi Cola. I Need Your Offerings to Get Food. Patent Applied For & Deliver Us From Evil. "It's true," Carl said, "with a kind of *merde*-y inner truth which shines forth as the objective correlative of what actually did happen, back home."

"Now, look at the way you made that 'm' and that 'n' there," Edward said. "The tops are pointed rather than rounded. That indicates aggressiveness and energy. The fact that they're also pointed rather than rounded at the bottom indicates a sarcastic, stubborn and irritable nature. See what I mean?"

"If you say so," Carl said.

"Your capitals are very small," Edward said, "indicating humility."

"My mother would be pleased," Carl said, "if she knew."

"On the other hand, the excessive size of the loops in your 'y' and your 'g' displays exaggeration and egoism."

"That's always been one of my problems," Carl answered.

"What's your whole name?" Edward asked, leaning against a building. They were on Fourteenth Street, near Broadway.

"Carl Maria von Weber," Carl said.

"Are you a drug addict?"

"Edward," Carl said, "you *are* a swinger."

"Are you a Muslim?"

Carl felt his long hair. "Have you read *As a Man Grows Older*, by Svevo? I really liked that one. I thought that one was fine."

"No, c'mon, Carl, answer the question," Edward insisted. "There's got to be frankness and honesty between the races. Are you one?"

"I think an accommodation can be reached and the government is doing all it can at the moment," Carl said. "I think there's something to be said on all sides of the question. This is not such a good place to hustle, you know that? I haven't got but two offerings all morning."

"People like people who look neat," Edward said. "You look kind of crummy, if you don't mind my saying so."

"You really think it's too long?" Carl asked, feeling his hair again.

"Do you think I'm a pretty color?" Edward asked. "Are you envious?"

"No," Carl said. "Not envious."

"See? Exaggeration and egoism. Just like I said."

"You're kind of boring, Edward. To tell the truth."

Edward thought about this for a moment. Then he said: "But I'm white."

"It's the color of choice," Carl said. "I'm tired of talking about color, though. Let's talk about values or something."

"Carl, I'm a fool," Edward said suddenly.

"Yes," Carl said.

"But I'm a *white* fool," Edward said. "That's what's so lovely about me."

"You *are* lovely, Edward," Carl said. "It's true. You have a nice look. Your aspect is good."

"Oh, hell," Edward said despondently. "You're very well-spoken," he said. "I noticed that."

"The reason for that is," Carl said, "I read. Did you read *The Cannibal* by John Hawkes? I thought that was a hell of a book."

"Get a haircut, Carl," Edward said. "Get a new suit. Maybe one of those new Italian suits with the tight coats. You could be upwardly mobile, you know, if you just put your back into it."

"Why are you worried, Edward? Why does my situation distress you? Why don't you just walk away and talk to somebody else?"

"You bother me," Edward confessed. "I keep trying to penetrate your inner reality, to find out what it is. Isn't that curious?"

"John Hawkes also wrote *The Beetle Leg* and a couple of

other books whose titles escape me at the moment," Carl said. "I think he's one of the best of our younger American writers."

"Carl," Edward said, "*what* is your inner reality? Blurt it out, baby."

"It's mine," Carl said quietly. He gazed down at his shoes, which resembled a pair of large dead brownish birds.

"Are you sure you didn't steal that dollar and a half mentioned on your sign?"

"Edward, I *told* you I didn't steal that dollar and a half." Carl stamped up and down in his sandwich boards. "It sure is *cold* here on Fourteenth Street."

"That's your imagination, Carl," Edward said. "This street isn't any colder than Fifth, or Lex. Your feeling that it's colder here probably just arises from your marginal status as a despised person in our society."

"Probably," Carl said. There was a look on his face. "You know I went to the government, and asked them to give me a job in the Marine Band, and they wouldn't do it?"

"Do you blow good, man? Where's your ax?"

"They wouldn't *give* me that cotton-pickin' job," Carl said. "What do you think of that?"

"This eschatological love," Edward said, "what kind of love is that?"

"That is later love," Carl said. "That's what I call it, anyhow. That's love on the other side of the Jordan. The term refers to a set of conditions which . . . It's kind of a story we black people tell to ourselves to make ourselves happy."

"Oh me," Edward said. "Ignorance and darkness."

"Edward," Carl said, "you don't *like* me."

"I do too like you, Carl," Edward said. "Where do you steal your books, mostly?"

"Mostly in drugstores," Carl said. "I find them good because mostly they're long and narrow and the clerks tend to stay near the prescription counters at the back of the store, whereas the books are usually in those little revolving racks near the front of the store. It's normally pretty easy to slip a couple in your overcoat pocket, if you're wearing an overcoat."

"But . . ."

"Yes," Carl said, "I know what you're thinking. If I'll steal books I'll steal other things. But stealing books is metaphysically different from stealing like money. Villon has something pretty good to say on the subject I believe."

"Is that in 'If I Were King'?"

"Besides," Carl added, "haven't *you* ever stolen anything? At some point in your life?"

"My life," Edward said. "Why do you remind me of it?"

"Edward, you're not satisfied with your life! I thought white lives were *nice!*" Carl said, surprised. "I love that word 'nice.' It makes me so happy."

"Listen Carl," Edward said, "why don't you just concentrate on improving your handwriting."

"My character, you mean."

"No," Edward said, "don't bother improving your character. Just improve your handwriting. Make larger capitals. Make smaller loops in your 'y' and your 'g.' Watch your word-spacing so as not to display disorientation. Watch your margins."

"It's an idea. But isn't that kind of a superficial approach to the problem?"

"Be careful about the spaces between the lines," Edward went on. "Spacing of lines shows clearness of thought. Pay attention to your finals. There are twenty-two different kinds of finals and each one tells a lot about a person. I'll lend you the book. Good handwriting is the key to advancement, or if not *the* key, at least *a* key. You could be the first man of your race to be Vice-President."

"That's something to shoot for, all right."

"Would you like me to go get the book?"

"I don't think so," Carl said, "no thanks. It's not that I don't have any faith in your solution. What I *would* like is to take a leak. Would you mind holding my sandwich boards for a minute?"

"Not at all," Edward said, and in a moment had slipped Carl's sandwich boards over his own slight shoulders. "Boy, they're kind of heavy, aren't they?"

"They cut you a bit," Carl said with a malicious smile. "I'll just go into this men's store here."

When Carl returned the two men slapped each other sharply in the face with the back of the hand—that beautiful part of the hand where the knuckles grow.

A Shower of Gold

Because he needed the money Peterson answered an ad that said "*We'll pay you* to be on TV if your opinions are strong enough or your personal experiences have a flavor of the unusual." He called the number and was told to come to Room 1551 in the Graybar Building on Lexington. This he did and after spending twenty minutes with a Miss Arbor who asked him if he had ever been in analysis was okayed for a program called *Who Am I?* "What do you have strong opinions about?" Miss Arbor asked. "Art," Peterson said, "life, money." "For instance?" "I believe," Peterson said, "that the learning ability of mice can be lowered or increased by regulating the amount of serotonin in the brain. I believe that schizophrenics have a high incidence of unusual fingerprints, including lines that make almost complete circles. I believe that the dreamer watches his dream in sleep, by moving his eyes." "*That's very interesting!*" Miss Arbor cried. "It's all in the *World Almanac*," Peterson replied.

"I see you're a sculptor," Miss Arbor said, "that's wonderful." "What is the nature of the program?" Peterson asked. "I've never seen it." "Let me answer your question with another question," Miss Arbor said. "Mr. Peterson, are you absurd?" Her enormous lips were smeared with a glowing white cream. "I beg your pardon?" "I mean," Miss Arbor said earnestly, "do you encounter your own existence as gratuitous? Do you feel *de trop?* Is there nausea?" "I have an enlarged liver," Peterson offered. "That's *excellent!*" Miss Arbor exclaimed. "That's a *very* good beginning. *Who Am I?* tries, Mr. Peterson, to discover what people *really are.* People today, we feel, are hidden away inside themselves, alienated, desperate, living in anguish, despair and bad faith. Why have we been thrown here, and abandoned? That's the question we try to answer, Mr. Peterson. Man stands alone in a featureless, anonymous landscape, in fear and trembling and sickness unto death. God is dead. Nothingness everywhere. Dread. Estrangement. Finitude. *Who Am I?* approaches these problems in a root radical way." "On television?" "We're interested in basics, Mr. Peterson. We don't play around." "I see," Peterson said, wondering about the amount of the fee. "What I want to know now, Mr. Peterson, is this: are you *interested* in absurdity?" "Miss Arbor," he said, "to tell you the truth, I don't know. I'm not sure I believe in it." "Oh, Mr. Peterson!" Miss Arbor said, shocked. "Don't *say* that! You'll be . . . " "Punished?" Peterson suggested. "*You* may not be interested in absurdity," she said firmly, "but absurdity is interested in *you*." "I have a lot of problems, if that helps," Peterson said. "Existence is problematic for you," Miss Arbor said, relieved. "The fee is two hundred dollars."

"I'm going to be on television," Peterson said to his dealer. "A terrible shame," Jean-Claude responded. "Is it unavoidable?" "It's unavoidable," Peterson said, "if I want to eat." "How much?" Jean-Claude asked and Peterson said: "Two hundred." He looked around the gallery to see if any of his works were on display. "A ridiculous compensation considering the infamy. Are you using your own name?" "You haven't by any chance . . ." "No one is buying," Jean-Claude said. "Undoubtedly it is the weather. People are thinking in terms of—what do you call those things?—Chris-Crafts. To boat with. You would not consider again what I spoke to you about before?" "No," Peterson said, "I wouldn't consider it." "Two little ones would move much, much faster than a single huge big one," Jean-Claude said, looking away: "To saw it across the middle would be a very simple matter." "It's supposed to be a work of art," Peterson said, as calmly as possible. "You don't go around sawing works of art across the middle, remember?" "That place where it saws," Jean-Claude said, "is not very difficult. I can put my two hands around it." He made a circle with his two hands to demonstrate. "Invariably when I look at that piece I see two pieces. Are you absolutely sure you didn't conceive it wrongly in the first instance?" "Absolutely," Peterson said. Not a single piece of his was on view, and his liver expanded in rage and hatred. "You have a very romantic impulse," Jean-Claude said. "I admire, dimly, the posture. You read too much in the history of art. It estranges you from those possibilities for authentic selfhood that inhere in the present century." "I know," Peterson said, "could you let me have twenty until the first?"

Peterson sat in his loft on lower Broadway drinking Rheingold and thinking about the President. He had always felt close to the President but felt now that he had, in agreeing to appear on the television program, done something slightly disgraceful, of which the President would not approve. But I needed the money, he told himself, the telephone is turned off and the kitten is crying for milk. And I'm running out of beer. The President feels that the arts should be encouraged, Peterson reflected, surely he doesn't want me to go without beer? He wondered if what he was feeling was simple guilt at having sold himself to television or something more elegant: nausea? His liver groaned within him and he considered a situation in which his new relationship with the President was announced. He was working in the loft. The piece in hand was to be called *Season's Greetings* and combined three auto radiators, one from a Chevrolet Tudor, one from a Ford pickup, one from a 1932 Essex, with part of a former telephone switchboard and other items. The arrangement seemed right and he began welding. After a time the mass was freestanding. A couple of hours had passed. He put down the torch, lifted off the mask. He walked over to the refrigerator and found a sandwich left by a friendly junk dealer. It was a sandwich made hastily and without inspiration: a thin slice of ham between two pieces of bread. He ate it gratefully nevertheless. He stood looking at the work, moving from time to time so as to view it from a new angle. Then the door to the loft burst open and the President ran in, trailing a sixteen-pound sledge. His first blow cracked the principal weld in *Season's Greetings*, the two halves parting like lovers, clinging for a moment and then rushing off in opposite directions. Twelve Secret Service men held Peterson in a paralyzing combination of secret grips. He's looking good, Peterson thought, very good, healthy, mature, fit, trustworthy. I like his suit. The President's second and third blows smashed the Essex radiator and the Chevrolet radiator. Then he attacked the welding torch, the plaster sketches on the workbench, the Rodin cast and the Giacometti stickman Peterson had bought in Paris. "*But Mr. President!*" Peterson shouted. "*I thought we were friends!*" A Secret Service man bit him in the back of the neck. Then the President lifted the sledge high in the air, turned toward Peterson, and said: "Your liver is diseased? That's a good sign. You're making progress. You're thinking."

"I happen to think that guy in the White House is doing a pretty darn good job." Peterson's barber, a man named Kitchen who was also a lay analyst and the author of four books titled *The Decision to Be*, was the only person in the world to whom he had confided his former sense of community with the President. "As far as his relationship with you personally goes," the barber continued, "it's essentially a kind of I-Thou relationship, if you know what I mean. You got to handle it with full awareness of the implications. In the end one experiences only oneself, Nietzsche said. When you're angry with the President, what you experience is self-as-angry-with-the-President. When things are okay between you and him, what you experience is self-as-swinging-with-the-President. Well and good. *But,*" Kitchen said, lathering up, "you want the relationship to be such that what you experience is the-President-as-swinging-with-you. You want *his* reality, get it? So that you can break out of the hell of solipsism. How about a little more off the sides?" "Everybody knows the language but me," Peterson said irritably. "Look," Kitchen said, "when you talk about me to somebody else, you say 'my barber,' don't you? Sure you do. In the same way, I look on you as being 'my customer,' get it?

But you don't regard yourself as being 'my' customer and I don't regard myself as 'your' barber. Oh, it's hell all right." The razor moved like a switchblade across the back of Peterson's neck. "Like Pascal said: 'The natural misfortune of our mortal and feeble condition is so wretched that when we consider it closely, nothing can console us.' " The razor rocketed around an ear. "Listen," Peterson said, "what do you think of this television program called *Who Am I?* Ever seen it?" "Frankly," the barber said, "it smells of the library. But they do a job on those people, I'll tell you that." "What do you mean?" Peterson said excitedly. "What kind of a job?" The cloth was whisked away and shaken with a sharp popping sound. "It's too horrible even to talk about," Kitchen said. "But it's what they deserve, those crumbs." "Which crumbs?" Peterson asked.

That night a tall foreign-looking man with a switchblade big as a butcherknife open in his hand walked into the loft without knocking and said "Good evening, Mr. Peterson, I am the cat-piano player, is there anything you'd particularly like to hear?" "Cat-piano?" Peterson said, gasping, shrinking from the knife. "What are you talking about? What do you want?" A biography of Nolde slid from his lap to the floor. "The cat-piano," said the visitor, "is an instrument of the devil, a diabolical instrument. You needn't sweat quite so much," he added, sounding aggrieved. Peterson tried to be brave. "I don't understand," he said. "Let me explain," the tall foreign-looking man said graciously. "The keyboard consists of eight cats—the octave—encased in the body of the instrument in such a way that only their heads and forepaws protrude. The player presses upon the appropriate paws, and the appropriate cats respond—with a kind of shriek. There is also provision made for pulling their tails. A tail-puller, or perhaps I should say tail *player*" (he smiled a disingenuous smile) "is stationed at the rear of the instrument, where the tails are. At the correct moment the tail-puller pulls the correct tail. The tail-note is of course quite different from the paw-note and produces sounds in the upper registers. Have you ever seen such an instrument, Mr. Peterson?" "No, and I don't believe it exists," Peterson said heroically. "There is an excellent early seventeenth-century engraving by Franz van der Wyngaert, Mr. Peterson, in which a cat-piano appears. Played, as it happens, by a man with a wooden leg. You will observe my own leg." The cat-piano player hoisted his trousers and a leglike contraption of wood, metal and plastic appeared. "And now, would you like to make a request? 'The Martyrdom of St. Sebastian'? The 'Romeo and Juliet' overture? 'Holiday for Strings'?" "But why—" Peterson began. "The kitten is crying for milk, Mr. Peterson. And whenever a kitten cries, the cat-piano plays." "But it's not my kitten," Peterson said reasonably. "It's just a kitten that wished itself on me. I've been trying to give it away. I'm not sure it's still around. I haven't seen it since the day before yesterday." The kitten appeared, looked at Peterson reproachfully, and then rubbed itself against the cat-piano player's mechanical leg. "Wait a minute!" Peterson exclaimed. "This thing is rigged! That cat hasn't been here in two days. What do you want from me? What am I supposed to do?" "Choices, Mr. Peterson, choices. You *chose* that kitten as a way of encountering that which you are not, that is to say, kitten. An effort on the part of the *pour-soi* to—" "But it chose me!" Peterson cried, "the door was open and the first thing I knew it was lying in my bed, under the Army blanket. I didn't have anything to do with it!" The cat-piano player repeated his disingenuous smile. "Yes, Mr. Peterson, I know, I know. Things are done to you, it is all a gigantic conspiracy. I've heard the story a hundred times. But the kitten is here, is it not? The kitten is weeping, is it not?" Peterson looked at the kitten, which was crying huge tigerish tears into its empty dish. "*Listen,* Mr. Peterson," the cat-piano player said, "*listen!*" The blade of his immense knife jumped back into the handle with a thwack! and the hideous music began.

The day after the hideous music began the three girls from California arrived. Peterson opened his door, hesitantly, in response to an insistent ringing, and found himself being stared at by three girls in blue jeans and heavy sweaters, carrying suitcases. "I'm Sherry," the first girl said, "and this is Ann and this is Louise. We're from California and we need a place to stay." They were homely and extremely purposeful. "I'm sorry," Peterson said, "I can't—" "We sleep anywhere," Sherry said, looking past him into the vastness of his loft, "on the floor if we have to. We've done it before." Ann and Louise stood on their toes to get a good look. "What's that funny music?" Sherry asked, "it sounds pretty far-out. We really won't be any trouble at all and it'll just be a little while until we make a connection." "Yes," Peterson said, "but why me?" "You're an artist," Sherry said sternly, "we saw the AIR sign downstairs." Peterson cursed the fire laws which made posting of the signs obligatory. "Listen," he said, "I can't even feed the cat. I can't even keep myself in beer. This is not the place. You won't be happy here. My work isn't authentic. I'm a minor artist." "The natural misfortune of our mortal and feeble condition is so wretched that when we consider it closely, nothing can console us," Sherry said. "That's Pascal." "I know," Peterson said, weakly. "Where is the john?" Louise asked. Ann marched into the kitchen and began to prepare, from supplies removed from her rucksack, something called *veal engagé*. "Kiss me," Sherry said, "I need love." Peterson flew to his friendly neighborhood bar, ordered a double brandy, and thrust himself into a telephone booth. "Miss Arbor? This is Hank Peterson. Listen, Miss Arbor, I can't do it. No, I mean really. I'm being punished horribly for even thinking about it. No, I mean it. You can't imagine what's going on around here. Please, get somebody else? I'd regard it as a great personal favor. Miss Arbor? Please?"

The other contestants were a young man in white pajamas named Arthur Pick, a karate expert, and an airline pilot in full uniform, Wallace E. Rice. "Just be natural," Miss Arbor said, "and of course be frank. We score on the basis of the validity of your answers, and of course that's measured by the polygraph." "What's this about a polygraph?" the airline pilot said. "The polygraph measures the validity of your answers," Miss Arbor said, her lips glowing whitely. "How else are we going to know if you're . . ." "Lying?" Wallace E. Rice supplied. The contestants were connected to the machine and the machine to a large illuminated tote board hanging over their heads. The master of ceremonies, Peterson noted without pleasure, resembled the President and did not look at all friendly.

The program began with Arthur Pick. Arthur Pick got up in his white pajamas and gave a karate demonstration in which he broke three half-inch pine boards with a single kick of his naked left foot. Then he told how he had disarmed a bandit, late at night at the A&P where he was an assistant manager, with a maneuver called a "rip-choong" which he demonstrated on the announcer. "How about that?" the announcer caroled. "Isn't that something? Audience?" The audience responded enthusiastically and Arthur Pick stood modestly with his hands behind his back. "Now," the announcer said, "let's play *Who Am I?* And here's your host, *Bill Lemmon!*" No, he doesn't look like the President, Peterson decided. "Arthur," Bill Lemmon said, "for twenty dollars—do you love your mother?" "Yes," Arthur Pick said. "Yes, of course." A bell rang, the tote board flashed, and the audience screamed. "He's lying!" the announcer shouted, "lying! lying! lying!" "Arthur," Bill Lemmon said, looking at his index cards, "the polygraph shows that the validity of your answer is . . . questionable. Would you like to try it again? Take another crack at it?" "You're crazy," Arthur Pick said. "Of course I love my mother." He was fishing around inside his pajamas for a handkerchief. "Is your mother watching the show tonight, Arthur?" "Yes, Bill, she is." "How long have you been studying karate?" "Two years, Bill." "And who paid for the lessons?" Arthur Pick hesitated. Then he said: "My mother, Bill." "They were pretty expensive, weren't they, Arthur?" "Yes, Bill, they were." "How expensive?" "Twelve dollars an hour." "Your mother doesn't make very much money, does she, Arthur?" "No, Bill, she doesn't." "Arthur, what does your mother do for a living?" "She's a garment worker, Bill. In the garment district." "And how long has she worked down there?" "All her life, I guess. Since my old man died." "And she doesn't make very much money, you said." "No. But she *wanted* to pay for the lessons.

She *insisted* on it." Bill Lemmon said: "She wanted a son who could break boards with his feet?" Peterson's liver leaped and the tote board spelled out, in huge, glowing white letters, the words BAD FAITH. The airline pilot, Wallace E. Rice, was led to reveal that he had been caught, on a flight from Omaha to Miami, with a stewardess sitting on his lap and wearing his captain's cap, that the flight engineer had taken a Polaroid picture, and that he had been given involuntary retirement after nineteen years of faithful service. "It was perfectly safe," Wallace E. Rice said, "you don't understand, the automatic pilot can fly that plane better than I can." He further confessed to a lifelong and intolerable itch after stewardesses which had much to do, he said, with the way their jackets fell just on top of their hips, and his own jacket with the three gold stripes on the sleeve darkened with sweat until it was black.

I was wrong, Peterson thought, the world is absurd. The absurdity is punishing me for not believing in it. I affirm the absurdity. On the other hand, absurdity is itself absurd. Before the emcee could ask the first question, Peterson began to talk. "Yesterday," Peterson said to the television audience, "in the typewriter in front of the Olivetti showroom on Fifth Avenue, I found a recipe for Ten Ingredient Soup that included a stone from a toad's head. And while I stood there marveling a nice old lady pasted on the elbow of my best Haspel suit a little blue sticker reading THIS INDIVIDUAL IS A PART OF THE COMMUNIST CONSPIRACY FOR GLOBAL DOMINATION OF THE ENTIRE GLOBE. Coming home I passed a sign that said in ten-foot letters COWARD SHOES and heard a man singing "Golden Earrings" in a horrible voice, and last night I dreamed there was a shoot-out at our house on Meat Street and my mother shoved me in a closet to get me out of the line of fire." The emcee waved at the floor manager to turn Peterson off, but Peterson kept talking. "In this kind of a world," Peterson said, "absurd if you will, possibilities nevertheless proliferate and escalate all around us and there are opportunities for beginning again. I am a minor artist and my dealer won't even display my work if he can help it but minor is as minor does and lightning may strike even yet. Don't be reconciled. Turn off your television sets," Peterson said, "cash in your life insurance, indulge in a mindless optimism. Visit girls at dusk. Play the guitar. How can you be alienated without first having been connected? Think back and remember how it was." A man on the floor in front of Peterson was waving a piece of cardboard on which something threatening was written but Peterson ignored him and concentrated on the camera with the little red light. The little red light jumped from camera to camera in an attempt to throw him off balance but Peterson was too smart for it and followed wherever it went. "My mother was a royal virgin," Peterson said, "and my father a shower of gold. My childhood was pastoral and energetic and rich in experiences which developed my character. As a young man I was noble in reason, infinite in faculty, in form express and admirable, and in apprehension . . ." Peterson went on and on and although he was, in a sense, lying, in a sense he was not.

Me and Miss Mandible

13 September

Miss Mandible wants to make love to me but she hesitates because I am officially a child; I am, according to the records, according to the gradebook on her desk, according to the card index in the principal's office, eleven years old. There is a misconception here, one that I haven't quite managed to get cleared up yet. I am in fact thirty-five, I've been in the Army, I am six feet one, I have hair in the appropriate places, my voice is a baritone, I know very well what to do with Miss Mandible if she ever makes up her mind.

In the meantime we are studying common fractions. I could, of course, answer all the questions, or at least most of them (there are things I don't remember). But I prefer to sit in this too-small seat with the desktop cramping my thighs and examine the life around me. There are thirty-two in the class, which is launched every morning with the pledge of allegiance to the flag. My own allegiance, at the moment, is divided between Miss Mandible and Sue Ann Brownly, who sits across the aisle from me all day long and is, like Miss Mandible, a fool for love. Of the two I prefer, today, Sue Ann; although between eleven and eleven and a half (she refuses to reveal her exact age) she is clearly a woman, with a woman's disguised aggression and a woman's peculiar contradictions.

15 September

Happily our geography text, which contains maps of all the principal land-masses of the world, is large enough to conceal my clandestine journal-keeping, accomplished in an ordinary black composition book. Every day I must wait until Geography to put down such thoughts as I may have had during the morning about my situation and my fellows. I have tried writing at other times and it does not work. Either the teacher is walking up and down the aisles (during this period, luckily, she sticks close to the map rack in the front of the room) or Bobby Vanderbilt, who sits behind me, is punching me in the kidneys and wanting to know what I am doing. Vanderbilt, I have found out from certain desultory conversations on the playground, is hung up on sports cars, a veteran consumer of *Road & Track*. This explains the continual roaring sounds which seem to emanate from his desk; he is reproducing a record album called *Sounds of Sebring*.

19 September

Only I, at times (only at times), understand that somehow a mistake has been made, that I am in a place where I don't belong. It may be that Miss Mandible also knows this, at some level, but for reasons not fully understood by me she is going along with the game. When I was first assigned to this room I wanted to protest, the error seemed obvious, the stupidest principal could have seen it; but I have come to believe it was deliberate, that I have been betrayed again.

Now it seems to make little difference. This life-role is as interesting as my former life-role, which was that of a claims adjuster for the Great Northern Insurance Company, a position which compelled me to spend my time amid the debris of our civilization: rumpled fenders, roofless sheds, gutted warehouses, smashed arms and legs. After ten years of this one has a tendency to see the world as a vast junkyard, looking at a man and seeing only his (potentially) mangled parts, entering a house only to trace the path of the inevitable fire. Therefore when I was installed here, although I knew an error had been made, I countenanced it, I was shrewd; I was aware that there might well be some kind of advantage to be gained from what seemed a disaster. The role of The Adjuster teaches one much.

22 September

I am being solicited for the volleyball team. I decline, refusing to take unfair profit from my height.

23 September

Every morning the roll is called: Bestvina, Bokenfohr, Broan, Brownly, Cone, Coyle, Crecelius, Darin, Durbin, Geiger, Guiswite, Heckler, Jacobs, Kleinschmidt, Lay, Logan, Masei, Mitgang, Pfeilsticker. It is like the litany chanted in the dim miserable dawns of Texas by the cadre sergeant of our basic training company.

In the Army, too, I was ever so slightly awry. It took me a fantastically long time to realize what the others grasped almost at once: that much of what we were doing was absolutely pointless, to no purpose. I kept wondering why. Then something happened that proposed a new question. One day we were commanded to whitewash, from the ground to the topmost leaves, all of the trees in our training area. The corporal who relayed the order was nervous and apologetic. Later an off-duty captain sauntered by and watched us, white-splashed and totally weary, strung out among the freakish shapes we had created. He walked away swearing. I understood the principle (orders are orders), but I wondered: Who decides?

29 September

Sue Ann is a wonder. Yesterday she viciously kicked my ankle for not paying attention when she was attempting to pass me a note during History. It is swollen still. But Miss Mandible was watching me, there was nothing I could do. Oddly enough Sue Ann reminds me of the wife I had in my former role, while Miss Mandible seems to be a child. She watches me constantly, trying to keep sexual significance out of her look; I am afraid the other children have noticed. I have already heard, on that ghostly frequency that is the medium of classroom communication, the words *"Teacher's pet!"*

2 October

Sometimes I speculate on the exact nature of the conspiracy which brought me here. At times I believe it was instigated by my wife of former days, whose name was . . . I am only pretending to forget. I know her name very well, as well as I know the name of my former motor oil (Quaker State) or my old Army serial number (US 54109268). Her name was Brenda.

7 October

Today I tiptoed up to Miss Mandible's desk (when there was no one else in the room) and examined its surface. Miss Mandible is a clean-desk teacher, I discovered. There was nothing except her gradebook (the one in which I exist as a sixth-grader) and a text, which was open at a page headed *Making the Processes Meaningful.* I read: "Many pupils enjoy working fractions when they understand what they are doing. They have confidence in their ability to take the right steps and to obtain correct answers. However, to give the subject full social significance, it is necessary that many realistic situations requiring the processes be found. Many interesting and lifelike problems involving the use of fractions should be solved . . ."

8 October

I am not irritated by the feeling of having been through all this before. Things are done differently now. The children, moreover, are in some ways different from those who accompanied me on my first voyage through the elementary schools: *"They have confidence in their ability to take the right steps and to obtain correct answers."* This is surely true. When Bobby Vanderbilt, who sits behind me and has the great tactical advantage of being able to maneuver in my disproportionate shadow, wishes to bust a classmate in the mouth he first asks Miss Mandible to lower the blind, saying that the sun hurts his eyes. When she does so, *bip!* My generation would never have been able to con authority so easily.

13 October

I misread a clue. Do not misunderstand me: it was a tragedy only from the point of view of the authorities. I conceived that it was my duty to obtain satisfaction for the injured, for an elderly lady (not even one of our policyholders, but a claimant against Big Ben Transfer & Storage, Inc.) from the company. The settlement was $165,000; the claim, I still believe, was just. But without my encouragement Mrs. Bichek would never have had the self-love to prize her injury so highly. The company paid, but its faith in me, in my efficacy in the role, was broken. Henry Goodykind, the district manager, expressed this thought in a few not altogether unsympathetic words, and told me at the same time that I was to have a new role. The next thing I knew I was here, at Horace Greeley Elementary, under the lubricious eye of Miss Mandible.

17 October

Today we are to have a fire drill. I know this because I am a Fire Marshal, not only for our room but for the entire right wing of the second floor. This distinction, which was awarded shortly after my arrival, is interpreted by some as another mark of my somewhat dubious relations with our teacher. My armband, which is red and decorated with white felt letters reading FIRE, sits on the little shelf under my desk, next to the brown paper bag containing the lunch I carefully make for myself each morning. One of the advantages of packing my own lunch (I have no one to pack it for me) is that I am able to fill it with things I enjoy. The peanut butter sandwiches that my mother made in my former existence, many years ago, have been banished in favor of ham and cheese. I have found that my diet has mysteriously adjusted to my new situation; I no longer drink, for instance, and when I smoke, it is in the boys' john, like everybody else. When school is out I hardly smoke at all. It is only in the matter of sex that I feel my own true age; this is apparently something that, once learned, can never be forgotten. I live in fear that Miss Mandible will one day keep me after school, and when we are alone, create a compromising situation. To avoid this I have become a model pupil: another reason for the pronounced dislike I have encountered in certain quarters. But I cannot deny that I am singed by those long glances from the vicinity of the chalkboard; Miss Mandible is in many ways, notably about the bust, a very tasty piece.

24 October

There are isolated challenges to my largeness, to my dimly realized position in the class as Gulliver. Most of my classmates are polite about this matter, as they would be if I had only one eye, or wasted, metal-wrapped legs. I am viewed as a mutation of some sort but essentially a peer. However Harry Broan, whose father has made himself rich manufacturing the Broan Bathroom Vent (with which Harry is frequently reproached, he is always being asked how things are in Ventsville), today inquired if I wanted to fight. An interested group of his followers had gathered to observe this suicidal undertaking. I replied that I didn't feel quite up to it, for which he was obviously grateful. We are now friends forever. He has given me to understand privately that he can get me all the bathroom vents I will ever need, at a ridiculously modest figure.

25 October

"*Many interesting and lifelike problems involving the use of fractions should be solved . . .*" The theorists fail to realize that everything that is either interesting or lifelike in the classroom proceeds from what they would probably call interpersonal relations: Sue Ann Brownly kicking me in the ankle. How lifelike, how womanlike, is her tender solicitude after the deed! Her pride in my newly acquired limp is transparent; everyone knows that she has set her mark upon me, that it is a victory in her unequal struggle with Miss Mandible for my great, overgrown heart. Even Miss Mandible knows, and counters in perhaps the only way she can, with sarcasm. "Are you wounded, Joseph?" Conflagrations smolder behind her eyelids, yearning for the Fire Marshal clouds her eyes. I mumble that I have bumped my leg.

30 October

I return again and again to the problem of my future.

4 November

The underground circulating library has brought me a copy of *Movie-TV Secrets*, the multicolor cover blazoned with the headline "Debbie's Date Insults Liz!" It is a gift from Frankie Randolph, a rather plain girl who until today has had not one word for me, passed on via Bobby Vanderbilt. I nod and smile over my shoulder in acknowledgment; Frankie hides her head under her desk. I have seen these magazines being passed around among the girls (sometimes one of the boys will condescend to inspect a particularly lurid cover). Miss Mandible confiscates them whenever she finds one. I leaf through *Movie-TV Secrets* and get an eyeful. "The exclusive picture on these pages isn't what it seems. We know how it looks and we know what the gossipers will do. So in the interests of a nice guy, we're publishing the facts first. Here's what really happened!" The picture shows a rising young movie idol in bed, pajama-ed and bleary-eyed, while an equally blowzy young woman looks startled beside him. I am happy to know that the picture is not really what it seems; it seems to be nothing less than divorce evidence.

What do these hipless eleven-year-olds think when they come across, in the same magazine, the full-page ad for Maurice de Paree, which features "Hip Helpers" or what appear to be padded rumps? ("A real undercover agent that adds appeal to those hips and derriere, both!") If they cannot decipher the language the illustrations leave nothing to the imagination. "Drive him frantic . . ." the copy continues. Perhaps this explains Bobby Vanderbilt's preoccupation with Lancias and Maseratis; it is a defense against being driven frantic.

Sue Ann has observed Frankie Randolph's overture, and catching my eye, she pulls from her satchel no less than seventeen of these magazines, thrusting them at me as if to prove that anything any of her rivals has to offer, she can top. I shuffle through them quickly, noting the broad editorial perspective:

"Debbie's Kids Are Crying"
"Eddie Asks Debbie: Will You . . . ?"
"The Nightmares Liz Has About Eddie!"
"The Things Debbie Can Tell About Eddie"
"The Private Life of Eddie and Liz"
"Debbie Gets Her Man Back?"
"A New Life for Liz"
"Love Is a Tricky Affair"
"Eddie's Taylor-Made Love Nest"
"How Liz Made a Man of Eddie"
"Are They Planning to Live Together?"
"Isn't It Time to Stop Kicking Debbie Around?"
"Debbie's Dilemma"
"Eddie Becomes a Father Again"
"Is Debbie Planning to Re-wed?"
"Can Liz Fulfill Herself?"
"Why Debbie Is Sick of Hollywood"

Who are these people, Debbie, Eddie, Liz, and how did they get themselves in such a terrible predicament? Sue Ann knows, I am sure; it is obvious that she has been studying their history as a guide to what she may expect when she is suddenly freed from this drab, flat classroom.

I am angry and I shove the magazines back at her with not even a whisper of thanks.

5 November

The sixth grade at Horace Greeley Elementary is a furnace of love, love, love. Today it is raining, but inside the air is heavy and tense with passion. Sue Ann is absent; I suspect that yesterday's exchange has driven her to her bed. Guilt hangs about me. She is not responsible, I know, for what she reads, for the models proposed to her by a venal publishing industry; I should not have been so harsh. Perhaps it is only the flu.

Nowhere have I encountered an atmosphere as charged with aborted sexuality as this. Miss Mandible is helpless; nothing goes right today. Amos Darin has been found drawing a dirty picture in the cloakroom. Sad and inaccurate, it was offered not as a sign of something else but as an act of love in itself. It has excited even those who have not seen it, even those who saw but understood only that it was dirty. The room buzzes with imperfectly comprehended titillation. Amos stands by the door, waiting to be taken to the principal's office. He wavers between fear and enjoyment of his temporary celebrity. From time to time Miss Mandible looks at me reproachfully, as if blaming me for the uproar. But I did not create this atmosphere, I am caught in it like all the others.

8 November

Everything is promised my classmates and me, most of all the future. We accept the outrageous assurances without blinking.

9 November

I have finally found the nerve to petition for a larger desk. At recess I can hardly walk; my legs do not wish to uncoil themselves. Miss Mandible says she will take it up with the custodian. She is worried about the excellence of my themes. Have I, she asks, been receiving help? For an instant I am on the brink of telling her my story. Something, however, warns me not to attempt it. Here I am safe, I have a place; I do not wish to entrust myself once more to the whimsy of authority. I resolve to make my themes less excellent in the future.

11 November

A ruined marriage, a ruined adjusting career, a grim interlude in the Army when I was almost not a person. This is the sum of my existence to date, a dismal total. Small wonder that re-education seemed my only hope. It is clear even to me that I need reworking in some fundamental way. How efficient is the society that provides thus for the salvage of its clinkers!

14 November

The distinction between children and adults, while probably useful for some purposes, is at bottom a specious one, I feel. There are only individual egos, crazy for love.

15 November

The custodian has informed Miss Mandible that our desks are all the correct size for sixth-graders, as specified by the Board of Estimate and furnished the schools by the Nu-Art Educational Supply Corporation of Englewood, California. He has pointed out that if the desk size is correct, then the pupil size must be incorrect. Miss Mandible, who has already arrived at this conclusion, refuses to press the matter further. I think I know why. An appeal to the administration might result in my removal from the class, in a transfer to some sort of setup for "exceptional children." This would be a disaster of the first magnitude. To sit in a room with child geniuses (or, more likely, children who are "retarded") would shrivel me in a week. Let my experience here be that of the common run, I say, let me be, please God, typical.

20 November

We read signs as promises. Miss Mandible understands by my great height, by my resonant vowels, that I will one day carry her off to bed. Sue Ann interprets these same signs to mean that I am unique among her male acquaintances, therefore most desirable, therefore her special property as is everything that is Most Desirable. If neither of these propositions works out then life has broken faith with them.

I myself, in my former existence, read the company motto ("Here to Help in Time of Need") as a description of the duty of the adjuster, drastically mislocating the company's deepest concerns. I believed that because I had obtained a wife who was made up of wife-signs (beauty, charm, softness, perfume, cookery) I had found love. Brenda, reading the same signs that have now misled Miss Mandible and Sue Ann Brownly, felt she had been promised that she would never be bored again. All of us, Miss Mandible, Sue Ann, myself, Brenda, Mr. Goodykind, still believe that the American flag betokens a kind of general righteousness.

But I say, looking about me in this incubator of future citizens, that signs are signs, and some of them are lies.

23 November

It may be that my experience as a child will save me after all. If only I can remain quietly in this classroom, making my notes while Napoleon plods through Russia in the droning voice of Harry Broan, reading aloud from our History text. All of the mysteries that perplexed me as an adult have their origins here. But Miss Mandible will not permit me to remain ungrown. Her hands rest on my shoulders too warmly, and for too long.

7 December

It is the pledges that this place makes to me, pledges that cannot be redeemed, that will confuse me later and make me feel I am not *getting anywhere.* Everything is presented as the result of some knowable process; if I wish to arrive at four I get there by way of two and two. If I wish to burn Moscow the route I must travel has already been marked out by another visitor. If, like Bobby Vanderbilt, I yearn for the wheel of the Lancia 2.4-liter coupé, I have only to go through the appropriate process, that is, get the money. And if it is money itself that I desire, I have only to *make* it. All of these goals are equally beautiful in the sight of the Board of Estimate; the proof is all around us, in the no-nonsense ugliness of this steel and glass building, in the straightline matter-of-factness with which Miss Mandible handles some of our less reputable wars. Who points out that arrangements sometimes slip, that errors are made, that signs are misread? *"They have confidence in their ability to take the right steps and to obtain correct answers."*

8 December

My enlightenment is proceeding wonderfully.

9 December

Disaster once again. Tomorrow I am to be sent to a doctor, for observation. Sue Ann Brownly caught Miss Mandible and me in the cloakroom, during recess, Miss Mandible's naked legs in a scissors around my waist. For a moment I thought Sue Ann was going to choke. She ran out of the room weeping, straight for the principal's office, certain now which of us was Debbie, which Eddie, which Liz. I am sorry to be the cause of her disillusionment, but I know that she will recover. Miss Mandible is ruined but fulfilled. Although she will be charged with contributing to the delinquency of a minor, she seems at peace; *her* promise has been kept. She knows now that everything she has been told about life, about America, is true.

I have tried to convince the school authorities that I am a minor only in a very special sense, that I am in fact mostly to blame—but it does no good. They are as dense as ever. My contemporaries are astounded that I present myself as anything other than an innocent victim. Like the Old Guard marching through the Russian drifts, the class marches to the conclusion that truth is punishment.

Bobby Vanderbilt has given me his copy of *Sounds of Sebring*, in farewell.

For I'm the Boy

On the trip back from the aerodrome Huber who was driving said: Still I don't see why we were required. You weren't required Bloomsbury said explicitly, you were invited. Invited then Huber said, I don't see what we were invited *for.* As friends of the family Bloomsbury said. You are both friends of the family. A tissue of truths he thought, delicate as the negotiations leading to the surrender. It was not enough Bloomsbury felt to say that his friends Huber and Whittle were as men not what he wished them to be. For it was very possible he was aware, that he was not what they wished him to be. Nevertheless there were times when he felt like crying aloud, that it was not right!

She was I thought quite calm Bloomsbury said. You also Huber said turning his head almost completely around. Of course she has been trained to weep in private Bloomsbury said looking out of the window. Training he thought, that's the great thing. Behind them aircraft rose and fell at intervals, he wondered if they should have waited for the take-off, if it would have been more respectful, or on the other hand less respectful, to have done so. Still I thought there'd certainly be weeping Whittle said from the front seat. I have observed that in situations involving birth, bereavement or parting forever there is usually some quantity of weeping. But he provided a crowd Huber said, precluding privacy. And thus weeping Whittle agreed. Yes, Bloomsbury said.

Ah Pelly where do you be goin'? T' grandmather's, bein' it please yer lardship. An' what a fine young soft young warm young thing ya have there Pelly on yer bicycle seat. Ooo yer lardship ye've an evil head on yer, I'll bet yer sez that t'all us guls. Naw Pelly an' the truth of the matter is, there's nivver a gul come down my street wi' such a fine one as yers. Yer a bold one yer worship, blast me if you are not. Lemme just feel of her a trifle Pelly, there's a good gul. Ooo Mishtar Bloomsbury I likes a bit o' fun as good as the next 'un but me husbing's watchin' from the porch wi' 'is field telescope. Pother Pelly it won't be leavin' any marks, we'll just slither behind this tree. Ring me bicycle bell yer lardship he'll think yer after sellin' the Eskimo Pies. That I will Pelly I'll give 'er a ring like she nivver had before. Ooo yer grace be keerful of me abdominal belt what's holdin' up me pedal pushers. Never fear Pelly I dealt wi' worse than that in my time I have.

Of course it's inaccurate to say that we are friends of the family Huber said. There no longer being any family. The family exists still I believe Whittle said, as a legal entity. Were you married? It would affect the legal question, whether or not the family *qua* family endures beyond the physical separation of the partners, which we have just witnessed. Bloomsbury understood that Whittle did not wish to be thought prying and understood also, or recalled rather, that Whittle's wife or former wife had flown away in an aircraft very similar to if not identical with the one in which Martha his own wife had elected to fly away. But as he considered the question a tiresome one, holding little interest in view of the physical separation already alluded to, which now claimed his attention to the exclusion of all other claims, he decided not to answer. Instead he said: She looked I thought quite pretty. Lovely Whittle acknowledged and Huber said: Stunning in fact.

Ah Martha coom now to bed there's a darlin' gul. Hump off blatherer I've no yet read me Mallarmé for this evenin'. Ooo Martha dear canna we noo let the dear lad rest this night? when th' telly's already shut doon an' th' man o' the hoose 'as a 'ard on? Don't be comin' round wit yer lewd proposals on a Tuesday night when ye know better. But Martha dear where is yer love for me that we talked about in 19 and 38? in the cemetary by the sea? Pish Mishtar Hard On ye'd better be lookin' after the Disposall what's got itself plogged up. Ding the Disposall! Martha me gul it's yer sweet hide I'm after havin'. Get yer hands from out of me Playtex viper, I'm dreadful bored wit' yer silly old tool. But Marthy dear what of th' poetry we read i' th' book, aboot th' curlew's cry an' th' white giant's thigh, in 19 and 38? that we consecrated our union wit'? That was then an' this is now, ye can be runnin' after that bicycle gul wi' th' tight pants if yer wants a bit o' the auld shiver 'n' shake. Ah Marthy it's no bicycle gul that's brakin' me heart but yer sweet self. Keep yer paws off me derriere dear yer makin' me lose me page i' th' book.

Rich girls always look pretty Whittle said factually and Huber said: I've heard that. Did she take the money with her? Whittle asked. Oh yes Bloomsbury said modestly (for had he not after all relinquished, at the same time he had relinquished Martha, a not inconsiderable fortune, amounting to thousands, if not more?). You could hardly have done otherwise I suppose Huber said. His eyes which fortunately remained on the road during this passage were steely-bright. And yet . . . Whittle began. Something for your trouble Huber suggested, a tidy bit, to put in the Postal Savings. It would have gone against the grain no doubt Whittle said. But there was trouble was there not? for which little or no compensation has been offered? Outrage Bloomsbury noted stiffened Whittle's neck which had always been inordinately long and thin, and stiff. The money he thought, there had been in truth a great deal. More than one person could easily dispose of. But just right as fate would have it for two.

A BEER WINE LIQUOR ICE sign appeared by the roadside. Huber stopped the car which was a Pontiac Chieftain and entering the store purchased, for $27.00, a bottle of 98-year-old brandy sealed on the top with a wax seal. The bottle was old and dirty but the brandy when Huber returned with it was tasty in the extreme. For the celebration Huber said generously offering the bottle first to Bloomsbury who had in their view recently suffered pain and thus deserved every courtesy, insofar as possible. Bloomsbury did not overlook this great-hearted attitude on the part of his friend. Although he has many faults Bloomsbury reflected, he has many virtues also. But the faults engaged his attention and sipping the old brandy he began to review them seriously, and those of Whittle also. One fault of Huber's which Bloomsbury considered and reconsidered was that of *not keeping his eye on the ball.* In the matter of the road for instance Bloomsbury said to himself, any Texaco Gasoline sign is enough to distract him from his clear duty, that of operating the vehicle. And there were other faults both mortal and venial which Bloomsbury thought about just as seriously as this. Eventually his thinking was interrupted by these words of Whittle's: Good old money!

It would have been wrong Bloomsbury said austerely, to have kept it. Cows flew by the windows in both directions. That during the years of our cohabitation it had been *our* money to cultivate and be proud of does not alter the fact that originally it was her money rather than my money he finished. You could have bought a boat Whittle said, or a horse or a house. Presents for your friends who have sustained you in the accomplishment of this difficult and if I may say so rather unpleasant task Huber added pushing the accelerator pedal to the floor so that the vehicle leaped ahead. While these things were being said Bloomsbury occupied himself by thinking of one of his favorite expressions, which was: *Everything will be revealed at the proper time.* He remembered too the several occasions on which Huber and Whittle had dined at his house. They had admired he recalled not only the tuck but also the wife of the house whose aspect both frontside and backside was scrutinized and commented upon by them. To the point that the whole enterprise (friendship) had become, for him, quite insupportable, and defeating. Huber had in one instance even reached out his hand to touch it, when it was near, and bent over, and sticking out, and Bloomsbury as host had been forced, by the logic of the situation, to rap his wrist with a soup spoon. Golden days Bloomsbury thought, in the sunshine of our happy youth.

It's idiotic Huber said, that we know nothing more of the circumstances surrounding the extinguishment of your union than you have chosen to tell us. What do you want to know? Bloomsbury asked, aware however that they would want *every-*

thing. It would be interesting I think as well as instructive Whittle said casually, to know for instance at what point the situation of living together became untenable, whether she wept when you told her, whether you wept when she told you, whether you were the instigator or she was the instigator, whether there were physical fights involving bodily blows or merely objects thrown on your part and on her part, if there were mental cruelties, cruelties of what order and on whose part, whether she had a lover or did not have a lover, whether you did or did not, whether you kept the television or she kept the television, the disposition of the balance of the furnishings including tableware, linens, light bulbs, beds and baskets, who got the baby if there was a baby, what food remains in the pantry at this time, what happened to the medicine bottles including Mercurochrome, rubbing alcohol, aspirin, celery tonic, milk of magnesia, No-Doze and Nembutal, was it a fun divorce or not a fun divorce, whether she paid the lawyers or you paid the lawyers, what the judge said if there was a judge, whether you asked her for a "date" after the granting of the decree or did not so ask, whether she was touched or not touched by this gesture if there was such a gesture, whether the date if there was such a date was a fun thing or not a fun thing—in short we'd like to get the feel of the event he said. We'd be pepped to know, Huber said. I remember how it was when my old wife Eleanor flew away Whittle said, but only dimly because of the years. Bloomsbury however was thinking.

Have ye heard the news Pelly, that Martha me wife has left me in a yareplane? on th' bloody Champagne Flight? O yer wonderfulness, wot a cheeky lot to be pullin' the plog on a lovely man like yerself. Well that's how the cock curls Pelly, there's naught left of 'er but a bottle of Drene Shampoo in th' boodwar. She was a bitch that she was to commit this act of lese majesty against th' sovereign person of yer mightiness. She locked 'erself i' th' john Pelly toward th' last an' wouldn't come out not even for Flag Day. Incredible Mishtar Bloomsbury to think that such as that coexist wi' us good guls side by side in the twentieth century. An' no more lovey-kindness than a stick, an' no more gratitude than the bloody Internal Revenue. What bought her clothes at the Salvation Army by th' look of her, on the Revolving Credit Plan. I fingerprinted her fingerpaintin's she said and wallowed in sex what is more. Coo, Mishtar Bloomsbury me husbing Jack brings th' telly right into th' bed wi' 'im, it's bumpin' me back all night long. I' th' bed? I' th' bed. It's been a weary long time Pelly since love 'as touched my hart. Ooo your elegance, there's not a young gul in the Western Hemisphere as could withstand the grandeur of such a swell person as you. It's marriage Pelly what has ruined me for love. It's a hard notion me Bloomie boy but tragically true nonetheless. I don't want pity Pelly there's little enough rapport between adults wi'out cloudin' th' issue wi' sentiment. I couldn't agree more yer gorgeousness damme if I haven't told Jack a thousand times, that rapport is the only thing.

Although customarily of a lively and even ribald disposition the friends of the family nevertheless maintained during these thoughts of Bloomsbury's attitudes of the most rigorous and complete solemnity, as were of course appropriate. However Whittle at length said: I remember from my own experience that the pain of parting was shall I say exquisite? Exquisite Huber said, what a stupid word. How would you know? Whittle asked, you've never been married. I may not know about marriage Huber said stoutly, but I know about words. Exquisite he pronounced giggling. You have no delicacy Whittle said, that is clear. Delicacy Huber said, you get better and better. He began weaving the car left and right on the highway, in delight. The brandy Whittle said, has been too much for you. Crud Huber said assuming a reliable look. You've suffered an insult to the brain Whittle said, better let me drive. You drive! Huber exclaimed, your ugly old wife Eleanor left you *precisely because* you were a mechanical idiot, she confided in me on the day of the hearing. A mechanical idiot! Whittle said in surprise, I wonder what she meant by that? Huber and Whittle then struggled for the wheel for a brief space but in a friendly way. The Pontiac Chieftain behaved very poorly during this struggle, zigging and zagging, but Bloomsbury who was preoccupied did not notice. It was interesting he thought that after so many years one could still be surprised by a flyaway wife. Surprise he thought, that's the great thing, it keeps the old tissues tense.

Well Whittle said how does it feel? It? Bloomsbury said, what is *it?*

The physical separation mentioned earlier Whittle said. We want to know how it feels. The question is not what is the feeling but what is the meaning? Bloomsbury said reasonably. Christ Huber said, I'll tell you about *my* affair. What about it? Bloomsbury asked. It was a Red Cross girl Huber said, named Buck Rogers. Of what did it consist? Whittle asked. It consisted Huber said, of going to the top of the Chrysler Building and looking out over the city. Not much meat there Whittle said disparagingly, how did it end? Badly Huber said. Did she jump? Whittle asked. I jumped Huber said. You were always a jumper Whittle said. Yes Huber said angrily, I had taken precautions. Did your chute open? Whittle asked. With a sound like timber falling Huber said, but she never knew. The end of the affair Whittle said sadly. But what a wonderful view of the city Huber commented. So now, Whittle said to Bloomsbury, *give us the feeling.*

We can discuss Bloomsbury said, the meaning but not the feeling. If there is emotion it is only just that you share it with your friends Whittle said. Who are no doubt all you have left in the world said Huber. Whittle had placed upon Huber's brow, which was large and red, handkerchiefs dampened in brandy, with a view toward calming him. But Huber would not be calmed. Possibly there are relatives Whittle pointed out, of one kind or another. Hardly likely Huber said, considering his circumstances, now that there is no more money I would hazard that there are no more relatives either. Emotion! Whittle exclaimed, when was the last time we had any? The war I expect Huber replied, all those chaps going West. I'll give you a hundred dollars Whittle said, for the feeling. No Bloomsbury said, I have decided not. We are fine enough to be a crowd at the airport so that your wife will not weep but not fine enough to be taken into your confidence I suppose Huber said bitterly. Not a matter of fine enough Bloomsbury said reflecting meanwhile upon the proposition that the friends of the family were *all he had left,* which was he felt quite a disagreeable notion. But probably true. God what manner of man is this! Whittle exclaimed and Huber said: Prick!

Once in a movie house Bloomsbury recalled Tuesday Weld had suddenly turned on the screen, looked him full in the face, and said: You are a good man. You are good, good, good. He had immediately gotten up and walked out of the theater, gratification singing in his heart. But that situation dear to him as it was helped him not a bit in this situation. And that memory memorable as it was did not prevent the friends of the family from stopping the car under a tree, and beating Bloomsbury in the face first with the brandy bottle, then with the tire iron, until at length the hidden feeling emerged, in the form of salt from his eyes and black blood from his ears, and from his mouth, all sorts of words.

Will You Tell Me?

I

Hubert gave Charles and Irene a nice baby for Christmas. The baby was a boy and its name was Paul. Charles and Irene who had not had a baby for many years were delighted. They stood around the crib and looked at Paul; they could not get enough of him. He was a handsome child with dark hair, dark eyes. Where did you get him Hubert? Charles and Irene asked. From the bank, Hubert said. It was a puzzling answer, Charles and Irene puzzled over it. Everyone drank mulled wine. Paul regarded them from the crib. Hubert was pleased to have been able to please Charles and Irene. They drank more wine.

Eric was born.

Hubert and Irene had a clandestine affair. It was important they felt that Charles not know. To this end they bought a bed which they installed in another house, a house some distance from the house in which Charles, Irene and Paul lived. The new bed was small but comfortable enough. Paul regarded Hubert and Irene thoughtfully. The affair lasted for twelve years and was considered very successful.

Hilda.

Charles watched Hilda growing from his window. To begin with, she was just a baby, then a four-year-old, then twelve years passed and she was Paul's age, sixteen. What a pretty young girl! Charles thought to himself. Paul agreed with Charles; he had already bitten the tips of Hilda's pretty breasts with his teeth. Hilda thought she was too old for most boys Paul's age, but not for Paul.

Hubert's son Eric wanted Hilda but could not have her.

In the cellar Paul continued making his bombs, by cellarlight. The bombs were made from tall Schlitz cans and a plastic substance which Paul refused to identify. The bombs were sold to other boys Paul's age to throw at their fathers. The bombs were to frighten them rather than to harm them. Hilda sold the bombs for Paul, hiding them under her black sweater when she went out on the street.

Hilda cut down a black pear tree in the back yard. Why?

Do you know that Hubert and Irene are having an affair? Hilda asked Paul. He nodded.

Then he said: But I don't care.

In Montreal they walked in the snow, leaving marks like maple leaves. Paul and Hilda thought: What is wonderful? It seemed to Paul and Hilda that this was the question. The people of Montreal were kind to them, and they thought about the question in an ambiance of kindness.

Charles of course had been aware of the affair between Hubert and Irene from the beginning. But Hubert gave us Paul, he thought to himself. He wondered why Hilda had cut down the black pear tree.

Eric sat by himself.

Paul put his hands on Hilda's shoulders. She closed her eyes. They held each other with their hands and thought about the question. France!

Irene bought Easter presents for everyone. How do I know which part of the beach Rosemarie will be lying upon? she asked herself. In Hilda's back yard the skeleton of the black pear tree whitened.

Dialogue between Paul and Ann:

—You say anything that crawls into your head, Paul, Ann objected.

—Go peddle your hyacinths, Hyacinth Girl.

It is a portrait, Hubert said, composed of all the vices of our generation in the fullness of their development.

Eric's bomb exploded with a great splash near Hubert. Hubert was frightened. What has been decided? he asked Eric. Eric could not answer.

Irene and Charles talked about Paul. I wonder how he is getting along in France? Charles wondered. I wonder if France likes him. Irene wondered again about Rosemarie. Charles wondered if the bomb that Eric had thrown at Hubert had been manufactured by his foster son, Paul. He wondered too about the strange word "foster," about which he had not wondered previously. From the bank? he wondered. What could Hubert have meant by that? What could Hubert have meant by "from the bank"? he asked Irene. I can't imagine, Irene said. The fire sparkled. It was evening.

In Silkeborg, Denmark, Paul regarded Hilda thoughtfully. You love Inge, she said. He touched her hand.

Rosemarie returned.

Paul grew older. Oh that poor fucker Eric, he said.

2

The quality of the love between Hubert and Irene:

This is a pretty good bed Hubert, Irene said. Except that it's not really quite wide enough.

You know that Paul is manufacturing bombs in your cellar don't you? Hubert asked.

Inge brushed her long gold hair in her red sweater.

Who was that man, Rosemarie asked, who wrote all those books about dogs?

Hilda sat in a café waiting for Paul to return from Denmark. In the café she met Howard. Go away Howard, Hilda said to Howard, I am waiting for Paul. Oh come on Hilda, Howard said in a dejected voice, let me sit down for just a minute. Just a minute. I won't bother you. I just want to sit here at your table and be near you. I was in the war you know. Hilda said: Oh all right. But don't touch me.

Charles wrote a poem about Rosemarie's dog, Edward. It was a sestina.

Daddy, why are you writing this poem about Edward? Rosemarie asked excitedly. Because you've been away Rosemarie, Charles said.

At Yale Eric walked around.

Irene said: Hubert I love you. Hubert said that he was glad. They lay upon the bed in the house, thinking about the same things, about Montreal's white snow and the blackness of the Black Sea.

The reason I cut down the black pear tree Howard, which I've never told anyone, was that it was just as old as I was at that time, sixteen, and it was beautiful, and *I* was beautiful I think, and we both were *there* the tree and me, and I couldn't stand it, Hilda said. You are still beautiful now, at nineteen, Howard said. But don't touch me, Hilda said.

Hubert was short in a rising market. He lost ten thousand. Can you pay the rent on this house for a while? he asked Irene. Of course darling, Irene said. How much is it? Ninety-three dollars a month, Hubert said, every month. That's not much really, Irene said. Hubert reached out his hand to caress Irene but decided not to.

Inge smiled in the candlelight from the victory candle.

Edward was tired of posing for Charles's poem. He stretched, growled, and bit himself.

In the cellar Paul mixed the plastic for another batch of bombs. A branch from the black pear tree lay on his work-table. Seeds fell into his toolbox. From the bank? he wondered. What was meant by "from the bank"? He remembered the kindness of Montreal. Hilda's black sweater lay across a chair. God is subtle, but he is not malicious, Einstein said. Paul held the tools in his hands. They included an awl. Now I shall have to find more Schlitz cans, he thought. Quickly.

Irene wondered if Hubert really loved her, or if he was merely saying so to be pleasant. She wondered how she could find out. Hubert was handsome. But so was Charles handsome for that matter. And I, I am still quite beautiful, she reminded herself. Not in the same way as young girls like Hilda and Rosemarie, but in a different way. I have a mature beauty.

From the bank? Inge wondered.

Eric came home for the holidays.

Rosemarie made a list of all the people who had not written her a letter that morning:

George Lewis
Peter Elkin
Joan Elkin
Howard Toff
Edgar Rich
Marcy Powers
Sue Brownly
and many others

Paul said to the man at the hardware store: I need a new awl. What size awl do you have in mind? the man asked. One about this size, Paul said, showing the man with his hands. Oh Hilda!

What is his little name? Charles and Irene asked Hubert. His name, Hubert said, is Paul. A small one, isn't he? Charles remarked. But well made, Hubert noted.

Can I buy you a drink? Howard asked Hilda. Have you had any *grappa* yet? It's one of the favorite drinks of this country. Your time is up Howard, Hilda said ruthlessly. Get out of this café. Now wait a minute, Howard said. This is a free country isn't it? No, Hilda said. No buddy, a free country is precisely what this is not insofar as your sitting at this table is concerned. Besides, I've decided to go to Denmark on the next plane.

The mailman (Rosemarie's mailman) persisted in his irritating habit of doing the other side of the street before he did her side of the street. Rosemarie ate a bowl of Three-Minute Oats.

Eric cut his nails with one of those 25¢ nail cutters.

The bomb Henry Jackson threw at his father failed to detonate. Why did you throw this Schlitz can at me Henry? Henry's father asked, and why is it ticking like a bomb?

Hilda appeared in Paul's cellar. Paul, she asked, can I borrow an ax? or a saw?

Hubert touched Irene's breast. You have beautiful breasts, he said to Irene. I like them. Do you think they're too mature? Irene asked anxiously.

Mature?

3

Ann the Hyacinth Girl wanted Paul but could not have him. He was sleeping with Inge in Denmark.

From his window Charles watched Hilda. She sat playing under the black pear tree. She bit deeply into a black pear. It tasted bad and Hilda looked at the tree inquiringly. Charles started to cry. He had been reading Bergson. He was surprised by his own weeping, and in a state of surprise, decided to get something to eat. Irene was not at home. There was nothing in the refrigerator. What was he going to do for lunch? Go to the drugstore?

Rosemarie looked at Paul. But of course he's far too young for me, she thought.

Edward and Eric met on the street.

Inge wrote the following letter to Ann to explain why Ann could not have Paul:

Dear Ann—

I deeply appreciate the sentiments expressed by you in our recent ship-to-shore telephone conversation. Is the Black Sea pleasant? I hope so and hope too that you are having a nice voyage. The Matson Line is one of my favorite lines. However I must tell you that Paul is at present deeply embedded in a love affair with me, Inge Grote, a very nice girl here in Copenhagen, and therefore cannot respond to your proposals, charming and well stated as they were. You have a very nice prose style on the telephone. Also, I might point out that if Paul loves any girl other than me in the near future it will surely be Hilda, that girl of girls. Hilda! what a remarkable girl! Of course there is also the possibility that he will love some girl he has not met yet—this is remote, I think. But thank you for the additional hyacinths anyway, and we promise to think of you from time to time.

Your friend,
Inge

Charles lay in bed with his wife, Irene. He touched a breast, one of Irene's. You have beautiful breasts Irene, Charles said. Thank you, Irene said, Charles.

Howard's wire to Eric was never delivered.

Hubert thought seriously about his Christmas present to Charles and Irene. What can I get for these dear friends that will absolutely shatter them with happiness? he asked himself. I wonder if they'd like a gamelan? a rag rug?

Oh Hilda, Paul said cheerfully, it has been so long since I've been near to you! Why don't the three of us go out for supper?

Charles! Irene exclaimed. You're hungry! And you've been crying! Your gray vest is stained with tears. Let me make you a ham and cheese sandwich. Luckily I have just come from the grocery store, where I bought some ham, cheese, bread, lettuce, mustard and paper napkins. Charles asked: Have you seen or heard from Hubert lately by the way? He regarded his gray tear-stained vest. Not in a long time, Irene said, Hubert's been acting sort of distant lately for some strange reason. Oh Charles, can I have an extra ninety-three dollars a month for the household budget? I need some floor polish and would also like to subscribe to the *National Geographic.*

Every month?

Ann looked over the ship's rail at the Black Sea. She threw hyacinths into it, not just one but a dozen or more. They floated upon the black surface of the water.

"Can you give me a urine sample?" asked the nurse.

Paul placed his new awl in the toolbox. Was that a shotgun Eric had been looking at in the hardware store?

Irene, Hubert said, I love you. I've always hesitated to mention it though because I was inhibited by the fact that you are married to my close friend, Charles. Now I feel close to you here in this newsreel theater, for almost the first time. I feel intimate. I feel like there might be some love in you for me, too. Then, Irene said, your giving me Paul for a Christmas present was symbolic?

Inge smiled.

Rosemarie smiled.

Ann smiled.

Goodbye, Inge, Paul said. Your wonderful blondness has been wonderful and I shall always remember you that way. Goodbye! Goodbye!

Howard cashed a check at American Express. What shall I do with this money? he wondered. Nothing financial has meaning any more now that Hilda has gone to Denmark. He returned to the café in the hope that Hilda had not really meant it.

Charles put some more wine on to mull.

Henry Jackson's father thought candidly: Henry is awfully young to be an anarchist isn't he?

Put those empty Schlitz cans over there in the corner by the furnace Harry, Paul said. And thank you for lending me your pickup truck in this cold weather. I think you had better get some snow tires pretty soon though, as I hear that snow is predicted for the entire region shortly. Deep snow.

Howard to Hilda: If you don't understand me, that's okay. I will just wilt here.

Where are you going Eric with that shotgun? Hubert asked.

It is virtually impossible to read one of Joel S. Goldsmith's books on the oneness of life without becoming a better person Eric, Rosemarie said.

Eric, take that shotgun out of your mouth! Irene shouted.

Eric!

4

Oh Hubert, why did you give me that damn baby? Paul I mean? Didn't you know he was going to grow?

The French countryside (the countryside of France) was covered with golden grass. I'm looking for a bar, they said, called the Cow on the Roof or something like that.

Inge stretched her right and left arms luxuriously. You have brought me so much marvelous happiness Paul that although I know you will go away soon to consort once more with Hilda, that all-time all-timer girl, it still pleases me to be here in this good Dansk bed with you. Do you want to talk about phenomenological reduction now? or do you want a muffin?

Edward counted his Pard.

From the bank? Rosemarie asked herself.

I have decided Charles to go to the Virgin Islands with Hubert. Do you mind? Since Hubert's position in the market has improved radically I feel he is entitled to a little relaxation in the golden sun. Okay?

The Black Sea patrol boat captain said: *Hy*acinths?

The new black pear tree reached sturdily for the sky on the grave, the very place, of the old black pear tree.

He wondered whether to wrap it as a gift, or simply take it over to Charles and Irene's in the box. He couldn't decide. He decided to have a drink. While Hubert was mixing his vodka martini Paul started to cry. I wonder if I'm making these drinks too strong?

The snow of Montreal banked itself against the red Rambler. Paul and Hilda embraced. What is wonderful? they thought. They thought the answer might be in their eyes, or in their mingled breath, but they couldn't be sure. It might be illusory.

The Balloon

The balloon, beginning at a point on Fourteenth Street, the exact location of which I cannot reveal, expanded northward all one night, while people were sleeping, until it reached the Park. There, I stopped it; at dawn the northernmost edges lay over the Plaza; the free-hanging motion was frivolous and gentle. But experiencing a faint irritation at stopping, even to protect the trees, and seeing no reason the balloon should not be allowed to expand upward, over the parts of the city it was already covering, into the "air space" to be found there, I asked the engineers to see to it. This expansion took place throughout the morning, soft imperceptible sighing of gas through the valves. The balloon then covered forty-five blocks north-south and an irregular area east-west, as many as six crosstown blocks on either side of the Avenue in some places. That was the situation, then.

But it is wrong to speak of "situations," implying sets of circumstances leading to some resolution, some escape of tension; there were no situations, simply the balloon hanging there—muted heavy grays and browns for the most part, contrasting with walnut and soft yellows. A deliberate lack of finish, enhanced by skillful installation, gave the surface a rough, forgotten quality; sliding weights on the inside, carefully adjusted, anchored the great, vari-shaped mass at a number of points. Now we have had a flood of original ideas in all media, works of singular beauty as well as significant milestones in the history of inflation, but at that moment there was only *this balloon*, concrete particular, hanging there.

There were reactions. Some people found the balloon "interesting." As a response this seemed inadequate to the immensity of the balloon, the suddenness of its appearance over the city; on the other hand, in the absence of hysteria or other societally induced anxiety, it must be judged a calm, "mature" one. There was a certain amount of initial argumentation about the "meaning" of the balloon; this subsided, because we have learned not to insist on meanings, and they are rarely even looked for now, except in cases involving the simplest, safest phenomena. It was agreed that since the meaning of the balloon could never be known absolutely, extended discussion was pointless, or at least less purposeful than the activities of those who, for example, hung green and blue paper lanterns from the warm gray underside, in certain streets, or seized the occasion to write messages on the surface, announcing their availability for the performance of unnatural acts, or the availability of acquaintances.

Daring children jumped, especially at those points where the balloon hovered close to a building, so that the gap between balloon and building was a matter of a few inches, or points where the balloon actually made contact, exerting an ever-so-slight pressure against the side of a building, so that balloon and building seemed a unity. The upper surface was so structured that a "landscape" was presented, small valleys as well as slight knolls, or mounds; once atop the balloon, a stroll was possible, or even a trip, from one place to another. There was pleasure in being able to run down an incline, then up the opposing slope, both gently graded, or in making a leap from one side to the other. Bouncing was possible, because of the pneumaticity of the surface, and even falling, if that was your wish. That all these varied motions, as well as others, were within one's possibilities, in experiencing the "up" side of the balloon, was extremely exciting for children, accustomed to the city's flat, hard skin. But the purpose of the balloon was not to amuse children.

Too, the number of people, children and adults, who took advantage of the opportunities described was not so large as it might have been: a certain timidity, lack of trust in the balloon, was seen. There was, furthermore, some hostility. Because we had hidden the pumps, which fed helium to the interior, and because the surface was so vast that the authorities could not determine the point of entry—that is, the point at which the gas was injected—a degree of frustration was evidenced by those city officers into whose province such manifestations normally fell. The apparent purposelessness of the balloon was vexing (as was the fact that it was "there" at all). Had we painted, in great letters, "LABORATORY TESTS PROVE" or "18% MORE EFFECTIVE" on the sides of the balloon, this difficulty would have been circumvented. But I could not bear to do so. On the whole, these officers were remarkably tolerant, considering the dimensions of the anomaly, this tolerance being the result of, first, secret tests conducted by night that convinced them that little or nothing could be done in the way of removing or destroying the balloon, and, secondly, a public warmth that arose (not uncolored by touches of the aforementioned hostility) toward the balloon, from ordinary citizens.

As a single balloon must stand for a lifetime of thinking about balloons, so each citizen expressed, in the attitude he chose, a complex of attitudes. One man might consider that the balloon had to do with the notion *sullied*, as in the sentence *The big balloon sullied the otherwise clear and radiant Manhattan sky*. That is, the balloon was, in this man's view, an imposture, something inferior to the sky that had formerly been there, something interposed between the people and their "sky." But in fact it was January, the sky was dark and ugly; it was not a sky you could look up into, lying on your back in the street, with pleasure, unless pleasure, for you, proceeded from having been threatened, from having been misused. And the underside of the balloon was a pleasure to look up into, we had seen to that, muted grays and browns for the most part, contrasted with walnut and soft, forgotten yellows. And so, while this man was thinking *sullied*, still there was an admixture of pleasurable cognition in his thinking, struggling with the original perception.

Another man, on the other hand, might view the balloon as if it were part of a system of unanticipated rewards, as when one's employer walks in and says, "Here, Henry, take this package of money I have wrapped for you, because we have been doing so well in the business here, and I admire the way you bruise the tulips, without which bruising your department would not be a success, or at least not the success that it is." For this man the balloon might be a brilliantly heroic "muscle and pluck" experience, even if an experience poorly understood.

Another man might say, "Without the example of ——, it is doubtful that —— would exist today in its present form," and find many to agree with him, or to argue with him. Ideas of "bloat" and "float" were introduced, as well as concepts of dream and responsibility. Others engaged in remarkably detailed fantasies having to do with a wish either to lose themselves in the balloon, or to engorge it. The private character of these wishes, of their origins, deeply buried and unknown, was such that they were not much spoken of; yet there is evidence that they were widespread. It was also argued that what was important was what you felt when you stood under the balloon; some people claimed that they felt sheltered, warmed, as never before, while enemies of the balloon felt, or reported feeling, constrained, a "heavy" feeling.

Critical opinion was divided:

"monstrous pourings"

"harp"

XXXXXXX "certain contrasts with darker portions"

"inner joy"

"large, square corners"

"conservative eclecticism that has so far governed modern balloon design"

:::::: "abnormal vigor"

"warm, soft lazy passages"

"Has unity been sacrificed for a sprawling quality?"

"*Quelle catastrophe!*"

"munching"

People began, in a curious way, to locate themselves in relation to aspects of the balloon: "I'll be at that place where it dips down into Forty-seventh Street almost to the sidewalk, near the Alamo Chile House," or, "Why don't we go stand on top, and take the air, and maybe walk about a bit, where it forms a tight, curving line with the façade of the Gallery of Modern Art—" Marginal intersections offered entrances within a given time duration, as well as "warm, soft, lazy passages" in which . . . But it is wrong to speak of "marginal intersections," each intersection was crucial, none could be ignored (as if, walking there, you might not find someone capable of turning your attention, in a flash, from old exercises to new exercises, risks and escalations). Each intersection was crucial, meeting of balloon and building, meeting of balloon and man, meeting of balloon and balloon.

It was suggested that what was admired about the balloon was finally this: that it was not limited, or defined. Sometimes a bulge, blister, or sub-section would carry all the way east to the river on its own initiative, in the manner of an army's movements on a map, as seen in a headquarters remote from the fighting. Then that part would be, as it were, thrown back again, or would withdraw into new dispositions; the next morning, that part would have made another sortie, or disappeared altogether. This ability of the balloon to shift its shape, to change, was very pleasing, especially to people whose lives were rather rigidly patterned, persons to whom change, although desired, was not available. The balloon, for the twenty-two days of its existence, offered the possibility, in its randomness, of mislocation of the self, in contradistinction to the grid of precise, rectangular pathways under our feet. The amount of specialized training currently needed, and the consequent desirability of long-term commitments, has been occasioned by the steadily growing importance of complex machinery, in virtually all kinds of operations; as this tendency increases, more and more people will turn, in bewildered inadequacy, to solutions for which the balloon may stand as a prototype, or "rough draft."

I met you under the balloon, on the occasion of your return from Norway; you asked if it was mine; I said it was. The balloon, I said, is a spontaneous autobiographical disclosure, having to do with the unease I felt at your absence, and with sexual deprivation, but now that your visit to Bergen has been terminated, it is no longer necessary or appropriate. Removal of the balloon was easy; trailer trucks carried away the depleted fabric, which is now stored in West Virginia, awaiting some other time of unhappiness, some time, perhaps, when we are angry with one another.

The President

I am not altogether sympathetic to the new President. He is, certainly, a strange fellow (only forty-eight inches high at the shoulder). But is strangeness alone enough? I spoke to Sylvia: "Is strangeness alone enough?" "I love you," Sylvia said. I regarded her with my warm kind eyes. "Your thumb?" I said. One thumb was a fiasco of tiny crusted slashes. "Pop-top beer cans," she said. "He is a *strange fellow,* all right. He has some magic charisma which makes people—" She stopped and began again. "When the band begins to launch into his campaign song, 'Struttin' with Some Barbecue,' I just . . . I can't . . ."

The darkness, strangeness, and complexity of the new President have touched everyone. There has been a great deal of fainting lately. Is the President at fault? I was sitting, I remember, in Row EE at City Center; the opera was *The Gypsy Baron*. Sylvia was singing in her green-and-blue gypsy costume in the gypsy encampment. I was thinking about the President. Is he, I wondered, right for this period? He is a *strange fellow,* I thought—not like the other Presidents we've had. Not like Garfield. Not like Taft. Not like Harding, Hoover, either of the Roosevelts, or Woodrow Wilson. Then I noticed a lady sitting in front of me, holding a baby. I tapped her on the shoulder. "Madam," I said, "your child has I believe fainted." "Giscard!" she cried, rotating the baby's head like a doll's. "Giscard, what has happened to you?" The President was smiling in his box.

"The President!" I said to Sylvia in the Italian restaurant. She raised her glass of warm red wine. "Do you think he liked me? My singing?" "He looked pleased," I said. "He was smiling."

"A brilliant whirlwind campaign, I thought," Sylvia stated. "Winning was brilliant," I said. "He is the first President we've had from City College," Sylvia said. A waiter fainted behind us. "But is he right for the period?" I asked. "Our period is perhaps not so choice as the previous period, still—"

"He thinks a great deal about death, like all people from City," Sylvia said. "The death theme looms large in his consciousness. I've known a great many people from City, and these people, with no significant exceptions, are hung up on the death theme. It's an obsession, as it were." Other waiters carried the waiter who had fainted out into the kitchen.

"Our period will be characterized in future histories as a period of tentativeness and uncertainty, I feel," I said. "A kind of parenthesis. When he rides in his black limousine with the plastic top I see a little boy who has blown an enormous soap bubble which has trapped him. The look on his face—" "The other candidate was dazzled by his strangeness, newness, smallness, and philosophical grasp of the death theme," Sylvia said. "The other candidate didn't have a prayer," I said. Sylvia adjusted her green-and-blue veils in the Italian restaurant. "Not having gone to City College and sat around the cafeterias there discussing death," she said.

I am, as I say, not entirely sympathetic. Certain things about the new President are not clear. I can't make out what he is thinking. When he has finished speaking I can never remember what he has said. There remains only an impression of strangeness, darkness . . . On television, his face clouds when his name is mentioned. It is as if hearing his name frightens him. Then he stares directly into the camera (an actor's preempting gaze) and begins to speak. One hears only cadences. Newspaper accounts of his speeches always say only that he "touched on a number of matters in the realm of . . ." When he has finished speaking he appears nervous and unhappy. The camera credits fade in over an image of the President standing stiffly, with his arms rigid at his sides, looking to the right and to the left, as if awaiting instructions. On the other hand, the handsome meliorist who ran against him, all zest and programs, was defeated by a fantastic margin.

People are fainting. On Fifty-seventh Street, a young girl dropped in her tracks in front of Henri Bendel. I was shocked to discover that she wore only a garter belt under her dress. I picked her up and carried her into the store with the help of a Salvation Army major—a very tall man with an orange hair-piece. "She fainted," I said to the floorwalker. We talked about the new President, the Salvation Army major and I. "I'll tell you what *I* think," he said. "I think he's got something up his sleeve nobody knows about. I think he's keeping it under wraps. One of these days . . ." The Salvation Army major shook my hand. "I'm not saying that the problems he faces aren't tremendous, staggering. The awesome burden of the Presidency. But if anybody—any *one man* . . ."

What is going to happen? What is the President planning? No one knows. But everyone is convinced that he will bring it off. Our exhausted age wishes above everything to plunge into the heart of the problem, to be able to say, *Here is the difficulty*. And the new President, that tiny, strange, and brilliant man, seems cankered and difficult enough to take us there. In the meantime, people are fainting. My secretary fell in the middle of a sentence. "Miss Kagle," I said. "Are you all right?" She was wearing an anklet of tiny silver circles. Each tiny silver circle held an initial: @@@@@@@@@@@@@@@@@. Who is this person "A"? What is he in your life, Miss Kagle?

I gave her water with a little brandy in it. I speculated about the President's mother. Little is known about her. She presents herself in various guises:

A little lady, 5' 2", with a cane.

A big lady, 7' 1", with a dog.

A wonderful old lady, 4' 3", with an indomitable spirit.

A noxious old sack, 6' 8", excaudate, because of an operation.

Little is known about her. We are assured, however, that the same damnable involvements that obsess us obsess her too. Copulation. Strangeness. Applause. She must be pleased that her son is what he is—loved and looked up to, a mode of hope for millions. "Miss Kagle. Drink it down. It will put you on your feet again, Miss Kagle." I regarded her with my warm kind eyes.

At Town Hall I sat reading the program notes to *The Gypsy Baron.* Outside the building, eight mounted policemen collapsed en bloc. The well-trained horses planted their feet delicately among the bodies. Sylvia was singing. They said a small man could never be President (only forty-eight inches high at the shoulder). Our period is not the one I would have chosen, but it has chosen me. The new President must have certain intuitions. I am convinced that he has these intuitions (although I am certain of very little else about him; I have reservations, I am not sure). I could tell you about his mother's summer journey, in 1919, to western Tibet—about the dandymen and the red bear, and how she told off the Pathan headman, instructing him furiously to rub up his English or get out of her service—but what order of knowledge is this? Let me instead simply note his smallness, his strangeness, his brilliance, and say that we expect great things of him. "I love you," Sylvia said. The President stepped through the roaring curtain. We applauded until our arms hurt. We shouted until the ushers set off flares enforcing silence. The orchestra tuned itself. Sylvia sang the second lead. The President was smiling in his box. At the finale, the entire cast slipped into the orchestra pit in a great, swooning mass. We cheered until the ushers tore up our tickets.

Game

Shotwell keeps the jacks and the rubber ball in his attaché case and will not allow me to play with them. He plays with them, alone, sitting on the floor near the console hour after hour, chanting "onesies, twosies, threesies, foursies" in a precise, well-modulated voice, not so loud as to be annoying, not so soft as to allow me to forget. I point out to Shotwell that two can derive more enjoyment from playing jacks than one, but he is not interested. I have asked repeatedly to be allowed to play by myself, but he simply shakes his head. "Why?" I ask. "They're mine," he says. And when he has finished, when he has sated himself, back they go into the attaché case.

It is unfair but there is nothing I can do about it. I am aching to get my hands on them.

Shotwell and I watch the console. Shotwell and I live under the ground and watch the console. If certain events take place upon the console, we are to insert our keys in the appropriate locks and turn our keys. Shotwell has a key and I have a key. If we turn our keys simultaneously the bird flies, certain switches are activated and the bird flies. But the bird never flies. In one hundred thirty-three days the bird has not flown. Meanwhile Shotwell and I watch each other. We each wear a .45 and if Shotwell behaves strangely I am supposed to shoot him. If I behave strangely Shotwell is supposed to shoot me. We watch the console and think about shooting each other and think about the bird. Shotwell's behavior with the jacks is strange. Is it strange? I do not know. Perhaps he is merely a selfish bastard, perhaps his character is flawed, perhaps his childhood was twisted. I do not know.

Each of us wears a .45 and each of us is supposed to shoot the other if the other is behaving strangely. How strangely is strangely? I do not know. In addition to the .45 I have a .38 which Shotwell does not know about concealed in my attaché case, and Shotwell has a .25 caliber Beretta which I do not know about strapped to his right calf. Sometimes instead of watching the console I pointedly watch Shotwell's .45, but this is simply a ruse, simply a maneuver, in reality I am watching his hand when it dangles in the vicinity of his right calf. If he decides I am behaving strangely he will shoot me not with the .45 but with the Beretta. Similarly Shotwell pretends to watch my .45 but he is really watching my hand resting idly atop my attaché case, my hand resting idly atop my attaché case, my hand. My hand resting idly atop my attaché case.

In the beginning I took care to behave normally. So did Shotwell. Our behavior was painfully normal. Norms of politeness, consideration, speech, and personal habits were scrupulously observed. But then it became apparent that an error had been made, that our relief was not going to arrive. Owing to an oversight. Owing to an oversight we have been here for one hundred thirty-three days. When it became clear that an error had been made, that we were not to be relieved, the norms were relaxed. Definitions of normality were redrawn in the agreement of January 1, called by us, The Agreement. Uniform regulations were relaxed, and mealtimes are no longer rigorously scheduled. We eat when we are hungry and sleep when we are tired. Considerations of rank and precedence were temporarily put aside, a handsome concession on the part of Shotwell, who is a captain, whereas I am only a first lieutenant. One of us watches the console at all times rather than two of us watching the console at all times, except when we are both on our feet. One of us watches the console at all times and if the bird flies then that one wakes the other and we turn our keys in the locks simultaneously and the bird flies. Our system involves a delay of perhaps twelve seconds but I do not care because I am not well, and Shotwell does not care because he is not himself. After the agreement was signed Shotwell produced the jacks and the rubber ball from his attaché case, and I began to write a series of descriptions of forms occurring in nature, such as a shell, a leaf, a stone, an animal. On the walls.

Shotwell plays jack and I write descriptions of natural forms on the walls.

Shotwell is enrolled in a USAFI course which leads to a master's degree in business administration from the University of Wisconsin (although we are not in Wisconsin, we are in Utah, Montana or Idaho). When we went down it was in either Utah, Montana or Idaho, I don't remember. We have been here for one hundred thirty-three days owing to an oversight. The pale green reinforced concrete walls sweat and the air conditioning zips on and off erratically and Shotwell reads *Introduction to Marketing* by Lassiter and Munk, making notes with a blue ballpoint pen. Shotwell is not himself, but I do not know it, he presents a calm aspect and reads *Introduction to Marketing* and makes his exemplary notes with a blue ballpoint pen, meanwhile controlling the .38 in my attaché case with one-third of his attention. I am not well.

We have been here one hundred thirty-three days owing to an oversight. Although now we are not sure what is oversight, what is plan. Perhaps the plan is for us to stay here permanently, or if not permanently at least for a year, for three hundred sixty-five days. Or if not for a year for some number of days known to them and not known to us, such as two hundred days. Or perhaps they are observing our behavior in some way, sensors of some kind, perhaps our behavior determines the number of days. It may be that they are pleased with us, with our behavior, not in every detail but in sum. Perhaps the whole thing is very successful, perhaps the whole thing is an experiment and the experiment is very successful. I do not know. But I suspect that the only way they can persuade sun-loving creatures into their pale green sweating reinforced concrete rooms under the ground is to say that the system is twelve hours on, twelve hours off. And then lock us below for some number of days known to them and not known to us. We eat well although the frozen enchiladas are damp when defrosted and the frozen devil's food cake is sour and untasty. We sleep uneasily and acrimoniously. I hear Shotwell shouting in his sleep, objecting, denouncing, cursing sometimes, weeping sometimes, in his sleep. When Shotwell sleeps I try to pick the lock on his attaché case, so as to get at the jacks. Thus far I have been unsuccessful. Nor has Shotwell been successful in picking the locks on my attaché case so as to get at the .38. I have seen the marks on the shiny surface. I laughed, in the latrine, pale green walls sweating and the air conditioning whispering, in the latrine.

I write descriptions of natural forms on the walls, scratching them on the tile surface with a diamond. The diamond is a two and one-half carat solitaire I had in my attaché case when we went down. It was for Lucy. The south wall of the room containing the console is already covered. I have described a shell, a leaf, a stone, animals, a baseball bat. I am aware that the baseball bat is not a natural form. Yet I described it. "The baseball bat," I said, "is typically made of wood. It is typically one meter in length or a little longer, fat at one end, tapering to afford a comfortable grip at the other. The end with the handhold typically offers a slight rim, or lip, at the nether extremity, to prevent slippage." My description of the baseball bat ran to 4500 words, all scratched with a diamond on the south wall. Does Shotwell read what I have written? I do not know. I am aware that Shotwell regards my writing-behavior as a little strange. Yet it is no stranger than his jacks-behavior, or the day he appeared in black bathing trunks with the .25 caliber Beretta strapped to his right calf and stood over the console, trying to span with his two arms outstretched the distance between the locks. He could not do it, I had already tried, standing over the console with my two arms outstretched, the distance is too great. I was moved to comment but did not comment, comment would have provoked countercomment, comment would have led God knows where. They had in their infinite patience, in their infinite foresight, in their infinite wisdom already imagined a man standing over the console with his two arms outstretched, trying to span with his two arms outstretched the distance between the locks.

Shotwell is not himself. He has made certain overtures. The burden of his message is not clear. It has something to do with the keys, with the locks. Shotwell is a strange person. He appears to be less affected by our situation than I. He goes about his business stolidly, watching the console, studying *Introduction to Marketing*, bouncing his rubber ball on the floor in a steady, rhythmical, conscientious manner. He appears to be less affected by our situation than I am. He is stolid. He says nothing. But he has made certain overtures, certain overtures have been made. I am not sure that I understand them. They have something to do with the keys, with the locks. Shotwell has something in mind. Stolidly he shucks the shiny silver paper from the frozen enchiladas, stolidly he stuffs them into the electric oven. But he has something in mind. But there must be a quid pro quo. I insist on a quid pro quo. I have something in mind.

I am not well. I do not know our target. They do not tell us for which city the bird is targeted. I do not know. That is planning. That is not my responsibility. My responsibility is to watch the console and when certain events take place upon the console, turn my key in the lock. Shotwell bounces the rubber ball on the floor in a steady, stolid, rhythmical manner. I am aching to get my hands on the ball, on the jacks. We have been here one hundred thirty-three days owing to an oversight. I write on the walls. Shotwell chants "onesies, twosies, threesies, foursies" in a precise, well-modulated voice. Now he cups the jacks and the rubber ball in his hands and rattles them suggestively. I do not know for which city the bird is targeted. Shotwell is not himself.

Sometimes I cannot sleep. Sometimes Shotwell cannot sleep. Sometimes when Shotwell cradles me in his arms and rocks me to sleep, singing Brahms' "Guten abend, gute Nacht," or I cradle Shotwell in my arms and rock him to sleep, singing, I understand what it is Shotwell wishes me to do. At such moments we are very close. But only if he will give me the jacks. That is fair. There is something he wants me to do with my key, while he does something with his key. But only if he will give me my turn. That is fair. I am not well.

Alice

twirling around on my piano stool my head begins to swim my head begins to swim twirling around on my piano stool twirling around on my piano stool a dizzy spell eventuates twirling around on my piano stool I begin to feel dizzy twirling around on my piano stool

I want to fornicate with Alice but my wife Regine would be insulted Alice's husband Buck would be insulted my child Hans would be insulted my answering service would be insulted tingle of insult running through this calm loving healthy productive tightly-knit

the hinder portion scalding-house good eating Curve B in addition to the usual baths and ablutions military police sumptuousness of the washhouse risking misstatements kept distances iris to iris queen of holes damp, hairy legs note of anger chanting and shouting konk sense of "mold" on the "muff" sense of "talk" on the "surface" konk[2] all sorts of chemical girl who delivered the letter give it a bone plummy bare legs saturated in every belief and ignorance rational living private client bad bosom uncertain workmen mutton-tugger obedience to the rules of the logical system Lord Muck hot tears harmonica rascal

that's chaos can you produce chaos? Alice asked certainly I can produce chaos I said I produced chaos she regarded the chaos chaos is handsome and attractive she said and more durable than regret I said and more nourishing than regret she said

I want to fornicate with Alice but it is a doomed project fornicating with Alice there are obstacles impediments preclusions estoppels I will exhaust them for you what a gas see cruel deprivements SECTION SEVEN moral ambiguities SECTION NINETEEN Alice's thighs are like SECTION TWENTY-ONE

I am an OB I obstetricate ladies from predicaments holding the bucket I carry a device connected by radio to my answering service bleeps when I am wanted can't even go to the films now for fear of bleeping during filmic highpoints can I in conscience *turn off* while fornicating with Alice?

Alice is married to Buck I am married to Regine Buck is my friend Regine is my wife regret is battologized in SECTIONS SIX THROUGH TWELVE and the actual intercourse intrudes somewhere in SECTION FORTY-THREE

I maintain an air of serenity which is spurious I manage this by limping my limp artful creation not an abject limp (Quasimodo) but a proud limp (Byron) I move slowly solemnly through the world miming a stiff leg this enables me to endure the gaze of strangers the hatred of pediatricians

we discuss discuss and discuss important considerations swarm and dither

for example in what house can I fornicate with Alice? in my house with Hans pounding on the bedroom door in her house with Buck shedding his sheepskin coat in the kitchen in some temporary rented house what joy

can Alice fornicate without her Malachi record playing? will Buck miss the Malachi record which Alice will have taken to the rented house? will Buck kneel before the rows and rows of records in his own house running a finger along the spines looking for the Malachi record? poignant poignant can Buck the honest architect with his acres of projects his mobs of draughtsmen the alarm bell which goes off in his office whenever the government decides to renovate a few blocks of blight can Buck object if I decide to renovate Alice?

and what of the boil on my ass the right buttock can I lounge in the bed in the rented house in such a way that Alice will not see will not start away from in fear terror revulsion

and what of rugs should I rug the rented house and what of cups what of leaning on an elbow in the Hertz Rent-All bed having fornicated with Alice and desiring a cup of black and what of the soap powder dish towels such a cup implies and what of a decent respect for the opinions of mankind and what of the hammer throw

I was a heavy man with the hammer once should there be a spare hammer for spare moments?

Alice's thighs are like great golden varnished wooden oars I assume I haven't seen them

chaos is tasty AND USEFUL TOO

colored clothes paper handkerchiefs super cartoons bit of fresh the Pope's mule inmission do such poor work together in various Poujadist manifestations deep-toned blacks waivers play to the gas Zentralbibliothek Zurich her bare ass with a Teddy bear blatty string kept in a state of suspended tension by a weight cut from the backs of alligators

you can do it too it's as easy as it looks

there is no game for that particular player white and violet over hedge and ditch clutching airbrush still single but wearing a ring the dry a better "feel" in use pretended to be doing it quite unconsciously fishes hammering long largish legs damp fine water dancer, strains of music, expenses of the flight Swiss emotion transparent thin alkaline and very slippery fluid danger for white rats little country telephone booths brut insults brought by mouth famous incidents

in bed regarding Alice's stomach it will be a handsome one I'm sure but will it not also resemble some others?

or would it be possible in the rented house to dispense with a bed to have only a mattress on the floor with all the values that attach to that or perhaps only a pair of blankets or perhaps only the skin of some slow-moving animal such as the slug the armadillo or perhaps only a pile of read newspapers

wise Alice tells you things you hadn't heard before in the world in Paris she recognizes the Ritz from the Babar books oh yes that's where the elephants stay

or would it be possible to use other people's houses at hours when these houses were empty would that be erotic? could love be made in doorways under hedges under the sprinting chestnut tree? can Alice forego her Malachi record so that Buck kneeling before the rows of records in his empty deserted abandoned and pace-setting house fingering the galore of spines there would *find* the Malachi record with little peeps of gree peeps of gree good for Buck!

shit

Magritte

what is good about Alice is first she likes chaos what is good about Alice is second she is a friend of Tom

SECTION NINETEEN TOM plaster thrashing gumbo of explanations grease on the Tinguely new plays sentimental songs sudden torrential rains carbon projects evidence of eroticism conflict between zones skin, ambiguous movements baked on the blue table 3 mm. a stone had broken my windshield hurricane damage impulsive behavior knees folded back lines on his tongue with a Magic Marker gape orange tips ligamenta lata old men buried upright delights of everyone's life uninteresting variations pygmy owl assumes the quadrupedal position in which the intestines sink forward measurement of kegs other sciences megapod nursemaid said very studied, hostile things she had long been saving up breakfast dream wonderful loftiness trank red clover uterine spasms guided by reason black envelopes highly esteemed archers wet leg critical menials making gestures chocolate ice pink and green marble weight of the shoes I was howling in the kitchen Tom was howling in the hall white and violet over hedge and ditch clutching oolfoo quiet street suburban in flavor quiet crowd only slightly restive as reports of the letters from Japan circulate

I am whispering to my child Hans my child Hans is whispering to me Hans whispers that I am faced with a problem in ethics the systems of the axiologicalists he whispers the systems of the deontologicalists but I am not privy to these systems I whisper try the New School he whispers the small device in my coat pocket goes bleep!

nights of ethics at the New School

is this "middle life"? can I hurry on to "old age"? I see Alice walking away from me carrying an A&P shopping bag the shopping bag is full of haunting melodies grid coordinates great expectations French ticklers magic marks

nights of ethics at the New School "good" and "bad" as terms with only an emotive meaning I like the Walrus best Alice whispered he ate more than the Carpenter though the instructor whispered then I like the Carpenter best Alice whispered but he ate as many as he could get the instructor whispered

yellow brick wall visible from rear bedroom window of the rented house

I see Alice walking away from me carrying a Primary Structure

MOVEMENT OF ALICE'S ZIPPER located at the rear of Alice's dress running from the neckhole to the bumhole yes I know the first is an attribute of the dress the second an attribute of the girl but I have located it for you in some rough way the zipper you could find it in the dark

a few crones are standing about next to them are some louts the crones and louts are talking about the movement of Alice's zipper

rap Alice on the rump standing in the rented bedroom I have a roller and a bucket of white paint requires a second coat perhaps a third who knows a fourth and fifth I sit on the floor next to the paint bucket regarding the yellow brick wall visible there a subway token on the floor I pick it up drop it into the paint bucket slow circles on the surface of the white paint

insurance?

confess that for many years I myself took no other measures, followed obediently in the footsteps of my teachers, copied the procedures I observed painted animals, frisky inventions, thwarted patrons, most great hospitals and clinics, gray gauzes transparent plastic containers Presidential dining room about 45 cm. coquetry and flirtation knit games beautiful tension beaten metal catchpenny devices impersonal panic Klinger's nude in tree tickling nose of bear with long branch or wand unbutton his boots fairly broad duct, highly elastic walls peerless piece "racing" Dr. Haacke has poppy-show pulled me down on the bed and started two ceiling-high trees astonishing and little known remark of Balzac's welter this field of honor financial difficulties what sort of figure did these men cut?

Alice's husband Buck calls me will I gather with him for a game of golf? I accept but on the shoe shelf I cannot find the correct shoes distractedness stupidity weak memory! I am boring myself what should be the punishment I am forbidden to pick my nose forevermore

Buck is rushing toward me carrying pieces of carbon paper big as bedsheets what is he hinting at? duplicity

bleep! it is the tipped uterus from Carson City calling

SECTION FORTY-THREE then I began chewing upon Alice's long and heavy breasts first one then the other the nipples brightened freshened then I turned her on her stomach and rubbed her back first slow then fast first the shoulders then the buttocks

possible attitudes found in books 1) I don't know what's happening to me 2) what does it mean? 3) seized with the deepest sadness, I know not why 4) I am lost, my head whirls, I know not where I am 5) I lose myself 6) I ask you, what have I come to? 7) I no longer know where I am, what is this country? 8) had I fallen from the skies, I could not be more giddy 9) a mixture of pleasure and confusion, that is my state 10) where am I, and when will this end? 11) what shall I do? I do not know where I am

but I do know where I am I am on West Eleventh Street shot with lust I speak to Alice on the street she is carrying a shopping bag I attempt to see what is in the shopping bag but she conceals it we turn to savor rising over the Women's House of Detention a particularly choice bit of "sisters" statistics on the longevity of life angelism straight as a loon's leg conceals her face behind *pneumatiques* hurled unopened scream the place down tuck mathematical models six hours in the confessional psychological comparisons scream the place down Mars yellow plights make micefeet of old cowboy airs cornflakes people pointing to the sea overboots nasal contact 7 cm. prune the audience dense car correctly identify chemical junk blooms of iron wonderful loftiness sentient populations

Robert Kennedy Saved from Drowning

K. at His Desk

He is neither abrupt with nor excessively kind to associates. Or he is both abrupt and kind.

The telephone is, for him, a whip, a lash, but also a conduit for soothing words, a sink into which he can hurl gallons of syrup if it comes to that.

He reads quickly, scratching brief comments ("Yes," "No") in corners of the paper. He slouches in the leather chair, looking about him with a slightly irritated air for new visitors, new difficulties. He spends his time sending and receiving messengers.

"I spend my time sending and receiving messengers," he says. "Some of these messages are important. Others are not."

Described by Secretaries

A: "Quite frankly I think he forgets a lot of things. But the things he forgets are those which are inessential. I even think he might forget deliberately, to leave his mind free. He has the ability to get rid of unimportant details. And he does."

B: "Once when I was sick, I hadn't heard from him, and I thought he had forgotten me. You know usually your boss will send flowers or something like that. I was in the hospital, and I was mighty blue. I was in a room with another girl, and *her* boss hadn't sent her anything either. Then suddenly the door opened and there he was with the biggest bunch of yellow tulips I'd ever seen in my life. And the other girl's boss was with him, and he had tulips too. They were standing there with all those tulips, smiling."

Behind the Bar

At a crowded party, he wanders behind the bar to make himself a Scotch and water. His hand is on the bottle of Scotch, his glass is waiting. The bartender, a small man in a beige uniform with gilt buttons, politely asks K. to return to the other side, the guests' side, of the bar. "You let one behind here, they all be behind here," the bartender says.

K. Reading the Newspaper

His reactions are impossible to catalogue. Often he will find a note that amuses him endlessly, some anecdote involving, say, a fireman who has propelled his apparatus at record-breaking speed to the wrong address. These small stories are clipped, carried about in a pocket, to be produced at appropriate moments for the pleasure of friends. Other manifestations please him less. An account of an earthquake in Chile, with its thousands of dead and homeless, may depress him for weeks. He memorizes the terrible statistics, quoting them everywhere and saying, with a grave look: "We must do something." Important actions often follow, sometimes within a matter of hours. (On the other hand, these two kinds of responses may be, on a given day, inexplicably reversed.)

The more trivial aspects of the daily itemization are skipped. While reading, he maintains a rapid drumming of his fingertips on the desktop. He receives twelve newspapers, but of these, only four are regarded as serious.

Attitude Toward His Work

"Sometimes I can't seem to do anything. The work is there, piled up, it seems to me an insurmountable obstacle, really out of reach. I sit and look at it, wondering where to begin, how to take hold of it. Perhaps I pick up a piece of paper, try to read it but my mind is elsewhere, I am thinking of something else, I can't seem to get the gist of it, it seems meaningless, devoid of interest, not having to do with human affairs, drained of life. Then, in an hour, or even a moment, everything changes suddenly: I realize I only have to *do* it, hurl myself into the midst of it, proceed mechanically, the first thing and then the second thing, that it is simply a matter of moving from one step to the next, plowing through it. I become interested, I become excited, I work very fast, things fall into place, I am exhilarated, amazed that these things could ever have seemed dead to me."

Sleeping on the Stones of Unknown Towns (Rimbaud)

K. is walking, with that familiar slight dip of the shoulders, through the streets of a small city in France or Germany. The shop signs are in a language which alters when inspected closely, MÖBEL becoming MEUBLES for example, and the citizens mutter to themselves with dark virtuosity a mixture of languages. K. is very interested, looks closely at everything, at the shops, the goods displayed, the clothing of the people, the tempo of street life, the citizens themselves, wondering about them. What are their water needs?

"In the West, wisdom is mostly gained at lunch. At lunch, people tell you things."

The nervous eyes of the waiters.

The tall bald cook, white apron, white T-shirt, grinning through an opening in the wall.

"Why is that cook looking at me?"

Urban Transportation

"The transportation problems of our cities and their rapidly expanding suburbs are the most urgent and neglected transportation problems confronting the country. In these heavily populated and industrialized areas, people are dependent on a system of transportation that is at once complex and inadequate. Obsolete facilities and growing demands have created seemingly insoluble difficulties and present methods of dealing with these difficulties offer little prospect of relief."

K. Penetrated with Sadness

He hears something playing on someone else's radio, in another part of the building.

The music is wretchedly sad; now he can (barely) hear it, now it fades into the wall.

He turns on his own radio. There it is, on his own radio, the same music. The sound fills the room.

Karsh of Ottawa

"We sent a man to Karsh of Ottawa and told him that we admired his work very much. Especially, I don't know, the Churchill thing and, you know, the Hemingway thing, and all that. And we told him we wanted to set up a sitting for K. sometime in June, if that would be convenient for him, and he said yes, that was okay, June was okay, and where did we want to have it shot, there or in New York or where. Well, that was a problem because we didn't know exactly what K.'s schedule would be for June, it was up in the air, so we tentatively said New York around the fifteenth. And he said, that was okay, he could do that. And he wanted to know how much time he could have, and we said, well, how much time do you need? And he said he didn't know, it varied from sitter to sitter. He said some people were very restless and that made it difficult to get just the right shot. He said there was one shot in each sitting that was, you know, the key shot, the right one. He said he'd have to see, when the time came."

Dress

He is neatly dressed in a manner that does not call attention to itself. The suits are soberly cut and in dark colors. He must at all times present an aspect of freshness difficult to sustain because of frequent movements from place to place under conditions which are not always the most favorable. Thus he changes clothes frequently, especially shirts. In the course of a day he changes his shirt many times. There are always extra shirts about, in boxes.

"Which of you has the shirts?"

A Friend Comments: K.'s Aloneness

"The thing you have to realize about K. is that essentially he's absolutely alone in the world. There's this terrible loneliness which prevents people from getting too close to him. Maybe it comes from something in his childhood, I don't know. But he's very hard to get to know, and a lot of people who think they know him rather well don't really know him at all. He says something or does something that surprises you, and you realize that all along you really didn't know him at all.

"He has surprising facets. I remember once we were out in a small boat. K. of course was the captain. Some rough weather came up and we began to head back in. I began worrying about picking up a landing and I said to him that I didn't think the anchor would hold, with the wind and all. He just looked at me. Then he said: 'Of course it will hold. That's what it's for.' "

K. on Crowds

"There are exhausted crowds and vivacious crowds.

"Sometimes, standing there, I can sense whether a particular crowd is one thing or the other. Sometimes the mood of the crowd is disguised, sometimes you only find out after a quarter of an hour what sort of crowd a particular crowd is.

"And you can't speak to them in the same way. The variations have to be taken into account. You have to say something to them that is meaningful to them *in that mood.*"

Gallery-going

K. enters a large gallery on Fifty-seventh Street, in the Fuller Building. His entourage includes several ladies and gentlemen. Works by a geometricist are on show. K. looks at the immense, rather theoretical paintings.

"Well, at least we know he has a ruler."

The group dissolves in laughter. People repeat the remark to one another, laughing.

The artist, who has been standing behind a dealer, regards K. with hatred.

K. Puzzled by His Children

The children are crying. There are several children, one about four, a boy, then another boy, slightly older, and a little girl, very beautiful, wearing blue jeans, crying. There are various objects on the grass, an electric train, a picture book, a red ball, a plastic bucket, a plastic shovel.

K. frowns at the children whose distress issues from no source immediately available to the eye, which seems indeed uncaused, vacant, a general anguish. K. turns to the mother of these children who is standing nearby wearing hip-huggers which appear to be made of linked marshmallows studded with diamonds but then I am a notoriously poor observer.

"Play with them," he says.

This mother of ten quietly suggests that K. himself "play with them."

K. picks up the picture book and begins to read to the children. But the book has a German text. It has been left behind, perhaps, by some foreign visitor. Nevertheless K. perseveres.

"A ist der Affe, er isst mit der Pfote." ("A is the Ape, he eats with his Paw.")

The crying of the children continues.

A Dream

Orange trees.

Overhead, a steady stream of strange aircraft which resemble kitchen implements, bread boards, cookie sheets, colanders.

The shiny aluminum instruments are on their way to complete the bombings of Sidi-Madani.

A farm in the hills.

Matters (from an Administrative Assistant)

"A lot of matters that had been pending came to a head right about that time, moved to the front burner, things we absolutely had to take care of. And we couldn't find K. Nobody knew where he was. We had looked everywhere. He had just withdrawn, made himself unavailable. There was this one matter that was probably more pressing than all the rest put together. Really crucial. We were all standing around wondering what to do. We were getting pretty nervous because this thing was really . . . Then K. walked in and disposed of it with a quick phone call. A quick phone call!"

Childhood of K. as Recalled by a Former Teacher

"He was a very alert boy, very bright, good at his studies, very thorough, very conscientious. But that's not unusual; that describes a good number of the boys who pass through here. It's not unusual, that is, to find these qualities which are after all the qualities that we look for and encourage in them. What *was* unusual about K. was his compassion, something very rare for a boy of that age—even if they have it, they're usually very careful not to display it for fear of seeming soft, girlish. I remember, though, that in K. this particular attribute was very marked. I would almost say that it was his strongest characteristic."

Speaking to No One but Waiters, He—

"The dandelion salad with bacon, I think."

"The *rysstafel.*"

"The poached duck."

"The black bean purée."

"The cod fritters."

K. Explains a Technique

"It's an expedient in terms of how not to destroy a situation which has been a long time gestating, or, again, how *to* break it up if it appears that the situation has changed, during the gestation period, into one whose implications are not quite what they were at the beginning. What I mean is that in this business things are constantly altering (usually for the worse) and usually you want to give the impression that you're not watching this particular situation particularly closely, that you're paying no special attention to it, until you're ready to make your move. That is, it's best to be sudden, if you can manage it. Of course you can't do that all the time. Sometimes you're just completely wiped out, cleaned out, totaled, and then the only thing to do is shrug and forget about it."

K. on His Own Role

"Sometimes it seems to me that it doesn't matter what I do, that it is enough to exist, to sit somewhere, in a garden for example, watching whatever is to be seen there, the small events. At other times, I'm aware that other people, possibly a great number of other people, could be affected by what I do or fail to do, that I have a responsibility, as we all have, to make the best possible use of whatever talents I've been given, for the common good. It is not enough to sit in that garden, however restful or pleasurable it might be. The world is full of unsolved problems, situations that demand careful, reasoned and intelligent action. In Latin America, for example."

As Entrepreneur

The original cost estimates for burying the North Sea pipeline have been exceeded by a considerable margin. Everyone wonders what he will say about this contretemps which does not fail to have its dangers for those responsible for the costly miscalculations, which are viewed in many minds as inexcusable.

He says only: "Exceptionally difficult rock conditions."

With Young People

K., walking the streets of unknown towns, finds himself among young people. Young people line these streets, narrow and curving, which are theirs, dedicated to them. They are everywhere, resting on the embankments, their guitars, small radios, long hair. They sit on the sidewalks, back to back, heads turned to stare. They stand implacably on street corners, in doorways, or lean on their elbows in windows, or squat in small groups at that place where the sidewalk meets the walls of buildings. The streets are filled with these young people who say nothing, reveal only a limited interest, refuse to declare themselves. Street after street contains them, a great number, more displayed as one turns a corner, rank upon rank stretching into the distance, drawn from the arcades, the plazas, staring.

He Discusses the French Writer, Poulet

"For Poulet, it is not enough to speak of *seizing the moment*. It is rather a question of, and I quote, 'recognizing in the instant which lives and dies, which surges out of nothingness and which ends in dream, an intensity and depth of significance which ordinarily attaches only to the whole of existence.'

"What Poulet is describing is neither an ethic nor a prescription but rather what he has discovered in the work of Marivaux. Poulet has taken up the Marivaudian canon and squeezed it with both hands to discover the essence of what may be called the Marivaudian being, what Poulet in fact calls the Marivaudian being.

"The Marivaudian being is, according to Poulet, a pastless futureless man, born anew at every instant. The instants are points which organize themselves into a line, but what is important is the instant, not the line. The Marivaudian being has in a sense no history. Nothing follows from what has gone before. He is constantly surprised. He cannot predict his own reaction to events. He is constantly being *overtaken* by events. A condition of breathlessness and dazzlement surrounds him. In consequence he exists in a certain freshness which seems, if I may say so, very desirable. This freshness Poulet, quoting Marivaux, describes very well."

K. Saved from Drowning

K. in the water. His flat black hat, his black cape, his sword are on the shore. He retains his mask. His hands beat the surface of the water which tears and rips about him. The white foam, the green depths. I throw a line, the coils leaping out over the surface of the water. He has missed it. No, it appears that he has it. His right hand (sword arm) grasps the line that I have thrown him. I am on the bank, the rope wound round my waist, braced against a rock. K. now has both hands on the line. I pull him out of the water. He stands now on the bank, gasping.

"Thank you."

—April 1968

Report

Our group is against the war. But the war goes on. I was sent to Cleveland to talk to the engineers. The engineers were meeting in Cleveland. I was supposed to persuade them not to do what they are going to do. I took United's 4:45 from LaGuardia arriving in Cleveland at 6:13. Cleveland is dark blue at that hour. I went directly to the motel, where the engineers were meeting. Hundreds of engineers attended the Cleveland meeting. I noticed many fractures among the engineers, bandages, traction. I noticed what appeared to be fracture of the carpal scaphoid in six examples. I noticed numerous fractures of the humeral shaft, of the os calcis, of the pelvic girdle. I noticed a high incidence of clay-shoveler's fracture. I could not account for these fractures. The engineers were making calculations, taking measurements, sketching on the blackboard, drinking beer, throwing bread, buttonholing employers, hurling glasses into the fireplace. They were friendly.

They were friendly. They were full of love and information. The chief engineer wore shades. Patella in Monk's traction, clamshell fracture by the look of it. He was standing in a slum of beer bottles and microphone cable. "Have some of this chicken à la Isambard Kingdom Brunel the Great Ingineer," he said. "And declare who you are and what we can do for you. What is your line, distinguished guest?"

"Software," I said. "In every sense. I am here representing a small group of interested parties. We are interested in your thing, which seems to be functioning. In the midst of so much dysfunction, function is interesting. Other people's things don't seem to be working. The State Department's thing doesn't seem to be working. The UN's thing doesn't seem to be working. The democratic left's thing doesn't seem to be working. Buddha's thing—"

"Ask us anything about our thing, which seems to be working," the chief engineer said. "We will open our hearts and heads to you, Software Man, because we want to be understood and loved by the great lay public, and have our marvels appreciated by that public, for which we daily unsung produce tons of new marvels each more life-enhancing than the last. Ask us anything. Do you want to know about evaporated thin-film metallurgy? Monolithic and hybrid integrated-circuit processes? The algebra of inequalities? Optimization theory? Complex high-speed micro-miniature closed and open loop systems? Fixed variable mathematical cost searches? Epitaxial deposition of semiconductor materials? Gross interfaced space gropes? We also have specialists in the cuckooflower, the doctorfish, and the dumdum bullet as these relate to aspects of today's expanding technology, and they do in the damnedest ways."

I spoke to him then about the war. I said the same things people always say when they speak against the war. I said that the war was wrong. I said that large countries should not burn down small countries. I said that the government had made a series of errors. I said that these errors once small and forgivable were now immense and unforgivable. I said that the government was attempting to conceal its original errors under layers of new errors. I said that the government was sick with error, giddy with it. I said that ten thousand of our soldiers had already been killed in pursuit of the government's errors. I said that tens of thousands of the enemy's soldiers and civilians had been killed because of various errors, ours and theirs. I said that we are responsible for errors made in our name. I said that the government should not be allowed to make additional errors.

"Yes, yes," the chief engineer said, "there is doubtless much truth in what you say, but we can't possibly *lose* the war, can we? And stopping is losing, isn't it? The war regarded as a process, stopping regarded as an abort? We don't know *how* to lose a war. That skill is not among our skills. Our array smashes their array, that is what we know. That is the process. That is what is.

"But let's not have any more of this dispiriting downbeat counterproductive talk. I have a few new marvels here I'd like to discuss with you just briefly. A few new marvels that are just about ready to be gaped at by the admiring layman. Consider for instance the area of realtime online computer-controlled wish evaporation. Wish evaporation is going to be crucial in meeting the rising expectations of the world's peoples, which are as you know rising entirely too fast."

I noticed then distributed about the room a great many transverse fractures of the ulna. "The development of the pseudoruminant stomach for underdeveloped peoples," he went on, "is one of our interesting things you should be interested in. With the pseudo-ruminant stomach they can chew cuds, that is to say, eat grass. Blue is the most popular color worldwide and for that reason we are working with certain strains of your native Kentucky *Poa pratensis,* or bluegrass, as the staple input for the p/r stomach cycle, which would also give a shot in the arm to our balance-of-payments thing don't you know. . . ." I noticed about me then a great number of metatarsal fractures in banjo splints. "The kangaroo initiative . . . eight hundred thousand harvested last year . . . highest percentage of edible protein of any herbivore yet studied . . ."

"Have new kangaroos been planted?"

The engineer looked at me.

"I intuit your hatred and jealousy of our thing," he said. "The ineffectual always hate our thing and speak of it as antihuman, which is not at all a meaningful way to speak of our thing. Nothing mechanical is alien to me," he said (amber spots making bursts of light in his shades), "because I am human, in a sense, and if I think it up, then 'it' is human too, whatever 'it' may be. Let me tell you, Software Man, we have been damned forbearing in the matter of this little war you declare yourself to be interested in. Function is the cry, and our thing is functioning like crazy. There are things we could do that we have not done. Steps we could take that we have not taken. These steps are, regarded in a certain light, the light of our enlightened self-interest, quite justifiable steps. We could, of course, get irritated. We could, of course, *lose patience.*

"We could, of course, release thousands upon thousands of self-powered crawling-along-the-ground lengths of titanium wire eighteen inches long with a diameter of .0005 centimeters (that is to say, invisible) which, scenting an enemy, climb up his trouser leg and wrap themselves around his neck. We have developed those. They are within our capabilities. We could, of course, release in the arena of the upper air our new improved pufferfish toxin which precipitates an identity crisis. No special technical problems there. That is almost laughably easy. We could, of course, place up to two million maggots in their rice within twenty-four hours. The maggots are ready, massed in secret staging areas in Alabama. We have hypodermic darts capable of piebalding the enemy's pigmentation. We have rots, blights, and rusts capable of attacking his alphabet. Those are dandies. We have a hut-shrinking chemical which penetrates the fibers of the bamboo, causing it, the hut, to strangle its occupants. This operates only after 10 P.M., when people are sleeping. Their mathematics are at the mercy of a suppurating surd we have invented. We have a family of fishes trained to attack their fishes. We have the deadly testicle-destroying telegram. The cable companies are coöperating. We have a green substance that, well, I'd rather not talk about. We have a secret word that, if pronounced, produces multiple fractures in all living things in an area the size of four football fields."

"That's why—"

"Yes. Some damned fool couldn't keep his mouth shut. The point is that the whole structure of enemy life is within our power to *rend, vitiate, devour,* and *crush*. But that's not the interesting thing."

"You recount these possibilities with uncommon relish."

"Yes, I realize that there is too much relish here. But *you* must realize that these capabilities represent in and of themselves highly technical and complex and interesting problems and hurdles on which our boys have expended many thousands of hours of hard work and brilliance. And that the effects are often grossly exaggerated by irresponsible victims. And that the whole thing represents a fantastic series of triumphs for the multi-disciplined problem-solving team concept."

"I appreciate that."

"We *could* unleash all this technology at once. You can imagine what would happen then. But that's not the interesting thing."

"What is the interesting thing?"

"The interesting thing is that we have a *moral sense*. It is on punched cards, perhaps the most advanced and sensitive moral sense the world has ever known."

"Because it is on punched cards?"

"It considers all considerations in endless and subtle detail," he said. "It even quibbles. With this great new moral tool, how can we go wrong? I confidently predict that, although we *could* employ all this splendid new weaponry I've been telling you about, *we're not going to do it.*"

"We're not going to do it?"

I took United's 5:44 from Cleveland arriving at Newark at 7:19. New Jersey is bright pink at that hour. Living things move about the surface of New Jersey at that hour molesting each other only in traditional ways. I made my report to the group. I stressed the friendliness of the engineers. I said, It's all right. I said, We have a moral sense. I said, *We're not going to do it.* They didn't believe me.

The Dolt

Edgar was preparing to take the National Writers' Examination, a five-hour fifty-minute examination, for his certificate. He was in his room, frightened. The prospect of taking the exam again put him in worlds of hurt. He had taken it twice before, with evil results. Now he was studying a book which contained not the actual questions from the examination but similar questions. "Barbara, if I don't knock it for a loop this time I don't know what we'll do." Barbara continued to address herself to the ironing board. Edgar thought about saying something to his younger child, his two-year-old daughter, Rose, who was wearing a white terry-cloth belted bathrobe and looked like a tiny fighter about to climb into the ring. They were all in the room while he was studying for the examination.

"The written part is where I fall down," Edgar said morosely, to everyone in the room. "The oral part is where I do best." He looked at the back of his wife which was pointed at him. "If I don't kick it in the head this time I don't know what we're going to do," he repeated. "Barb?" But she failed to respond to this implied question. She felt it was a false hope, taking this examination which he had already failed miserably twice and which always got him very worked up, black with fear, before he took it. Now she didn't wish to witness the spectacle any more so she gave him her back.

"The oral part," Edgar continued encouragingly, "is A-okay. I can for instance give you a list of answers, I know it so well. Listen, here is an answer, can you tell me the question?" Barbara, who was very sexually attractive (that was what made

Edgar tap on her for a date, many years before) but also deeply mean, said nothing. She put her mind on their silent child, Rose.

"Here is the answer," Edgar said. "The answer is Julia Ward Howe. What is the question?"

This answer was too provocative for Barbara to resist long, because she knew the question. "Who wrote 'The Battle Hymn of the Republic'?" she said. "There is not a grown person in the United States who doesn't know that."

"You're right," Edgar said unhappily, for he would have preferred that the answer had been a little more recherché, one that she would not have known the question to. But she had been a hooker for a period before their marriage and he could resort to this area if her triumph grew too great. "Do you want to try another one?"

"Edgar I don't *believe in* that examination any more," she told him coldly.

"I don't believe in you Barbara," he countered.

This remark filled her with remorse and anger. She considered momentarily letting him have one upside the head but fear prevented her from doing it so she turned her back again and thought about the vaunted certificate. With a certificate he could write for all the important and great periodicals, and there would be some money in the house for a change instead of what they got from his brother and the Unemployment.

"It isn't you who has to pass this National Writers' Examination," he shot past her. Then, to mollify, he gave her another answer. "Brand, tuck, glave, claymore."

"Is that an answer?" she asked from behind her back.

"It is indeed. What's the question?"

"I don't know," she admitted, slightly pleased to be put back in a feminine position of not knowing.

"Those are four names for a sword. They're archaic."

"That's why I didn't know them, then."

"Obviously," said Edgar with some malice, for Barbara was sometimes given to saying things that were obvious, just to fill the air. "You put a word like that in now and then to freshen your line," he explained. "Even though it's an old word, it's so old it's new. But you have to be careful, the context has to let people know what the thing is. You don't want to be simply obscure." He liked explaining the tricks of the trade to Barb, who made some show of interest in them.

"Do you want me to read you what I've written for the written part?"

Barb said yes, with a look of pain, for she still felt acutely what he was trying to do.

"This is the beginning," Edgar said, preparing his yellow manuscript paper.

"What is the title?" Barbara asked. She had turned to face him.

"I haven't got a title yet," Edgar said. "Okay, this is the beginning." He began to read aloud. "*In the town of A——, in the district of Y——, there lived a certain Madame A——, wife of that Baron A—— who was in the service of the young Friedrich II of Prussia. The Baron, a man of uncommon ability, is chiefly remembered for his notorious and inexplicable blunder at the Battle of Kolin: by withdrawing the column under his command at a crucial moment in the fighting, he earned for himself the greatest part of the blame for Friedrich's defeat, which resulted in a loss, on the Prussian side, of 13,000 out of 33,000 men. Now as it happened, the château in which Madame A—— was sheltering lay not far from the battlefield, in fact, the removal of her husband's corps placed the château itself in the gravest danger, and at the moment Madame A—— learned, from a Captain Orsini, of her husband's death by his own hand, she was also told that a detachment of pandours, the brutal and much-feared Hungarian light irregular cavalry, was hammering at the château gates.*"

Edgar paused to breathe.

Barb looked at him in some surprise. "The beginning turns me on," she said. "More than usual, I mean." She began to have some faint hope, and sat down on the sofabed.

"Thank you," Edgar said. "Do you want me to read you the development?"

"Go ahead."

Edgar drank some water from a glass near to hand.

"The man who brought this terrible news enjoyed a peculiar status in regard to the lady, he was her lover, and he was not. Giacomo Orsini, second son of a noble family of Siena, had as a young man a religious vocation. He had become a priest, not the grander sort of priest who makes a career in Rome and in great houses, but a modest village priest in the north of his country. Here befell him a singular misfortune. It was the pleasure of Friedrich Wilhelm I, father of the present ruler, to assemble, as is well known, the finest army in Europe. Tiny Prussia was unable to supply men in sufficient numbers to satisfy this ambition, his recruiters ranged over the whole of Europe, and those whom they could not persuade, with promises of liberal bounties, into the king's service, they kidnapped. Now Friedrich was above all else fond of very tall men, and had created, for his personal guard, a regiment of giants, much mocked at the time, but nonetheless a brave and formidable sight. It was the bad luck of the priest Orsini to be a very tall man, and of impressive mien and bearing withal; he was abducted straight from the altar, as he was saying mass, the Host in his hands—"

"This is very exciting," Barb broke in, her eyes showing genuine pleasure and enthusiasm.

"Thank you," Edgar said, and continued his reading.

"—and served ten years in the regiment of giants. On the death of Friedrich Wilhelm, the regiment was disbanded, among other economies; but the former priest, by now habituated to military life, and even zestful for it, enlisted under the new young king, with the rank of captain."

"Is this historically accurate?" Barbara asked.

"It does not contradict what is known," Edgar assured her.

"Assigned to the staff of Baron A——, and much in the latter's house in consequence, he was thrown in with the lovely Inge. Madame A——, a woman much younger than her husband, and possessed of many excellent qualities. A deep sympathy established itself between them, with this idiosyncrasy, that it was never pressed to a conclusion, on his part, or acknowledged in any way, on hers. But both were aware that it

existed, and drew secret nourishment from it, and took much delight in the nearness, one to the other. But this pleasant state of affairs also had a melancholy aspect, for Orsini, although exercising the greatest restraint in the matter, nevertheless considered that he had, in even admitting to himself that he was in love with Madame A——, damaged his patron the Baron, whom he knew to be a just and honorable man, and one who had, moreover, done him many kindnesses. In this humor Orsini saw himself as a sort of jackal skulking about the periphery of his benefactor's domestic life, which had been harmonious and whole, but was now, in whatsoever slight degree, compromised."

Rose, the child, stood in her white bathrobe looking at her father who was talking for such a long time, and in such a dramatic shaking voice.

"The Baron, on his side, was not at all insensible of the passion that was present, as it were in a condition of latency, between his young wife and the handsome Sienese. In truth, his knowledge of their intercourse, which he imagined had ripened far beyond the point it had actually reached, had flung him headlong into a horrible crime: for his withholding of the decisive troops at Kolin, for which history has judged him so harshly, was neither an error of strategy nor a display of pusillanimity, but a willful act, having as its purpose the exposure of the château, and thus the lovers, whom he had caused to be together there, to the blood-lust of the pandours. And as for his alleged suicide, that too was a cruel farce, he lived, in a hidden place."

Edgar stopped.

"It's swift-moving," Barbara complimented.

"Well, do you want me to read you the end?"

"The end? Is it the end already?"

"Do you want me to read you the end?" he repeated.

"Yes."

"I've got the end but I don't have the middle," Edgar said, a little ashamed.

"You don't have the middle?"

"Do you want me to read you the end or don't you?"

"Yes, read me the end." The possibility of a semiprofessional apartment, which she had entertained briefly, was falling out of her head with this news, that there was no middle.

"The last paragraph is this:

"During these events Friedrich, to console himself for the debacle at Kolin, composed in his castle at Berlin a flute sonata, of which the critic Guilda has said, that it is not less lovely than the sonatas of Georg Philip Telemann."

"That's ironic," she said knowingly.

"Yes," Edgar agreed, impatient. He was as volatile as popcorn.

"But what about the middle?"

"I don't have the middle!" he thundered.

"Something has to happen between them, Inge and what's his name," she went on. "Otherwise there's no story." Looking at her he thought: she is still streety although wearing her housewife gear. The child was a perfect love, however, and couldn't be told from the children of success.

Barb then began telling a story she knew that had happened to a friend of hers. This girl had had an affair with a man and had become pregnant. The man had gone off to Seville, to see if hell was a city much like it, and she had spontaneously aborted, in Chicago. Then she had flown over to parley, and they had walked in the streets and visited elderly churches and like that. And the first church they went into, there was this tiny little white coffin covered with flowers, right in the sanctuary.

"Banal," Edgar pronounced.

She tried to think of another anecdote to deliver to him.

"I've got to get that certificate!" he suddenly called out desperately.

"I don't think you can pass the National Writers' Examination with what you have on that paper," Barb said then, with great regret, because even though he was her husband she didn't want to hurt him unnecessarily. But she had to tell the truth. "Without a middle."

"I wouldn't have been great, even with the certificate," he said.

"Your views would have become known. You would have been something."

At that moment the son manqué entered the room. The son manqué was eight feet tall and wore a serape woven out of two hundred transistor radios, all turned on and tuned to different stations. Just by looking at him you could hear Portland and Nogales, Mexico.

"No grass in the house?"

Barbara got the grass which was kept in one of those little yellow and red metal canisters made for sending film back to Eastman Kodak.

Edgar tried to think of a way to badmouth this immense son leaning over him like a large blaring building. But he couldn't think of anything. Thinking of anything was beyond him. I sympathize. I myself have these problems. Endings are elusive, middles are nowhere to be found, but worst of all is to begin, to begin, to begin.

See the Moon?

I know you think I'm wasting my time. You've made that perfectly clear. But I'm conducting these very important lunar hostility studies. And it's not you who'll have to leave the warm safe capsule. And dip a toe into the threatening lunar surround.

I am still wearing my yellow flower which has lasted wonderfully.

My methods may seem a touch irregular. Have to do chiefly with folded paper airplanes at present. But the paper must be folded *in the right way.* Lots of calculations and worrying about edges.

Show me a man who worries about edges and I'll show you a natural-born winner. Cardinal Y. agrees. Columbus himself worried, the Admiral of the Ocean Sea. But he kept it quiet.

The sun so warm on this screened porch, it reminds me of my grandmother's place in Tampa. The same rusty creaky green glider and the same faded colored canvas cushions. And at night the moon graphed by the screen wire, if you squint. The Sea of Tranquillity occupying squares 47 through 108.

See the moon? It hates us.

My methods are homely but remember Newton and the apple. And when Rutherford started out he didn't even have a decently heated laboratory. And then there's the matter of my security check—I'm waiting for the government. Somebody told it I'm insecure. *That's true.*

I suffer from a frightful illness of the mind, light-mindedness. It's not catching. You needn't shrink.

You've noticed the wall? I pin things on it, souvenirs. There is the red hat, there the book of instructions for the Ant Farm. And this is a traffic ticket written on a saint's day (which saint? I don't remember) in 1954 just outside a fat little town (which town? I don't remember) in Ohio by a cop who asked me what I did. I said I wrote poppycock for the president of a university, true then.

You can see how far I've come. Lunar hostility studies aren't for everyone.

It's my hope that these . . . souvenirs . . . will someday merge, blur—cohere is the word, maybe—into something meaningful. A grand word, meaningful. What do I look for? A work of art, I'll not accept anything less. Yes I know it's shatteringly ingenuous but I wanted to be a painter. They get away with murder in my view; Mr. X. on the *Times* agrees with me. You don't know how I envy them. They can pick up a Baby Ruth wrapper on the street, glue it to the canvas (in the *right place*, of course, there's that), and lo! people crowd about and cry, "A real Baby Ruth wrapper, by God, what could be realer than that!" Fantastic metaphysical advantage. You hate them, if you're ambitious:

The Ant Farm instructions are a souvenir of Sylvia. The red hat came from Cardinal Y. We're friends, in a way.

I wanted to be one, when I was young, a painter. But I couldn't stand stretching the canvas. Does things to the fingernails. And that's the first place people look.

Fragments are the only forms I trust.

Light-minded or no, I'm . . . riotous with mental health. I measure myself against the Russians, that's fair. I have here a clipping datelined Moscow, four young people apprehended strangling a swan. *That*'s boredom. The swan's name, Borka. The sentences as follows: Tsarev, metalworker, served time previously for stealing public property, four years in a labor camp, strict regime. Roslavtsev, electrician, jailed previously for taking a car on a joyride, three years and four months in a labor camp, semistrict regime. Tatyana Voblikova (only nineteen and a Komsomol member too), technician, one and a half years in a labor camp, degree of strictness unspecified. Anna G.

Kirushina, technical worker, fine of twenty percent of salary for one year. Anna objected to the strangulation, but softly: she helped stuff the carcass into a bag.

The clipping is tacked up on my wall. I inspect it from time to time, drawing the moral. Strangling swans is wrong.

My brother who is a very distinguished pianist . . . has no fingernails at all. Don't look it's horrible. He plays under another name. And tunes his piano peculiarly, some call it sour. And renders *ragas* he wrote himself. A night *raga* played at noon can cause darkness, did you know that? It's extraordinary.

He wanted to be an Untouchable, Paul did. That was his idea of a contemporary career. But then a girl walked up and touched him (slapped him, actually; it's a complicated story). And he joined us, here in the imbroglio.

My father on the other hand is perfectly comfortable, and that's not a criticism. He makes flags, banners, bunting (sometimes runs me up a shirt). There was never any question of letting my father drink from the public well. He was on the Well Committee, he decided who dipped and who didn't. That's not a criticism. Exercises his creativity, nowadays, courtesy the emerging nations. Green for the veldt that nourishes the gracile Grant's gazelle, white for the purity of our revolutionary aspirations. The red for blood is understood. That's not a criticism. It's what they all ask for.

A call tonight from Gregory, my son by my first wife. Seventeen and at MIT already. Recently he's been asking questions. Suddenly he's conscious of himself as a being with a history.

The telephone rings. Then, without a greeting: *Why did I have to take those little pills?* What little pills? *Little white pills with a "W" on them.* Oh. Oh yes. You had some kind of a nervous disorder, for a while. *How old was I?* Eight. Eight or nine. *What was it? Was it epilepsy?* Good God no, nothing so fancy. We never found out what it was. It went away. *What did I do? Did I fall down?* No no. Your mouth trembled, that was all. You couldn't control it. *Oh, OK. See you.*

The receiver clicks.

Or: *What did my great-grandfather do? For a living I mean?* He was a ballplayer, semi-pro ballplayer, for a while. Then went into the building business. *Who'd he play for?* A team called the St. Augustine Rowdies, I think it was. *Never heard of them.* Well . . . *Did he make any money? In the building business?* Quite a bit. *Did your father inherit it?* No, it was tied up in a lawsuit. When the suit was over there wasn't anything left. *Oh. What was the lawsuit?* Great-grandfather diddled a man in a land deal. So the story goes. *Oh. When did he die?* Let's see, 1938 I think. *What of?* Heart attack. *Oh. OK. See you.*

End of conversation.

Gregory, you didn't listen to my advice. I said try the Vernacular Isles. Where fish are two for a penny and women two for a fish. But you wanted MIT and electron-spin-resonance spectroscopy. You didn't even crack a smile in your six-ply heather hopsacking.

Gregory you're going to have a half brother now. You'll like that, won't you? Will you half like it?

We talked about the size of the baby, Ann and I. What could be deduced from the outside.

I said it doesn't look very big to me. She said it's big enough for *us*. I said we don't need such a great roaring big one after all. She said they cost the earth, those extra-large sizes. Our holdings in Johnson's Baby Powder to be considered too. We'd need acres and acres. I said we'll put it in a Skinner box maybe. She said no child of hers. Displayed under glass like a rump roast. I said you haven't wept lately. She said I keep getting bigger whether I laugh or cry.

Dear Ann. I don't think you've quite . . .

What you don't understand is, it's like somebody walks up to you and says, I have a battleship I can't use, would you like to have a battleship? And you say, yes yes, I've never had a battleship, I've always wanted one. And he says, it has four sixteen-inch guns forward, and a catapult for launching scout planes. And you say, I've always wanted to launch scout planes. And he says, *it's yours,* and then you have this battleship. And then you have to paint it, because it's rusting, and clean it, because it's dirty, and anchor it somewhere, because the Police Department wants you to get it off the streets. And the crew is crying, and there are silverfish in the chartroom and a funny knocking noise in Fire Control, water rising in the No. 2 hold, and the chaplain can't find the Palestrina tapes for the Sunday service. And you can't get anybody to sit with it. And finally you discover that what you have here is this great, big, pink-and-blue rockabye *battleship.*

Ann. I'm going to keep her ghostly. Just the odd bit of dialogue.

"What is little Gog doing."

"Kicking."

I don't want her bursting in on us with the freshness and originality of her observations. What we need here is *perspective*. She's good with Gregory though. I think he half likes her.

Don't go. The greased-pig chase and balloon launchings come next.

I was promising once. After the Elgar, a *summa cum laude.* The university was proud of me. It was a bright shy white new university on the Gulf Coast. Gulls and oleanders and quick howling hurricanes. The teachers brown burly men with power boats and beer cans. The president a retired admiral who'd done beautiful things in the Coral Sea.

"You will be a credit to us, George," the admiral said. That's not my name.

Applause from the stands filled with mothers and brothers. Then following the mace in a long line back to the field house to ungown. Ready to take my place at the top.

But a pause at Pusan, and the toy train to the Chorwon Valley. Walking down a road wearing green clothes. Korea green and black and silent. The truce had been signed. I had a carbine to carry. My buddy Bo Tagliabue the bonus baby, for whom the Yanks had paid thirty thousand. We whitewashed rocks to enhance our area. Colonels came crowding to feel Bo's hurling arm. Mine the whitest rocks.

I lunched with Thais from Thailand, hot curry from great galvanized washtubs. Engineers banging down the road in six-by-sixes raising red dust. My friend Gib Mandell calling Elko, Nevada, on his canvas-covered field telephone. "Operator I crave Elko, Nevada."

Then I was a sergeant with stripes, getting the troops out of the sun. Tagliabue a sergeant too. *Triste* in the Tennessee Tea Room in Tokyo, yakking it up in Yokohama. Then back to our little tent town on the side of a hill, boosting fifty-gallon drums of heating oil tentward in the snow.

Ozzie the jeep driver waking me in the middle of the night. "They got Julian in the Tango Tank." And up and alert as they taught us in Leadership School, over the hills to Tango, seventy miles away. Whizzing through Teapot, Tempest, Toreador, with the jeep's canvas top flapping. Pfc. Julian drunk and disorderly and beaten up. The MP sergeant held out a receipt book. I signed for the bawdy remains.

Back over the pearly Pacific in a great vessel decorated with oranges. A trail of orange peel on the plangent surface. Sitting in the bow fifty miles out of San Francisco, listening to the Stateside disc jockeys chattering cha cha cha. Ready to grab my spot at the top.

My clothes looked old and wrong. The city looked new with tall buildings raised while my back was turned. I rushed here and there visiting friends. They were burning beef in their backyards, brown burly men with beer cans. The beef black on the outside, red on the inside. My friend Horace had fidelity. "Listen to that bass. That's sixty watts' worth of bass, boy."

I spoke to my father. "How is business?" "If Alaska makes it," he said, "I can buy a Hasselblad. And we're keeping an eye on Hawaii." Then he photographed my veteran face, f.6 at 300. My father once a cheerleader at a great Eastern school. Jumping in the air and making fierce angry down-the-field gestures at the top of his leap.

That's not a criticism. We have to have cheerleaders.

I presented myself at the Placement Office. I was on file. My percentile was the percentile of choice.

"How come you were headman of only one student organization, George?" the Placement Officer asked. Many hats for top folk was the fashion then.

I said I was rounded, and showed him my slash. From the Fencing Club.

"But you served your country in an overseas post."

"And regard my career plan on neatly typed pages with wide margins."

"Exemplary," the Placement Officer said. "You seem married, mature, malleable, how would you like to affiliate yourself with us here at the old school? We have a spot for a poppycock man, to write the admiral's speeches. Have you ever done poppycock?"

I said no but maybe I could fake it.

"Excellent, excellent," the Placement Officer said. "I see you have grasp. And you can sup at the Faculty Club. And there is a ten-percent discount on tickets for all home games."

The admiral shook my hand. "You will be a credit to us, George," he said. I wrote poppycock, sometimes cockypap. At four o'clock the faculty hoisted the cocktail flag. We drank daiquiris on each other's sterns. I had equipped myself—a fiberglass runabout, someplace to think. In the stadia of friendly shy new universities we went down the field on Gulf Coast afternoons with gulls, or exciting nights under the tall toothpick lights. The crowd roared. Sylvia roared. Gregory grew.

There was no particular point at which I stopped being promising.

Moonstruck I was, after a fashion. Sitting on a bench by the practice field, where the jocks chanted secret signals in their underwear behind tall canvas blinds. Layabout babies loafing on blankets, some staked out on twelve-foot dog chains. Brown mothers squatting knee to knee in shifts of scarlet and green. I stared at the moon's pale daytime presence. It seemed . . . inimical.

Moonstruck.

We're playing Flinch. You flinched.

The simplest things are the most difficult to explain, all authorities agree. Say I was tired of p***yc**k, if that pleases you. It's true enough.

Sylvia went up in a puff of smoke. She didn't like unsalaried life. And couldn't bear a male acquaintance moon-staring in the light of day. Decent people look at night.

We had trouble with Gregory: who would get which part. She settled for three-fifths, and got I think the worst of it, the dreaming raffish Romany part that thinks science will save us. I get matter-of-fact midnight telephone calls: *My EE instructor shot me down.* What happened? *I don't know, he's an ass anyhow.* Well that may be but still— *When's the baby due?* January, I told you. *Yeah, can I go to Mexico City for the holidays?* Ask your mother, you know she— *There's this guy, his old man has a villa. . . .* Well, we can talk about it. *Yeah, was grandmother a Communist?* Nothing so distinguished, she— *You said she was kicked out of Germany.* Her family was anti-Nazi. *Adler means eagle in German.* That's true. There was something called the Weimar Republic, her father— *I read about it.*

We had trouble with Gregory, we wanted to be scientific. Toys from Procreative Playthings of Princeton. O Gregory, that Princeton crowd got you coming and going. Procreative Playthings at one end and the Educational Testing Service at the other. And that serious-minded co-op nursery, that was a mistake. "A growing understanding between parent and child through shared group experience." I still remember poor Henry Harding III. Under "Sibs" on the membership roll they listed his, by age:

26
25
23
20
19
15
10
9
8
6

O Mrs. Harding, haven't you heard? They have these little Christmas-tree ornaments for the womb now, they work wonders.

Did we do "badly" by Gregory? Will we do "better" with Gog? Such questions curl the hair. It's wiser not to ask.

I mentioned Cardinal Y. (the red hat). He's a friend, in a way. Or rather, the subject of one of my little projects.

I set out to study cardinals, about whom science knows nothing. It seemed to me that cardinals could be known in the same way we know fishes or roses, by classification and enumeration. A perverse project, perhaps, but who else has embraced this point of view? Difficult nowadays to find a point of view kinky enough to call one's own, with Sade himself being carried through the streets on the shoulders of sociologists, cheers and shouting, ticker tape unwinding from high windows . . .

The why of Cardinal Y. You're entitled to an explanation.

The Cardinal rushed from the Residence waving in the air his hands, gloved in yellow pigskin it appeared, I grasped a hand, "Yes, yellow pigskin!" the Cardinal cried. I wrote in my book, *yellow pigskin.*

Significant detail. The pectoral cross contains nine diamonds, the scarlet soutane is laundered right on the premises.

I asked the Cardinal questions, we had a conversation.

"I am thinking of a happy island more beautiful than can be imagined," I said.

"I am thinking of a golden mountain which does not exist," he said.

"Upon what does the world rest?" I asked.

"Upon an elephant," he said.

"Upon what does the elephant rest?"

"Upon a tortoise."

"Upon what does the tortoise rest?"

"Upon a red lawnmower."

I wrote in my book, *playful.*

"Is there any value that has value?" I asked.

"If there is any value that has value, then it must lie outside the whole sphere of what happens and is the case, for all that happens and is the case is accidental," he said. He was not serious. I wrote in my book, *knows the drill.*

(Oh I had heard reports, how he slunk about in the snow telling children he was Santa Claus, how he disbursed funds in unauthorized disbursements to unshaven men who came to the kitchen door, how his housekeeper pointedly rolled his red socks together and black socks together hinting red with red and black with black, the Cardinal patiently unrolling a red ball to get a red sock and a black ball to get a black sock, which he then wore together. . . .)

Cardinal Y. He's sly.

I was thorough. I popped the Cardinal on the patella with a little hammer, and looked into his eyes with a little light. I tested the Cardinal's stomach acidity using Universal Indicator Paper, a scale of one to ten, a spectrum of red to blue. The pH value was 1 indicating high acidity. I measured the Cardinal's ego strength using the Minnesota Multiphastic Muzzle Map, he had an MMMM of four over three. I sang to the Cardinal, the song was "Stella by Starlight," he did not react in any way. I calculated the number of gallons needed to fill the Cardinal's bath to a depth of ten inches (beyond which depth, the Cardinal said, he never ventured). I took the Cardinal to the ballet, the ballet was *The Conservatory*. The Cardinal applauded at fifty-seven points. Afterward, backstage, the Cardinal danced with Plenosova, holding her at arm's length with a good will and an ill grace. The skirts of the scarlet soutane stood out to reveal high-button shoes, and the stagehands clapped.

I asked the Cardinal his views on the moon, he said they were the conventional ones, and that is how I know all I know about cardinals. Not enough perhaps to rear a science of cardinalogy upon, but enough perhaps to form a basis for the investigations of other investigators. My report is over there, in the blue binding, next to my copy of *La Géomancie et la Néomancie des Anciens* by the Seigneur of Salerno.

Cardinal Y. One can measure and measure and miss the most essential thing. I liked him. I still get the odd blessing in the mail now and then.

Too, maybe I was trying on the role. Not for myself. When a child is born, the locus of one's hopes . . . shifts, slightly. Not altogether, not all at once. But you feel it, this displacement. You speak up, strike attitudes, like the mother of a tiny Lollobrigida. Drunk with possibility once more.

I am still wearing my yellow flower which has lasted wonderfully.

"What is Gog doing?"

"Sleeping."

You see, Gog of mine, Gog o' my heart, I'm just trying to give you a little briefing here. I don't want you unpleasantly surprised. I can't stand a startled look. Regard me as a sort of Distant Early Warning System. Here is the world and here are the knowledgeable knowers knowing. What can I tell you? What has been pieced together from the reports of travelers.

Fragments are the only forms I trust.

Look at my wall, it's all there. That's a leaf, Gog, stuck up with Scotch Tape. No no, the Scotch Tape is the shiny transparent stuff, the leaf the veined irregularly shaped . . .

There are several sides to this ax, Gog, consider the photostat, "Mr. W. B. Yeats Presenting Mr. George Moore to the Queen of the Fairies." That's a civilized gesture, I mean Beerbohm's. And when the sculptor Aristide Maillol went into the printing business he made the paper by *chewing the fibers himself*. That's dedication. And here is a Polaroid photo, shows your Aunt Sylvia and me putting an Ant Farm together. That's how close we were in those days. Just an Ant Farm apart.

See the moon? It hates us.

And now comes J. J. Sullivan's orange-and-blue Gulf Oil truck to throw kerosene into the space heater. Driver in green siren suit, red face, blond shaved head, the following rich verbal transaction:

"Beautiful day."

"Certainly is."

And now settling back in this green glider with a copy of *Man*. Dear Ann when I look at *Man* I don't want you. Unfolded Ursala Herring seems eversomuchmore desirable. A clean girl too and with interests, cooking, botany, pornographic novels. Someone new to show my slash to.

In another month Gog leaps fully armed from the womb. What can I do for him? I can get him into AA, I have influence. And make sure no harsh moonlight falls on his new soft head.

Hello there Gog. We hope you'll be very happy here.

The Indian Uprising

We defended the city as best we could. The arrows of the Comanches came in clouds. The war clubs of the Comanches clattered on the soft, yellow pavements. There were earthworks along the Boulevard Mark Clark and the hedges had been laced with sparkling wire. People were trying to understand. I spoke to Sylvia. "Do you think this is a good life?" The table held apples, books, long-playing records. She looked up. "No."

Patrols of paras and volunteers with armbands guarded the tall, flat buildings. We interrogated the captured Comanche. Two of us forced his head back while another poured water into his nostrils. His body jerked, he choked and wept. Not believing a hurried, careless and exaggerated report of the number of casualties in the outer districts where trees, lamps, swans had been reduced to clear fields of fire we issued entrenching tools to those who seemed trustworthy and turned the heavy-weapons companies so that we could not be surprised from that direction. And I sat there getting drunker and drunker and more in love and more in love. We talked.

"Do you know Fauré's 'Dolly'?"

"Would that be Gabriel Fauré?"

"It would."

"Then I know it," she said. "May I say that I play it at certain times, when I am sad, or happy, although it requires four hands."

"How is that managed?"

"I accelerate," she said, "ignoring the time signature."

And when they shot the scene in the bed I wondered how you felt under the eyes of the cameramen, grips, juicers, men in the mixing booth: excited? stimulated? And when they shot the scene in the shower I sanded a hollow-core door working carefully against the illustrations in texts and whispered instructions from one who had already solved the problem. I had made after all other tables, one while living with Nancy, one while living with Alice, one while living with Eunice, one while living with Marianne.

Red men in waves like people scattering in a square startled by something tragic or a sudden, loud noise accumulated against the barricades we had made of window dummies, silk, thoughtfully planned job descriptions (including scales for the orderly progress of other colors), wine in demijohns, and robes. I analyzed the composition of the barricade nearest me and found two ashtrays, ceramic, one dark brown and one dark brown with an orange blur at the lip; a tin frying pan; two-liter bottles of red wine; three-quarter-liter bottles of Black & White, aquavit, cognac, vodka, gin, Fad #6 sherry; a hollow-core door in birch veneer on black wrought-iron legs; a blanket, red-orange with faint blue stripes; a red pillow and a blue pillow; a woven straw wastebasket; two glass jars for flowers; corkscrews and can openers; two plates and two cups, ceramic, dark brown; a yellow-and-purple poster; a Yugoslavian carved flute, wood, dark brown; and other items. I decided I knew nothing.

The hospitals dusted wounds with powders the worth of which was not quite established, other supplies having been exhausted early in the first day. I decided I knew nothing. Friends put me in touch with a Miss R., a teacher, unorthodox they said, excellent they said, successful with difficult cases, steel shutters on the windows made the house safe. I had just learned via an International Distress Coupon that Jane had been beaten up by a dwarf in a bar on Tenerife but Miss R. did not allow me to speak of it. "You know nothing," she said, "you feel nothing, you are locked in a most savage and terrible ignorance, I despise you, my boy, *mon cher*, my heart. You may attend but you must not attend now, you must attend later, a day or a week or an hour, you are making me ill. . . ." I nonevaluated these remarks as Korzybski instructed. But it was difficult. Then they pulled back in a feint near the river and we rushed into that sector with a reinforced battalion hastily formed among the Zouaves and cabdrivers. This unit was crushed in the afternoon of a day that began with spoons and letters in hallways and under windows where men tasted the history of the heart, cone-shaped muscular organ that maintains *circulation of the blood.*

But it is you I want now, here in the middle of this Uprising, with the streets yellow and threatening, short, ugly lances with fur at the throat and inexplicable shell money lying in the grass. It is when I am with you that I am happiest, and it is for you that I am making this hollow-core door table with black wrought-iron legs. I held Sylvia by her bear-claw necklace. "Call off your braves," I said. "We have many years left to live." There was a sort of muck running in the gutters, yellowish, filthy stream suggesting excrement, or nervousness, a city that does not know what it has done to deserve baldness, errors, infidelity. "With luck you will survive until matins," Sylvia said. She ran off down the Rue Chester Nimitz, uttering shrill cries.

Then it was learned that they had infiltrated our ghetto and that the people of the ghetto instead of resisting had joined the smooth, well-coordinated attack with zip guns, telegrams, lockets, causing that portion of the line held by the IRA to swell and collapse. We sent more heroin into the ghetto, and hyacinths, ordering another hundred thousand of the pale, delicate flowers. On the map we considered the situation with its strung-out inhabitants and merely personal emotions. Our parts were blue and their parts were green. I showed the blue-and-green map to Sylvia. "Your parts are green," I said. "You gave me heroin first a year ago," Sylvia said. She ran off down George C. Marshall Allée, uttering shrill cries. Miss R. pushed me into a large room painted white (jolting and dancing in the soft light, and I was excited! and there were people watching!) in which there were two chairs. I sat in one chair and Miss R. sat in the other. She wore a blue dress containing a red figure. There was nothing exceptional about her. I was disappointed by her plainness, by the bareness of the room, by the absence of books.

The girls of my quarter wore long blue mufflers that reached to their knees. Sometimes the girls hid Comanches in their rooms, the blue mufflers together in a room creating a great blue fog. Block opened the door. He was carrying weapons, flowers, loaves of bread. And he was friendly, kind, enthusiastic, so I related a little of the history of torture, reviewing the technical literature quoting the best modern sources, French, German, and American, and pointing out the flies which had gathered in anticipation of some new, cool color.

"What is the situation?" I asked.

"The situation is liquid," he said. "We hold the south quarter and they hold the north quarter. The rest is silence."

"And Kenneth?"

"That girl is not in love with Kenneth," Block said frankly. "She is in love with his coat. When she is not wearing it she is huddling under it. Once I caught it going down the stairs by itself. I looked inside. Sylvia."

Once I caught Kenneth's coat going down the stairs by itself but the coat was a trap and inside a Comanche who made a thrust with his short, ugly knife at my leg which buckled and tossed me over the balustrade through a window and into another situation. Not believing that your body brilliant as it was and your fat, liquid spirit distinguished and angry as it was were stable quantities to which one could return on wires more than once, twice, or another number of times I said: "See the table?"

In Skinny Wainwright Square the forces of green and blue swayed and struggled. The referees ran out on the field trailing chains. And then the blue part would be enlarged, the green diminished. Miss R. began to speak. "A former king of Spain, a Bonaparte, lived for a time in Bordentown, New Jersey. But that's no good." She paused. "The ardor aroused in men by the beauty of women can only be satisfied by God. That is *very* good (it is Valéry) but it is not what I have to teach you, goat, muck, filth, heart of my heart." I showed the table to Nancy. "See the table?" She stuck out her tongue red as a blood test. "I made such a table once," Block said frankly. "People all over America have made such tables. I doubt very much whether one can enter an American home without finding at least one such table, or traces of its having been there, such as faded places in the carpet." And afterward in the garden the men of the 7th Cavalry played Gabrieli, Albinoni, Marcello, Vivaldi, Boccherini. I saw Sylvia. She wore a yellow ribbon, under a long blue muffler. "Which side are you on," I cried, "after all?"

"The only form of discourse of which I approve," Miss R. said in her dry, tense voice, "is the litany. I believe our masters and teachers as well as plain citizens should confine themselves to what can safely be said. Thus when I hear the words *pewter, snake, tea, Fad #6 sherry, serviette, fenestration, crown, blue* coming from the mouth of some public official, or some raw youth, I am not disappointed. Vertical organization is also possible," Miss R. said, "as in

pewter
snake
tea
Fad #6 sherry
serviette
fenestration
crown
blue.

I run to liquids and colors," she said, "but you, you may run to something else, my virgin, my darling, my thistle, my poppet, my own. Young people," Miss R. said, "run to more and more unpleasant combinations as they sense the nature of our society. Some people," Miss R. said, "run to conceits or wisdom but I hold to the hard, brown, nutlike word. I might point out that there is enough aesthetic excitement here to satisfy anyone but a damned fool." I sat in solemn silence.

Fire arrows lit my way to the post office in Patton Place where members of the Abraham Lincoln Brigade offered their last, exhausted letters, postcards, calendars. I opened a letter but inside was a Comanche flint arrowhead played by Frank Wedekind in an elegant gold chain and congratulations. Your earring rattled against my spectacles when I leaned forward to touch the soft, ruined place where the hearing aid had been. "Pack it in! Pack it in!" I urged, but the men in charge of the Uprising refused to listen to reason or to understand that it was real and that our water supply had evaporated and that our credit was no longer what it had been, once.

We attached wires to the testicles of the captured Comanche. And I sat there getting drunker and drunker and more in love and more in love. When we threw the switch he spoke. His name, he said, was Gustave Aschenbach. He was born at L——, a country town in the province of Silesia. He was the son of an upper official in the judicature, and his forebears had all been officers, judges, departmental functionaries. . . . And you can never touch a girl in the same way more than once, twice, or another number of times however much you may wish to hold, wrap, or otherwise fix her hand, or look, or some other quality, or incident, known to you previously. In Sweden the little Swedish children cheered when we managed nothing more remarkable than getting off a bus burdened with packages, bread and liver paste and beer. We went to an old church and sat in the royal box. The organist was practicing. And then into the graveyard next to the church. *Here lies Anna Pedersen, a good woman.* I threw a mushroom on the grave. The officer commanding the garbage dump reported by radio that the garbage had begun to move.

Jane! I heard via an International Distress Coupon that you were beaten up by a dwarf in a bar on Tenerife. That doesn't sound like you, Jane. Mostly you kick the dwarf in his little dwarf groin before he can get his teeth into your tasty and nice-looking leg, don't you, Jane? Your affair with Harold is reprehensible, you know that, don't you, Jane? Harold is married to Nancy. And there is Paula to think about (Harold's kid), and Billy (Harold's other kid). I think your values are peculiar, Jane! Strings of language extend in every direction to bind the world into a rushing, ribald whole.

And you can never return to felicities in the same way, the brilliant body, the distinguished spirit recapitulating moments that occur once, twice, or another number of times in rebellions, or water. The rolling consensus of the Comanche nation smashed our inner defenses on three sides. Block was firing a grease gun from the upper floor of a building designed by Emery Roth & Sons. "See the table?" "Oh, pack it in with your bloody table!" The city officials were tied to trees. Dusky warriors padded with their forest tread into the mouth of the mayor. "Who do you want to be?" I asked Kenneth and he said he wanted to be Jean-Luc Godard but later when time permitted conversations in large, lighted rooms, whispering galleries with black-and-white Spanish rugs and problematic sculpture on calm, red catafalques. The sickness of the quarrel lay thick in the bed. I touched your back, the white, raised scars.

We killed a great many in the south suddenly with helicopters and rockets but we found that those we had killed were children and more came from the north and from the east and from other places where there are children preparing to live. "Skin," Miss R. said softly in the white, yellow room. "This is the Clemency Committee. And would you remove your belt and shoelaces." I removed my belt and shoelaces and looked (rain shattering from a great height the prospects of silence and clear, neat rows of houses in the subdivisions) into their savage black eyes, paint, feathers, beads.

Views of My Father Weeping

An aristocrat was riding down the street in his carriage. He ran over my father.

•

After the ceremony I walked back to the city. I was trying to think of the reason my father had died. Then I remembered: he was run over by a carriage.

•

I telephoned my mother and told her of my father's death. She said she supposed it was the best thing. I too supposed it was the best thing. His enjoyment was diminishing. I wondered if I should attempt to trace the aristocrat whose carriage had run him down. There were said to have been one or two witnesses.

•

Yes it is possible that it is not my father who sits there in the center of the bed weeping. It may be someone else, the mailman, the man who delivers the groceries, an insurance salesman or tax collector, who knows. However, I must say, it resembles my father. The resemblance is very strong. He is not smiling through his tears but frowning through them. I remember once we were out on the ranch shooting peccadillos (result of a meeting, on the plains of the West, of the collared peccary and the nine-banded armadillo). My father shot and missed. He wept. This weeping resembles that weeping.

•

"Did you see it?" "Yes but only part of it. Part of the time I had my back turned." The witness was a little girl, eleven or twelve. She lived in a very poor quarter and I could not imagine that, were she to testify, anyone would credit her. "Can you recall what the man in the carriage looked like?" "Like an aristocrat," she said.

•

The first witness declares that the man in the carriage looked "like an aristocrat." But that might be simply the carriage itself. Any man sitting in a handsome carriage with a driver on the box and perhaps one or two footmen up behind tends to look like an aristocrat. I wrote down her name and asked her to call me if she remembered anything else. I gave her some candy.

•

I stood in the square where my father was killed and asked people passing by if they had seen, or knew of anyone who had seen, the incident. At the same time I felt the effort was wasted. Even if I found the man whose carriage had done the job, what would I say to him? "You killed my father." "Yes," the aristocrat would say, "but he ran right in under the legs of the horses. My man tried to stop but it happened too quickly. There was nothing anyone could do." Then perhaps he would offer me a purse full of money.

•

The man sitting in the center of the bed looks very much like my father. He is weeping, tears coursing down his cheeks. One can see that he is upset about something. Looking at him I see that something is wrong. He is spewing like a fire hydrant with its lock knocked off. His yammer darts in and out of all the rooms. In a melting mood I lay my paw on my breast and say, "Father." This does not distract him from his plaint, which rises to a shriek, sinks to a pule. His range is great, his ambition commensurate. I say again, "Father," but he ignores me. I don't know whether it is time to flee or will not be time to flee until later. He may suddenly stop, assume a sternness. I have kept the door open and nothing between me and the door, and moreover the screen unlatched, and on top of that the motor running, in the Mustang. But perhaps it is not my father weeping there, but another father: Tom's father, Phil's father, Pat's father, Pete's father, Paul's father. Apply some sort of test, voiceprint reading or

•

My father throws his ball of knitting up in the air. The orange wool hangs there.

•

My father regards the tray of pink cupcakes. Then he jams his thumb into each cupcake, into the top. Cupcake by cupcake. A thick smile spreads over the face of each cupcake.

•

Then a man volunteered that he had heard two other men talking about the accident in a shop. "What shop?" The man pointed it out to me, a draper's shop on the south side of the square. I entered the shop and made inquiries. "It was your father, eh? He was bloody clumsy if you ask me." This was the clerk behind the counter. But another man standing nearby, well-dressed, even elegant, a gold watchchain stretched across his vest, disagreed. "It was the fault of the driver," the second man said. "He could have stopped them if he had cared to." "Nonsense," the clerk said, "not a chance in the world. If your father hadn't been drunk—" "He wasn't drunk," I said. "I arrived on the scene soon after it happened and I smelled no liquor."

•

This was true. I had been notified by the police, who came to my room and fetched me to the scene of the accident. I bent over my father, whose chest was crushed, and laid my cheek against his. His cheek was cold. I smelled no liquor but blood from his mouth stained the collar of my coat. I asked the people standing there how it had happened. "Run down by a carriage," they said. "Did the driver stop?" "No, he whipped up the horses and went off down the street and then around the corner at the end of the street, toward King's New Square." "You have no idea as to whose carriage . . ." "None." Then I made the arrangements for the burial. It was not until several days later that the idea of seeking the aristocrat in the carriage came to me.

•

I had had in my life nothing to do with aristocrats, did not even know in what part of the city they lived, in their great houses. So that even if I located someone who had seen the incident and could identify the particular aristocrat involved, I would be faced with the further task of finding his house and gaining admittance (and even then, might he not be abroad?). "No, the driver was at fault," the man with the gold watch-chain said. "Even if your father was drunk—and I can't say about that, one way or another, I have no opinion—even if your father was drunk, the driver could have done more to avoid the accident. He was dragged, you know. The carriage dragged him about forty feet." I had noticed that my father's clothes were torn in a peculiar way. "There was one thing," the clerk said, "don't tell anyone I told you, but I can give you one hint. The driver's livery was blue and green."

•

It is someone's father. That much is clear. He is fatherly. The gray in the head. The puff in the face. The droop in the shoulders. The flab on the gut. Tears falling. Tears falling. Tears falling. Tears falling. More tears. It seems that he intends to go further along this salty path. The facts suggest that this is his program, weeping. He has something in mind, more weeping. O lud lud! But why remain? Why watch it? Why tarry? Why not fly? Why subject myself? I could be somewhere else, reading a book, watching the telly, stuffing a big ship into a little bottle, dancing the Pig. I could be out in the streets feeling up eleven-year-old girls in their soldier drag, there are thousands, as alike as pennies, and I could be— Why doesn't he stand up, arrange his clothes, dry his face? He's trying to embarrass us. He wants attention. He's trying to make himself interesting. He wants his brow wrapped in cold cloths perhaps, his hands held perhaps, his back rubbed, his neck kneaded, his wrists patted, his elbows anointed with rare oils, his toenails painted with tiny scenes representing God blessing America. I won't do it.

•

My father has a red bandana tied around his face covering the nose and mouth. He extends his right hand in which there is a water pistol. "Stick 'em up!" he says.

•

But blue and green livery is not unusual. A blue coat with green trousers, or the reverse, if I saw a coachman wearing such livery I would take no particular notice. It is true that most livery tends to be blue and buff, or blue and white, or blue and a sort of darker blue (for the trousers). But in these days one often finds a servant aping the more exquisite color combinations affected by his masters. I have even seen them in red trousers although red trousers used to be reserved, by unspoken agreement, for the aristocracy. So that the colors of the driver's livery were not of much consequence. Still it was something. I could now go about in the city, especially in stables and gin shops and such places, keeping a weather eye for the livery of the lackeys who gathered there. It was possible that more than one of the gentry dressed his servants in this blue and green livery, but on the other hand, unlikely that there were as many as half a dozen. So that in fact the draper's clerk had offered a very good clue indeed, had one the energy to pursue it vigorously.

•

There is my father, standing alongside an extremely large dog, a dog ten hands high at the very least. My father leaps on the dog's back, straddles him. My father kicks the large dog in the ribs with his heels. "Giddyap!"

•

My father has written on the white wall with his crayons.

•

I was stretched out on my bed when someone knocked at the door. It was the small girl to whom I had given candy when I had first begun searching for the aristocrat. She looked frightened, yet resolute; I could see that she had some information for me. "I know who it was," she said. "I know his name." "What is it?" "First you must give me five crowns." Luckily I had five crowns in my pocket; had she come later in the day, after I had eaten, I would have had nothing to give her. I handed over the money and she said, "Lars Bang." I looked at her in some surprise. "What sort of name is that for an aristocrat?" "His coachman," she said. "The coachman's name is Lars Bang." Then she fled.

•

When I heard this name, which in its sound and appearance is rude, vulgar, not unlike my own name, I was seized with repugnance, thought of dropping the whole business, although the piece of information she had brought had just cost me five crowns. When I was seeking him and he was yet nameless, the aristocrat and, by extension, his servants, seemed vulnerable: they had, after all, been responsible for a crime, or a sort of crime. My father was dead and they were responsible, or at least involved; and even though they were of the aristocracy or servants of the aristocracy, still common justice might be sought for; they might be required to make reparation, in some measure, for what they had done. Now, having the name of the coachman, and being thus much closer to his master than when I merely had the clue of the blue and green livery, I became afraid. For, after all, the unknown aristocrat must be a very powerful man, not at all accustomed to being called to account by people like me; indeed, his contempt for people like me was so great that, when one of us was so foolish as to stray into the path of his carriage, the aristocrat dashed him down, or permitted his coachman to do so, dragged him along the cobblestones for as much as forty feet, and then went gaily on his way, toward King's New Square. Such a man, I reasoned, was not very likely to take kindly to what I had to say to him. Very possibly there would be no purse of money at all, not a crown, not an öre; but rather he would, with an abrupt, impatient nod of his head, set his servants upon me. I would be beaten, perhaps killed. Like my father.

•

But if it is not my father sitting there in the bed weeping, why am I standing before the bed, in an attitude of supplication? Why do I desire with all my heart that this man, my father, cease what he is doing, which is so painful to me? Is it only that my position is a familiar one? That I remember, before, desiring with all my heart that this man, my father, cease what he is doing?

•

Why! . . . there's my father! . . . sitting in the bed there! . . . and he's *weeping!* . . . as though his heart would burst! . . . Father! . . . how is this? . . . who has wounded you? . . . name the man! . . . why I'll . . . I'll . . . here, Father, take this handkerchief! . . . and this handkerchief! . . . and this handkerchief! . . . I'll run for a towel . . . for a doctor . . . for a priest . . . for a good fairy . . . is there . . . can you . . . can I . . . a cup of hot tea? . . . bowl of steaming soup? . . . shot of Calvados? . . . a joint? . . . a red jacket? . . . a blue jacket? . . . Father, please! . . . look at me, Father . . . who has insulted you? . . . are you, then, compromised? . . . ruined? . . . a slander is going around? . . . an obloquy? . . . a traducement? . . . 'sdeath! . . . I won't permit it! . . . I won't abide it! . . . I'll . . . move every mountain . . . climb every river . . . etc.

•

My father is playing with the salt and pepper shakers, and with the sugar bowl. He lifts the cover off the sugar bowl, and shakes pepper into it.

•

Or: My father thrusts his hand through a window of the doll's house. His hand knocks over the doll's chair, knocks over the doll's chest of drawers, knocks over the doll's bed.

•

The next day, just before noon, Lars Bang himself came to my room. "I understand that you are looking for me." He was very much of a surprise. I had expected a rather burly, heavy man, of a piece with all of the other coachmen one saw sitting up on the box; Lars Bang was, instead, slight, almost feminine-looking, more the type of the secretary or valet than the coachman. He was not threatening at all, contrary to my fears; he was almost helpful, albeit with the slightest hint of malice in his helpfulness. I stammeringly explained that my father, a good man although subject to certain weaknesses, including a love of the bottle, had been run down by an aristocrat's coach, in the vicinity of King's New Square, not very many days previously; that I had information that the coach had dragged him some forty feet; and that I was eager to establish certain facts about the case. "Well then," Lars Bang said, with a helpful nod, "I'm your man, for it was my coach that was involved. A sorry business! Unfortunately I haven't the time right now to give you the full particulars, but if you will call around at the address written on this card, at six o'clock in the evening, I believe I will be able to satisfy you." So saying, he took himself off, leaving me with the card in my hand.

•

I spoke to Miranda, quickly sketching what had happened. She asked to see the white card; I gave it to her, for the address meant nothing to me. "Oh my," she said. "17 rue du Bac, that's over by the Vixen Gate—a very special quarter. Only aristocrats of the highest rank live there, and common people are not even allowed into the great park that lies between the houses and the river. If you are found wandering about there at night, you are apt to earn yourself a very severe beating." "But I have an appointment," I said. "An appointment with a coachman!" Miranda cried, "how foolish you are! Do you think the men of the watch will believe that, or even if they believe it (you have an honest enough face) will allow you to prowl that rich quarter, where so many thieves would dearly love to be set free for an hour or so, after dark? Go to!" Then she advised me that I must carry something with me, a pannier of beef or some dozen bottles of wine, so that if apprehended by the watch, I could say that I was delivering to such and such a house, and thus be judged an honest man on an honest errand, and escape a beating. I saw that she was right; and going out, I purchased at the wine merchant's a dozen bottles of a rather good claret (for it would never do to be delivering wine no aristocrat would drink); this cost me thirty crowns, which I had borrowed from Miranda. The bottles we wrapped round with straw, to prevent them banging into one another, and the whole we arranged in a sack, which I could carry on my back. I remember thinking, how they rhymed, fitted together, *sack* and *back*. In this fashion I set off across the city.

•

There is my father's bed. In it, my father. Attitude of dejection. Graceful as a mule deer once, the same large ears. For a nanosecond, there is a nanosmile. Is he having me on? I remember once we went out on the ups and downs of the West (out past Vulture's Roost) to shoot. First we shot up a lot of old beer cans, then we shot up a lot of old whiskey bottles, better because they shattered. Then we shot up some mesquite bushes and some parts of a Ford pickup somebody'd left lying around. But no animals came to our party (it was noisy, I admit it). A long list of animals failed to arrive, no deer, quail, rabbit, seals, sea lions, condylarths. It was pretty boring shooting up mesquite bushes, so we hunkered down behind some rocks, Father and I, he hunkered down behind his rocks and I hunkered down behind my rocks, and we commenced to shooting at each other. That was interesting.

•

My father is looking at himself in a mirror. He is wearing a large hat (straw) on which there are a number of blue and yellow plastic jonquils. He says: "How do I look?"

•

Lars Bang took the sack from me and without asking permission reached inside, withdrawing one of the straw-wrapped bottles of claret. "Here's something!" he exclaimed, reading the label. "A gift for the master, I don't doubt!" Then, regarding me steadily all the while, he took up an awl and lifted the cork. There were two other men seated at the pantry table, dressed in the blue-and-green livery, and with them a dark-haired, beautiful girl, quite young, who said nothing and looked at no one. Lars Bang obtained glasses, kicked a chair in my direction, and poured drinks all round. "To your health!" he said (with what I thought an ironical overtone) and we drank. "This young man," Lars Bang said, nodding at me, "is here seeking our advice on a very complicated business. A murder, I believe you said?" "I said nothing of the kind. I seek information about an accident." The claret was soon exhausted. Without looking at me, Lars Bang opened a second bottle and set it in the center of the table. The beautiful dark-haired girl ignored me along with all the others. For my part, I felt I had conducted myself rather well thus far. I had not protested when the wine was made free of (after all, they would be accustomed to levying a sort of tax on anything entering through the back door). But also I had not permitted his word "murder" to be used, but instead specified the use of the word "accident." Therefore I was, in general, comfortable sitting at the table drinking the wine, for which I have no better head than had my father. "Well," said Lars Bang at length, "I will relate the circumstances of the accident, and you may judge for yourself as to whether myself and my master, the Lensgreve Aklefeldt, were at fault." I absorbed this news with a slight shock. A count! I had selected a man of very high rank indeed to put my question to. In a moment my accumulated self-confidence drained away. A count! Mother of God, have mercy on me.

•

There is my father, peering through an open door into an empty house. He is accompanied by a dog (small dog; not the same dog as before). He looks into the empty room. He says: "Anybody home?"

•

There is my father, sitting in his bed, weeping.

•

"It was a Friday," Lars Bang began, as if he were telling a tavern story. "The hour was close upon noon and my master directed me to drive him to King's New Square, where he had some business. We were proceeding there at a modest easy pace, for he was in no great hurry. Judge of my astonishment when, passing through the draper's quarter, we found ourselves set upon by an elderly man, thoroughly drunk, who flung himself at my lead pair and began cutting at their legs with a switch, in the most vicious manner imaginable. The poor dumb brutes reared, of course, in fright and fear, for," Lars Bang said piously, "they are accustomed to the best of care, and never a blow do they receive from me, or from the other coachman, Rik, for the count is especially severe upon this point, that his animals be well-treated. The horses, then, were rearing and plunging; it was all I could do to hold them; I shouted at the man, who fell back for an instant. The count stuck his head out of the window, to inquire as to the nature of the trouble, and I told him that a drunken man had attacked our horses. Your father, in his blindness, being not content with the mischief he had already worked, ran back in again, close to the animals, and began madly cutting at their legs with his stick. At this renewed attack the horses, frightened out of their wits, jerked the reins from my hands, and ran headlong over your father, who fell beneath their hooves. The heavy wheels of the carriage passed over him (I felt two quite distinct thumps), his body caught upon a projection under the boot, and he was dragged some forty feet, over the cobblestones. I was attempting, with all my might, merely to hang on to the box, for, having taken the bit between their teeth, the horses were in no mood to tarry; nor could any human agency have stopped them. We flew down the street . . ."

•

My father is attending a class in good behavior.

"Do the men rise when friends greet us while we are sitting in a booth?"

"The men do not rise when they are seated in a booth," he answers, "although they may half-rise and make apologies for not fully rising."

•

". . . the horses turning into the way that leads to King's New Square; and it was not until we reached that place that they stopped and allowed me to quiet them. I wanted to go back and see what had become of the madman, your father, who had attacked us; but my master, vastly angry and shaken up, forbade it. I have never seen him in so fearful a temper as that day; if your father had survived, and my master got his hands on him, it would have gone ill with your father, that's a certainty. And so, you are now in possession of all the facts. I trust you are satisfied, and will drink another bottle of this quite fair claret you have brought us, and be on your way." Before I had time to frame a reply, the dark-haired girl spoke. "Bang is an absolute bloody liar," she said.

•

Etc.

Paraguay

The upper part of the plain that we had crossed the day before was now white with snow, and it was evident that there was a storm raging behind us and that we had only just crossed the Burji La in time to escape it. We camped in a slight hollow at Sekbachan, eighteen miles from Malik Mar, the night as still as the previous one and the temperature the same; it seemed as if the Deosai Plains were not going to be so formidable as they had been described; but the third day a storm of hail, sleet, and snow alternately came at noon when we began to ascend the Sari Sangar Pass, 14,200 feet, and continued with only a few minutes' intermission till four o'clock. The top of the pass is a fairly level valley containing two lakes, their shores formed of boulders that seemed impossible to ride over. The men slid and stumbled so much that I would not let anyone lead my pony for fear of pulling him over; he was old and slow but perfectly splendid here, picking his way among the rocks without a falter. At the summit there is a cairn on which each man threw a stone, and here it is customary to give payment to the coolies. I paid each man his agreed-upon wage, and, alone, began the descent. Ahead was Paraguay.[1]

Where Paraguay Is

Thus I found myself in a strange country. This Paraguay is not the Paraguay that exists on our maps. It is not to be found on

1 Quoted from *A Summer Ride Through Western Tibet*, by Jane E. Duncan, Collins, London, 1906. Slightly altered.

the continent, South America; it is not a political subdivision of that continent, with a population of 2,161,000 and a capital city named Asunción. This Paraguay exists elsewhere. Now, moving toward the first of the "silver cities," I was tired but also elated and alert. Flights of white meat moved through the sky overhead in the direction of the dim piles of buildings.

Jean Mueller

Entering the city I was approached, that first day, by a dark girl wrapped in a red shawl. The edges of the shawl were fringed, and the tip of each strand of fringe was a bob of silver. The girl at once placed her hands on my hips, standing facing me; she smiled, and exerted a slight pull. I was claimed as her guest; her name was Jean Mueller. "*Teníamos grandes deseos de conocerlo,*" she said. I asked how she knew I had arrived and she said, "Everyone knows." We then proceeded to her house, a large, modern structure some distance from the center of the city; there I was shown into a room containing a bed, a desk, a chair, bookcases, a fireplace, a handsome piano in a cherry-wood case. I was told that when I had rested I might join her downstairs and might then meet her husband; before leaving the room she sat down before the piano, and, almost mischievously, played a tiny sonata of Bibblemann's.

Temperature

Temperature controls activity to a remarkable degree. By and large, adults here raise their walking speed and show more spontaneous movement as the temperature rises. But the temperature-dependent pattern of activity is complex. For instance, the males move twice as fast at 60 degrees as they do at 35 degrees, but above 60 degrees speed decreases. The females show more complicated behavior; they increase spontaneous activity as the temperature rises from 40 to 48 degrees, become less active between 49 and 66 degrees, and above 66 degrees again go into a rising tempo of spontaneous movements up to the lethal temperature of 77 degrees. Temperature also (here as elsewhere) plays a critical role in the reproductive process. In the so-called "silver cities" there is a particular scale—66, 67, 68, 69 degrees—at which intercourse occurs (and only within that scale). In the "gold" areas, the scale does not, apparently, apply.

Herko Mueller

Herko Mueller walks through gold and silver leaves, awarded, in the summer months, to those who have produced the best pastiche of the emotions. He is smiling because he did not win one of these prizes, which the people of Paraguay seek to avoid. He is tall, brown, wears a funny short beard, and is fond of zippered suits in brilliant colors: yellow, green, violet. He is, professionally, an arbiter of comedy. "A sort of drama critic?" "More what you would term an umpire. The members of the audience are given a set of rules and the rules constitute the comedy. Our comedies seek to reach the imagination. When you are looking at something, you cannot imagine it." In the evenings I have wet sand to walk upon—long stretches of beach with the sea tasting the edges. Getting back into my clothes after a swim, I discover a strange thing: a sand dollar under my shirt. It is strange because this sand is sifted twice daily to remove impurities and maintain whiteness. And the sea itself, the New Sea, is not programmed for echinoderms.

Error

A government error resulting in the death of a statistically insignificant portion of the population (less than one-fortieth of one per cent) has made people uneasy. A skelp of questions and answers is fused at high temperature (1400° C) and then passed through a series of protracted caresses. Amelioration of the condition results. Paraguay is not old. It is new, a new country. Rough sketches suggest its "look." Heavy yellow drops like pancake batter fall from its sky. I hold a bouquet of umbrellas in each hand. A phrase of Herko Mueller's: *"Y un 60% son mestizos: gloria, orgullo, presente y futuro del*

Paraguay" (". . . the glory, pride, present and future of Paraguay"). The country's existence is "predictive," he says, and I myself have noticed a sort of frontier ambiance. There are problems. The problem of shedding skin. Thin discarded shells like disposable plastic gloves are found in the street.

Rationalization

The problems of art. New artists have been obtained. These do not object to, and indeed argue enthusiastically for, the rationalization process. Production is up. Quality-control devices have been installed at those points where the interests of artists and audience intersect. Shipping and distribution have been improved out of all recognition. (It is in this area, they say in Paraguay, that traditional practices were most blameworthy.) The rationalized art is dispatched from central art dumps to regional art dumps, and from there into the lifestreams of cities. Each citizen is given as much art as his system can tolerate. Marketing considerations have not been allowed to dictate product mix; rather, each artist is encouraged to maintain, in his software, highly personal, even idiosyncratic, standards (the so-called "hand of the artist" concept). Rationalization produces simpler circuits and, therefore, a saving in hardware. Each artist's product is translated into a statement in symbolic logic. The statement is then "minimized" by various clever methods. The simpler statement is translated back into the design of a simpler circuit. Foamed by a number of techniques, the art is then run through heavy steel rollers. Flip-flop switches control its further development. Sheet art is generally dried in smoke and is dark brown in color. Bulk art is air-dried, and changes color in particular historical epochs.

Skin

Ignoring a letter from the translator Jean sat on a rubber pad doing exercises designed to loosen the skin. Scores of diamond-shaped lights abraded her arms and legs. The light placed a pattern of false information in those zones most susceptible to tearing. Whistling noises accompanied the lights. The process of removing the leg skin is private. Tenseness is eased by the application of a cream, heavy yellow drops like pancake batter. I held several umbrellas over her legs. A man across the street pretending not to watch us. Then the skin placed in the green official receptacles.

The Wall

Our design for the lift tower left us with a vast blind wall of *in situ* concrete. There was thus the danger of having a dreary expanse of blankness in that immensely important part of the building. A solution had to be found. The great wall space would provide an opportunity for a gesture of thanks to the people of Paraguay; a stone would be placed in front of it, and, instead of standing in the shadows, the Stele of the Measures would be brought there also. The wall would be divided, by means of softly worn paths, into doors. These, varying in size from the very large to the very small, would have different colors and thicknesses. Some would open, some would not, and this would change from week to week, or from hour to hour, or in accord with sounds made by people standing in front of them. Long lines or tracks would run from the doors into the roaring public spaces.[2]

Silence

In the larger stores silence (damping materials) is sold in paper sacks like cement. Similarly, the softening of language usually lamented as a falling off from former practice is in fact a clear response to the proliferation of surfaces and stimuli. Imprecise sentences lessen the strain of close tolerances. Silence is also available in the form of white noise. The extension of white noise to the home by means of leased wire from a central generating point has been useful, Herko says. The analogous

2 Quoted from *The Modular*, by Le Corbusier, MIT Press, Cambridge, 1954. Slightly altered.

establishment of "white space" in a system paralleling the existing park system has also been beneficial. Anechoic chambers placed randomly about the city (on the model of telephone booths) are said to have actually saved lives. Wood is becoming rare. They are now paying for yellow pine what was formerly paid for rosewood. Relational methods govern the layout of cities. Curiously, in some of the most successful projects the design has been swung upon small collections of rare animals spaced (on the lost-horse principle) on a lack of grid. Carefully calculated mixes: mambas, the black wrasse, the giselle. Electrolytic jelly exhibiting a capture ratio far in excess of standard is used to fix the animals in place.

Terror

We rushed down to the ends of the waves, apertures through which threatening lines might be seen. Arbiters registered serial numbers of the (complex of threats) with ticks on a great, brown board. Jean meanwhile, unaffected, was casting about on the beach for driftwood, brown washed pieces of wood laced with hundreds of tiny hairline cracks. Such is the smoothness of surfaces in Paraguay that anything not smooth is valuable. She explains to me that in demanding (and receiving) explanations you are once more brought to a stop. You have got, really, no farther than you were before. "Therefore we try to keep everything open, go forward avoiding the final explanation. If we inadvertently receive it, we are instructed to 1) pretend that it is just another error, or 2) misunderstand it. Creative misunderstanding is crucial." Creation of new categories of anxiety which must be bandaged or "patched." The expression "put a patch on it." There are "hot" and "cold" patches and specialists in the application of each. Rhathymia is the preferred mode of presentation of the self.

The Temple

Turning sharply to the left I came upon, in a grove of trees, a temple of some sort, abandoned, littered with empty boxes, the floor coated with a thin layer of lime. I prayed. Then drawing out my flask I refreshed myself with apple juice. Everyone in Paraguay has the same fingerprints. There are crimes but people chosen at random are punished for them. Everyone is liable for everything. An extension of the principle, there but for the grace of God go I. Sexual life is very free. There are rules but these are like the rules of chess, intended to complicate and enrich the game. I made love to Jean Mueller while her husband watched. There have been certain technical refinements. The procedures we use (called here "impalement") are used in Paraguay but also new techniques I had never before encountered, "dimidiation" and "quartering." These I found very refreshing.

Microminiaturization

Microminiaturization leaves enormous spaces to be filled. Disposability of the physical surround has psychological consequences. The example of the child's anxiety occasioned by the family's move to a new home may be cited. Everything physical in Paraguay is getting smaller and smaller. Walls thin as a thought, locomotive-substitutes no bigger than ball-point pens. Paraguay, then, has big empty spaces in which men wander, trying to touch something. Preoccupation with skin (on and off, wrinkling, the new skin, pink, fresh, taut) possibly a response to this. Stories about skin, histories of particular skins. But no jokes! Some 700,000 photographs of nuclear events were lost when the great library of Paraguay burned. Particle identification was set back many years. Rather than re-create the former physics, a new physics based on the golden section (proliferation of golden sections) was constructed. As a system of explanation almost certain to be incorrect it enjoys enormous prestige here.

Behind the Wall

Behind the wall there is a field of red snow. I had expected that to enter it would be forbidden, but Jean said no, walk about in it, as much as you like. I had expected that walking in it one would leave no footprints, or that there would be some other anomaly of that kind, but there were no anomalies; I left footprints and felt the cold of the snow underfoot. I said to Jean Mueller, "What is the point of this red snow?" "The intention of the red snow, the reason it is isolated behind the wall, yet not forbidden, is its soft glow—as if it were lighted from beneath. You must have noticed it; you've been standing here for twenty minutes." "But what does it do?" "Like any other snow, it invites contemplation and walking about in." The snow rearranged itself into a smooth, red surface without footprints. It had a red glow, as if lighted from beneath. It seemed to proclaim itself a mystery, but one there was no point in solving—an ongoing low-grade mystery.

Departure

Then I was shown the plan, which is kept in a box. Herko Mueller opened the box with a key (everyone has a key). "Here is the plan," he said. "It governs more or less everything. It is a way of allowing a very wide range of tendencies to interact." The plan was a number of analyses of Brownian motion equipped, at each end, with alligator clips. Then the bell rang and the space became crowded, hundreds of men and women standing there waiting for the marshals to establish some sort of order. I had been chosen, Herko said, to head the column (on the principle of the least-likely-leader). We robed; I folded my arms around the mace. We began the descent (into? out of?) Paraguay.

On Angels

The death of God left the angels in a strange position. They were overtaken suddenly by a fundamental question. One can attempt to imagine the moment. How did they *look* at the instant the question invaded them, flooding the angelic consciousness, taking hold with terrifying force? The question was, "What are angels?"

New to questioning, unaccustomed to terror, unskilled in aloneness, the angels (we assume) fell into despair.

The question of what angels "are" has a considerable history. Swedenborg, for example, talked to a great many angels and faithfully recorded what they told him. Angels look like human beings, Swedenborg says. "That angels are human forms, or men, has been seen by me a thousand times." And again: "From all of my experience, which is now of many years, I am able to state that angels are wholly men in form, having faces, eyes, ears, bodies, arms, hands, and feet . . ." But a man cannot see angels with his bodily eyes, only with the eyes of the spirit.

Swedenborg has a great deal more to say about angels, all of the highest interest: that no angel is ever permitted to stand behind another and look at the back of his head, for this would disturb the influx of good and truth from the Lord; that angels have the east, where the Lord is seen as a sun, always before their eyes; and that angels are clothed according to their intelligence. "Some of the most intelligent have garments that blaze as if with flame, others have garments that glisten as if with light; the less intelligent have garments that are glistening white or white without the effulgence; and the still less intelligent have garments of various colors. But the angels of the inmost heaven are not clothed."

All of this (presumably) no longer obtains.

Gustav Davidson, in his useful *Dictionary of Angels*, has brought together much of what is known about them. Their names are called: the angel Elubatel, the angel Friagne, the angel Gaap, the angel Hatiphas (genius of finery), the angel Murmur (a fallen angel), the angel Mqttro, the angel Or, the angel Rash, the angel Sandalphon (taller than a five hundred years' journey on foot), the angel Smat. Davidson distinguishes categories: Angels of Quaking, who surround the heavenly throne; Masters of Howling and Lords of Shouting, whose work is praise; messengers, mediators, watchers, warners. Davidson's *Dictionary* is a very large book; his bibliography lists more than eleven hundred items.

The former angelic consciousness has been most beautifully described by Joseph Lyons (in a paper titled *The Psychology of Angels*, published in 1957). Each angel, Lyons says, knows all that there is to know about himself and every other angel. "No angel could ever ask a question, because questioning proceeds out of a situation of not knowing, and of being in some way aware of not knowing. An angel cannot be curious; he has nothing to be curious about. He cannot wonder. Knowing all that there is to know, the world of possible knowledge must appear to him as an ordered set of facts which is completely behind him, completely fixed and certain and within his grasp . . ."

But this, too, no longer obtains.

It is a curiosity of writing about angels that, very often, one turns out to be writing about men. The themes are twinned. Thus one finally learns that Lyons, for example, is really writing not about angels but about schizophrenics—thinking about men by invoking angels. And this holds true of much other writing on the subject—a point, we may assume, that was not lost on the angels when they began considering their new relation to the cosmos, when the analogues (is an angel more like a quetzal or more like a man? or more like music?) were being handed about.

We may further assume that some attempt was made at self-definition by function. An angel is what he does. Thus it was necessary to investigate possible new roles (you are reminded that this is impure speculation). After the lamentation had gone on for hundreds and hundreds of whatever the angels use for time, an angel proposed that lamentation be the function of angels eternally, as adoration was formerly. The mode of lamentation would be silence, in contrast to the unceasing chanting of Glorias that had been their former employment. But it is not in the nature of angels to be silent.

A counterproposal was that the angels affirm chaos. There were to be five great proofs of the existence of chaos, of which the first was the absence of God. The other four could surely be located. The work of definition and explication could, if done nicely enough, occupy the angels forever, as the contrary work has occupied human theologians. But there is not much enthusiasm for chaos among the angels.

The most serious because most radical proposal considered by the angels was refusal—that they would remove themselves from being, not be. The tremendous dignity that would accrue to the angels by this act was felt to be a manifestation of spiritual pride. Refusal was refused.

There were other suggestions, more subtle and complicated, less so, none overwhelmingly attractive.

I saw a famous angel on television; his garments glistened as if with light. He talked about the situation of angels now. Angels, he said, are like men *in some ways*. The problem of adoration is felt to be central. He said that for a time the angels had tried adoring each other, as we do, but had found it, finally, "not enough." He said they are continuing to search for a new principle.

The Phantom of the Opera's Friend

I have never visited him in his sumptuous quarters five levels below the Opera, across the dark lake.

But he has described them. Rich divans, exquisitely carved tables, amazing silk and satin draperies. The large, superbly embellished mantelpiece, on which rest two curious boxes, one containing the figure of a grasshopper, the other the figure of a scorpion . . .

He can, in discoursing upon his domestic arrangements, become almost merry. For example, speaking of the wine he has stolen from the private cellar of the Opera's Board of Directors:

"A *very* adequate Montrachet! Four bottles! Each director accusing every other director! I tell you, it made me feel like a director myself! As if I were worth two or three millions and had a fat, ugly wife! And the trout was admirable. You know what the Poles say—fish, to taste right, must swim three times: in water, butter, and wine. All in all, a splendid evening!"

But he immediately alters the mood by making some gloomy observation. "Our behavior is mocked by the behavior of dogs."

It is not often that the accents of joy issue from beneath that mask.

Monday. I am standing at the place I sometimes encounter him, a little door at the rear of the Opera (the building has 2,531 doors to which there are 7,593 keys). He always appears "suddenly"—a *coup de théâtre* that is, to tell the truth, more annoying than anything else. We enact a little comedy of surprise.

"It's you!"

"Yes."

"What are you doing here?"

"Waiting."

But today no one appears, although I wait for half an hour. I have wasted my time. Except—

Faintly, through many layers of stone, I hear organ music. The music is attenuated but unmistakable. It is his great work *Don Juan Triumphant.* A communication of a kind.

I rejoice in his immense, buried talent.

But I know that he is not happy.

His situation is simple and terrible. He must decide whether to risk life aboveground or to remain forever in hiding, in the cellars of the Opera.

His tentative, testing explorations in the city (always at night) have not persuaded him to one course or the other. Too, the city is no longer the city he knew as a young man. Its meaning has changed.

At a café table, in a place where the light from the streetlamps is broken by a large tree, we sit silently over our drinks.

Everything that can be said has been said many times.

I have no new observations to make. The decision he faces has been tormenting him for decades.

"If after all I—"

But he cannot finish the sentence. We both know what is meant.

I am distracted, a bit angry. How many nights have I spent this way, waiting upon his sighs?

In the early years of our friendship I proposed vigorous measures. A new life! Advances in surgery, I told him, had made a normal existence possible for him. New techniques in—

"I'm too old."

One is never too old, I said. There were still many satisfactions open to him, not the least the possibility of service to others. His music! A home, even marriage and children were not out of the question. What was required was boldness, the will to break out of old patterns . . .

Now as these thoughts flicker through our brains, he smiles ironically.

Sometimes he speaks of Christine:

"That voice!

"But I was perhaps overdazzled by the circumstances . . .

"A range from low C to the F above high C!

"Flawed, of course . . .

"Liszt heard her. *'Que, c'est beau!'* he cried out.

"Possibly somewhat deficient in temperament. But I had temperament enough for two.

"Such goodness! Such gentleness!

"I would pull down the very doors of heaven for a—"

Tuesday. A few slashes of lightning in the sky . . .

Is one man entitled to fix himself at the center of a cosmos of hatred, and remain there?

The acid . . .

The lost love . . .

Yet all of this is generations cold. There have been wars, inventions, assassinations, discoveries . . .

Perhaps *practical affairs* have assumed, in his mind, a towering importance. Does he fear the loss of the stipend (20,000 francs per month) that he has not ceased to extort from the directors of the Opera?

But I have given him assurances. He shall want for nothing.

Occasionally he is overtaken by what can only be called fits of grandiosity:

"One hundred million cells in the brain! All intent on being the Phantom of the Opera!"

"Between three and four thousand human languages! And I am the Phantom of the Opera in every one of them!"

This is quickly followed by the deepest despair. He sinks into a chair, passes a hand over his mask.

"Forty years of it!"

Why must I have *him* for a friend?

I wanted a friend with whom one could be seen abroad.

With whom one could exchange country weekends, on our respective estates!

I put these unworthy reflections behind me . . .

Gaston Leroux was tired of writing *The Phantom of the Opera.* He replaced his pen in its penholder.

"I can always work on *The Phantom of the Opera* later—in the fall, perhaps. Right now I feel like writing *The Secret of the Yellow Room.*"

Gaston Leroux took the manuscript of *The Phantom of the Opera* and put it on a shelf in the closet.

Then, seating himself once more at his desk, he drew toward him a clean sheet of foolscap. At the top he wrote the words, *The Secret of the Yellow Room.*

Wednesday. I receive a note urgently requesting a meeting. "*All men that are ruined are ruined on the side of their natural propensities,*" the note concludes.

This is surely true. Yet the vivacity with which he embraces ruin is unexampled, in my experience.

When we meet he is pacing nervously in an ill-lit corridor just off the room where the tympani are stored.

I notice that his dress, always so immaculate, is disordered, slept-in-looking. A button hangs by a thread from his waistcoat.

"I have brought you a newspaper," I say.

"Thank you. I wanted to tell you . . . that I have made up my mind."

His hands are trembling. I hold my breath.

"I have decided to take your advice. Sixty-five is not after all the end of one's life! I place myself in your hands. Make whatever arrangements you wish. Tomorrow night at this time I quit the Opera forever."

Blind with emotion, I can think of nothing to say.

A firm handclasp, and he is gone.

A room is prepared. I tell my servants that I am anticipating a visitor who will be with us for an indefinite period.

I choose for him a room with a splendid window, a view of the Seine; but I am careful also to have installed heavy velvet curtains, so that the light, with which the room is plentifully supplied, will not come as an assault.

The degree of light *he* wishes.

And when I am satisfied that the accommodations are all that could be desired, I set off to interview the doctor I have selected.

"You understand that the operation, if he consents to it, will have specific . . . psychological consequences?"

I nod.

And he shows me in a book pictures of faces with terrible burns, before and after having been reconstructed by his science. It is indeed an album of magical transformations.

"I would wish first to have him examined by my colleague Dr. W., a qualified alienist."

"This is possible. But I remind you that he has had no intercourse with his fellow men, myself excepted, for—"

"But was it not the case that *originally,* the violent emotions of revenge and jealousy—"

"Yes. But replaced now, I believe, by a melancholy so deep, so all-pervading—"

Dr. Mirabeau assumes a mock-sternness.

"Melancholy, sir, is an ailment with which I have had some slight acquaintance. We shall see if his distemper can resist a little miracle."

And he extends, into the neutral space between us, a shining scalpel.

But when I call for the Phantom on Thursday, at the appointed hour, he is not there.

What vexation!

Am I not slightly relieved?

Can it be that *he doesn't like me?*

I sit down on the curb, outside the Opera. People passing look at me. I will wait here for a hundred years. Or until the hot meat of romance is cooled by the dull gravy of common sense once more.

City Life

1.

Elsa and Ramona entered the complicated city. They found an apartment without much trouble, several rooms on Porter Street. Curtains were hung. Bright paper things from a Japanese store were placed here and there.

—You'd better tell Charles that he can't come see us until everything is ready.

Ramona thought: I don't want him to come at all. He will go into a room with Elsa and close the door. I will be sitting outside reading the business news. Britain Weighs Economic Curbs. Bond Rate Surge Looms. Time will pass. Then, they will emerge. Acting as if nothing had happened. Elsa will make coffee. Charles will put brandy from his flat silver flask into the coffee. We will all drink the coffee with the brandy in it. Ugh!

—Where shall we put the telephone books?

—Put them over there, by the telephone.

Elsa and Ramona went to the $2 plant store. A man stood outside selling individual peacock feathers. Elsa and Ramona bought several hanging plants in white plastic pots. The proprietor put the plants in brown paper bags.

—Water them every day, girls. Keep them wet.

—We will.

Elsa uttered a melancholy reflection on life: It goes faster and faster! Ramona said: It's so difficult!

Charles accepted a position with greater responsibilities in another city.

—I'll be able to get in on weekends sometimes.

—Is this a real job?

—Of course, Elsa. You don't think I'd fool you, do you?

Clad in an extremely dark gray, if not completely black, suit, he had shaved his mustache.

—This outfit doesn't let you wear them.

Ramona heard Elsa sobbing in the back bedroom. I suppose I should sympathize with her. But I don't.

2.

Ramona received the following letter from Charles:

> Dear Ramona—
>
> Thank you, Ramona, for your interesting and curious letter. It is true that I have noticed you sitting there, in the living room, when I visit Elsa. I have many times made mental notes about your appearance, which I consider in no way inferior to that of Elsa herself. I get a pretty electric reaction to your taste in clothes, too. Those upper legs have not been lost on me. But the trouble is, when two girls are living together, one must make a choice. One can't have them both, in our society. This prohibition is enforced by you girls, chiefly, together with older ladies, who if the truth were known probably don't care, but nevertheless feel that standards must be upheld, somewhere. I have Elsa, therefore I can't have you. (I know that there is a philosophical problem about "being" and "having" but I can't discuss that now because I'm a little rushed due to the pressures of my new assignment.) So that's what obtains at the moment, most excellent Ramona. That's where we stand. Of course the future may be different. It not infrequently is.
>
> Hastily,
> Charles

—What are you reading?

—Oh, it's just a letter.

—Who is it from?

—Oh, just somebody I know.

—Who?

—Oh, nobody.

—Oh.

Ramona's mother and father came to town from Montana. Ramona's thin father stood on the Porter Street sidewalk wearing a business suit and a white cowboy hat. He was watching his car. He watched from the steps of the house for a while, and then watched from the sidewalk a little, and then watched from the steps again. Ramona's mother looked in the suitcases for the present she had brought.

—Mother! You shouldn't have brought me such an expensive present!

—Oh, it wasn't all that expensive. We wanted you to have something for the new apartment.

—An original gravure by René Magritte!

—Well, it isn't very big. It's just a small one.

Whenever Ramona received a letter forwarded to her from her Montana home, the letter had been opened and the words "Oops! Opened by mistake!" written on the envelope. But she forgot that in gazing at the handsome new Magritte print, a picture of a tree with a crescent moon cut out of it.

—It's fantastically beautiful! Where shall we hang it?

—How about on the wall?

3.

At the University the two girls enrolled in the Law School.

—I hear the Law School's tough, Elsa stated, but that's what we want, a tough challenge.

—You are the only two girls ever to be admitted to our Law School, the Dean observed. Mostly, we have men. A few foreigners. Now I am going to tell you three things to keep an eye on: 1) Don't try to go too far too fast. 2) Wear plain clothes. And 3) Keep your notes clean. And if I hear the words "Yoo hoo" echoing across the quadrangle, you will be sent down instantly. We don't use those words in this school.

—I like what I already know, Ramona said under her breath.

Savoring their matriculation, the two girls wandered out to sample the joys of Pascin Street. They were closer together at this time than they had ever been. Of course, they didn't want to get too close together. They were afraid to get too close together.

Elsa met Jacques. He was deeply involved in the struggle.

—What is this struggle about, exactly, Jacques?

—My God, Elsa, your eyes! I have never seen that shade of umber in anyone's eyes before. Ever.

Jacques took Elsa to a Mexican restaurant. Elsa cut into her *cabrito con queso.*

—To think that this food was once a baby goat!

Elsa, Ramona, and Jacques looked at the dawn coming up over the hanging plants. Patterns of silver light and so forth.

—You're not afraid that Charles will bust in here unexpectedly and find us?

—Charles is in Cleveland. Besides, I'd say you were with Ramona. Elsa giggled.

Ramona burst into tears.

Elsa and Jacques tried to comfort Ramona.

—Why don't you take a twenty-one-day excursion-fare trip to "preserves of nature"?

—If I went to a "preserve of nature," it would turn out to be nothing but a terrible fen!

Ramona thought: He will go into a room with Elsa and close the door. Time will pass. Then they will emerge, acting as if nothing had happened. Then the coffee. Ugh!

4·

Charles in Cleveland.

"Whiteness"

"Vital skepticism"

Charles advanced very rapidly in the Cleveland hierarchy. That sort of situation that develops sometimes wherein managers feel threatened by gifted subordinates and do not assign them really meaningful duties but instead shunt them aside into dead areas where their human potential is wasted did not develop in Charles' case. His devoted heart lifted him to the highest levels. It was Charles who pointed out that certain operations had been carried out more efficiently "when the cathedrals were white," and in time the entire Cleveland structure was organized around his notions: "whiteness," "vital skepticism."

Two men held Charles down on the floor and a third slipped a needle into his hip.

He awakened in a vaguely familiar room.

—Where am I? he asked the nurselike person who appeared to answer his ring.

—Porter Street, this creature said. Mlle. Ramona will see you shortly. In the meantime, drink some of this orange juice.

Well, Charles thought to himself, I cannot but admire the guts and address of this brave girl, who wanted me so much that she engineered this whole affair—my abduction from Cleveland and removal to these beloved rooms, where once I was entertained by the beautiful Elsa. And now I must see whether my key concepts can get me out of this "fix," for "fix" it is. I shouldn't have written that letter. Perhaps if I wrote another letter? A follow-up?

Charles formed the letter to Ramona in his mind.

Dear Ramona—

Now that I am back in your house, tied down to this bed with these steel bands around my ankles, I understand that perhaps my earlier letter to you was subject to misinterpretation etc. etc.

Elsa entered the room and saw Charles tied down on the bed.

—That's against the law!

—Sit down, Elsa. Just because you are a law student you want to proclaim the rule of law everywhere. But some things don't have to do with the law. Some things have to do with the heart. The heart, which was our great emblem and cockade, when the cathedrals were white.

—I'm worried about Ramona, Elsa said. She has been missing lectures. And she has been engaging in hilarity at the expense of the law.

—Jokes?

—Gibes. And now this extralegality. Your sequestration.

Charles and Elsa looked out of the window at the good day.

—See that blue in the sky. How wonderful. After all the gray we've had.

5.

Elsa and Ramona watched the Motorola television set in their pajamas.

—What else is on? Elsa asked.

Ramona looked in the newspaper.

—On 7 there's *Johnny Allegro* with George Raft and Nina Foch. On 9 *Johnny Angel* with George Raft and Claire Trevor. On 11 there's *Johnny Apollo* with Tyrone Power and Dorothy Lamour. On 13 is *Johnny Concho* with Frank Sinatra and Phyllis Kirk. On 2 is *Johnny Dark* with Tony Curtis and Piper Laurie. On 4 is *Johnny Eager* with Robert Taylor and Lana Turner. On 5 is *Johnny O'Clock* with Dick Powell and Evelyn Keyes. On 31 is *Johnny Trouble* with Stuart Whitman and Ethel Barrymore.

—What's this one we're watching?

—What time is it?

—Eleven thirty-five.

—*Johnny Guitar* with Joan Crawford and Sterling Hayden.

6.

Jacques, Elsa, Charles and Ramona sat in a row at the sun dance. Jacques was sitting next to Elsa and Charles was sitting next to Ramona. Of course Charles was also sitting next to Elsa but he was leaning toward Ramona mostly. It was hard to tell what his intentions were. He kept his hands in his pockets.

—How is the struggle coming, Jacques?

—Quite well, actually. Since the Declaration of Rye we have accumulated many hundreds of new members.

Elsa leaned across Charles to say something to Ramona.

—Did you water the plants?

The sun dancers were beating the ground with sheaves of wheat.

—Is that supposed to make the sun shine, or what? Ramona asked.

—Oh, I think it's just sort of to . . . honor the sun. I don't think it's supposed to make it do anything.

Elsa stood up.

—That's against the law!

—Sit down Elsa.

Elsa became pregnant.

7.

"This young man, a man though only eighteen . . ."

A large wedding scene

Charles measures the church

Elsa and Jacques bombarded with flowers

Fathers and mothers riding on the city railway

The minister raises his hands

Evacuation of the sacristy: bomb threat

Black limousines with ribbons tied to their aerials

Several men on balconies who appear to be signaling, or applauding

Traffic lights

Pieces of blue cake

Champagne

8.

—Well, Ramona, I am glad we came to the city. In spite of everything.

—Yes, Elsa, it has turned out well for you. You are Mrs. Jacques Tope now. And soon there will be a little one.

—Not so soon. Not for eight months. I am sorry, though, about one thing. I hate to give up Law School.

—Don't be sorry. The Law needs knowledgeable civilians as well as practitioners. Your training will not be wasted.

—That's dear of you. Well, goodbye.

Elsa and Jacques and Charles went into the black bedroom. Ramona remained outside with the newspaper.

—Well, I suppose I might as well put the coffee on, she said to herself. Rats!

9.

Laughing aristocrats moved up and down the corridors of the city.

Elsa, Jacques, Ramona and Charles drove out to the combined racetrack and art gallery. Ramona had a Heineken and everyone else had one too. The tables were crowded with laughing aristocrats. More laughing aristocrats arrived in their carriages drawn by dancing matched pairs. Some drifted in from Flushing and São Paulo. Management of the funded indebtedness was discussed; the Queen's behavior was discussed. All of the horses ran very well, and the pictures ran well too. The laughing aristocrats sucked on the heads of their gold-headed canes some more.

Jacques held up his degrees from the New Yorker Theatre, where he had been buried in the classics, when he was twelve.

—I remember the glorious debris underneath the seats, he said, and I remember that I hated then, as I do now, laughing aristocrats.

The aristocrats heard Jacques talking. They all raised their canes in the air, in rage. A hundred canes shattered in the sun, like a load of antihistamines falling out of an airplane. More laughing aristocrats arrived in phaetons and tumbrels.

As a result of absenting himself from Cleveland for eight months, Charles had lost his position there.

—It is true that I am part of the laughing-aristocrat structure, Charles said. I don't mean I am one of them. I mean I am their creature. They hold me in thrall.

Laughing aristocrats who invented the cost-plus contract . . .

Laughing aristocrats who invented the real estate broker . . .

Laughing aristocrats who invented Formica . . .

Laughing aristocrats wiping their surfaces clean with a damp cloth . . .

Charles poured himself another brilliant green Heineken.

—To the struggle!

10.

The Puerto Rican painters have come, as they do every three years, to paint the apartment!

The painters, Emmanuel and Curtis, heaved their buckets, rollers, ladders and drop cloths up the stairs into the apartment.

—What shade of white do you want this apartment painted? A consultation.

—How about plain white?

—Fine, Emmanuel said. That's a mighty good-looking Motorola television set you have there. Would you turn it to Channel 47, *por favor?* There's a film we'd like to see. We can paint and watch at the same time.

—What's the film?

—*Victimas de Pecado,* with Pedro Vargas and Ninon Sevilla.

Elsa spoke to her husband, Jacques.

—Ramona has frightened me.

—How?

—She said one couldn't sleep with someone more than four hundred times without being bored.

—How does she know?

—She saw it in a book.

—Well, Jacques said, we only do what we really want to do about eleven percent of the time. In our lives.

—Eleven percent!

At the Ingres Gardens, the great singer Moonbelly sang a song of rage.

11.

Vercingetorix, leader of the firemen, reached for his red telephone.

—Hello, is this Ramona?

—No, this is Elsa. Ramona's not home.

—Will you tell her that the leader of all the firemen called?

Ramona went out of town for a weekend with Vercingetorix. They went to his farm, about eighty miles away. In the kitchen of the farm, bats attacked them. Vercingetorix could not find his broom.

—Put a paper bag over them. Where is a paper bag?

—The groceries, Vercingetorix said.

Ramona dumped the groceries on the floor. The bats were zooming around the room uttering audible squeaks. With the large paper bag in his hands Vercingetorix made weak capturing gestures toward the bats.

—God, if one gets in my hair, Ramona said.

—They don't want to fly into the bag, Vercingetorix said.

—Give me the bag, if one gets in my hair I'll croak right here in front of you.

Ramona put the paper bag over her head just as a bat banged into her.

—What was that?

—A bat, Vercingetorix said, but it didn't get into your hair.

—Damn you, Ramona said, inside the bag, why can't you stay in the city like other men?

Moonbelly emerged from the bushes and covered her arms with kisses.

12.

Jacques persuaded Moonbelly to appear at a benefit for the signers of the Declaration of Rye, who were having a little legal trouble. Three hundred younger people sat in the church. Paper plates were passed up and down the rows. A number of quarters were collected.

Moonbelly sang a new song called "The System Cannot Withstand Close Scrutiny."

> The system cannot withstand close scrutiny
> The system cannot withstand close scrutiny
> The system cannot withstand close scrutiny
> The system cannot withstand close scrutiny
> Etc.

Jacques spoke briefly and well. A few more quarters showered down on the stage.

At the party after the benefit Ramona spoke to Jacques, because he was handsome and flushed with triumph.

—Tell me something.

—All right Ramona what do you want to know?

—Do you promise to tell me the truth?

—Of course. Sure.

—Can one be impregnated by a song?

—I think not. I would say no.

—While one is asleep, possibly?

—It's not very likely.

—What sort of people have hysterical pregnancies?

—Well, you know. Sort of nervous girls.

—If a hysterical pregnancy results in a birth, is it still considered hysterical?

—No.

—Rats!

13.

Charles and Jacques were trying to move a parked Volkswagen. When a Volkswagen is parked with its parking brake set you need three people to move it, usually.

A third person was sighted moving down the street.

—Say, buddy, could you give us a hand for a minute?

—Sure, the third person said.

Charles, Jacques, and the third person grasped the VW firmly in their hands and heaved. It moved forward opening up a new parking space where only half a space had been before.

—Thanks, Jacques said. Now would you mind helping us unload this panel truck here? It contains printed materials pertaining to the worldwide struggle for liberation from outmoded ways of thought that hold us in thrall.

—I don't mind.

Charles, Jacques, and Hector carried the bundles of printed material up the stairs into the Porter Street apartment.

—What does this printed material say, Jacques?

—It says that the government has promised to give us some of our money back if it loses the war.

—Is that true?

—No. And now, how about a drink?

Drinking their drinks they regarded the black trombone case which rested under Hector's coat.

—Is that a trombone case?

Hector's eyes glazed.

Moonbelly sat on the couch, his great belly covered with plants and animals.

—It's good to be what one is, he said.

14.

Ramona's child was born on Wednesday. It was a boy.

—But Ramona! Who is responsible? Charles? Jacques? Moonbelly? Vercingetorix?

—It was a virgin birth, unfortunately, Ramona said.

—But what does this imply about the child?

—Nothing, Ramona said. It was just an ordinary virgin birth. Don't bother your pretty head about it, Elsa dear.

However much Ramona tried to soft-pedal the virgin birth,

people persisted in getting excited about it. A few cardinals from the Sacred Rota dropped by.

—What is this you're claiming here, foolish girl?

—I claim nothing, Your Eminence. I merely report.

—Give us the name of the man who has compromised you!

—It was a virgin birth, sir.

Cardinal Maranto frowned in several directions.

—There can't be another Virgin Birth!

Ramona modestly lowered her eyes. The child, Sam, was wrapped in a blanket with his feet sticking out.

—Better cover those feet.

—Thank you, Cardinal. I will.

15.

Ramona went to class at the Law School carrying Sam on her hip in a sling.

—What's that?

—My child.

—I didn't know you were married.

—I'm not.

—That's against the law! I think.

—What law is it against?

The entire class regarded the teacher.

—Well there is a law against fornication on the books, but of course it's not enforced very often ha ha. It's sort of difficult to enforce ha ha.

—I have to tell you, Ramona said, that this child is not of human man conceived. It was a virgin birth. Unfortunately.

A few waves of smickers washed across the classroom.

A law student named Harold leaped to his feet.

—Stop this smickering! What are we thinking of? To make mock of this fine girl! Rot me if I will permit it! Are we gentlemen? Is this lady our colleague? Or are we rather beasts of the field? This Ramona, this trull . . . No, that's not what I mean. I mean that we should think not upon her peculations but on our own peculations. For, as Augustine tells us, if for some error or sin of our own, sadness seizes us, let us not only bear in mind that an afflicted spirit is a sacrifice to God but also the words: for as water quencheth a flaming fire, so almsgiving quencheth sin; and for I desire, He says, mercy rather than sacrifice. As, therefore, if we were in danger from fire, we should, of course, run for water with which to extinguish it, and should be thankful if someone showed us water nearby, so if some flame of sin has arisen from the hay of our passions, we should take delight in this, that the ground for a work of great mercy is given to us. Therefore—

Harold collapsed, from the heat of his imagination.

A student in a neighboring seat looked deeply into Sam's eyes.

—They're brown.

16.

Moonbelly was fingering his ax.

—A birth hymn? Do I really want to write a birth hymn?

—What do I really think about this damn birth?

—Of course it's within the tradition.

—Is this the real purpose of cities? Is this why all these units have been brought together, under the red, white and blue?

—Cities are erotic, in a depressing way. Should that be my line?

—Of course I usually do best with something in the rage line. However—

—C . . . F . . . C . . . F . . . C . . . F . . . G7 . . .

Moonbelly wrote "Cities Are Centers of Copulation."

The recording company official handed Moonbelly a gold record marking the sale of a million copies of "Cities Are Centers of Copulation."

17.

Charles and Jacques were still talking to Hector Guimard, the former trombone player.

—Yours is not a modern problem, Jacques said. The problem today is not angst but lack of angst.

—Wait a minute, Jacques. Although I myself believe that there is nothing wrong with being a trombone player, I can understand Hector's feeling. I know a painter who feels the same way about being a painter. Every morning he gets up, brushes his teeth, and stands before the empty canvas. A terrible feeling of being *de trop* comes over him. So he goes to the corner and buys the *Times*, at the corner newsstand. He comes back home and reads the *Times*. During the period in which he's coupled with the *Times* he is all right. But soon the *Times* is exhausted. The empty canvas remains. So (usually) he makes a mark on it, some kind of mark that is not what he means. That is, any old mark, just to have something on the canvas. Then he is profoundly depressed because what is there is not what he meant. And it's time for lunch. He goes out and buys a pastrami sandwich at the deli. He comes back and eats the sandwich meanwhile regarding the canvas with the wrong mark on it out of the corner of his eye. During the afternoon, he paints out the mark of the morning. This affords him a measure of satisfaction. The balance of the afternoon is spent in deciding whether or not to venture another mark. The new mark, if one is ventured, will also, inevitably, be misconceived. He ventures it. It is misconceived. It is, in fact, the worst kind of vulgarity. He paints out the second mark. Anxiety accumulates. However, the canvas is now, in and of itself, because of the wrong moves and the painting out, becoming rather interesting-looking. He goes to the A&P and buys a TV Mexican dinner and many bottles of Carta Blanca. He comes back to his loft and eats the Mexican dinner and drinks a couple of Carta Blancas, sitting in front of his canvas. The canvas is, for one thing, no longer empty. Friends drop in and congratulate him on having a not-empty canvas. He begins feeling better. A something has been wrested from the nothing. The quality of the something is still at issue—he is by no means home free. And of course all of painting—the whole art—has moved on somewhere else, it's not where his head is, and he knows that, but nevertheless he—

—How does this apply to trombone playing? Hector asked.

—I had the connection in my mind when I began, Charles said.

—As Goethe said, theory is gray, but the golden tree of life is green.

18.

Everybody in the city was watching a movie about an Indian village menaced by a tiger. Only Wendell Corey stood between the village and the tiger. Furthermore Wendell Corey had dropped his rifle—or rather the tiger had knocked it out of his hands—and was left with only his knife. In addition, the tiger had Wendell Corey's left arm in his mouth up to the shoulder.

Ramona thought about the city.

—I have to admit we are locked in the most exquisite mysterious muck. This muck heaves and palpitates. It is multidirectional and has a mayor. To describe it takes many hundreds of thousands of words. Our muck is only a part of a much greater muck—the nation-state—which is itself the creation of that muck of mucks, human consciousness. Of course all these things also have a touch of sublimity—as when Moonbelly sings, for example, or all the lights go out. What a happy time that was, when all the electricity went away! If only we could re-create that paradise! By, for instance, all forgetting to pay our electric bills at the same time. All nine million of us. Then we'd all get those little notices that say unless we remit within five days the lights will go out. We all stand up from our chairs with the notice in our hands. The same thought drifts across the furrowed surface of nine million minds. We wink at each other, through the walls.

At the Electric Company, a nervousness appeared as Ramona's thought launched itself into parapsychological space.

Ramona arranged names in various patterns.

Vercingetorix
Moonbelly
Charles

Moonbelly
Charles
Vercingetorix

Charles
Vercingetorix
Moonbelly

—Upon me, their glance has fallen. The engendering force was, perhaps, the fused glance of all of them. From the millions of units crawling about on the surface of the city, their wavering desirous eye selected me. The pupil enlarged to admit more light: more me. They began dancing little dances of suggestion and fear. These dances constitute an invitation of unmistakable import—an invitation which, if accepted, leads one down many muddy roads. I accepted. What was the alternative?

Kierkegaard Unfair to Schlegel

A: I use the girl on the train a lot. I'm on a train, a European train with compartments. A young girl enters and sits opposite me. She is blond, wearing a short-sleeved sweater, a short skirt. The sweater has white and blue stripes, the skirt is dark blue. The girl has a book, *Introduction to French* or something like that. We are in France but she is not French. She has a book and a pencil. She's extremely self-conscious. She opens the book and begins miming close attention, you know, making marks with the pencil at various points. Meanwhile I am carefully looking out of the window, regarding the terrain. I'm trying to avoid looking at her legs. The skirt has raised itself a bit, you see, there is a lot of leg to look at. I'm also trying to avoid looking at her breasts. They appear to be free under the white-and-blue sweater. There is a small gold pin pinned to the sweater on the left side. It has lettering on it. I can't make out what it says. The girl shifts in her seat, moves from side to side, adjusting her position. She's very very self-aware. All her movements are just a shade overdone. The book is in her lap. Her legs are fairly wide apart, very tanned, the color of—

Q: That's a very common fantasy.
A: All my fantasies are extremely ordinary.
Q: Does it give you pleasure?
A: A poor . . . A rather unsatisfactory . . .
Q: What is the frequency?
A: Oh God who knows. Once in a while. Sometimes.
Q: You're not cooperating.
A: I'm not interested.

Q: I might do an article.
A: I don't like to have my picture taken.
Q: Solipsism plus triumphantism.
A: It's possible.

Q: You're not political?
A: I'm extremely political in a way that does no good to anybody.
Q: You don't participate?
A: I participate. I make demands, sign newspaper advertisements, vote. I make small campaign contributions to the candidate of my choice and turn my irony against the others. But I accomplish nothing. I march, it's ludicrous. In the last march, there were eighty-seven thousand people marching, by the most conservative estimate, and yet being in the midst of them, marching with them . . . I wanted to march with the Stationary Engineers, march under their banner, but two cops prevented me, they said I couldn't enter at that point, I had to go back to the beginning. So I went back to the beginning and marched with the Food Handlers for Peace and Freedom.
Q: What sort of people were they?
A: They looked just like everybody else. It's possible they weren't real food handlers. Maybe just the two holding the sign. I don't know. There were a lot of girls in black pajamas and peasant straw hats, very young girls, high-school girls, running, holding hands in a long chain, laughing. . . .
Q: You've been pretty hard on our machines. You've withheld your enthusiasm, that's damaging . . .
A: I'm sorry.
Q: Do you think your irony could be helpful in changing the government?
A: I think the government is very often in an ironic relation to itself. And that's helpful. For example: we're spending a great deal of money for this army we have, a very large army, beautifully equipped. We're spending something on the order of twenty billions a year for it. Now, the whole point of an army is—what's the word?—deterrence. And the nut of deterrence is credibility. So what does the government do? It goes

and sells off its surplus uniforms. And the kids start wearing them, uniforms or parts of uniforms, because they're cheap and have some sort of style. And immediately you get this vast clown army in the streets parodying the real army. And they mix periods, you know, you get parody British grenadiers and parody World War I types and parody Sierra Maestra types. So you have all these kids walking around wearing these filthy uniforms with wound stripes, hash marks, Silver Stars, but also ostrich feathers, Day-Glo vests, amulets containing powdered rhinoceros horn . . . You have this splendid clown army in the streets standing over against the real one. And of course the clown army constitutes a very serious attack on all the ideas which support the real army including the basic notion of having an army at all. The government has opened itself to all this, this undermining of its own credibility, just because it wants to make a few dollars peddling old uniforms. . . .

Q: How is my car?
Q: How is my nail?
Q: How is the taste of my potato?
Q: How is the cook of my potato?
Q: How is my garb?
Q: How is my button?
Q: How is the flower bath?
Q: How is the shame?
Q: How is the plan?
Q: How is the fire?
Q: How is the flue?
Q: How is my mad mother?
Q: How is the aphorism I left with you?

Q: You are an ironist.
A: It's useful.
Q: How is it useful?
A: Well, let me tell you a story. Several years ago I was living in a rented house in Colorado. The house was what is called a rancher—three or four bedrooms, knotty pine or some such on

the inside, cedar shakes or something like that on the outside. It was owned by a ski instructor who lived there with his family in the winter. It had what seemed to be hundreds of closets and we immediately discovered that these closets were filled to overflowing with all kinds of play equipment. Never in my life had I seen so much play equipment gathered together in one place outside, say, Abercrombie's. There were bows and arrows and shuffleboard and croquet sets, putting greens and trampolines and things that you strapped to your feet and jumped up and down on, table tennis and jai alai and poker chips and home roulette wheels, chess and checkers and Chinese checkers and balls of all kinds, hoops and nets and wickets, badminton and books and a thousand board games, and a dingus with cymbals on top that you banged on the floor to keep time to the piano. The merest drawer in a bedside table was choked with marked cards and Monopoly money.

Now, suppose I had been of an ironical turn of mind and wanted to make a joke about all this, some sort of joke that would convey that I had noticed the striking degree of boredom implied by the presence of all this impedimenta and one which would also serve to comment upon the particular way of struggling with boredom that these people had chosen. I might have said, for instance, that the remedy is worse than the disease. Or quoted Nietzsche to the effect that the thought of suicide is a great consolation and had helped him through many a bad night. Either of these perfectly good jokes would do to annihilate the situation of being uncomfortable in this house. The shuffleboard sticks, the barbells, balls of all kinds—my joke has, in effect, thrown them out of the world. An amazing magical power!

Now, suppose that I am suddenly curious about this amazing magical power. Suppose I become curious about how my irony actually works—how it functions. I pick up a copy of Kierkegaard's *The Concept of Irony* (the ski instructor is also a student of Kierkegaard) and I am immediately plunged into difficulties. The situation bristles with difficulties. To begin with, Kierkegaard says that the outstanding feature of irony is that it confers upon the ironist a subjective freedom. The subject, the speaker, is negatively free. If what the ironist says is not his meaning, or is the opposite of his meaning, he is free both in relation to others and in relation to himself. He is not bound by what he has said. Irony is a means of depriving the object of its reality in order that the subject may feel free.

Irony deprives the object of its reality when the ironist says something about the object that is not what he means. Kierkegaard distinguishes between the phenomenon (the word) and the essence (the thought or meaning). Truth demands an identity of essence and phenomenon. But with irony quote the phenomenon is not the essence but the opposite of the essence unquote page 264. The object is deprived of its reality by what I have said about it. Regarded in an ironical light, the object shivers, shatters, disappears. Irony is thus destructive and what Kierkegaard worries about a lot is that irony has nothing to put in the place of what it has destroyed. The new actuality—what the ironist has said about the object—is peculiar in that it is a comment upon a former actuality rather than a new actuality. This account of Kierkegaard's account of irony is grossly oversimplified. Now, consider an irony directed not against a given object but against the whole of existence. An irony directed against the whole of existence produces, according to Kierkegaard, estrangement and poetry. The ironist, serially successful in disposing of various objects of his irony, becomes drunk with freedom. He becomes, in Kierkegaard's words, lighter and lighter. Irony becomes an infinite absolute negativity. Quote irony no longer directs itself against this or that particular phenomenon, against a particular thing unquote. Quote the whole of existence has become alien to the ironic subject unquote page 276. For Kierkegaard, the actuality of irony is poetry. This may be clarified by reference to Kierkegaard's treatment of Schlegel.

Schlegel had written a book, a novel, called *Lucinde*. Kierkegaard is very hard on Schlegel and *Lucinde*. Kierkegaard characterizes this novel of Schlegel's as quote poetical unquote page 308. By which he means to suggest that Schlegel has constructed an actuality which is superior to the historical actuality and a substitute for it. By negating the historical actuality poetry quote opens up a higher actuality, expands and transfigures the imperfect into the perfect, and thereby softens and mitigates that deep pain which would darken and obscure all things unquote page 312. That's beautiful. Now this would seem to be a victory for Schlegel, and indeed Kierkegaard says that poetry is a victory over the world. But it is not the case that *Lucinde* is a victory for Schlegel. What is wanted, Kierkegaard says, is not a victory over the world but a reconciliation with the world. And it is soon discovered that although poetry is a kind of reconciliation, the distance between the new actuality, higher and more perfect than the historical actuality, and the historical actuality, lower and more imperfect than the new actuality, produces not a reconciliation but animosity. Quote so that it often becomes no reconciliation at all but rather animosity unquote same page. What began as a victory eventuates in animosity. The true task is reconciliation with actuality and the true reconciliation, Kierkegaard says, is religion. Without discussing whether or not the true reconciliation is religion (I have a deep bias against religion which precludes my discussing the question intelligently) let me say that I believe that Kierkegaard is here unfair to Schlegel. I find it hard to persuade myself that the relation of Schlegel's novel to actuality is what Kierkegaard says it is. I have reasons for this (I believe, for example, that Kierkegaard fastens upon Schlegel's novel in its prescriptive aspect—in which it presents itself as a text telling us how to live—and neglects other aspects, its objecthood for one) but my reasons are not so interesting. What is interesting is my making the statement that I think Kierkegaard is unfair to Schlegel. And that the whole thing is a damned shame!

Because that is not what I think at all. We have to do here with my own irony. Because of course Kierkegaard was "fair" to Schlegel. In making a statement to the contrary I am attempting to . . . I might have several purposes—simply being provocative, for example. But mostly I am trying to annihilate Kierkegaard in order to deal with his disapproval.

Q: Of Schlegel?

A: Of me.

Q: What is she doing now?

A: She appears to be—

Q: How does she look?

A: Self-absorbed.

Q: That's not enough. You can't just say, "Self-absorbed." You have to give more . . . You've made a sort of promise which . . .

A:

Q: Are her eyes closed?

A: Her eyes are open. She's staring.

Q: What is she staring at?

A: Nothing that I can see.

Q: And?

A: She's caressing her breasts.

Q: Still wearing the blouse?

A: Yes.

Q: A yellow blouse?

A: Blue.

A: Sunday. We took the baby to Central Park. At the Children's Zoo she wanted to ride a baby Shetland pony which appeared to be about ten minutes old. Howled when told she could not. Then into a meadow (not a real meadow but an excuse for a meadow) for ball-throwing. I slept last night on the couch rather than in the bed. The couch is harder and when I can't sleep I need a harder surface. Dreamed that my father told me that my work was garbage. Mr. Garbage, he called me in the dream. Then, at dawn, the baby woke me again. She had taken off her nightclothes and climbed into a pillowcase. She was standing by the couch in the pillowcase, as if at the starting line of a sack race. When we got back from the park I finished reading the Hitchcock-Truffaut book. In the Hitchcock-Truffaut book there is a passage in which Truffaut comments on *Psycho*. "If I'm not mistaken, out of your fifty works, this is the only film showing . . ." Janet Leigh in a bra. And Hitchcock says: "But the scene would have been more interesting if the girl's bare breasts had been rubbing against the man's chest." *That's true*. H. and S. came for supper. Veal Scaloppine Marsala and very well done, with green noodles and salad. Buckets of vodka before and buckets of brandy after. The brandy depressed me. Some talk about the new artists' tenement being made out of an old warehouse building. H. said, "I hear it's going to be very classy. I hear it's going to have white rats." H. spoke about his former wife and toothbrushes: "She was always at it, fiercely, many hours a day and night." I don't know if this stuff is useful . . .

Q: I'm not your doctor.

A: Pity.

A: But I love my irony.

Q: Does it give you pleasure?

A: A poor . . . A rather unsatisfactory. . . .

Q: The unavoidable tendency of everything particular to emphasize its own particularity.

A: Yes.

Q: You could interest yourself in these interesting machines. They're hard to understand. They're time-consuming.

A: I don't like you.

Q: I sensed it.

A: These imbecile questions . . .

Q: Inadequately answered. . . .

A: . . . imbecile questions leading nowhere . . .

Q: The personal abuse continues.

A: . . . that voice, confident and shrill . . .

Q: (aside): He has given away his gaiety, and now has nothing.

Q: But consider the moment when Pasteur, distracted, ashamed, calls upon Mme. Boucicault, widow of the department-store owner. Pasteur stammers, sweats; it is clear that he is there to ask for money, money for his Institute. He becomes more firm, masters himself, speaks with force, yet he is not sure that she knows who he is, that he is Pasteur. "The least contribution," he says finally. "But of course," she (equally embarrassed) replies. She writes a check. He looks at the check. One million francs. They both burst into tears.

A (bitterly): Yes, that makes up for everything, that you know that story. . . .

The Falling Dog

Yes, a dog jumped on me out of a high window. I think it was the third floor, or the fourth floor. Or the third floor. Well, it knocked me down. I had my chin on the concrete. Well, he didn't bark before he jumped. It was a silent dog. I was stretched out on the concrete with the dog on my back. The dog was looking at me, his muzzle curled round my ear, his breath was bad, I said, "Get off."

He did. He walked away looking back over his shoulder. "Christ," I said. Crumbs of concrete had been driven into my chin. "For God's sake," I said. The dog was four or five meters down the sidewalk, standing still. Looking back at me over his shoulder.

gay dogs falling
sense in which you would say of a thing,
it's a dog, as you would say, it's a lemon
rain of dogs like rain of frogs
or shower of objects dropped to confuse enemy radar

Well, it was a standoff. I was on the concrete. He was standing there. Neither of us spoke. I wondered what he was like (the dog's life). I was curious about the dog. Then I understood why I was curious.

wrapped or bandaged, vulnerability but also
aluminum
plexiglass

anti-hairy materials
vaudeville (the slide for life)

(Of course I instantly made up a scenario to explain everything. Involving a mysterious ((very beautiful)) woman. Her name is Sophie. I follow the dog to her house. "The dog brought me." There is a ringing sound. "What is that ringing?" "That is the electric eye." "Did I break a beam?" "You and the dog together. The dog is only admitted if he brings someone." "What is that window he jumped out of?" "That is his place." "But he comes here because . . ." "His food is here." Sophie smiles and puts a hand on my arm: "Now you must go." "Take the dog back to his place and then come back here?" "No, just take the dog back to his place. That will be enough. When he has finished eating." "Is that all there is to it?" "I needed the beam broken," Sophie says with a piteous look ((Sax Rohmer)). "When the beam is broken, the bell rings. The bell summons a man." "Another man." "Yes. A Swiss." "I could do whatever it is he does." "No. You are for breaking the beam and taking the dog back to his place." I hear him then, the Swiss. I hear his motorcycle. The door opens, he enters, a real brute, muscled, lots of fur ((Olympia Press)). "Why is the dog still here?" "This man refuses to take him back." The Swiss grabs the dog under the muzzle mock-playfully. "He wants to stay!" the Swiss says, to the dog. *"He wants to stay!"* Then the Swiss turns to me. "You're not going to take the dog back?" Threatening look, gestures, etc., etc. "No," I say. "The dog jumped on my back, out of a window. A very high window, the third floor or the fourth floor. My chin was driven into the concrete." "What do I care about your flaming chin? I don't think you understand your function. Your function is to get knocked down by the dog, follow the dog here and break the beam, then take the dog back to his place. There's no reason in the world why we should stand here and listen to a lot of flaming nonsense about your flaming etc. etc. . . .")

I looked at the dog. He looked at me.

who else has done dogs?
Baskin, Bacon, Landseer, Hogarth, Hals

with leashes trailing as they fall

with dog materials following:
bowl, bone, collar, license, Gro-pup

I noticed that he was an Irish setter, rust-colored. He noticed that I was a Welsh sculptor, buff-colored (no, really, what did he notice? how does he think?). I reflected that he was probably a nice dog from a good home (bourgeois dog) but with certain unfortunate habits like jumping on people from high windows (rationalization: he is a member of the television generation and thus—)

Well, I read a letter, then. A letter that had come to me from Germany, that had been in my pocket. I hadn't wanted to read it before but now I read it. It seemed a good time.

Mr. XXXX XXXXXXXX
c/o Blue Gallery
Madison and Eighty-first St.
New York, N.Y.

Dear Mr. XXXXXXXX:

For the above-mentioned publishers I am preparing a book of recent American sculptors. This work shall not become a collection of geegaws and so, it tries to be an aimed presentation of the qualitative best recent American sculptors. I personally am fascinated by your collected YAWNING MAN series of sculptors as well as the YAWNING lithographs. For this reason I absolutely want to include a new figure or figures from you if there are new ones. The critiques of your first show in Basel had been very bad. The German reviewers are coming from such immemorial conceptions of art that they did not know what to do with your sculptors. And I wish a better welcome to your contribution to this book when it is published here. Please send recent photographs of the work plus explanatory text on the YAWNING MAN.

Many thanks! and kindest regards!

Yours,
R. Rondorfer

Well, I was right in not wanting to read that letter. It was kind of this man to be interested in something I was no longer interested in. How was he to know that I was in that unhappiest of states, between images?

But now something new had happened to me.

dogs as a luxury (what do we need them for?)
hounds of heaven
fallen in the sense of fallen angels
flayed dogs falling? musculature
sans skeleton?

But it is well to be suspicious. Sometimes an image is not an image at all but merely an idea. People have wasted years.

I wanted the dog's face. Whereas my old image, the Yawning Man, had been faceless (except for a gap where the mouth was, the yawn itself), I wanted the dog's face. I wanted his expression, falling. I thought of the alternatives: screaming, smiling. And things in between.

dirty and clean dogs
ultraclean dogs, laboratory animals
thrown or flung dogs
in series, Indian file
an exploded view of the Falling Dog:
head, heart, liver, lights

to the dogs
putting on the dog:
I am telling him something which isn't true

and we are both falling

dog tags!
but forget puns. Cloth falling dogs, the
gingham dog and the etc., etc. Pieces
of cloth dogs falling. Or quarter-inch
plywood in layers, the layers separated
by an inch or two of airspace. Like old
triple-wing aircraft

dog-ear (pages falling with corners bent back)

Tray: cafeteria trays of some obnoxious brown plastic
But enough puns

Group of tiny hummingbird-sized falling dogs
Massed in upper corners of a room with high ceilings,
14–17 foot
in rows, in ranks, on their backs

Well, I understood then that this was my new image, The Falling Dog. My old image, the Yawning Man, was played out. I had done upward of two thousand Yawning Men in every known material, and I was tired of it. Images fray, tatter, empty themselves. I had seven good years with that image, the Yawning Man, but—

But now I had the Falling Dog, what happiness.

(flights? sheets?)
of falling dogs, flat falling dogs like sails
Day-Glo dogs falling

am I being sufficiently skeptical?
try it out

die like a
dog-eat-dog

proud as a dog in shoes
dogfight
doggerel
dogmatic

am I being over-impressed by the circumstances
suddenness
pain
but it's a gift. thank you

love me love my

Styrofoam?

Well, I got up and brushed off my chin, then. The silent dog was still standing there. I went up to him carefully. He did not move. I had to wonder about what it meant, the Falling Dog, but I didn't have to wonder about it now, I could wonder later. I wrapped my arms around his belly and together we rushed to the studio.

The Policemen's Ball

Horace, a policeman, was making Rock Cornish Game Hens for a special supper. The Game Hens are frozen solid, Horace thought. He was wearing his blue uniform pants.

Inside the Game Hens were the giblets in a plastic bag. Using his needlenose pliers Horace extracted the frozen giblets from the interior of the birds. Tonight is the night of the Policemen's Ball, Horace thought. We will dance the night away. But first, these Game Hens must go into a three-hundred-and-fifty-degree oven.

Horace shined his black dress shoes. Would Margot "put out" tonight? On this night of nights? Well, if she didn't—Horace regarded the necks of the birds which had been torn asunder by the pliers. No, he reflected, that is not a proper thought. Because I am a member of the force. I must try to keep my hatred under control. I must try to be an example for the rest of the people. Because if they can't trust us . . . the blue men . . .

In the dark, outside the Policemen's Ball, the horrors waited for Horace and Margot.

Margot was alone. Her roommates were in Provincetown for the weekend. She put pearl-colored lacquer on her nails to match the pearl of her new-bought gown. Police colonels and generals will be there, she thought. The Pendragon of Police himself. Whirling past the dais, I will glance upward. The pearl of my eyes meeting the steel gray of high rank.

Margot got into a cab and went over to Horace's place. The cabdriver was thinking: A nice-looking piece. I could love her.

Horace removed the birds from the oven. He slipped little

gold frills, which had been included in the package, over the ends of the drumsticks. Then he uncorked the wine, thinking: This is a town without pity, this town. For those whose voices lack the crack of authority. Luckily the uniform . . . Why won't she surrender her person? Does she think she can resist the force? The force of the force?

"These birds are delicious."

Driving Horace and Margot smoothly to the Armory, the new cabdriver thought about basketball.

Why do they always applaud the man who makes the shot?

Why don't they applaud the ball?

It is the ball that actually goes into the net.

The man doesn't go into the net.

Never have I seen a man going into the net.

Twenty thousand policemen of all grades attended the annual fête. The scene was Camelot, with gay colors and burgees. The interior of the Armory had been roofed with lavish tenting. Police colonels and generals looked down on the dark uniforms, white gloves, silvery ball gowns.

"Tonight?"

"Horace, not now. This scene is so brilliant. I want to remember it."

Horace thought: It? Not me?

The Pendragon spoke. "I ask you to be reasonable with the citizens. They pay our salaries after all. I know that they are difficult sometimes, obtuse sometimes, even criminal sometimes, as we often run across in our line of work. But I ask you despite all to be reasonable. I know it is hard. I know it is not easy. I know that for instance when you see a big car, a '70 Biscayne hardtop, cutting around a corner at a pretty fair clip, with three in the front and three in the back, and they are all mixed up, ages and sexes and colors, your natural impulse is to— I know your first thought is, All those people! Together! And your second thought is, Force! But I must ask you in the name of force itself to be restrained. For force, that great principle, is most honored in the breach and the observance. And that is where you men are, in the breach. You are fine men, the finest. You are Americans. So for the sake of America, be careful. Be reasonable. Be slow. In the name of the Father and of the Son and of the Holy Ghost. And now I would like to introduce Vercingetorix, leader of the firemen, who brings us a few words of congratulation from that fine body of men."

Waves of applause for the Pendragon filled the tented area.

"He is a handsome older man," Margot said.

"He was born in a Western state and advanced to his present position through raw merit," Horace told her.

The government of Czechoslovakia sent observers to the Policemen's Ball. "Our police are not enough happy," Colonel-General Čepicky explained. "We seek ways to improve them. This is a way. It may not be the best way of all possible ways, but . . . Also I like to drink the official whiskey! It makes me gay!"

A bartender thought: Who is that yellow-haired girl in the pearl costume? She is stacked.

The mood of the Ball changed. The dancing was more serious now. Margot's eyes sparkled from the jorums of champagne she had drunk. She felt Horace's delicately Game Hen-flavored breath on her cheek. I will give him what he wants, she decided. Tonight. His heroism deserves it. He stands between us and them. He represents what is best in the society: decency, order, safety, strength, sirens smoke. No, he does not represent smoke. Firemen represent smoke. Great billowing oily black clouds. That Vercingetorix has a noble look. With whom is Vercingetorix dancing, at present?

The horrors waited outside patiently. Even policemen, the horrors thought. We get even policemen, in the end.

In Horace's apartment, a gold frill was placed on a pearl toe.

The horrors had moved outside Horace's apartment. Not even policemen and their ladies are safe, the horrors thought. No one is safe. Safety does not exist. Ha ha ha ha ha ha ha ha ha ha!

The Glass Mountain

1. I was trying to climb the glass mountain.

2. The glass mountain stands at the corner of Thirteenth Street and Eighth Avenue.

3. I had attained the lower slope.

4. People were looking up at me.

5. I was new in the neighborhood.

6. Nevertheless I had acquaintances.

7. I had strapped climbing irons to my feet and each hand grasped a sturdy plumber's friend.

8. I was 200 feet up.

9. The wind was bitter.

10. My acquaintances had gathered at the bottom of the mountain to offer encouragement.

11. "Shithead."

12. "Asshole."

13. Everyone in the city knows about the glass mountain.

14. People who live here tell stories about it.

15. It is pointed out to visitors.

16. Touching the side of the mountain, one feels coolness.

17. Peering into the mountain, one sees sparkling blue-white depths.

18. The mountain towers over the part of Eighth Avenue like some splendid, immense office building.

19. The top of the mountain vanishes into the clouds, or on cloudless days, into the sun.

20. I unstuck the righthand plumber's friend leaving the left-hand one in place.

21. Then I stretched out and reattached the righthand one a

little higher up, after which I inched my legs into new positions.

22. The gain was minimal, not an arm's length.

23. My acquaintances continued to comment.

24. "Dumb motherfucker."

25. I was new in the neighborhood.

26. In the streets were many people with disturbed eyes.

27. Look for yourself.

28. In the streets were hundreds of young people shooting up in doorways, behind parked cars.

29. Older people walked dogs.

30. The sidewalks were full of dogshit in brilliant colors: ocher, umber, Mars yellow, sienna, viridian, ivory black, rose madder.

31. And someone had been apprehended cutting down trees, a row of elms broken-backed among the VWs and Valiants.

32. Done with a power saw, beyond a doubt.

33. I was new in the neighborhood yet I had accumulated acquaintances.

34. My acquaintances passed a brown bottle from hand to hand.

35. "Better than a kick in the crotch."

36. "Better than a poke in the eye with a sharp stick."

37. "Better than a slap in the belly with a wet fish."

38. "Better than a thump on the back with a stone."

39. "Won't he make a splash when he falls, now?"

40. "I hope to be here to see it. Dip my handkerchief in the blood."

41. "Fart-faced fool."

42. I unstuck the lefthand plumber's friend leaving the righthand one in place.

43. And reached out.

44. To climb the glass mountain, one first requires a good reason.

45. No one has ever climbed the mountain on behalf of science, or in search of celebrity, or because the mountain was a challenge.

46. Those are not good reasons.

47. But good reasons exist.

48. At the top of the mountain there is a castle of pure gold, and in a room in the castle tower sits . . .

49. My acquaintances were shouting at me.

50. "Ten bucks you bust your ass in the next four minutes!"

51. . . . a beautiful enchanted symbol.

52. I unstuck the righthand plumber's friend leaving the left-hand one in place.

53. And reached out.

54. It was cold there at 206 feet and when I looked down I was not encouraged.

55. A heap of corpses both of horses and riders ringed the bottom of the mountain, many dying men groaning there.

56. "A weakening of the libidinous interest in reality has recently come to a close." (Anton Ehrenzweig)

57. A few questions burned in my mind.

58. Does one climb a glass mountain, at considerable personal discomfort, simply to disenchant a symbol?

59. Do today's stronger egos still *need* symbols?

60. I decided that the answer to these questions was "yes."

61. Otherwise what was I doing there, 206 feet above the power-sawed elms, whose white meat I could see from my height?

62. The best way to fail to climb the mountain is to be a knight in full armor—one whose horse's hoofs strike fiery sparks from the sides of the mountain.

63. The following-named knights had failed to climb the mountain and were groaning in the heap: Sir Giles Guilford, Sir Henry Lovell, Sir Albert Denny, Sir Nicholas Vaux, Sir Patrick Grifford, Sir Gisbourne Gower, Sir Thomas Grey, Sir Peter Coleville, Sir John Blunt, Sir Richard Vernon, Sir Walter Willoughby, Sir Stephen Spear, Sir Roger Faulconbridge, Sir Clarence Vaughan, Sir Hubert Ratcliffe, Sir James Tyrrel, Sir Walter Herbert, Sir Robert Brakenbury, Sir Lionel Beaufort, and many others.

64. My acquaintances moved among the fallen knights.

65. My acquaintances moved among the fallen knights, collecting rings, wallets, pocket watches, ladies' favors.

66. "Calm reigns in the country, thanks to the confident wisdom of everyone." (M. Pompidou)

67. The golden castle is guarded by a lean-headed eagle with blazing rubies for eyes.

68. I unstuck the lefthand plumber's friend, wondering if—

69. My acquaintances were prising out the gold teeth of not-yet-dead knights.

70. In the streets were people concealing their calm behind a façade of vague dread.

71. "The conventional symbol (such as the nightingale, often associated with melancholy), even though it is recognized only through agreement, is not a sign (like the traffic light) because, again, it presumably arouses deep feelings and is regarded as possessing properties beyond what the eye alone sees." *(A Dictionary of Literary Terms)*

72. A number of nightingales with traffic lights tied to their legs flew past me.

73. A knight in pale pink armor appeared above me.

74. He sank, his armor making tiny shrieking sounds against the glass.

75. He gave me a sideways glance as he passed me.

76. He uttered the word "*Muerte*" as he passed me.

77. I unstuck the righthand plumber's friend.

78. My acquaintances were debating the question, which of them would get my apartment?

79. I reviewed the conventional means of attaining the castle.

80. The conventional means of attaining the castle are as follows: "The eagle dug its sharp claws into the tender flesh of the youth, but he bore the pain without a sound, and seized the bird's two feet with his hands. The creature in terror lifted him high up into the air and began to circle the castle. The youth held on bravely. He saw the glittering palace, which by the pale rays of the moon looked like a dim lamp; and he saw the windows and balconies of the castle tower. Drawing a small knife from his belt, he cut off both the eagle's feet. The bird rose up in the air with a yelp, and the youth dropped lightly onto a broad balcony. At the same moment a door opened, and he saw a courtyard filled with flowers and trees,

and there, the beautiful enchanted princess." (*The Yellow Fairy Book*)

81. I was afraid.

82. I had forgotten the Band-Aids.

83. When the eagle dug its sharp claws into my tender flesh—

84. Should I go back for the Band-Aids?

85. But if I went back for the Band-Aids I would have to endure the contempt of my acquaintances.

86. I resolved to proceed without the Band-Aids.

87. "In some centuries, his [man's] imagination has made life an intense practice of all the lovelier energies." (John Masefield)

88. The eagle dug its sharp claws into my tender flesh.

89. But I bore the pain without a sound, and seized the bird's two feet with my hands.

90. The plumber's friends remained in place, standing at right angles to the side of the mountain.

91. The creature in terror lifted me high in the air and began to circle the castle.

92. I held on bravely.

93. I saw the glittering palace, which by the pale rays of the moon looked like a dim lamp; and I saw the windows and balconies of the castle tower.

94. Drawing a small knife from my belt, I cut off both the eagle's feet.

95. The bird rose up in the air with a yelp, and I dropped lightly onto a broad balcony.

96. At the same moment a door opened, and I saw a courtyard filled with flowers and trees, and there, the beautiful enchanted symbol.

97. I approached the symbol, with its layers of meaning, but when I touched it, it changed into only a beautiful princess.

98. I threw the beautiful princess headfirst down the mountain to my acquaintances.

99. Who could be relied upon to deal with her.

100. Nor are eagles plausible, not at all, not for a moment.

Critique de la Vie Quotidienne

While I read the *Journal of Sensory Deprivation*, Wanda, my former wife, read *Elle*. *Elle* was an incitement to revolt to one who had majored in French in college and now had nothing much to do with herself except take care of a child and look out of the window. Wanda empathized with the magazine. *"Femmes enceintes, ne mangez pas de bifteck cru!"* *Elle* once proclaimed, and Wanda complied. Not a shred of *bifteck cru* passed her lips during the whole period of her pregnancy. She cultivated, as *Elle* instructed, *un petit air naïf*, or the schoolgirl look. She was always pointing out to me four-color photographs of some handsome restored mill in Brittany which had been redone with Arne Jacobsen furniture and bright red and orange plastic things from Milan: *"Une Maison Qui Capte la Nature."* During this period *Elle* ran something like four thousand separate *actualité* pieces on Anna Karina, the film star, and Wanda actually came to resemble her somewhat.

Our evenings lacked promise. The world in the evening seems fraught with the absence of promise, if you are a married man. There is nothing to do but go home and drink your nine drinks and forget about it.

Slumped there in your favorite chair, with your nine drinks lined up on the side table in soldierly array, and your hand never far from them, and your other hand holding on to the plump belly of the overfed child, and perhaps rocking a bit, if the chair is a rocking chair as mine was in those days, then it is true that a tiny tendril of contempt—strike that, *content*—might curl up from the storehouse where the world's content is kept, and reach into your softened brain and take hold there, persuading you that this, at last, is the fruit of all your labors, which you'd been wondering about in some such terms as, "Where is the fruit?" And so, newly cheered and warmed by this false insight, you reach out with your free hand (the one that is not clutching the nine drinks) and pat the hair of the child, and the child looks up into your face, gauging your mood as it were, and says, "Can I have a horse?", which is after all a perfectly reasonable request, in some ways, but in other ways is total ruin to that state of six-o'clock equilibrium you have so painfully achieved, because it, the child's request, is of course absolutely out of the question, and so you say "No!" as forcefully as possible—a bark rather like a bite—in such a way as to put the quietus on this project, having a horse, once and for all, permanently. But, placing yourself in the child's ragged shoes, which look more like used Brillo pads than shoes now that you regard them closely, you remember that time long ago on the other side of the Great War when you too desired a horse, and so, pulling yourself together, and putting another drink in your mouth (that makes three, I believe), you assume a thoughtful look (indeed, the same grave and thoughtful look you have been wearing all day, to confuse your enemies and armor yourself against the indifference of your friends) and begin to speak to the child softly, gently, cunningly even, explaining that the genus horse prefers the great open voids, where it can roam, and graze, and copulate with other attractive horses, to the confined space of a broken-down brownstone apartment, and that a horse if obtained would not be happy here, in the child's apartment, and does he, the child, want an unhappy horse, moping and brooding, and lying all over the double bed in the bedroom, and perhaps vomiting at intervals, and maybe even kicking down a wall or two, to express its rage? But the child, sensing the way the discussion is trending, says impatiently, with a chop of its tiny little hand, "No, I don't *mean* that," giving you to understand that it, the child, had not intended what you are arguing against but had intended something else altogether: a horse personally owned by it, the child, but pastured at a stable in the park, a horse such as Otto has—"Otto has a horse?" you say in astonishment—Otto being a schoolfellow of the child, and indeed the same age, and no brighter as far as the naked eye can determine but perhaps a shade more fortunate in the wealth dimension, and the child nods, yes, Otto has a horse, and a film of tears is squeezed out and presented to you, over its eyes, and with liberal amounts of anathematization for Otto's feckless parents and the profound hope that the fall of the market has ruined them beyond repair you push the weeping child with its filmic tears off your lap and onto the floor and turn to your wife, who has been listening to all of this with her face turned to the wall, and no doubt a look upon her face corresponding to that which St. Catherine of Siena bent upon poor Pope Gregory whilst reproaching him for the luxury of Avignon, if you could see it (but of course you cannot, as her face is turned to the wall)—you look, as I say, to your wife, as the cocktail hour fades, there being only two drinks left of the nine (and you have sworn a mighty oath never to take more than nine before supper, because of what it does to you), and inquire in the calmest tones available what is for supper and would she like to take a flying fuck at the moon for visiting this outrageous child upon you. She, rising with a regal sweep of her *air naïf,* and not failing to let you have a good look at her handsome legs, those legs you could have, if you were good, motors out of the room and into the kitchen, where she throws the dinner on the floor, so that when you enter the kitchen to get some more ice you begin skidding and skating about in a muck of pork chops, squash, *sauce diable,* Danish stainless-steel flatware, and Louis Martini Mountain Red. So, this being the content of your happy hour, you decide to break your iron-clad rule, that rule of rules, and have eleven drinks instead of the modest nine with which you had been wont to stave off the song of twilight, when the lights are low, and the flickering shadows, etc., etc. But, opening the refrigerator, you discover that the slovenly bitch has failed to fill up the ice trays so there is *no more ice* for your tenth and eleventh sloshes. On discovering this you are just about ready to throw in the entire enterprise, happy home, and go to the bordel for the evening, where at least you can be sure that everyone will be kind to you, and not ask you for a horse, and the floor will not be a muck of *sauce diable* and pork chops. But when you put your hand in your pocket you discover that there are only three dollars there—not enough to cover a sortie to the bordel, where Master Charge is not accepted, so that the entire scheme, going to the bordel, is blasted. Upon making these determinations, which are not such as to bring the hot flush of excitement to the old cheek, you measure out your iceless over-the-limit drinks, using a little cold water as a make-do, and return to what is called the "living" room, and prepare to live, for a little while longer, in a truce with your circumstances—aware that there are wretches worse off than you, people whose trepanations have not been successful, girls who have not been invited to the sexual revolution, priests still frocked. It is seven-thirty.

I remember once we were sleeping in a narrow bed, Wanda and I, in a hotel, on a holiday, and the child crept into bed with us.

"If you insist on overburdening the bed," we said, "you must sleep at the bottom, with the feet." "But I don't want to sleep with the feet," the child said. "Sleep with the feet," we said, "they won't hurt you." "The feet kick," the child said, "in the middle of the night." "The feet or the floor," we said. "Take your choice." "Why can't I sleep with the heads," the child asked, "like everybody else?" "Because you are a child," we said, and the child subsided, whimpering, the final arguments in the case having been presented and the verdict in. But in truth the child was not without recourse, it urinated in the bed, in the vicinity of the feet. "God damn it," I said, inventing this formulation at the instant of need. "What the devil is happening, at the bottom of the bed?" "I couldn't help it," the child said. "It just came out." "I forgot to bring the plastic sheet," Wanda said. "Holy hell," I said. "Is there to be no end to this *family life?*"

I spoke to the child and the child spoke to me and the merest pleasantry trembled with enough animus to bring down an elephant.

"Clean your face," I said to the child. "It's dirty." "It's not," the child said. "By God it is," I said, "filth adheres in nine areas which I shall enumerate." "That is because of the dough," the child said. "We were taking death masks." "Dough!" I exclaimed, shocked at the idea that the child had wasted flour and water and no doubt paper too in this lightsome pastime, taking death masks. "Death!" I exclaimed for added emphasis. "What do you know of death?" "It is the end of the world," the child said, "for the death-visited individual. The world ends," the child said, "when you turn out your eyes." This was true, I could not dispute it. I returned to the main point. "Your father is telling you to wash your face," I said, locating myself in the abstract where I was more comfortable. "I know that," the child said, "that's what you always say." "Where are they, the masks?" I asked. "Drying," the child said, "on the heaterator"—its word for radiator. I then went to the place where the heaterator stood and looked. Sure enough, four tiny life masks. My child and three of its tiny friends lay there, grinning. "Who taught you how to do this?" I asked, and the child said, "We learned it in school." I cursed the school then, in my mind. It was not the first time I had cursed the school, in my mind. "Well, what will you do with them?" I asked, demonstrating an interest in childish projects. "Hang them on the wall?" the child suggested. "Yes, yes, hang them on the wall, why not?" I said. "Intimations of mortality," the child said, with a sly look. "Why the look?" I asked. "What is that supposed to mean?" "Ho ho," the child said, sniggering—a palpable snigger. "Why the snigger?" I asked, for the look in combination with the snigger had struck fear into my heart, a place where no more fear was needed. "You'll find out," the child said, testing the masks with a dirty finger to determine if they had dried. "I'll find out!" I exclaimed. "What does that mean, I'll find out?" "You'll be sorry," the child said, with a piteous glance at itself, in the mirror. But I was ahead of him, I was already sorry. "Sorry!" I cried, "I've been sorry all my life!" "Not without reason," the child said, a wise look replacing the piteous look. I am afraid that a certain amount of physical abuse of the child ensued. But I shall not recount it, because of the shame.

"You can have the seven years," I said to Wanda. "What seven years?" Wanda asked. "The seven years by which you will, statistically, outlive me," I said. "Those years will be yours, to do with as you wish. Not a word of reproof or critique will you hear from me, during those years. I promise." "I cannot wait," she said.

I remember Wanda in the morning. Up in the morning reading the *Times* I was walked past by Wanda, already sighing although not thirty seconds out of bed. At night I drank and my hostility came roaring out of its cave like a jet-assisted banshee. When we played checkers I'd glare at her so hotly she'd often miss a triple jump.

I remember that I fixed the child's bicycle, once. That brought me congratulations, around the fireside. That was a good, a fatherly thing to do. It was a cheap bicycle, $29.95 or some such, and the seat wobbled and the mother came home from the park with the bicycle in an absolute fury because the child was being penalized by my penury, in the matter of the seat. "I will fix it," I said. I went to the hardware store and bought a two-and-one-half-inch piece of pipe which I used as a collar around the seat's stem to accommodate the downward thrust. Then I affixed a flexible metal strap about eight inches in length first to the back of the seat and then to the chief upright, by means of screws. This precluded side-to-side motion of the seat. A triumph of field expediency. Everyone was loving and kind that night. The child brought me my nine drinks very prettily, setting them on the side table and lining them up with the aid of a meterstick, into a perfect straight line. "Thank you," I said. We beamed at each other contesting as to who could maintain the beam the longest.

I visited the child's nursery school, once. Fathers were invited seriatim, one father a day. I sat there on a little chair while the children ran to and fro and made sport. I was served a little cake. A tiny child not my own attached herself to me. Her father was in England, she said. She had visited him there and his apartment was full of cockroaches. I wanted to take her home with me.

After the separation, which came about after what is known as the breaking point was reached, Wanda visited me in my bachelor setup. We were drinking healths. "Health to the child!" I proposed. Wanda lifted her glass. "Health to your projects!" she proposed, and I was pleased. That seemed very decent of her. I lifted my glass. "Health to the republic!" I proposed. We drank to that. Then Wanda proposed a health. "Health to abandoned wives!" she said. "Well now," I said. " 'Abandoned,' that's a little strong." "Pushed out, jettisoned, abjured, thrown away," she said. "I remember," I said, "a degree of mutuality, in our parting." "And when guests came," she said, "you always made me sit in the kitchen." "I thought you liked it in the kitchen," I said. "You were forever telling me to get out of the bloody kitchen." "And when my overbite required correction," she said, "you would not pay for the apparatus." "Seven years of sitting by the window with your thumb in your mouth," I said. "What did you expect?" "And when I needed a new frock," she said, "you hid the Master Charge." "There was nothing wrong with the old one," I said, "that a few well-placed patches couldn't have fixed." "And when we were invited to the Argentine Embassy," she said, "you made me drive the car in a chauffeur's cap, and park the car, and stand about with the other drivers outside while you chatted up the Ambassador." "You know no Spanish," I pointed out. "It was not the happiest of marriages," she said, "all in all." "There has been a sixty percent increase in single-person households in the last ten years, according to the Bureau of the Census," I told her. "Perhaps we are part of a trend." That thought did not seem to console her much. "Health to the child!" I proposed, and she said, "We've already done that." "Health to the mother of the child!" I said, and she said, "I'll drink to that." To tell the truth we were getting a little wobbly on our pins, at this point. "It is probably not necessary to rise each time," I said, and she said, "Thank

God," and sat. I looked at her then to see if I could discern traces of what I had seen in the beginning. There were traces but only traces. Vestiges. Hints of a formerly intact mystery never to be returned to its original wholeness. "I know what you're doing," she said, "you are touring the ruins." "Not at all," I said. "You look very well, considering." "Considering!" she cried, and withdrew from her bosom an extremely large horse pistol. "Health to the dead!" she proposed, meanwhile waving the horse pistol in the air in an agitated manner. I drank that health, but with misgivings, because who was she talking about? "The sacred dead," she said with relish. "The well-beloved, the well-esteemed, the well-remembered, the well-ventilated." She attempted to ventilate me then, with the horse pistol. The barrel wavered to the right of my head, and to the left of my head, and I remembered that although its guidance system was primitive its caliber was large. The weapon discharged with a blurt of sound and the ball smashed a bottle of J&B on the mantel. She wept. The place stank of Scotch. I called her a cab.

Wanda is happier now, I think. She has taken herself off to Nanterre, where she is studying Marxist sociology with Lefebvre (not impertinently, the author of the *Critique de la Vie Quotidienne*). The child is being cared for in an experimental nursery school for the children of graduate students run, I understand, in accord with the best Piagetian principles. And I, I have my J&B. The J&B company keeps manufacturing it, case after case, year in and year out, and there is, I am told, no immediate danger of a dearth.

The Sandman

Dear Dr. Hodder,

I realize that it is probably wrong to write a letter to one's girlfriend's shrink but there are several things going on here that I think ought to be pointed out to you. I thought of making a personal visit but the situation then, as I'm sure you understand, would be completely untenable—I would be *visiting a psychiatrist.* I also understand that in writing to you I am in some sense interfering with the process but you don't have to discuss with Susan what I have said. Please consider this an "eyes only" letter. Please think of it as personal and confidential.

You must be aware, first, that because Susan is my girlfriend pretty much everything she discusses with you she also discusses with me. She tells me what she said and what you said. We have been seeing each other for about six months now and I am pretty familiar with her story, or stories. Similarly, with your responses, or at least the general pattern. I know, for example, that my habit of referring to you as "the sandman" annoys you but let me assure you that I mean nothing unpleasant by it. It is simply a nickname. The reference is to the old rhyme: "Sea-sand does the sandman bring/Sleep to end the day/He dusts the children's eyes with sand/And steals their dreams away." (This is a variant; there are other versions, but this is the one I prefer.) I also understand that you are a little bit shaky because the prestige of analysis is now, as I'm sure you know far better than I, at a nadir. This must tend to make you nervous and who can blame you? One always tends to get a little bit shook when one's methodology is in question.

Of course! (By the bye, let me say that I am very pleased that you are one of the ones that talk, instead of just sitting there. I think that's a good thing, an excellent thing, I congratulate you.)

To the point. I fully understand that Susan's wish to terminate with you and buy a piano instead has disturbed you. You have every right to be disturbed and to say that she is not electing the proper course, that what she says conceals something else, that she is evading reality, etc., etc. Go ahead. But there is one possibility here that you might be, just might be, missing. Which is that she means it.

Susan says: "I want to buy a piano."

You think: She wishes to terminate the analysis and escape into the piano.

Or: Yes, it is true that her father wanted her to be a concert pianist and that she studied for twelve years with Goetzmann. But she does not really want to reopen that can of maggots. She wants me to disapprove.

Or: Having failed to achieve a career as a concert pianist, she wishes to fail again. She is now too old to achieve the original objective. The spontaneous organization of defeat!

Or: She is flirting again.

Or:

Or:

Or:

Or:

The one thing you cannot consider, by the nature of your training and of the discipline itself, is that she really might want to terminate the analysis and buy a piano. That the piano might be more necessary and valuable to her than the analysis.[1]

What we really have to consider here is the locus of hope. Does hope reside in the analysis or rather in the piano? As a shrink rather than a piano salesman you would naturally tend to opt for the analysis. But there are differences. The piano salesman can stand behind his product; you, unfortunately,

1 For an admirable discussion of this sort of communication failure and many other matters of interest see Percy, "Toward a Triadic Theory of Meaning," *Psychiatry*, Vol. 35 (February 1972), pp. 6–14 *et seq.*

cannot. A Steinway is a known quantity, whereas an analysis can succeed or fail. I don't reproach you for this, I simply note it. (An interesting question: Why do laymen feel such a desire to, in plain language, fuck over shrinks? As I am doing here, in a sense? I don't mean hostility in the psychoanalytic encounter, I mean in general. This is an interesting phenomenon and should be investigated by somebody.)

It might be useful if I gave you a little taste of my own experience of analysis. I only went five or six times. Dr. Behring was a tall thin man who never said anything much. If you could get a "What comes to mind?" out of him you were doing splendidly. There was a little incident that is, perhaps, illustrative. I went for my hour one day and told him about something I was worried about. (I was then working for a newspaper down in Texas.) There was a story that four black teenagers had come across a little white boy, about ten, in a vacant lot, sodomized him repeatedly and then put him inside a refrigerator and closed the door (this was before they had that requirement that abandoned refrigerators had to have their doors removed) and he suffocated. I don't know to this day what actually happened, but the cops had picked up *some* black kids and were reportedly beating the shit out of them in an effort to make them confess. I was not on the police run at that time but one of the police reporters told me about it and I told Dr. Behring. A good liberal, he grew white with anger and said what was I doing about it? It was the first time he had talked. So I was shaken—it hadn't occurred to me that I was required to do something about it, he was right—and after I left I called my then sister-in-law, who was at that time secretary to a City Councilman. As you can imagine, such a position is a very powerful one—the councilmen are mostly off making business deals and the executive secretaries run the office—and she got on to the chief of police with an inquiry as to what was going on and if there was any police brutality involved and if so, how much. The case was a very sensational one, you see; *Ebony* had a writer down there trying to cover it but he couldn't get in to see the boys and the cops had roughed him up some, they couldn't understand at that time that there could be such a thing as a black reporter. They understood that they had to be a little careful with the white reporters, but a black reporter was beyond them. But my sister-in-law threw her weight (her Councilman's weight) around a bit and suggested to the chief that if there was a serious amount of brutality going on the cops had better stop it, because there was too much outside interest in the case and it would be extremely bad PR if the brutality stuff got out. I also called a guy I knew pretty high up in the sheriff's department and suggested that *he* suggest to his colleagues that they cool it. I hinted at unspeakable political urgencies and he picked it up. The sheriff's department was separate from the police department but they both operated out of the Courthouse Building and they interacted quite a bit, in the normal course. So the long and short of it was that the cops decided to show the four black kids at a press conference to demonstrate that they weren't really beat all to rags, and that took place at four in the afternoon. I went and the kids looked OK, except for one whose teeth were out and who the cops said had fallen down the stairs. Well, we all know the falling-down-the-stairs story but the point was the *degree* of mishandling and it was clear that the kids had not been half-killed by the cops, as the rumor stated. They were walking and talking naturally, although scared to death, as who would not be? There weren't any TV pictures because the newspaper people always pulled out the plugs of the TV people, at important moments, in those days—it was a standard thing. Now while I admit it sounds callous to be talking about the degree of brutality being minimal, let me tell you that it was no small matter, in that time and place, to force the cops to show the kids to the press at all. It was an achievement, of sorts. So about eight o'clock I called Dr. Behring at home, I hope interrupting his supper, and told him that the kids were OK, relatively, and he said that was fine, he was glad to hear it. They were later no-billed and I stopped seeing him. That was my experience of analysis and that it may have left me a little sour, I freely grant. Allow for this bias.

To continue. I take exception to your remark that Susan's "openness" is a form of voyeurism. This remark interested me for a while, until I thought about it. Voyeurism I take to be an eroticized expression of curiosity whose chief phenomenological characteristic is the distance maintained between the voyeur and the object. The tension between the desire to draw near the object and the necessity to maintain the distance becomes a libidinous energy nondischarge, which is what the voyeur seeks.[2] The tension. But your remark indicates, in my opinion, a radical misreading of the problem. Susan's "openness"—a willingness of the heart, if you will allow such a term—is not at all comparable to the activities of the voyeur. Susan draws near. Distance is not her thing—not by a long chalk. Frequently, as you know, she gets burned, but she always tries again. What is operating here, I suggest, is an attempt on your part to "stabilize" Susan's behavior in reference to a state-of-affairs that you feel should obtain. Susan gets married and lives happily ever after. Or: There is within Susan a certain amount of creativity which should be liberated and actualized. Susan becomes an artist and lives happily ever after.

But your norms are, I suggest, skewing your view of the problem, and very badly.

Let us take the first case. You reason: If Susan is happy or at least functioning in the present state of affairs (that is, moving from man to man as a silver dollar moves from hand to hand), then why is she seeing a shrink? Something is wrong. New behavior is indicated. Susan is to get married and live happily ever after. May I offer another view? That is, that "seeing a shrink" might be precisely a maneuver in a situation in which Susan *does not want* to get married and live happily ever after? That getting married and living happily ever after might be, for Susan, the worst of fates, and that in order to validate her nonacceptance of this norm she defines herself to herself as shrink-needing? That you are actually certifying the behavior which you seek to change? (When she says to you that she's not shrinkable, you should listen.)

Perhaps, Dr. Hodder, my logic is feeble, perhaps my intu-

2 See, for example, Straus, "Shame as A Historiological Problem," in *Phenomenological Psychology* (New York: Basic Books, 1966), p. 219.

itions are frail. It is, God knows, a complex and difficult question. Your perception that Susan is an artist of some kind *in potentia* is, I think, an acute one. But the proposition "Susan becomes an artist and lives happily ever after" is ridiculous. (I realize that I am couching the proposition in such terms—"happily ever after"—that it is ridiculous on the face of it, but there is ridiculousness piled upon ridiculousness.) Let me point out, if it has escaped your notice, that what an artist does, is fail. Any reading of the literature[3] (I mean the theory of artistic creation), however summary, will persuade you instantly that the paradigmatic artistic experience is that of failure. The actualization fails to meet, equal, the intuition. There is something "out there" which cannot be brought "here." This is standard. I don't mean bad artists, I mean good artists. There is no such thing as a "successful artist" (except, of course, in worldly terms). The proposition should read, "Susan becomes an artist and lives unhappily ever after." This is the case. Don't be deceived.

What I am saying is, that the therapy of choice is not clear. I deeply sympathize. You have a dilemma.

I ask you to note, by the way, that Susan's is not a seeking after instant gratification as dealt out by so-called encounter or sensitivity groups, nude marathons, or dope. None of this is what is going down. "Joy" is not Susan's bag. I praise her for seeking out you rather than getting involved with any of this other idiocy. Her forte, I would suggest, is mind, and if there are games being played they are being conducted with taste, decorum, and some amount of intellectual rigor. Not-bad games. When I take Susan out to dinner she does not order chocolate-covered ants, even if they are on the menu. (Have you, by the way, tried Alfredo's, at the corner of Bank and Hudson streets? It's wonderful.) (Parenthetically, the problem of analysts sleeping with their patients is well known and I understand that Susan has been routinely seducing you—a reflex, she can't help it—throughout the analysis. I understand that

3 Especially, perhaps, Ehrenzweig, *The Hidden Order of Art* (University of California Press, 1966), pp. 234–9.

there is a new splinter group of therapists, behaviorists of some kind, who take this to be some kind of ethic? Is this true? Does this mean that they do it only when they want to, or whether they want to or not? At a dinner party the other evening a lady analyst was saying that three cases of this kind had recently come to her attention and she seemed to think that this was rather a lot. The problem of maintaining mentorship is, as we know, not easy. I think you have done very well in this regard, and God knows it must have been difficult, given those skirts Susan wears that unbutton up to the crotch and which she routinely leaves unbuttoned to the third button.)

Am I wandering too much for you? Bear with me. The world is waiting for the sunrise.

We are left, I submit, with the problem of her depressions. They are, I agree, terrible. Your idea that I am not "supportive" enough is, I think, wrong. I have found, as a practical matter, that the best thing to do is to just do ordinary things, read the newspaper for example, or watch basketball, or wash the dishes. That seems to allow her to come out of it better than any amount of so-called "support." (About the *chasmus hystericus* or hysterical yawning I don't worry any more. It is masking behavior, of course, but after all, you must allow us our tics. The world is waiting for the sunrise.) What do you do with a patient who finds the world unsatisfactory? The world *is* unsatisfactory; only a fool would deny it. I know that your own ongoing psychic structuralization is still going on—you are thirty-seven and I am forty-one—but you must be old enough by now to realize that shit is shit. Susan's perception that America has somehow got hold of the greed ethic and that the greed ethic has turned America into a tidy little hell is not, I think, wrong. What do you do with such a perception? Apply Band-Aids, I suppose. About her depressions, I wouldn't do anything. I'd leave them alone. Put on a record.[4]

Let me tell you a story.

One night we were at her place, about three A.M., and this man called, another lover, quite a well-known musician who is

4 For example, Harrison, "Wah Wah," Apple Records, STCH 639, Side One, Track 3.

very good, very fast—a good man. He asked Susan "Is he there?", meaning me, and she said "Yes," and he said "What are you doing?", and she said, "What do you think?", and he said, "When will you be finished?", and she said, "Never." Are you, Doctor dear, in a position to appreciate the beauty of this reply, in this context?

What I am saying is that Susan is wonderful. *As is.* There are not so many things around to which that word can be accurately applied. Therefore I must view your efforts to improve her with, let us say, a certain amount of ambivalence. If this makes me a negative factor in the analysis, so be it. I will be a negative factor until the cows come home, and cheerfully. I can't help it, Doctor, I am voting for the piano.

With best wishes,

Träumerei

So there you are, Daniel, reclining, reclining on the chaise, a lovely picture, white trousers, white shirt, red cummerbund, scarlet rather, white suède jacket, sunflower in buttonhole, beard neatly combed, let's have a look at the fingernails. Daniel, your fingernails are a disgrace. Have a herring. We are hungry, Daniel, we could eat the hind leg off a donkey. Quickly, Daniel, quickly to the bath, it's time to bathe, the bath is drawn, the towels laid out, the soap in the soap dish, the new bath mat laid down, the bust of Puccini over the tub polished, the choir is ready, it will sing the *Nelson Mass* of Haydn, soaping to begin with the Kyrie, luxuriating from the Kyrie to the Credo, serious scrubbing from the Credo to the Sanctus, toweling to commence with the Agnus Dei. Daniel, walk the dog and frighten the birds, we can't abide birdsong. Spontini is eternal, Daniel, we knew him well, he sat often in that very chair, the chair you sit in, Spontini sat there, hawking and spitting, coughing blood into a plaid handkerchief, he was not in the best of health after he left Berlin, we were very close, Daniel, Spontini and we, *Agnes von Hohenstaufen* was his favorite among his works, "not lacking in historical significance," he used to say of it, in his modest way, and of course he was right, *Agnes von Hohenstaufen* is eternal. Daniel, do you know a Putzi, no Putzi appears in the register, what is this, Daniel, a new Putzi and not recorded in the register, what marches, are you conducting a little fiddle here, Daniel, Putzi is on the telephone, hurry to the telephone, Daniel. Daniel, you may begin bringing in the sheaves. Do you want *all* the herring, Daniel? For a day, Daniel, we sat before a Constable sketch in a dream, an entire day, twenty-four hours, the light failed and we had candles brought, we cried "Ho! Candles, this way, lights, lights, lights!" and candles were brought, and we gazed additionally, some additional gazes, at the Constable sketch, in a dream. Have a shot of aquavit, Daniel. And there's an old croquet ball! It's been so long since we've played, almost forgotten how, perhaps some evening in the cool, while the light lasts, we'll have a game, we were very apt once, probably you are not, but we'll teach you, pure pleasure, Daniel, pure and unrestricted pleasure, while the light lasts, indulgence at its fiery height, you will lust after the last wicket, you will rush for the stake, and miss it, very likely, the untutored amateur in his eagerness, you'll be hit off into the shrubbery, we will place our ball next to your ball, and place a foot on our ball, and give it a good bash, your ball will go flying off into the shrubbery, what a pleasure, it frightens the birds. That is our croquet elegy, Daniel. Repair the dog cart, Daniel. Or have another herring, we were ripping up a herring with Mascagni once, some decades ago, the eternal Mascagni, a wonderful man, Pietro, a great laugher, he would laugh and laugh, and then stop laughing, and grow gray, a disappointed man, Pietro, brought a certain amount of grayness into one's drawing room, relieved of course by the laughing, from time to time, he was a rocket, Mascagni, worldwide plaudits and then pop! nothing, not a plaudit in a carload, he grew a bit morose, in his last years, and gray, perhaps that's usual when one's plaudits have been taken away, a darling man, and wonderful with the stick, always on the road in his last years, opera orchestras, he was the devil with your work-shy element, was Pietro, your work-shy element might as well bend to it when Pietro was in the pit. You may go to your room now, Daniel. She loves you still, we can't understand it, they all profess an unexhausted passion, the whole string, that's remarkable, Putzi too, you're to be congratulated and we are never the last to offer our congratulations, the persistence of memory as the poet puts it, would that be the case do you think, would that be the explanation, hurry to the cellar and bring up a cask of herring and four bottles of aquavit, we're going to let you work on the wall. We had a man working on the wall, Daniel, a good man, Buller by name, knew his trade, did Buller, but he went away, to the West, an offer from the Corps of Engineers, they were straightening a river, somewhere in the West, Buller had straightened streams in his youth but never a river, he couldn't resist, gave us a turkey by way of farewell, it was that season, we gave him a watch, inscribed TO BULLER, FAITHFUL POURER OF FOOTINGS, and then he hove out of view, hove over the horizon, run to the wall, Daniel, you'll find the concrete block stacked on the site, and mind your grout, Daniel, mind your grout. Daniel, you're looking itchy, we know that itch, we are not insensible of your problem, in our youth we whored after youth, on the one hand, and whored after beauty, on the other, very often these were combined in the same object, a young girl for example, a simplification, one does not have to whore after youth and whore after beauty consecutively, running first to the left, down dark streets, whoring after youth, and then to the right, through the arcades, whoring after beauty, and generally whoring oneself ragged, please, Daniel, don't do that, throwing the cat against the wall *injures the cat.* Your women, Daniel, have arrayed themselves on the garden gate. There's a racket down at the garden gate, Daniel, see to it, and the damned birds singing, and think for a while about delayed gratification, it's what distinguishes us from the printed circuits, Daniel, your printed circuit can't delay a gratification worth a damn. Daniel, run and buy a barrel of herring from the herringvolk. For we deny no man his mead, after a hard day at the wall. Your grout is lovely, Daniel. Daniel, have you noticed this herring, it looks very much like the President, do you think so, we are soliciting your opinion, although we are aware that most people think the President looks not like a herring but like a foot, what is your opinion, Daniel. Glazunov is eternal, of course, eight symphonies, two piano concertos, a violin concerto, a cello concerto, a concerto for saxophone, six overtures, seven quartets, a symphonic poem, serenades, fantasias, incidental music, and the Hymn to Pushkin. Pass the aquavit, Daniel. There was a moment when we thought we were losing our mind. Yes, we, losing our mind, the wall not even started at that period, we were open to the opinions of mankind, vulnerable, anyone could come along, as you did, Daniel, and have an opinion contrary to our opinion, we remember when the Monsignor came to inspect our miracle, a wonderful little miracle that had happened to us, still believers, at that period, we had the exhibits spread out on the rug, neatly tagged, Exhibit A, Exhibit B, and so forth, the Monsignor tickled the exhibits with his toe, toed the exhibits reflectively, or perhaps he was merely trying to give that impression, they're cunning, you never know, we had prostrated ourselves of course, then he tickled the tops of our heads with his toe and said, "Get up, you fools, get up and pour me a glass of that sherry I spy there, on the sideboard," we got up and poured him a glass, with trembling hands you may be sure, and the damned birds singing, he sipped, a smile appeared on the monsignorial mug, "Well boys," he said, "a few cases of this spread around the chancellery won't do your petition any harm," we immediately went to the cellar, loaded six cases upon a dray and caused them to be drayed to the chancellery, but to no avail, spurious they said, of our miracle, we were crushed, blasted, we thought we were losing our mind. You, Daniel, can be the new miracle, in your white trousers, white suède jacket, red cummerbund, scarlet rather, yellow sunflower in the buttonhole, a miracle of nullity, pass the aquavit. Have a reindeer steak, Daniel, it's Dancer, Dancer or Prancer, no, no, that's a joke, Daniel, and while you're at it bring the accounts, your pocket money must be accounted for, thirty-five cents a week times thirteen weeks, what? Thirty-five cents a week times twenty-six weeks, we did not realize that your option had been picked up, you will be the comfort of our old age, Daniel, if you live. Give the herb garden a weed, Daniel. The telephone is ringing, Daniel, answer it, we'll be here, sipping hock and listening on the extensions. Your backing and filling, your excuses, their reproaches, the weeping, all very well in a way, stimulating even, but it palls, your palaver, after a time, these ladies, poor girls, the whole string, Martha, Mary, all the rest, Claudia or is it Claudine, we can't remember, amusing, yes, for a time, for a time, until the wall is completed, a perfect circle or is it a perfect rhomboid, we can't remember. We remember browsing in the dictionary, page something or other, pumpernickel to puppyish, keeping the mind occupied, until the wall is completed, young whelp, what are you now, thirty-eight, thirty-nine, almost a neonate, have a herring, and count your blessings, and mind your grout, and give the fingernails a buff, spurious they said, of our miracle, that was a downer, and the damned birds singing, we're spared nothing, and the cat with its head cracked, thanks to you, Daniel, the garden gate sprung, thanks to you, Daniel, Mascagni gone, Glazunov gone, and the damned birds singing, and the croquet balls God knows where, and the damned birds singing.

The Rise of Capitalism

The first thing I did was make a mistake. I thought I had understood capitalism, but what I had done was assume an attitude—melancholy sadness—toward it. This attitude is not correct. Fortunately your letter came, at that instant. "Dear Rupert, I love you every day. You are the world, which is life. I love you I adore you I am crazy about you. Love, Marta." Reading between the lines, I understood your critique of my attitude toward capitalism. Always mindful that the critic must *"studiare da un punto di vista formalistico e semiologico il rapporto fra lingua di un testo e codificazione di un—"* But here a big thumb smudges the text—the thumb of capitalism, which we are all under. Darkness falls. My neighbor continues to commit suicide, once a fortnight. I have his suicides geared into my schedule because my role is to save him; once I was late and he spent two days unconscious on the floor. But now that I have understood that I have not understood capitalism, perhaps a less equivocal position toward it can be "hammered out." My daughter demands more Mr. Bubble for her bath. The shrimp boats lower their nets. A book called *Humorists of the 18th Century* is published.

•

Capitalism places every man in competition with his fellows for a share of the available wealth. A few people accumulate big piles, but most do not. The sense of community falls victim to this struggle. Increased abundance and prosperity are tied to growing "productivity." A hierarchy of functionaries interposes itself between the people and the leadership. The good of the private corporation is seen as prior to the public good. The world market system tightens control in the capitalist countries and terrorizes the Third World. All things are manipulated to these ends. The King of Jordan sits at his ham radio, inviting strangers to the palace. I visit my assistant mistress. "Well, Azalea," I say, sitting in the best chair, "what has happened to you since my last visit?" Azalea tells me what has happened to her. She has covered a sofa, and written a novel. Jack has behaved badly. Roger has lost his job (replaced by an electric eye). Gigi's children are in the hospital being detoxified, all three. Azalea herself is dying of love. I stroke her buttocks, which are perfection, if you can have perfection, under the capitalistic system. "It is better to marry than to burn," St. Paul says, but St. Paul is largely discredited now, for the toughness of his views does not accord with the experience of advanced industrial societies. I smoke a cigar, to disoblige the cat.

•

Meanwhile Marta is getting angry. "Rupert," she says, "you are no better than a damn dawg! A plain dawg has more sensibility than you, when it comes to a woman's heart!" I try to explain that it is not my fault but capitalism's. She will have none of it. "I stand behind the capitalistic system," Marta says. "It has given us everything we have—the streets, the parks, the great avenues and boulevards, the promenades and malls—and other things, too, that I can't think of right now." But what has the market been doing? I scan the list of the fifteen Most Loved Stocks:

Occident Pet	983,100	20⅝	+ 3¾
Natomas	912,300	58⅜	+ 18½

What chagrin! Why wasn't I into Natomas, as into a fine garment, that will win you social credit when you wear it to the ball? I am not rich again this morning! I put my head between Marta's breasts, to hide my shame.

•

Honoré de Balzac went to the movies. He was watching his favorite flick, *The Rise of Capitalism*, with Simone Simon and Raymond Radiguet. When he had finished viewing the film, he went out and bought a printing plant, for fifty thousand francs. "Henceforth," he said, "I will publish myself, in handsome expensive de-luxe editions, cheap editions, and foreign editions, duodecimo, sextodecimo, octodecimo. I will also publish atlases, stamp albums, collected sermons, volumes of sex education, remarks, memoirs, diaries, railroad timetables, daily newspapers, telephone books, racing forms, manifestos, libretti, abecedaries, works on acupuncture, and cookbooks." And then Honoré went out and got drunk, and visited his girlfriend's house, and, roaring and stomping on the stairs, frightened her husband to death. And the husband was buried, and everyone stood silently around the grave, thinking of where they had been and where they were going, and the last handfuls of wet earth were cast upon the grave, and Honoré was sorry.

•

The Achievements of Capitalism:

(a) The curtain wall
(b) Artificial rain
(c) Rockefeller Center
(d) Casals
(e) Mystification

•

"Capitalism sure is sunny!" cried the unemployed Laredo toolmaker, as I was out walking, in the streets of Laredo. "None of that noxious Central European miserabilism for us!" And indeed, everything I see about me seems to support his position. Laredo is doing very well now, thanks to application of the brilliant principles of the "new capitalism." Its Gross Laredo Product is up, and its internal contradictions are down.

Catfish-farming, a new initiative in the agribusiness sector, has worked wonders. The dram-house and the card-house are each nineteen stories high. "No matter," Azalea says. "You are still a damn dawg, even if you have 'unveiled existence.' " At the Laredo Country Club, men and women are discussing the cathedrals of France, where all of them have just been. Some liked Tours, some Lyon, some Clermont. "A pious fear of God makes itself felt in this spot."

•

Capitalism arose and took off its pajamas. Another day, another dollar. Each man is valued at what he will bring in the marketplace. Meaning has been drained from work and assigned instead of remuneration. Unemployment obliterates the world of the unemployed individual. Cultural underdevelopment of the worker, as a technique of domination, is found everywhere under late capitalism. Authentic self-determination by individuals is thwarted. The false consciousness created and catered to by mass culture perpetuates ignorance and powerlessness. Strands of raven hair floating on the surface of the Ganges . . . Why can't they clean up the Ganges? If the wealthy capitalists who operate the Ganges wig factories could be forced to install sieves, at the mouths of their plants . . . And now the sacred Ganges is choked with hair, and the river no longer knows where to put its flow, and the moonlight on the Ganges is swallowed by the hair, and the water darkens. By Vishnu! This is an intolerable situation! Shouldn't something be done about it?

•

Friends for dinner! The *crudités* are prepared, green and fresh . . . The good paper napkins are laid out . . . Everyone is talking about capitalism (although some people are talking about the psychology of aging, and some about the human use of human beings, and some about the politics of experience). "How can you say that?" Azalea shouts, and Marta shouts, "What about the air?" As a flower moves toward the florist, women move toward men who are not good for them. Self-actualization is not to be achieved in terms of another person, but you don't know that, when you begin. The negation of the negation is based on a correct reading of the wrong books. The imminent heat-death of the universe is not a bad thing, because it is a long way off. Chaos is a position, but a weak one, related to that "unfocusedness" about which I have forgotten to speak. And now the saints come marching in, saint upon saint, to deliver their message! Here are St. Albert (who taught Thomas Aquinas), and St. Almachius (martyred trying to put an end to gladiatorial contests), and St. Amadour (the hermit), and St. Andrew of Crete (whose "Great Kanon" runs to two hundred and fifty strophes), and St. Anthony of the Caves, and St. Athanasius the Athonite, and St. Aubry of the Pillar, and many others. "Listen!" the saints say. "He who desires true rest and happiness must raise his hope from things that perish and pass away and place it in the Word of God, so that, cleaving to that which abides forever, he may also together with it abide forever." Alas! It is the same old message. "Rupert," Marta says, "the embourgeoisment of all classes of men has reached a disgusting nadir in your case. A damn hawg has more sense than you. At least a damn hawg doesn't go in for 'the bullet wrapped in sugar,' as the Chinese say." She is right.

•

Smoke, rain, abulia. What can the concerned citizen do to fight the rise of capitalism, in his own community? Study of the tides of conflict and power in a system in which there is structural inequality is an important task. A knowledge of European intellectual history since 1789 provides a useful background. Information theory offers interesting new possibilities. Passion is helpful, especially those types of passion which are nonlicit. Doubt is a necessary precondition to meaningful action. Fear is the great mover, in the end.

A City of Churches

"Yes," Mr. Phillips said, "ours is a city of churches all right."

Cecelia nodded, following his pointing hand. Both sides of the street were solidly lined with churches, standing shoulder to shoulder in a variety of architectural styles. The Bethel Baptist stood next to the Holy Messiah Free Baptist, St. Paul's Episcopal next to Grace Evangelical Covenant. Then came the First Christian Science, the Church of God, All Souls, Our Lady of Victory, the Society of Friends, the Assembly of God, and the Church of the Holy Apostles. The spires and steeples of the traditional buildings were jammed in next to the broad imaginative flights of the "contemporary" designs.

"Everyone here takes a great interest in church matters," Mr. Phillips said.

Will I fit in? Cecelia wondered. She had come to Prester to open a branch office of a car-rental concern.

"I'm not especially religious," she said to Mr. Phillips, who was in the real-estate business.

"Not *now*," he answered. "Not *yet*. But we have many fine young people here. You'll get integrated into the community soon enough. The immediate problem is, where are you to live? Most people," he said, "live in the church of their choice. All of our churches have many extra rooms. I have a few belfry apartments that I can show you. What price range were you thinking of?"

They turned a corner and were confronted with more churches. They passed St. Luke's, the Church of the Epiphany, All Saints Ukrainian Orthodox, St. Clement's, Fountain Baptist, Union Congregational, St. Anargyri's, Temple Emanuel, the First Church of Christ Reformed. The mouths of all the churches were gaping open. Inside, lights could be seen dimly.

"I can go up to a hundred and ten," Cecelia said. "Do you have any buildings here that are *not* churches?"

"None," said Mr. Phillips. "Of course many of our fine church structures also do double duty as something else." He indicated a handsome Georgian façade. "That one," he said, "houses the United Methodist and the Board of Education. The one next to it, which is Antioch Pentecostal, has the barbershop."

It was true. A red-and-white striped barber pole was attached inconspicuously to the front of the Antioch Pentecostal.

"Do many people rent cars here?" Cecelia asked. "Or would they, if there was a handy place to rent them?"

"Oh, I don't know," said Mr. Phillips. "Renting a car implies that you want to go somewhere. Most people are pretty content right here. We have a lot of activities. I don't think I'd pick the car-rental business if I was just starting out in Prester. But you'll do fine." He showed her a small, extremely modern building with a severe brick, steel, and glass front. "That's St. Barnabas. Nice bunch of people over there. Wonderful spaghetti suppers."

Cecelia could see a number of heads looking out of the windows. But when they saw that she was staring at them, the heads disappeared.

"Do you think it's healthy for so many churches to be gathered together in one place?" she asked her guide. "It doesn't seem . . . *balanced,* if you know what I mean."

"We are famous for our churches," Mr. Phillips replied. "They are harmless. Here we are now."

He opened a door and they began climbing many flights of dusty stairs. At the end of the climb they entered a good-sized room, square, with windows on all four sides. There was a bed, a table, and two chairs, lamps, a rug. Four very large bronze bells hung in the exact center of the room.

"What a view!" Mr. Phillips exclaimed. "Come here and look."

"Do they actually ring these bells?" Cecelia asked.

"Three times a day," Mr. Phillips said, smiling. "Morning, noon, and night. Of course when they're rung you have to be pretty quick at getting out of the way. You get hit in the head by one of these babies and that's all she wrote."

"God Almighty," said Cecelia involuntarily. Then she said, "Nobody lives in the belfry apartments. That's why they're empty."

"You think so?" Mr. Phillips said.

"You can only rent them to new people in town," she said accusingly.

"I wouldn't do that," Mr. Phillips said. "It would go against the spirit of Christian fellowship."

"This town is a little creepy, you know that?"

"That may be, but it's not for you to say, is it? I mean, you're new here. You should walk cautiously, for a while. If you don't want an upper apartment I have a basement over at Central Presbyterian. You'd have to share it. There are two women in there now."

"I don't want to share," Cecelia said. "I want a place of my own."

"Why?" the real-estate man asked curiously. "For what purpose?"

"Purpose?" asked Cecelia. "There is no particular purpose. I just want—"

"That's not usual here. Most people live with other people. Husbands and wives. Sons with their mothers. People have roommates. That's the usual pattern."

"Still, I prefer a place of my own."

"It's very unusual."

"Do you have any such places? Besides bell towers, I mean?"

"I guess there are a few," Mr. Phillips said, with clear reluctance. "I can show you one or two, I suppose."

He paused for a moment.

"It's just that we have different values, maybe, from some of the surrounding communities," he explained. "We've been written up a lot. We had four minutes on the CBS Evening News one time. Three or four years ago. *A City of Churches*, it was called."

"Yes, a place of my own is essential," Cecelia said, "if I am to survive here."

"That's kind of a funny attitude to take," Mr. Phillips said. "What denomination are you?"

Cecelia was silent. The truth was, she wasn't anything.

"I said, what denomination are you?" Mr. Phillips repeated.

"I can will my dreams," Cecelia said. "I can dream whatever I want. If I want to dream that I'm having a good time, in Paris or some other city, all I have to do is go to sleep and I will dream that dream. I can dream whatever I want."

"What do you dream, then, mostly?" Mr. Phillips said, looking at her closely.

"Mostly sexual things," she said. She was not afraid of him.

"Prester is not that kind of a town," Mr. Phillips said, looking away.

They went back down the stairs.

The doors of the churches were opening, on both sides of the street. Small groups of people came out and stood there, in front of the churches, gazing at Cecelia and Mr. Phillips.

A young man stepped forward and shouted, "*Everyone in this town already has a car! There is no one in this town who doesn't have a car!*"

"Is that true?" Cecelia asked Mr. Phillips.

"Yes," he said. "It's true. No one would rent a car here. Not in a hundred years."

"Then I won't stay," she said. "I'll go somewhere else."

"You must stay," he said. "There is already a car-rental office for you. In Mount Moriah Baptist, on the lobby floor. There is a counter and a telephone and a rack of car keys. And a calendar."

"I won't stay," she said. "Not if there's not any sound business reason for staying."

"We want you," said Mr. Phillips. "We want you standing

behind the counter of the car-rental agency, during regular business hours. It will make the town complete."

"I won't," she said. "Not me."

"You must. It's essential."

"I'll dream," she said. "Things you won't like."

"We are discontented," said Mr. Phillips. "Terribly, terribly discontented. Something is wrong."

"I'll dream the Secret," she said. "You'll be sorry."

"We are like other towns, except that we are perfect," he said. "Our discontent can only be held in check by perfection. We need a car-rental girl. Someone must stand behind that counter."

"I'll dream the life you are most afraid of," Cecelia threatened.

"You are ours," he said, gripping her arm. "Our car-rental girl. Be nice. There is nothing you can do."

"Wait and see," Cecelia said.

Daumier

We Have All Misunderstood Billy the Kid

I was speaking to Amelia.

"Not self-slaughter in the crude sense. Rather the construction of surrogates. Think of it as a transplant."

"Daumier," she said, "you are not making me happy."

"The false selves in their clatter and boister and youthful brio will slay and bother and push out and put to all types of trouble the original, authentic self, which is a dirty great villain, as can be testified and sworn to by anyone who has ever been awake."

"The self also dances," she said, "sometimes."

"Yes," I said, "I have noticed that, but one pays dear for the occasional schottische. Now, here is the point about the self: It is insatiable. It is always, always hankering. It is what you might call rapacious to a fault. The great flaming mouth to the thing is never in this world going to be stuffed full. I need only adduce the names of Alexander, Bonaparte, Messalina, and Billy the Kid."

"You have misunderstood Billy the Kid," she murmured.

"Whereas the surrogate, the construct, is in principle satiable. We design for satiability."

"Have you taken action?" she asked. "Or is all this just the usual?"

"I have one out now," I said, "a Daumier, on the plains and pampas of consciousness, and he is doing very well, I can tell you that. He has an important post in a large organization. I get regular reports."

"What type of fellow is he?"

"A good true fellow," I said, "and knows his limits. He doesn't overstep. Desire has been reduced in him to a minimum. Just enough left to make him go. Loved and respected by all."

"Tosh," she said. "Tosh and bosh."

"You will want one," I said, "when you see what they are like."

"We have all misunderstood Billy the Kid," she said in parting.

A Long Sentence in Which the Miracle of Surrogation Is Performed Before Your Eyes

Now in his mind's eye which was open for business at all times even during the hours of sleep and dream and which was the blue of bedcovers and which twinkled and which was traced with blood a trifle at all times and which was covered at all times with a monocle of good quality, the same being attached by long thin black streamy ribands to his mind's neck, now in this useful eye Daumier saw a situation.

Mr. Bellows, Mr. Hawkins, The Traffic, Chilidogs

Two men in horse-riding clothes stood upon a plain, their attitudes indicating close acquaintance or colleagueship. The plain presented in its foreground a heavy yellow oblong salt lick rendered sculptural by the attentions over a period of time of sheep or other salt-loving animals. Two horses in the situation's upper lefthand corner watched the men with nervous horse-gaze.

Mr. Bellows spoke to his horse.

"Stand still, horse."

Mr. Hawkins sat down atop the salt lick and filled a short brass pipe Oriental in character.

"Are they quiet now?"

"Quiet as the grave," Mr. Bellows said. "Although I don't know what we'll be doin' for quiet when the grass gives out."

"That'll be a while yet."

"And Daumier?"

"Scoutin' the trail ahead," said Mr. Hawkins.

"He has his problems you must admit."

"Self-created in my opinion."

Mr. Hawkins took a deep draw upon his pipelet.

"The herd," he said.

"And the queen."

"And the necklace."

"And the cardinal."

"It's the old story," Mr. Hawkins stated. "One word from the queen and he's off tearing about the countryside and let business go hang."

"There's such a thing as tending to business, all right," said Mr. Bellows. "Some people never learned it."

"And him the third generation in the Traffic," Mr. Hawkins added. Then, after a moment: "Lovely blue flowers there a while back. I don't suppose you noticed."

"I noticed," said Mr. Bellows. "I picked a bunch."

"Did you, now. Where are they at?"

"I give um to someone," Mr. Bellows said.

"Someone. What someone?"

There was a silence.

"You are acquainted with the Rules, I believe," Mr. Hawkins said.

"Nothing in the Rules about bestowal of bluebonnets, I believe," Mr. Bellows replied.

"Bluebonnets, were they? Now, that's nice. That's very nice."

"Bluebonnets or indeed flowers of any kind are not mentioned in the Rules."

"We are promised to get this here shipment—"

"I have not interfered with the shipment."

"We are promised to get this here herd of *au-pair* girls to the railhead intact in both mind and body," Mr. Hawkins stated. "And I say that bestowal of bluebonnets is interferin' with a girl's mind and there's no two ways about it."

"She was looking very down-in-the-mouth."

"Not your affair. Not your affair."

Mr. Bellows moved to change the subject. "Is Daumier likely to be back for chow do you think?"

"What is for chow?"

"Chilidogs."

"He'll be back. Daumier does love his chilidog."

Résumé of the Plot or Argument

Ignatius Loyola XVIII, with a band of hard-riding fanatical Jesuits under his command, has sworn to capture the herd and release the girls from the toils so-called of the Traffic, in which Daumier, Mr. Hawkins, and Mr. Bellows are prominent executives of long standing. Daumier meanwhile has been distracted from his proper business by a threat to the queen, the matter of the necklace (see Dumas, *The Queen's Necklace*, pp. 76–105).

Description of Three O'Clock in the Afternoon

I left Amelia's place and entered the October afternoon. The afternoon was dying giving way to the dark night, yet some amount of sunglow still warmed the cunning-wrought cobbles of the street. Many citizens both male and female were hurrying hither and thither on errands of importance, each *agitato* step compromising slightly the sheen of the gray fine-troweled sidewalk. Immature citizens in several sizes were massed before a large factorylike structure where advanced techniques transformed them into true-thinking right-acting members of the three social classes, lower, middle, and upper middle. Some number of these were engaged in ludic agon with basketballs, the same being hurled against passing vehicles producing an unpredictable rebound. Dispersed amidst the hurly and burly of the children were their tenders, shouting. Inmixed with this broil were ordinary denizens of the quarter—shopmen, *rentiers*, churls, sellers of vicious drugs, stum-drinkers, aunties, girls whose jeans had been improved with appliqué rose blossoms in the cleft of the buttocks, practicers of the priest hustle, and the like. Two officers of the Shore Patrol were hitting an imbecile Sea Scout with long shapely well-modeled nightsticks under the impression that they had jurisdiction. A man was swearing fine-sounding swearwords at a small yellow motorcar of Italian extraction, the same having joined its bumper to another bumper, the two bumpers intertangling like shameless lovers in the act of love. A man in the organic-vegetable hustle stood in the back of a truck praising tomatoes, the same being abulge with tomato-muscle and ablaze with minimum daily requirements. Several members of the madman profession made the air sweet with their imprecating and their moans and the subtle music of the tearing of their hair.

Thought

Amelia is skeptical, I thought.

List of Research Materials Consulted

My plan for self-transplants was not formulated without the benefit of some amount of research. I turned over the literature, which is immense, the following volumes sticking in the mind as having been particularly valuable: *The Self: An Introduction* by Meyers, *Self-Abuse*, by Samuels, *The Armed Self* by Crawlie, Burt's *The Concept of Self*, *Self-Congratulation* by McFee, Fingarette's *Self-Deception*, *Self Defense for Women and Young Girls* by Birch, Winterman's *Self-Doubt*, *The Effaced Self* by Lilly, *Self-Hatred in Vermin* by Skinner, LeBett's *Selfishness*, Gordon's *Self-Love*, *The Many-Colored Self* by Winsor and Newton, Paramananda's *Self-Mastery*, *The Misplaced Self* by Richards, *Nastiness* by Bertini, *The Self Prepares* by Teller, Flaxman's *The Self as Pretext*, Hickel's *Self-Propelled Vehicles*, Sørensen's *Self-Slaughter*, *Self and Society in Ming Thought* by DeBary, *The Sordid Self* by Clute, and *Techniques of Self-Validation* by Wright. These works underscored what I already knew, that the self is a dirty great villain, an interrupter of sleep, a deviler of awakeness, an intersubjective atrocity, a mouth, a maw. Transplantation of neutral or partially inert materials into the cavity was in my view the one correct solution.

Neutral or Partially Inert Materials Cross a River

A girl appeared holding a canteen.

"Is there any wine *s'il vous plaît?*"

"More demands," said Mr. Hawkins. "They accumulate."

"Some people do not know they are a member of a herd," said Mr. Bellows.

The girl turned to Daumier.

"Is it your intention to place all of us in this dirty water?" she asked, pointing to the river. "Together with our clothes and personal belonging as well?"

"There is a ford," said Daumier. "The water is only knee-high."

"And on the other bank, shooters? Oh, that's very fine. *Très intelligent.*"

"What's your name, Miss?"

"Celeste," said the girl. "Possibly there are vipers in the water? Poisonmouths?"

"Possibly," said Daumier. "But they won't hurt you. If you see one, just go around him."

"Myself, I will stay here, thank you. The other girls, they stay here too, I think."

"Celeste, you wouldn't be telling them about poisonmouths in the water, would you?"

"It is not necessary. They can look for their own selves." She paused. "Possibly you have a very intelligent plan for avoiding the shooters?"

She is not pretty, Daumier thought. But a good figure.

"My papa is a lawyer," she said. "An *avocat*."

"So?"

"There was no word in the agreement about marching through great floods filled with vipers and catfishes."

"The problem is not the water but the Jesuits on the other side," said Daumier.

"The noble Loyola. Our resuscitator."

"You want to spend the next year in a convent? Wearing a long dress down to your feet and reading *The Lives of the Saints* and not a chilidog to your name?"

"He will take us to the convent?"

"Yes."

"What a thing. I did not know."

"Daumier," said Mr. Hawkins. "What is your *très intelligent* plan?"

"What if we send some of the girls in to bathe?"

"What for?"

"And while the enemy is struck blind by the dazzling beauty of our girls bathing, we cross the rest of them down yonder at the other ford."

"Ah, you mean bathing, uh—"

"Right."

"Could you get them to do it?"

"I don't know." He turned to Celeste. "What about it?"

"There is nothing in the agreement about making Crazy Horse shows in the water. But on the other hand, the cloister . . ."

"Yes," said Daumier.

Soon seven girls wearing towels were approaching the water.

"You and Mr. Bellows cross the herd down there. I'll watch out for these," Daumier said to Mr. Hawkins.

"Oh, you will," said Mr. Hawkins. "That's nice. That's very nice indeed. That is what I call nice, that is."

"Mr. Hawkins," said Daumier.

Then Daumier looked at Celeste and saw that the legs on her were as long and slim as his hope of Heaven and the thighs on her were as strong and sweet-shaped as ampersands and the buttocks on her were as pretty as two pictures and the waist on her was as neat and incurved as the waist of a fiddle and the shoulders on her were as tempting as sex crimes and the hair on her was as long and black as Lent and the movement of the whole was honey, and he sank into a swoon.

When he awoke, he found Mr. Hawkins lifting him by his belt and lowering him to the ground again, repeatedly.

"A swoon most likely," said Mr. Hawkins. "He was always given to swoonin'."

The girls were gathered about him, fully dressed and combing their damp hair.

"He looks extremely charming when he is swooned," said Celeste. "I don't like the eagle gaze so much."

"And his father and grandfather before him," said Mr. Hawkins, "they were given to swoonin'. The grandfather particularly. Physical beauty it was that sent the grandfather to the deck. There are those who have seen him fall at the mere flash of a kneecap."

"Is the herd across?" asked Daumier.

"Every last one of um," said Mr. Hawkins. "Mr. Bellows is probably handing out the TV dinners right now."

"We made a good exhibition, I think," said Celeste. "Did you see?"

"A little," said Daumier. "Let's push across and join the others."

They crossed the river and climbed a ridge and went through some amount of brush and past a broke-down abandoned farmhouse with no roof and through a pea patch that nobody had tended for so many years that the peas in their pods were as big as Adam's apples. On the other side of the pea patch they found Mr. Bellows tied to a tree by means of a great many heavy ropes around his legs, stomach, and neck, and his mouth stuffed full of pages torn from a breviary. The herd was nowhere to be seen.

Two Whiskeys with a Friend

"The trouble with you," said Gibbon, "is that you are a failure."

"I am engaged upon a psychological thimblerig which may have sound commercial applications," I said. "Vistas are opening."

"Faugh," he said.

"Faugh?"

"The trouble with you is that you are an idiot," Gibbon said. "You lack a sense of personal worthlessness. A sense of personal worthlessness is the motor that drives the overachiever to his splendid overachievements that we all honor and revere."

"I have it!" I said. "A deep and abiding sense of personal worthlessness. One of the best."

"It was your parents I expect," said Gibbon. "They were possibly too kind. The family of orientation is charged above all with developing the sense of personal worthlessness. Some are sloppy about it. Some let this responsibility slide and the result is a child with no strong sense of personal worthlessness, thus no drive to prove that the view he holds of himself is not correct, the same being provable only by conspicuous and distinguished achievement above and beyond the call of reasonableness."

I thought: His tosh is better than my tosh.

"I myself," said Gibbon, "am slightly underdone in the personal worthlessness line. It was Papa's fault. He used no irony. The communications mix offered by the parent to the child is as you know twelve percent do this, eighty-two percent don't do that, and six percent huggles and endearments. That is standard. Now, to avoid boring himself or herself to death during this monition the parent enlivens the discourse with wit, usually irony of the cheaper sort. The irony ambigufies the message, but more importantly establishes in the child the sense of personal lack-of-worth. Because the child understands that one who is talked to in this way is not much of a something. Ten years of it goes a long way. Fifteen is better. That is where Pap fell down. He eschewed irony. Did you bring any money?"

"Sufficient."

"Then I'll have another. What class of nonsense is this that you are up to with the surrogate?"

"I have made up a someone who is taking the place of myself. I think about him rather than about me."

"The trouble with you is that you are simpleminded. No wonder you were sacked from your job in the think tank."

"I was thinking but I was thinking about the wrong things."

"Does it work? This transplant business?"

"I have not had a thought about myself in seven days."

"Personally," said Gibbon, "I am of the opinion that the answer is Krishna Socialism."

Mr. Bellows Is Sprung; Arrival of a Figure; Popcorn Available in the Lower Lobby

"Our herd is rustled," said Mr. Hawkins.

Mr. Bellows was having pages of the Word removed from his mouth.

"Fifteen hundred head," said Daumier. "My mother will never forgive me."

"How many men did he have with him?" asked Mr. Hawkins.

"Well I only *saw* about four. Coulda been more. They jumped me just as we come outa the tree line. Two of 'em come at me from the left and two of 'em come at me from the right, and they damn near pulled me apart between 'em. And himself sittin' there on his great black horse with the five black hats on him and laughin' and gigglin' to beat all bloody hell. Then they yanked me off my horse and throwed me to the ground terrible hard and two of 'em sat on me while himself made a speech to the herd."

"What type of speech would that be?"

"It begun, 'Dearly beloved.' The gist of it was that Holy Mother the Church had arranged to rescue all the girls from the evil and vicious and low and reprehensible toils of the Traffic—meaning us—and the hardships and humiliations and degradations of *au-pair* life through the God-smiled-upon intervention of these hard-riding pure-of-heart Jesuits."

"How did the herd take it?"

"Then he said confessions would be between two and four in the afternoon, and that evening services would be at eight sharp. Then there was a great lot of groanin'. That was from the herd. Then the girls commenced to ask the padres about the hamburger ration and the grass ration and which way was the john and all that, and the boys in black got a little bit flustered. They realized they had fifteen hundred head of ravenous *au-pair* girls on their hands."

"He seems a good thinker," said Celeste. "To understand your maneuver beforehand, and to defeat it with his own very much superior maneuver—"

At that moment a figure of some interest approached the group. The figure was wearing on the upper of his two lips a pair of black fine-curled mustachios and on the top of his head a hat with a feather or plume of a certain swash and on his shoulders a cape of dark-blue material of a certain swagger and on his trunk a handsome leather doublet with pot-metal clasps and on the bottom of him a pair of big blooming breeches of a peach velvet known to interior decorators for its appositeness in the upholstering of loveseats and around his waist a sling holding a long resplendent rapier and on his two hands great gauntlets of pink pigskin and on his fine-chiseled features an expression of high-class arrogance. The figure was in addition mounted upon the top of a tall-standing well-curried fast-trotting sheep.

"What is it?" asked Mr. Bellows.

"Beats me," said Mr. Hawkins. "I think it is an actor."

"I know what it is," said Daumier. "It is a musketeer."

Further Boiling of the Plot in Summary Form

The musketeer carries a letter from the queen which informs Daumier that Jeanne de Valois, a bad person attached to the court, has obtained the necklace, which is worth 1,600,000 francs, by persuading the Cardinal de Rohan, an admirer of the queen, to sign a personal note for the amount, he thinking he is making a present to the queen, she thinking that the necklace has been returned to the jewelers, Jeanne de Valois having popped the diamonds into an unknown hiding place. The king is very likely going to find out about the whole affair and become very angry, in several directions. Daumier is begged to come to the capital and straighten things out. He does so.

History of the Society of Jesus

Driven from England, 1579
Driven from France, 1594
Driven from Venice, 1606
Driven from Spain, 1767
Driven from Naples, 1768
Suppressed entirely by Clement XIV, 1773
Revived, 1814

Something Is Happening

I then noticed that I had become rather fond—fond to a fault—of a person in the life of my surrogate. It was of course the girl Celeste. My surrogate obviously found her attractive and no less did I, this was a worry. I began to wonder how I could get her out of his life and into my own.

Amelia Objects

"What about me?"

Quotation from La Fontaine

"I must have the new, though there be none left in the world."

The Parry

"You are insatiable," she said.

"I am in principle fifty percent sated," I said. "Had I two surrogates I would be one hundred percent sated. Two are necessary so that no individual surrogate gets the big head. My identification with that Daumier who is even now cleaning up all sorts of trouble in the queen's service is wonderful but there must be another. I see him as a quiet, thoughtful chap who leads a contemplative-type life. Maybe in the second person."

The New Surrogate Given a Trial Run

This is not the worst time for doing what you are doing, and you are therefore pleased with yourself—not wildly, but a little.

There are several pitfalls you have avoided. Other people have fallen into them. Standing at the rim of the pit, looking down at the sharpened stakes, you congratulate yourself on your good luck (because you know good sense cannot be credited) and move on. The conditions governing your life have been codified and set down in a little book, but no one has ever given you a copy, and when you have sought it in libraries, you are told that someone else has it on extended loan. Still, you are free to seek love, to the best of your ability, or to wash your clothes in the machines that stand with their round doors temptingly open, or to buy something in one of the many shops in this area—a puppy perhaps. Pausing before a show window full of puppies, brown and black and mixtures, you notice that they are very appealing. If only you could have one that would stay a puppy, and not grow into a full-sized dog. Your attachments are measured. Not that you are indifferent by nature—you want nothing so much as a deep-going, fundamental involvement—but this does not seem to happen. Your attachments are measured; each seems to last exactly two years. Why is that? On the last lap of a particular liaison, you feel that it is *time to go,* as if you were a guest at a dinner party and the host's offer of another brandy had a peculiar falseness to it. Full of good will, you attempt to pretend that you do not feel this way, you attempt to keep the level of cheerfulness and hope approximately where it has always been, to keep alive a sense of "future." But no one is fooled. Optimistic plans are made, but within each plan is another plan, allowing for the possible absence of one of the planners. You eye the bed, the record-player, the pictures, already making lists of who will take what. What does this say about you—that you move from person to person, a tourist of the emotions? Is this the meaning of failure? Perhaps it is too soon to decide. It has occurred to you that you, Daumier, may yet do something great. A real solid durable something, perhaps in the field of popular music, or light entertainment in general. These fields are not to be despised, although you are aware that many people look down on them. But perhaps a better-conceived attack might contain a shade less study. It is easy to be satisfied if you get out of things what inheres in them, but you must look closely, take nothing for granted, let nothing become routine. You must fight against the cocoon of habituation which covers everything, if you let it. There are always openings, if you can find them. There is always something to do.

A Sampling of Critical Opinion

"He can maunder."

"Can't he maunder!"

"I have not heard maundering of this quality since—"

"He is a maundering fool."

Celeste Motors from One Sphere to Another Sphere

"She has run away," said Mr. Hawkins.

"Clean as a whistle," said Mr. Bellows.

"Herd-consciousness is a hard thing to learn," said Mr. Hawkins. "Some never learn it."

"Yes," said Mr. Bellows, "there's the difficulty, the iddyological. You can get quite properly banjaxed there, with the iddyological."

Food

I was preparing a meal for Celeste—a meal of a certain elegance, as when arrivals or other rites of passage are to be celebrated.

First off there were Saltines of the very best quality and of a special crispness, squareness, and flatness, obtained at great personal sacrifice by making representations to the National Biscuit Company through its authorized nuncios in my vicinity.

Upon these was spread with a hand lavish and not stinting Todd's Liver Pâté, the same having been robbed from geese and other famous animals and properly adulterated with cereals and other well-chosen extenders and the whole delicately spiced with calcium propionate to retard spoilage. Next there were rare cheese products from Wisconsin wrapped in gold foil in exquisite tints with interesting printings thereon, including some very artful representations of cows, the same being clearly in the best of health and good humor. Next there were dips of all kinds including clam, bacon with horseradish, onion soup with sour cream, and the like, which only my long acquaintance with some very high-up members of the Borden company allowed to grace my table. Next there were Fritos curved and golden to the number of 224 (approx.), or the full contents of the bursting 53¢ bag. Next there were Frozen Assorted Hors d'Oeuvres of a richness beyond description, these wrested away from an establishment catering only to the nobility, the higher clergy, and certain selected commoners generally agreed to be comers in their particular areas of commonality, calcium propionate added to retard spoilage. In addition there were Mixed Nuts assembled at great expense by the Planters concern from divers strange climes and hanging gardens, each nut delicately dusted with a salt that has no peer. Furthermore there were cough drops of the manufacture of the firm of Smith Fils, brown and savory and served in a bowl once the property of Brann the Iconoclast. Next there were young tender green olives into which ripe red pimentos had been cunningly thrust by underpaid Portuguese, real and true handwork every step of the way. In addition there were pearl onions meticulously separated from their nonstandard fellows by a machine that had caused the Board of Directors of the S & W concern endless sleepless nights and had passed its field trials just in time to contribute to the repast I am describing. Additionally there were gherkins whose just fame needs no further words from me. Following these appeared certain cream cheeses of Philadelphia origin wrapped in costly silver foil, the like of which a pasha could not have afforded in the dear dead days. Following were Mock Ortolans Manqués made of the very best soybean aggregate, the like of which could not be found on the most sophisticated tables of Paris, London, and Rome. The whole washed down with generous amounts of Tab, a fiery liquor brewed under license by the Coca-Cola Company which will not divulge the age-old secret recipe no matter how one begs and pleads with them but yearly allows a small quantity to circulate to certain connoisseurs and bibbers whose credentials meet the very rigid requirements of the Cellarmaster. All of this stupendous feed being a mere scherzo before the announcement of the main theme, chilidogs.

"What is all this?" asked sweet Celeste, waving her hands in the air. "Where is the food?"

"You do not recognize a meal spiritually prepared," I said, hurt in the self-love.

"We will be very happy together," she said. "I cook."

Conclusion

I folded Mr. Hawkins and Mr. Bellows and wrapped them in tissue paper and put them carefully away in a drawer along with the king, the queen, and the cardinal. I was temporarily happy and content but knew that there would be a time when I would not be happy and content; at that time I could unwrap them and continue their pilgrimages. The two surrogates, the third-person Daumier and the second-person Daumier, were wrapped in tissue paper and placed in the drawer; the second-person Daumier especially will bear watching and someday when my soul is again sickly and full of sores I will take him out of the drawer and watch him. Now Celeste is making a *daube* and I will go into the kitchen and watch Celeste making the *daube*. She is placing strips of optional pork in the bottom of a pot. Amelia also places strips of optional pork in the bottom of a pot, when she makes a *daube*, but somehow— The self cannot be escaped, but it can be, with ingenuity and hard work, distracted. There are always openings, if you can find them, there is always something to do.

The Party

I went to a party and corrected a pronunciation. The man whose voice I had adjusted fell back into the kitchen. I praised a Bonnard. It was not a Bonnard. My new glasses, I explained, and I'm terribly sorry, but significant variations elude me, vodka exhausts me, I was young once, essential services are being maintained. Drums, drums, drums, outside the windows. I thought that if I could persuade you to say "No," then my own responsibility would be limited, or changed, another sort of life would be possible, different from the life we had previously, somewhat skeptically, enjoyed together. But you had wandered off into another room, testing the effect on members of the audience of your ruffled blouse, your long magenta skirt. Giant hands, black, thick with fur, reaching in through the windows. Yes, it was King Kong, back in action, and all of the guests uttered loud exclamations of fatigue and disgust, examining the situation in the light of their own needs and emotions, hoping that the ape was real or papier-mâché according to their temperaments, or wondering whether other excitements were possible out in the crisp, white night.

"Did you see him?"

"Let us pray."

The important tasks of a society are often entrusted to people who have fatal flaws. Of course we tried hard, it was intelligent to do so, extraordinary efforts were routine. Your zest was, and is, remarkable. But carrying over into private life attitudes that have been successful in the field of public administration is not, perhaps, a good idea. Zest is not fun for everybody. I am aware that roles change. Kong himself is now an adjunct professor of art history at Rutgers, co-author of a text on tomb sculpture; if he chooses to come to a party through the window he is simply trying to make himself interesting. A lady spoke to me, she had in her hand a bunch of cattleyas. "I have attempted to be agreeable," she said, "but it's like teaching iron to swim, with this group." Zest is not fun for everybody. When whippoorwills called, you answered. And then I would go out, with the lantern, up and down the streets, knocking on doors, asking perfect strangers if they had seen you. OK. That is certainly one way of doing it. This is not a complaint. But wouldn't it be better to openly acknowledge your utter reliance on work, on specific, carefully formulated directions, agreeing that, yes, a certain amount of anesthesia is derived from what other people would probably think of as some kind of a career? Excel if you want, but remember that there are gaps. You told me that you had thought, as a young girl, that masturbation was "only for men." Couldn't you be mistaken about other things, too?

The two sisters were looking at television in the bedroom, on the bed, amidst the coats and hats, umbrellas, airline bags. I gave them each a drink and we watched the game together, the *Osservatore Romano* team vs. the Diet of Worms, Worms leading by six points. I had never seen khaki-colored punch before. The hostess said there would be word games afterward, some of the people outside would be invited in, peasant food served in big wooden bowls—wine, chicken, olive oil, bread. Everything would improve, she said. I could still hear, outside, the drums; whistles had been added, there were both whistles and drums. I was surprised. The present era, with its emphasis on emotional cost control as well as its insistent, almost annoying lucidity, does not favor splinter groups, because they can't win. Small collective manifestations are OK insofar as they show "stretch marks"—traces of strain which tend to establish that public policy is not a smooth, seamless achievement, like an egg, but has rather been hacked out at some cost to the policymakers. Kong got to his feet. "Louise loves me," he said, pointing to a girl, "but I would rather sleep with Cynthia Garmonsway. It's just one of those things. Human experience is different, in some ways, from ape experience, but that doesn't mean that I don't like perfumed nights, too." I know what he means. The mind carries you with it, away from what you are supposed to do, toward things that cannot be explained rationally, toward difficulty, lack of clarity, late-afternoon light.

"Francesca. Do you want to go?"

"I want to stay."

Now the sisters have begun taking their interminable showers, both bathrooms are tied up, I must either pretend not to know them or accept the blame. In the larger rooms tender fawns and pinks have replaced the earlier drab, sad colors. I noticed that howls and rattles had been added to the whistles and drums. Is it some kind of a revolution? Maybe a revolution in taste, as when Mannerism was overthrown by the Baroque. Kong is being curried by Cynthia Garmonsway. She holds the steel curry comb in her right hand and pulls it gently through the dark thick fur. Cynthia formerly believed in the "enormous diversity of things"; now she believes in Kong. The man whose pronunciation I had corrected emerged from the kitchen. "Probably it is music," he said, nodding at the windows, "the new music, which we older men are too old to understand."

You, of course, would never say such a thing to me, but you have said worse things. You told me that Kafka was not a thinker, and that a "genetic" approach to his work would disclose that much of it was only a kind of very imaginative whining. That was during the period when you were going in for wrecking operations, feeling, I suppose, that the integrity of your own mental processes was best maintained by a series of strong, unforgiving attacks. You made quite an impression on everyone, in those days: your ruffled blouse, your long magenta skirt slit to the knee, the dagger thrust into your boot. "Is that a metaphor?" I asked, pointing to the dagger; you shook your head, smiled, said no. Now that you have had a change of heart, now that you have joined us in finding Kafka, and Kleist, too, the awesome figures that we have agreed that they are, the older faculty are more comfortable with you, are ready to promote you, marry you, even, if that is your wish. But you don't have to make up your mind tonight. Relax and enjoy the party, to the extent that it is possible to do so; it is not over yet. The game has ended, a news program has begun. "Emerald mines in the northwest have been nationalized." A number of young people standing in a meadow, holding hands, singing. Can the life of the time be caught in an advertisement? Is that how it is, really, in the meadows of the world?

And where are all the new people I have come here to meet? I have met only a lost child, dressed in rags, real rags, holding an iron hook attached to a fifty-foot rope. I said, "What is that for?" The child said nothing, placed the hook quietly on the floor at my feet, opened a bottle and swallowed twenty aspirin. Is six too young for a suicide attempt? We fed her milk, induced vomiting, the police arrived within minutes. When one has spoken a lot one has already used up all of the ideas one has. You must change the people you are speaking to so that you appear, to yourself, to be still alive. But the people here don't look new; they look like emerald-mine owners, in fact, or proprietors of some other sector of the economy that something bad has just happened to. I'm afraid that going up to them and saying "Travel light!", with a smile, will not really lift their spirits. Why am I called upon to make them happier, when it is so obviously beyond my competence? Francesca, you have selected the wrong partner, in me. You made the mistake a long time ago. I am not even sure that I like you now. But it is true that I cannot stop thinking about you, that every small daily problem—I will never be elected to the Academy, Richelieu is against me and d'Alembert is lukewarm—is examined in the light of your possible reaction, or displeasure. At one moment you say that the Academy is a joke, at another that you are working industriously to sway Webster to my cause. Damned capricious! In the silence, an alphorn sounds. Then the noise again, drums, whistles, howls, rattles, alphorns. Attendants place heavy purple veils or shrouds over statuary, chairs, the buffet table, members of the orchestra. People are clustered in front of the bathrooms holding fine deep-piled towels, vying to dry the beautiful sisters. The towels move sensuously over the beautiful surfaces. I too could be excited by this tissue.

Dear Francesca, tell me, is this a successful party, in your view? Is this the best we can do? I know that you have always wanted to meet Kong; now that you have met him and he has said whatever he has said to you (I saw you smiling), can we go home? I mean you to your home, me to my home, all these others to their own homes, cells, cages? I am feeling a little ragged. What made us think that we could escape things like bankruptcy, alcoholism, being disappointed, having children? Say "No," refuse me once and for all, let me try something else. Of course we did everything right, insofar as we were able to imagine what "right" was. Is it really important to know that this movie is fine, and that one terrible, and to talk intelligently about the difference? Wonderful elegance! No good at all!

Eugénie Grandet

> Balzac's novel *Eugénie Grandet* was published in 1833. Grandet, a rich miser, has an only child, Eugénie. She falls in love with her young cousin, Charles. When she learns he is financially ruined, she lends him her savings. Charles goes to the West Indies, secretly engaged to marry Eugénie on his return. Years go by. Grandet dies and Eugénie becomes an heiress. But Charles, ignorant of her wealth, writes to ask her for his freedom: he wants to marry a rich girl. Eugénie releases him, pays his father's debts, and marries without love an old friend of the family, Judge de Bonfons.
>
> —*The Thesaurus of Book Digests*

"Oh, oh, where's Old Grandet going so early in the morning, running as though his house were on fire?"

"He'll end up by buying the whole town of Saumur!"

"He doesn't even notice the cold, his mind is always on his business!"

"Everything he does is significant!"

"He knows the secrets and mysteries of the life and death of money!"

•

"It looks as though I'm going to be quite successful here in Saumur," thought Charles, unbuttoning his coat.

•

A great many people are interested in the question: Who will obtain Eugénie Grandet's hand?

•

Eugénie Grandet's hand:

•

Judge de Bonfons arrives carrying flowers.

•

"Mother, have you noticed that this society we're in tends to be a little . . . repressive?"

"What does that mean, Eugénie? What does that mean, that strange new word, 'repressive,' that I have never heard before?"

"It means . . . it's like when you decide to do something, and you get up out of your chair to do it, and you take a step, and then become aware of frosty glances being directed at you from every side."

"Frosty glances?"

"Your desires are stifled."

"What desires are you talking about?"

"Just desires in general. Any desires. It's a whole . . . I guess atmosphere is the word . . . a tendency on the part of the society . . ."

"You'd better sew some more pillow cases, Eugénie."

•

Part of a letter:

. . . And now he's ruined a
friends will desert him, and
humiliation. Oh, I wish I ha
straight to heaven, where his
but this is madness . . . I re
that of Charles.

I have sent him to you so
news of my death to him and
in store for him. Be a father to
not tear him away from his
would kiss him. I beg him on m
which, as his mother's heir, he
But this is a superfluous ple
will realize that he must not
Persuade him to give up all his
time comes. Reveal to him th
which he must live from now
still has any love for me, tell
not lost for him. Yes, work wh
give him back the fortune I ha
And if he is willing to listen
who for his sake would like to

•

"Please allow me to retire," Charles said. "I must begin a long and sad correspondence."

"Certainly, nephew."

•

"The painter is here from Paris!"

"Good day, painter. What is your name?"

"My name, sir, is John Graham!"

"John Graham! That is not a French name!"

"No, sir. I am an American. My dates are 1881–1961."

"Well, you have an air of competence. Is that your equipment there, on the stagecoach platform?"

"Yes. That is my equipment. That is my easel, my palette, and my paint box containing tins of paints as well as the finest camel's-hair brushes. In this bag, here, are a few changes of clothes, for I anticipate that this portrait will take several days."

"Well, that is fine. How do you like our country?"

"It appears to be a very fine country. I imagine a lot of painting could get done in this country."

"Yes, we have some pretty good painters of our own. That is why I am surprised to find that they sent an American painter, rather than a French one, to do Mlle. Eugénie's portrait. But I'm sure you will do a first-class job. We're paying you enough."

"Yes, the fee is quite satisfactory."

"Have you brought any examples of your work, so we can see what kind of thing you do?"

"Well, in this album here . . . this is a portrait of Ellen West . . . this one is Mrs. Margot Heap . . . that's an Indian chief . . . that's Patsy Porker . . ."

"Why are they all cross-eyed?"

"Well, that's just the way I do it. I don't see anything wrong with that. It often occurs in nature."

"But *every one* is . . ."

"Well, what's so peculiar about that? I just like . . . that's just the way I do it. I *like* . . ."

•

"In my opinion, Eugénie wasn't fondled enough as a child."

"Adolphe des Grassins wasn't fondled enough either!"

"And Judge de Bonfons?"

"Who could bring himself to fondle Judge de Bonfons!"

"And Charles Grandet?"

"His history in this regard is not known. But it has been observed that he is forever *patting himself*, pat pat pat, on the hair, on the kneecap, pat pat pat pat pat pat. This implies—"

"These children need fondling!"

"The state should fondle these poor children!"
"Balzac himself wasn't fondled enough!"
"Men are fools!"

•

Eugénie Grandet with ball:

•

Charles and Eugénie understand each other.
They speak only with their eyes.
The poor ruined dandy withdraws into a corner and remains there in calm, proud silence.
But from time to time his cousin's gentle, caressing glance

•

"No more butter, Eugénie. You've already used up a whole half pound this month."
"But, Father . . . the butter for Charles's éclair!"

•

Butter butter butter butter butter butter butter butter butter butter butter butter butter butter butter butter butter butter butter

butter butter

•

Eugénie Grandet decides to kill her father.

•

Charles decides to try his luck in the Indies—that deadliest of climates.

•

"Here, Charles, take this money of mine. This money that my father gave me. This money that if he finds out I gave it to you, all hell will break loose. I want you to have it, to finance your operations in the Indies—that deadliest of climates."

"No, Eugénie, I couldn't do that. I couldn't take your money. No, I won't do it. No."

"No, I mean it, Charles. Take the money and use it for worthy purposes. Please. See, here is a ducat, minted in 1756 and still bright as day. And here are some doubloons, worth two escudos each. And here are some shiny quadroons, of inestimable value. And here in this bag are thalers and bobs, and silver quids and copper bawbees. Altogether, nearly six thousand francs. Take it, it's yours."

"No, Eugénie, I can't take your money. I can't do it."

"No, Charles, take my money. My little hoard."

"OK."

•

In order not to interrupt the course of events which took place within the Grandet family, we must now glance ahead at the operations which the old man carried out in Paris by means of the des Grassins. A month after the banker's departure, Grandet was in possession of enough government stock, purchased at eighty francs a share, to yield him an income of a hundred thousand francs a year. The information given after his death by the inventory of his property never threw the slightest light on the means by which his wary mind conceived to exchange the price of the certificate for the certificate itself. Monsieur Cruchot believed that Nanon had unwittingly been the trusty instrument by which the money was delivered. It was at about that time that she went away for five days on the pretext of putting something in order at Froidfond, as though the old man were capable of leaving anything in disorder!

With regard to the affairs of the house of Guillaume Grandet, all the old man's expectations were realized. As is well known, the Bank of France has precise information on all the large fortunes of Paris and the provinces. The names of des Grassins and Félix Grandet of Saumur were well known there and enjoyed the respect granted to all noted financial figures whose wealth is based on enormous holdings of unmortgaged land. The arrival of the banker from Saumur, who was said to be under orders to liquidate, for the sake of honor, the house of Grandet in Paris, was therefore enough to spare the deceased merchant's memory the shame of protested notes. The seals were broken in the presence of the creditors, who

•

"Here's a million and a half francs, Judge," Eugénie said, drawing from her bosom a certificate for a hundred shares in the Bank of France.

•

Charles in the Indies. He sold:

Chinese
Negroes
swallows' nests
children
artists

Photograph of Charles in the Indies:

The letter:

Dear Cousin,

I have decided to marry a Mlle. d'Aubrion, and not you. Her nose turns red, under certain circumstances: but I have contrived a way of not looking at her, at those times—all will be well. If my children are to get into the École Normale, the marriage is essential; and we have to live for the children, don't we? A brilliant life awaits me, is what I am trying to say to you, if I don't marry you, and that is why I am marrying this other girl, who is hideously ugly but possessed of a notable, if decayed, position in the aristocracy. Therefore those binding promises we exchanged, on the bench, are, to all intents and purposes, mooted. If I have smothered your hopes at the same time, what can I do? We get the destiny we deserve, and I have done so many evil things, in the Indies, that I am no longer worthy of you, probably. Knowing chuckles will doubtless greet this news, the news of my poor performance, in Saumur—I ask you to endure them, for the sake of

Your formerly loving,

Charles

•

"I have decided to give everything to the Church."
"An income of eight hundred thousand a year!"
"Yes."
"It will kill your father."
"You think it will kill him if I give everything to the Church?"
"I certainly do."
"Run and fetch the curé this instant."

•

Old Grandet clutches his chest, and capitulates. Eight hundred thousand a year! He gasps. A death by gasping.

•

Adolphe des Grassins, an unsuccessful suitor of Eugénie Grandet, follows his father to Paris. He becomes a worthless scoundrel there.

Nothing:
A Preliminary Account

It's not the yellow curtains. Nor curtain rings. Nor is it bran in a bucket, not bran, nor is it the large, reddish farm animal eating the bran from the bucket, the man who placed the bran in the bucket, his wife, or the raisin-faced banker who's about to foreclose on the farm. None of these is nothing. A damselfish is not nothing, it's a fish, a *Pomacentrus,* it likes warm water, coral reefs—perhaps even itself, for all we know. Nothing is not a nightshirt or a ninnyhammer, ninety-two, or Nineveh. It is not a small jungle in which, near a river, a stone table has been covered with fruit. It is not the handsome Indian woman standing next to the stone table holding the blond, kidnapped child. Neither is it the proposition *esse est percipi,* nor is it any of the refutations of that proposition. Nor is it snuff. Hurry. There is not much time, and we must complete, or at least attempt to complete, the list. Nothing is not a tongue depressor; splendid, hurry on. Not a tongue depressor on which a distinguished artist has painted part of a nose, part of a mouth, a serious, unsmiling eye. Good, we got that in. Hurry on. We are persuaded that nothing is not the yellow panties. The yellow panties edged with white on the floor under the black chair. And it's not the floor or the black chair or the two naked lovers standing up in the white-sheeted bed having a pillow fight during the course of which the male partner will, unseen by his beloved, load his pillowcase with a copy of *Webster's Third International*. We are nervous. There is not much time. Nothing is not a Gregorian chant or indeed a chant of any kind unless it be the howl of the null muted to inaudibility by the laws of language strictly construed. It's not an "O" or an asterisk or what Richard is thinking or that thing we can't name at the moment but which we use to clip papers together. It's not the ice cubes disappearing in the warmth of our whiskey nor is it the town in Scotland where the whiskey is manufactured nor is it the workers who, while reading the Bible and the local newspaper and Rilke, are sentiently sipping the product through eighteen-foot-long, almost invisible nylon straws.

And it's not a motor hotel in Dib (where the mudmen live) and it's not pain or *pain* or the mustard we spread on the *pain* or the mustard plaster we spread on the pain, fee simple, the roar of fireflies mating, or meat. Nor is it lobster protected from its natural enemies by its high price or true grit or false grit or thirst. It's not the yellow curtains, we have determined that, and it's not what is behind the yellow curtains which we cannot mention out of respect for the King's rage and the Queen's reputation. Hurry. Not much time. Nothing is not a telephone number or any number whatsoever including zero. It's not science and in particular it's not black-hole physics, which is not nothing but physics. And it's not (quickly now, quickly) Benjamin Franklin trying to seduce, by mail, the widow of the French thinker Claude Adrien Helvétius, and it is not the nihilism of Gorgias, who asserts that nothing exists and even if something did exist it could not be known and even if it could be known that knowledge could not be communicated, no, it's not that although the tune is quite a pretty one. I am sorry to say that it is not Athos, Porthos, or Aramis, or anything that ever happened to them or anything that may yet happen to them if, for example, an Exxon tank truck exceeding the speed limit outside of Yuma, Arizona, runs over a gila monster which is then reincarnated as Dumas *père*. It's not weather of any kind, fair, foul, or undecided, and it's not mental weather of any kind, fair, foul, or partly cloudy, and it's neither my psychiatrist nor your psychiatrist or either of their psychiatrists, let us hurry on. And it is not what is under the bed because even if you tell us "There is nothing under the bed" and we think, *At last! Finally! Pinned to the specimen board!* still you are only informing us of a local, only temporarily stable situation, you have not delivered nothing itself. Only the list can present us with nothing itself, pinned, finally, at last, let us press on. We are aware of the difficulties of proving a negative, such as the statement "There is not a hipphilosamus in my living room," and that even if you show us a photograph of your living room with no hipphilosamus in it, and adduce as well a tape recording on which no hipphilosamus tread is discernible, how can we be sure that the photograph has not been retouched, the tape cunningly altered, or that both do not either pre- or postdate the arrival of the hipphilosamus? That large, verbivorous animal which is able to think underwater for long periods of time? And while we are mentioning verbs, can we ask the question, of nothing, what does nothing *do?*

Quickly, quickly. Heidegger suggests that "Nothing nothings" —a calm, sensible idea with which Sartre, among others, disagrees. (What Heidegger thinks about nothing is not nothing.) Heidegger points us toward dread. Having borrowed a cup of dread from Kierkegaard, he spills it, and in the spreading stain he finds (like a tea-leaf reader) Nothing. Original dread, for Heidegger, is what intolerabilizes all of what-is, offering us a momentary glimpse of what is not, finally a way of bumping into Being. But Heidegger is far too grand for us; we applaud his daring but are ourselves performing a homelier task, making a list. Our list can in principle never be completed, even if we summon friends or armies to help out (nothing is not an army nor is it an army's history, weapons, morale, doctrines, victories, or defeats—there, that's done). And even if we were able, with much labor, to exhaust the possibilities, get it all *inscribed,* name everything nothing is not, down to the last rogue atom, the one that rolled behind the door, and had thoughtfully included ourselves, the makers of the list, on the list—the list itself would remain. Who's got a match?

But if we cannot finish, we can at least begin. If what exists is in each case the totality of the series of appearances which manifests it, then nothing must be characterized in terms of its non-appearances, no-shows, incorrigible tardiness. Nothing is what keeps us waiting (forever). And it's not *Charlie Is My*

Darling, nor would it be Mary if I had a darling so named nor would it be my absence-of-darling had I neglected to search out and secure one. And it is not the yellow curtains behind which fauns and astronauts embrace, behind which flesh crawls in all directions and flickertail squirrels fall upward into the trees. And death is not nothing and the cheering sections of consciousness ("Do not go gentle into that good night") are not nothing nor are holders of the contrary view ("Burning to be gone," says Beckett's Krapp, into his Sony). What can I tell you about the rape of Lucrece by the beastly nephew of proud Tarquin? Only this: the rapist wore a coat with raglan sleeves. Not much, but not nothing. Put it on the list. For an ampler account, see Shakespeare. And you've noted the anachronism, Lord Raglan lived long after the event, but errors, too, are not nothing. Put it on the list. Nothing ventured, nothing gained. What a wonderful list! How joyous the notion that, try as we may, we cannot do other than fail and fail absolutely and that the task will remain always before us, like a meaning for our lives. Hurry. Quickly. Nothing is not a nail.

A Manual for Sons

(1) Mad fathers
(2) Fathers as teachers
(3) On horseback, etc.
(4) The leaping father
(5) Best way to approach
(6) Ys
(7) Names of
(8) Voices of
Sample voice, A
B
C
(9) Fanged, etc.
(10) Hiram or Saul
(11) Color of fathers
(12) Dandling
(13) A tongue-lashing
(14) The falling father
(15) Lost fathers
(16) Rescue of fathers
(17) Sexual organs
(18) Yamos
(19) "Responsibility"
(20) Death of
(21) Patricide a poor idea, and summation

Mad fathers stalk up and down the boulevards, shouting. Avoid them, or embrace them, or tell them your deepest thoughts—it makes no difference, they have deaf ears. If their dress is covered with sewn-on tin cans and their spittle is like a string of red boiled crayfish running head-to-tail down the front of their tin cans, serious impairment of the left brain is present. If, on the other hand, they are simply barking (no tin cans, spittle held securely in the pouch of the cheek), they have been driven to distraction by the intricacies of living with others. Go up to them and, stilling their wooden clappers by putting your left hand between the hinged parts, say you're sorry. If the barking ceases, this does not mean that they have heard you, it only means they are experiencing erotic thoughts of abominable luster. Permit them to enjoy these images for a space, and then strike them sharply in the nape with the blade of your tanned right hand. Say you're sorry again. It won't get through to them (because their brains are mush) but in pronouncing the words your body will assume an attitude that conveys, in every country of the world, sorrow—this language they can understand. Gently feed them with bits of leftover meat you are carrying in your pockets. First hold the meat in front of their eyes, so that they can see what it is, and then point to their mouths, so that they know that the meat is for them. Mostly, they will open their mouths at this point. If they do not, throw the meat in between barks. If the meat does not get all the way into the mouth but lands upon (say) the upper lip, hit them again in the neck; this often causes the mouth to pop open and the meat sticking to the upper lip to fall into the mouth. Nothing may work out in the way I have described; in this eventuality, you can do not much for a mad father except listen, for a while, to his babble. If he cries aloud, *"Stomp it, emptor!"*, then you must attempt to figure out the code. If he cries aloud, *"The fiends have killed your horse!"*, note down in your notebook the frequency with which the words "the" and "your" occur in his tirade. If he cries aloud, *"The cat's in its cassock and flitter-te-hee moreso stomp it!"*, remember that he has already asked you once to "stomp it" and that this must refer to something you are doing. So stomp it.

•

Fathers are teachers of the true and not-true, and no father ever knowingly teaches what is not true. In a cloud of unknowing, then, the father proceeds with his instruction. Tough meat should be hammered well between two stones before it is placed on the fire, and should be combed with a hair comb and brushed with a hairbrush before it is placed on the fire. On arriving at night, with thirsty cattle, at a well of doubtful character, one deepens the well first with a rifle barrel, then with a pigsticker, then with a pencil, then with a ramrod, then with an icepick, "bringing the well in" finally with needle and thread. Do not forget to clean your rifle barrel immediately. To find honey, tie a feather or straw to the leg of a bee, throw him into the air, and peer alertly after him as he flies slowly back to the hive. Nails, boiled for three hours, give off a rusty liquid that, when combined with oxtail soup, dries to a flame color, useful for warding off tuberculosis or attracting native women. Do not forget to hug the native women immediately. To prevent feet from blistering, soap the inside of the stocking with a lather of raw egg and steel wool, which together greatly soften the leather of the foot. Delicate instruments (such as surveying instruments) should be entrusted to a porter who is old and enfeebled; he will totter along most carefully. For a way of making an ass not to bray at night, lash a heavy child to his tail; it appears that when an ass wishes to bray he elevates his tail; and if the tail cannot be elevated, he has not the heart. Savages are easily satisfied with cheap beads in the following colors: dull white, dark blue, and vermillion red. Expensive beads are often spurned by them. Nonsavages should be given cheap books in the following colors: dead white, brown, and seaweed. Books praising the sea are much sought after. Satanic operations should not be conducted without first consulting the Bibliothèque Nationale. When Satan at last appears to you, try not to act surprised. Then get down to hard bargaining. If he likes neither the beads nor the books, offer him a cold beer. Then—

Fathers teach much that is of value. Much that is not.

•

Fathers in some countries are like cotton bales; in others, like clay pots or jars; in others, like reading, in a newspaper, a long account of a film you have already seen and liked immensely but do not wish to see again, or read about. Some fathers have triangular eyes. Some fathers, if you ask them for the time of day, spit silver dollars. Some fathers live in old filthy cabins high in the mountains, and make murderous noises deep in their throats when their amazingly sharp ears detect, on the floor of the valley, an alien step. Some fathers piss either perfume or medicinal alcohol, distilled by powerful body processes from what they have been, all day long, drinking. Some fathers have only one arm. Others have an extra arm, in addition to the normal two, hidden inside their coats. On that arm's fingers are elaborately wrought golden rings that, when a secret spring is pressed, dispense charity. Some fathers have made themselves over into convincing replicas of beautiful sea animals, and some into convincing replicas of people they hated as children. Some fathers are goats, some are milk, some teach Spanish in cloisters, some are exceptions, some are capable of attacking world economic problems and killing them, but have not yet done so; they are waiting for one last vital piece of data. Some fathers strut but most do not, except inside; some fathers pose on horseback but most do not, except in the eighteenth century; some fathers fall off the horses they mount but most do not; some fathers, after falling off the horse, shoot the horse, but most do not; some fathers fear horses but most fear, instead, women; some fathers masturbate because they fear women; some fathers sleep with hired women because they fear women who are free; some fathers never sleep at all, but are endlessly awake, staring at their features, which are behind them.

•

The leaping father is not encountered often, but exists. Two leaping fathers together in a room can cause accidents. The best idea is to chain heavy-duty truck tires to them, one in front, one in back, so that their leaps become pathetic small hops. That is all their lives amount to anyhow, and it is good for them to be able to see, in the mirror, their whole life-histories performed, in a sequence perhaps five minutes long, of upward movements which do not, really, get very far or achieve very much. Without the tires, the leaping father has a nuisance value which may rapidly transform itself into a serious threat. Ambition is the core of this problem (it may even be ambition *for you,* in which case you are in even greater danger than had been supposed), and the core may be removed by open-liver surgery (the liver being the home of the humours, as we know). There is something very sad about all leaping fathers, about leaping itself. I prefer to keep my feet on the ground, in situations where the ground has not been cut out from under me, by the tunneling father. The latter is usually piebald in color, and supremely notable for his nonflogitiousness.

•

The best way to approach a father is from behind. Thus if he chooses to hurl his javelin at you, he will probably miss. For in the act of twisting his body around, and drawing back his hurling arm, and sighting along the shaft, he will give you time to run, to make reservations for a flight to another country. To Rukmani, there are no fathers there. In that country virgin corn gods huddle together under a blanket of ruby chips and flexible cement, through the long wet Rukmanian winter, and in some way not known to us produce offspring. The new citizens are greeted with dwarf palms and certificates of worth, are led (or drawn on runnerless sleds) out into the zocalo, the main square of the country, and their *augensheinlich* parentages recorded upon a great silver bowl. Look! In the walnut paneling of the dining hall, a javelin! The paneling is wounded in a hundred places.

•

I knew a father named Ys who had many many children and sold every one of them to the bone factories. The bone factories will not accept angry or sulking children, therefore Ys was, to his children, the kindest and most amiable father imaginable. He fed them huge amounts of calcium candy and the milk of minks, told them interesting and funny stories, and led them each day in their bone-building exercises. "Tall sons," he said, "are best." Once a year the bone factories sent a little blue van to Ys's house.

•

The names of fathers. Fathers are named:

A'albiel	Adeo
Aariel	Adityas
Aaron	Adlai
Aba	Adnai
Ababaloy	Adoil
Abaddon	Adossia
Aban	Aeon
Abathur	Aeshma
Abbott	Af
Abdia	Afkiel
Abel	Agason
Abiou	Agwend
Achsah	Albert
Adam	

•

Fathers have voices, and each voice has a *terribilità* of its own. The sound of a father's voice is various: like film burning, like marble being pulled screaming from the face of a quarry, like the clash of paper clips by night, lime seething in a lime pit, or batsong. The voice of a father can shatter your glasses. Some fathers have tetchy voices, others tetched-in-the-head voices. It is understood that fathers, when not robed in the father-role, may be farmers, heldentenors, tinsmiths, racing drivers, fistfighters, or salesmen. Most are salesmen. Many fathers did not wish, especially, to be fathers; the thing came upon them, seized them, by accident, or by someone else's careful design, or by simple clumsiness on someone's part.

Nevertheless this class of father—the inadvertent—is often among the most tactful, light-handed, and beautiful of fathers. If a father has fathered twelve or twenty-seven times, it is well to give him a curious look—this father does not loathe himself enough. This father frequently wears a blue wool watch cap, on stormy nights, to remind himself of a manly past—action in the North Atlantic. Many fathers are blameless in all ways, and these fathers are either sacred relics people are touched with to heal incurable illnesses, or texts to be studied, generation after generation, to determine how this idiosyncrasy may be maximized. Text-fathers are usually bound in blue.

The father's voice is an instrument of the most terrible pertinaciousness.

SAMPLE VOICE, A.

Son, I got bad news for you. You won't understand the whole purport of it, 'cause you're only six, a little soft in the head too, that fontanelle never did close properly, I wonder why. But I can't delay it no longer, son, I got to tell you the news. There ain't no malice in it, son, I hope you believe me. The thing is, you got to go to school, son, and get socialized. That's the news. You're turnin' pale, son, I don't blame you. It's a terrible thing, but there it is. We'd socialize you here at home, your mother and I, except that we can't stand to watch it, it's that dreadful. And your mother and I who love you and always have and always will are a touch sensitive, son. We don't want to hear your howls and screams. It's going to be miserable, son, but you won't hardly feel it. And I know you'll do well and won't do anything to make us sad, your mother and I who love you. I know you'll do well and won't run away or fall down in fits either. Son, your little face is pitiful. Son, we can't just let you roam the streets like some kind of crazy animal. Son, you got to get your natural impulses curbed. You got to get your corners knocked off, son, you got to get realistic. They going to vamp on you at that school, kid. They going to tear up your ass. They going to learn you how to think, you'll get your letters there, your letters and your figures, your verbs and all that. Your mother and I could socialize you here at home but it would be too painful for your mother and I who love you. You're going to meet the stick, son, the stick going to walk up to you and say howdy-do. You're going to learn about your country at that school, son, oh beautiful for spacious skies. They going to lay just a raft of stuff on you at that school and I caution you not to resist, it ain't appreciated. Just take it as it comes and you'll be fine, son, just fine. You got to do right, son, you got to be realistic. They'll be other kids in that school, kid, and ever' last one of 'em will be after your lunch money. But don't give 'em your lunch money, son, put it in your shoe. If they come up against you tell 'em the other kids already got it. That way you fool 'em, you see, son? What's the matter with you? And watch out for the custodian, son, he's mean. He don't like his job. He wanted to be president of a bank. He's not. It's made him mean. Watch out for that sap he carries on his hip. Watch out for the teacher, son, she's sour. Watch out for her tongue, it'll cut you. She's got a bad mouth on her, son, don't balk her if you can help it. I got nothin' against the schools, kid, they just doin' their job. Hey kid what's the matter with you kid? And if this school don't do the job we'll find one that can. We're right behind you, son, your mother and I who love you. You'll be gettin' your sports there, your ball sports and your blood sports and watch out for the coach, he's a disappointed man, some say a sadist but I don't know about that. You got to develop your body, son. If they shove you, shove back. Don't take nothin' off nobody. Don't show fear. Lay back and watch the guy next to you, do what he does. Except if he's a damn fool. If he's a damn fool you'll know he's a damn fool 'cause everybody'll be hittin' on him. Let me tell you 'bout that school, son. They do what they do 'cause I told them to do it. That's why they do it. They didn't think up those ideas their own selves. I told them to do it. Me and your mother who love you, we told them to do it. Behave yourself, kid! Do right! You'll be fine there, kid, just fine. What's the matter with you, kid? Don't be that way. I hear the ice-cream man outside, son. You want to go and see the ice-cream man?

Go get you an ice cream, son, and make sure you get your sprinkles. Go give the ice-cream man your quarter, son. And hurry back.

B.

Hey son. Hey boy. Let's you and me go out and throw the ball around. Throw the ball around. You don't want to go out and throw the ball around? How come you don't want to go out and throw the ball around? I know why you don't want to go out and throw the ball around. It's 'cause you— Let's don't discuss it. It don't bear thinkin' about. Well let's see, you don't want to go out and throw the ball around, you can hep me work on the patio. You want to hep me work on the patio? Sure you do. Sure you do. We gonna have us a fine-lookin' patio there, boy, when we get it finished. Them folks across the street are just about gonna fall out when they see it. C'mon kid, I'll let you hold the level. And this time I want you to hold the fucking thing straight. I want you to hold it straight. It ain't difficult, any idiot can do it. A nigger can do it. We're gonna stick it to them mothers across the street, they think they're so fine. Flee from the wrath to come, boy, that's what I always say. Seen it on a sign one time. Flee from the Wrath to Come. Crazy guy goin' down the street holdin' this sign, see, flee from the wrath to come, it tickled me. Went round for days sayin' it out loud to myself, flee from the wrath to come, flee from the wrath to come. Couldn't get it outa my head. See they're talkin' 'bout God there, that's what that's all about, God, see boy, God. It's this God crap they try and hand you, see, they got a whole routine, see, let's don't talk about it, it fries my ass. Your mother goes for all that, see, and of course your mother is a fine woman and a sensible woman but she's just a little bit ape on this church thing we don't discuss it. She has her way and I got mine, we don't discuss it. She's a little bit ape on this subject, see, I don't blame her it was the way she was raised. Her mother was ape on this subject. That's how the churches make their money, see, they get the women. All these dumb-ass women. *Hold it straight kid.* That's better. Now run me a line down that form with the pencil. I gave you the pencil. What'd you do with the goddamn pencil? Jesus Christ kid *find the pencil.* OK go in the house and get me another pencil. Hurry up I can't stand here holdin' this all day. Wait a minute here's the pencil. OK. I got it. Now hold it straight and run me a line down that form. *Not that way dummy,* on the horizontal. You think we're buildin' a barn? That's right. Good. Now run the line. Good. OK, now go over there and fetch me the square. Square's the flat one, looks like a L. Like this, look. Good. Thank you. OK now hold that mother up against the form where you made the line. That's so we get this side of it square, see? OK now hold the board and lemme just put in the stakes. HOLD IT STILL DAMN IT. How you think I can put in the stakes with you wavin' the damn thing around like that? Hold it still. Check it with the square again. OK, is it square? Now hold it still. Still. OK. That's got it. How come you're tremblin'? Nothin' to it, all you got to do is hold one little bitty piece of one-by-six straight for two minutes and you go into a fit? Now stop that. Stop it. I said stop it. Now just take it easy. You like heppin' me with the patio, don'tcha? Just think 'bout when it's finished and we be sittin' out here with our drinks drinkin' our drinks and them jackasses 'cross the street will be havin' a hemorrhage. From green envy. Flee from the wrath to come, boy, flee from the wrath to come. He he.

C.

Hey son come here a minute. I want you and me to have a little talk. You're turnin' pale. How come you always turn pale when we have a little talk? You *delicate?* Pore delicate little flower? Naw you ain't, you're a *man,* son, or will be someday the good Lord willin'. But you got to do right. That's what I want to talk to you about. Now put down that comic book and come on over here and sit by me. Sit right there. Make yourself comfortable. Now, you comfortable? Good. Son, I want to talk to you about your personal habits. Your personal habits. We ain't never talked about your personal habits and now it's time. I been watchin' you, kid. Your personal habits are admirable. Yes they are. They are flat admirable. I like the way you pick up your room. You run a clean room, son, I got to hand it to you. And I like the way you clean your teeth. You brush right, in the right direction, and you brush *a lot.* You're goin' to have good gums, kid, good healthy gums. We ain't gonna have to lay out no money to get your teeth fixed, your mother and I, and that's a blessing and we thank you. And you keep yourself clean, kid, clothes neat, hands clean, face clean, knees clean, that's the way to hop, way to hop. There's just one little thing, son, one little thing that puzzles me. I been studyin' 'bout it and I flat don't understand it. How come you spend so much time washin' your hands, kid? I been watchin' you. You spend an hour after breakfast washin' your hands. Then you go wash 'em again 'bout ten-thirty, ten-forty, 'nother fifteen minutes washin' your hands. Then just before lunch, maybe a half hour, washin' your hands. Then after lunch, sometimes an hour, sometimes less, it varies. I been noticin'. Then in the middle of the afternoon back in there washin' your hands. Then before supper and after supper and before you go to bed and sometimes you get up in the middle of the night and go on in there and wash your hands. Now I'd think you were in there playin' with your little pecker, 'cept you a shade young for playin' with your little pecker and besides you leave the door open, most kids close the door when they go in there to play with their little peckers but you leave it open. So I see you in there and I see what you're doin', you're washin' your hands. And I been keepin' track of it son, you spend 'bout three-quarters of your wakin' hours *washin' your hands.* And I think there's somethin' a little bit *strange* about that, son. It ain't natural. So what I want to know is how come you spend so much time washin' your hands, son? Can you tell me? Huh? Can you give me a rational explanation? Well, can you? Huh? You got anything to say on this subject? Well, what's the matter? You're just sittin' there. Well come on, son, what you got to say for yourself? What's the explanation? Now it won't do you no good to start cryin', son, that don't help anything. OK kid stop crying. *I said stop it!* I'm goin' to whack you, kid, you don't stop cryin'. Now cut that out. This minute. Now cut it out. Goddamn baby. Come on now kid, get ahold of yourself. Now go wash your face and come on back in here, I want to talk to you some more. Wash your face, but don't do that other. Now go on in there and get back in here right quick. I want to talk to you 'bout bumpin' your head, son, against the wall, 'fore you go to sleep. I don't like it. You're too old to do that. It disturbs me. I can hear you in there, when you go to bed, bump bump bump bump bump bump bump bump bump. It's disturbing. It's monotonous. It's a very disturbing sound. I don't like it. I don't like listenin' to it. I want you to stop it. I want you to get ahold of yourself. I don't like to hear that noise when I'm sittin' in here tryin' to read the paper or whatever I'm doin', I don't like to hear it and it bothers your mother. It gets her all upset and I don't like your mother to be all upset, just on accounta you. Bump bump bump bump bump bump bump bump bump, what are you, kid, some kind of animal? I cain't figure you out, kid. I just flat cain't understand it, bump bump bump bump bump bump bump. Dudden't hurtcha? Dudden't hurtcha head? Well, never mind about that right now. Go on in there and wash your face, and then come on back in here and we'll talk some more. And don't do none of that other, just wash your face. You got three minutes.

•

Fathers are like blocks of marble—giant cubes, highly polished, with veins and seams—placed squarely in your path. They block your path. They cannot be climbed over, neither can they be slithered past. They are the "past," and very likely the slither, if the slither is thought of as that accommodating maneuver you make to escape notice, or get by unscathed. If you attempt to go around one, you will find that another (winking at the first) has mysteriously appeared athwart the trail. Or maybe it is the same one, moving with the speed of paternity. Look closely at color and texture. Is this giant square block of marble similar in color and texture to a slice of rare roast beef? Your very father's complexion! Do not try to draw too many conclusions from this; the obvious ones are sufficient and correct. Some fathers like to dress up in black robes and go out and give away the sacraments, adding to their black robes the chasuble, stole, and alb, in reverse order. Of these "fathers" I shall not speak, except to commend them for their lack of ambition and sacrifice, especially the sacrifice of the "franking privilege," or the privilege of naming the first male child after yourself: Franklin Edward A'albiel, Jr. Of all possible fathers, the fanged father is the least desirable. If you can get your lariat around one of his fangs, and quickly wrap the other end of it several times around your saddle horn, and if your horse is a trained roping horse and knows what to do, how to plant his front feet and then back up with small nervous steps, keeping the lariat taut, then you have a chance. Do not try to rope both fangs at the same time; concentrate on the right. Do the thing fang by fang, and then you will be safe, or more nearly so. I have seen some old, yellowed six-inch fangs that were drawn in this way, and once, in a whaling museum in a seaport town, a twelve-inch fang, mistakenly labeled as the tusk of a walrus. But I recognized it at once, it was a father fang, which has its own peculiarly shaped, six-pointed root. I am pleased never to have met that father. . . .

•

If your father's name is Hiram or Saul, flee into the woods. For these names are the names of kings, and your father Hiram, or your father Saul, will not be a king, but will retain, in hidden places in his body, the memory of kingship. And there is no one more blackhearted and surly than an ex-king, or a person who harbors, in the dark channels of his body, the memory of kingship. Fathers so named consider their homes to be Camelots, and their kith and kin courtiers, to be elevated or depressed in rank according to the lightest whinges of their own mental weather. And one can never know for sure if one is "up" or "down" at a particular moment; one is a feather, floating, one has no place to stand. Of the rage of the king-father I will speak later, but understand that fathers named Hiram,

Saul, Charles, Francis, or George rage (when they rage) exactly in the manner of their golden and noble namesakes. Flee into the woods, at such times, or earlier, before the mighty scimitar or yataghan leaps from its scabbard. The proper attitude toward such fathers is that of the toad, lickspittle, smellfeast, carpet knight, pickthank, or tuft-hunter. When you cannot escape to the trees, genuflect, and stay down there, on one knee with bowed head and clasped hands, until dawn. By this time he will probably have drunk himself into a sleep, and you may creep away and seek your bed (if it has not been taken away from you) or, if you are hungry, approach the table and see what has been left there, unless the ever-efficient cook has covered everything with clear plastic and put it away. In that case, you may suck your thumb.

•

The color of fathers: The bay-colored father can be trusted, mostly, whether he is standard bay, blood bay, or mahogany bay. He is useful (1) in negotiations between warring tribes, (2) as a catcher of red-hot rivets when you are building a bridge, (3) in auditioning possible bishops for the Synod of Bishops, (4) in the co-pilot's seat, and (5) for carrying one corner of an eighteen-meter-square mirror through the city's streets. Dun-colored fathers tend to shy at obstacles, and therefore you do not want a father of this color, because life, in one sense, is nothing but obstacles, and his continual shying will reduce your nerves to grease. The liver-chestnut-colored father has a reputation for decency and good sense; if God commands him to take out his knife and slice through your neck with it, he will probably say "No, thanks." The dusty-chestnut father will reach for his knife. The light-chestnut father will ask for another opinion. The standard-chestnut father will look the other way, to the east, where another vegetation ceremony, with more interesting dances, is being held. Sorrel-colored fathers are easily excitable and are employed most often where a crowd, or mob, is wanted, as for coronations, lynchings, and the like. The bright-sorrel father, who glows, is an exception; he is content with his glow, with his name (John), and with his life membership in the Knights of the Invisible Empire. In bungled assassinations, the assassin will frequently be a blond-sorrel father who forgot to take the lens cap off his telescopic sight. Buckskin-colored fathers know the Law and its mangled promise, and can help you in your darker projects, such as explaining why a buckskin-colored father sometimes has a black stripe down the spine from the mane to the root of the tail; it is because he has been whoring after Beauty, and thinks himself more beautiful with the black stripe, which sets off his tanned deer-hide color most wonderfully, than without it. Red roan-colored fathers, blue roan-colored fathers, rose gray-colored fathers, grulla-colored fathers are much noted for bawdiness, and this should be encouraged, for bawdiness is a sacrament that does not, usually, result in fatherhood; it is its own reward. Spots, paints, pintos, piebalds, and Appaloosas have a sweet dignity that proceeds from their inferiority, and excellent senses of smell. The color of a father is not an absolute guide to the character and conduct of that father but tends to be a self-fulfilling prophecy, because when he sees what color he is, he hastens out into the world to sell more goods and services, so that he may keep pace with his destiny.

•

Fathers and dandling: If a father fathers daughters, then our lives are eased. Daughters are for dandling, and are often dandled up until their seventeenth or eighteenth year. The hazard here, which must be faced, is that the father will want to sleep with his beautiful daughter, who is after all *his* in a way that even his wife is not, in a way that even his most delicious mistress is not. Some fathers just say "Publish and be damned!" and go ahead and sleep with their new and amazingly sexual daughters, and accept what pangs accumulate afterward; most do not. Most fathers are sufficiently disciplined in this regard, by mental straps, so that the question never arises. When fathers are giving their daughters their "health" instruction (that is to say, talking to them about the reproductive process) (but this is most often done by mothers, in my experience) it is true that a subtle rinse of desire may be tinting the situation slightly (when you are hugging and kissing the small woman sitting on your lap it is hard to know when to stop, it is hard to stop yourself from proceeding as if she were a bigger woman not related to you by blood). But in most cases, the taboo is observed, and additional strictures imposed, such as "Mary, you are never to allow that filthy John Wilkes Booth to lay a hand upon your bare, white, new breast." Although in the modern age some fathers are moving rapidly in the opposite direction, toward the future, saying, "Here, Mary, here is your blue fifty-gallon drum of babykilling foam, with your initials stamped on it in a darker blue—see, there on the top?" But the important thing about daughter-fathers is that, as fathers, they don't count. Not to their daughters, I don't mean—I have heard daughter-stories that would toast your hair—but to themselves. Fathers of daughters see themselves as *hors concours* in the great exhibition, and this is a great relief. They do not have to teach hurling the caber. They tend, therefore, to take a milder, gentler hand (meanwhile holding on, with an iron grip, to all the fierce prerogatives that fatherhood of any kind conveys—the guidance system of a slap is an example). To say more than this about fathers of daughters is beyond me, even though I am father of a daughter.

•

A tongue-lashing: "Whosoever hath within himself the deceivableness of unrighteousness and hath pleasure in unrighteousness and walketh disorderly and hath turned aside into vain jangling and hath become a manstealer and liar and perjured person and hath given over himself to wrath and doubting and hath been unthankful and hath been a lover of his own self and hath gendered strife with foolish and unlearned questions and hath crept into houses leading away silly women with divers lusts and hath been the inventor of evil things and hath embraced contentiousness and obeyed slanderousness and hath filled his mouth with cursing and bitterness and hath made of his throat an open sepulcher and hath the poison of asps under his lips and hath boasted and hath hoped against hope and hath been weak in faith and hath polluted the land with his whoredoms and hath profaned holy things and hath despised mine holy things and hath committed lewdness and hath mocked and hath daubed himself with untempered mortars, and whosoever, if a woman, hath journeyed to the Assyrians there to have her breasts pressed by lovers clothed in blue, captains and rulers, desirable young men, horsemen riding upon horses, horsemen riding upon horses who lay upon her and discovered her nakedness and bruised the breasts of her virginity and poured their whoredoms upon her, and hath doted upon them captains and rulers clothed most gorgeously, horsemen riding upon horses, girdled with girdles upon their loins, and hath multiplied her whoredoms with her paramours whose flesh is as the flesh of asses and whose issue is like the issue of horses, great lords and rulers clothed in blue and riding on horses: This man and this woman I say shall be filled with drunkenness and sorrow like a pot whose scum is therein and whose scum hath not gone out of it and under which the pile for the fire is and on which the wood is heaped and the fire kindled and the pot spiced and the bones burned and then the pot set empty on the coals that the brass of it may be hot and may burn and that the filthiness of it may be molten in it, that the scum may be consumed, for ye have wearied yourselves with lies and your great scum went not forth out of you, your scum shall be in the fire and I will take away the desire of thine eyes. Remember ye not that when I was yet with you I told you these things?"

•

There are twenty-two kinds of fathers, of which only nineteen are important. The drugged father is not important. The lionlike father (rare) is not important. The Holy Father is not important, for our purposes. There is a certain father who is falling through the air, heels where his head should be, head where his heels should be. The falling father has grave meaning for all of us. The wind throws his hair in every direction. His cheeks are flaps almost touching his ears. His garments are shreds, telltales. This father has the power of curing the bites of mad dogs, and the power of choreographing the interest rates.

What is he thinking about, on the way down? He is thinking about emotional extravagance. The Romantic Movement, with its exploitation of the sensational, the morbid, the occult, the erotic! The falling father has noticed Romantic tendencies in several of his sons. The sons have taken to wearing slices of raw bacon in their caps, and speaking out against the interest rates. After all he has done for them! Many bicycles! Many *gardes-bébés!* Electric guitars uncountable! Falling, the falling father devises his iron punishment, resolved not to err again on the side of irresponsible mercy. He is also thinking about his upward mobility, which doesn't seem to be doing so well at the moment. There is only one thing to do: work harder! He decides that if he can ever halt the "downturn" that he seems to be in, he will redouble his efforts, really put his back into it, this time. The falling father is important because he embodies the "work ethic," which is a dumb one. The "fear ethic" should be substituted, as soon as possible. Peering upward at his endless hurtling, let us simply shrug, fold up the trampoline we were going to try to catch him in, and place it once again on top of the rafters, in the garage.

•

To find a lost father: The first problem in finding a lost father is to lose him, decisively. Often he will wander away from home and lose himself. Often he will remain at home but still be "lost" in every true sense, locked away in an upper room, or in a workshop, or in the contemplation of beauty, or in the contemplation of a secret life. He may, every evening, pick up his gold-headed cane, wrap himself in his cloak, and depart, leaving behind, on the coffee table, a sealed laundry bag in which there is an address at which he may be reached, in case of war. War, as is well known, is a place at which many fathers are lost, sometimes temporarily, sometimes forever. Fathers are frequently lost on expeditions of various kinds (the journey to the interior). The five best places to seek this kind of lost father are Nepal, Rupert's Land, Mount Elbrus, Paris, and the agora. The five kinds of vegetation in which fathers most often lose themselves are needle-leaved forest, broad-leaved forest mainly evergreen, broad-leaved forest mainly deciduous, mixed needle-leaved and broad-leaved forest, and tundra. The five kinds of things fathers were wearing when last seen are caftans, bush jackets, parkas, Confederate gray, and ordinary business suits. Armed with these clues, then, you may place an advertisement in the newspaper: *Lost, in Paris, on or about February 24, a broad-leaf-loving father, 6' 2", wearing a blue caftan, may be armed and dangerous, we don't know, answers to the name Old Hickory. Reward.* Having completed this futile exercise, you are then free to think about what is really important. Do you really want to find this father? What if, when you find him, he speaks to you in the same tone he used before he lost himself? Will he again place nails in your mother, in her elbows and back of the knee? Remember the javelin. Have you any reason to believe that it will not, once again, flash through the seven-o'clock-in-the-evening air? What we are attempting to determine is simple: Under what conditions do you wish to live? Yes, he "nervously twiddles the stem of his wineglass." Do you wish to watch him do so on into the last decade of the present century? I don't think so. Let him take those mannerisms, and what they portend, to Borneo, they will be new to Borneo. Perhaps in Borneo he will also nervously twiddle the stem of, etc., but he will not be brave enough to manufacture there the explosion of which this is a sign. Throwing the roast through the mirror. Thrusting a belch big as an opened umbrella into the middle of something someone else is trying to say. Beating you, either with a wet, knotted rawhide or with an ordinary belt. Ignore that empty chair at the head of the table. Give thanks.

•

On the rescue of fathers: Oh they hacked him pretty bad, they hacked at him with axes and they hacked at him with hacksaws but me and my men got there fast, wasn't as bad as it might have been, first we fired smoke grenades in different colors, yellow and blue and green, that put a fright into them but they wouldn't quit, they opened up on us with 81-mm. mortars and meanwhile continued to hack. I sent some of the boys out to the left to flank them but they'd put some people over there to prevent just that and my men got into a firefight with their support patrol, no other way to do the thing but employ a frontal assault, which we did, at least it took the pressure off him, they couldn't continue to hack and deal with our assault at the same time. We cleaned their clocks for them, I will say that, they fell back to the left and linked up with their people over there, my flanking party broke off contact as I had instructed and let them flee unpursued. We came out of it pretty well, had a few wounded but that's all. We turned immediately to the task of bandaging him in the hacked places, bloody great wounds but our medics were very good, they were all over him, he never made a complaint or uttered a sound, not a whimper out of him, not a sign. This took place at the right arm, just above the elbow, we left some pickets there for a few days until the arm had begun to heal, I think it was a successful rescue, we returned to our homes to wait for the next time. I think it was a successful rescue. It was an adequate rescue.

Then they attacked him with sumo wrestlers, giant fat men in loincloths. We countered with loincloth snatchers—some of our best loincloth snatchers. We were successful. The hundred naked fat men fled. I had rescued him again. Then we sang "Genevieve, Oh Genevieve." All the sergeants gathered before the veranda and sang it, and some enlisted men too—some enlisted men who had been with the outfit for a long time. They sang it, in the twilight, pile of damp loincloths blazing fitfully off to the left. When you have rescued a father from whatever terrible threat menaces him, then you feel, for a moment, that you are the father and he is not. For a moment. This is the only moment in your life you will feel this way.

•

The sexual organs of fathers: The penises of fathers are traditionally hidden from the inspection of those who are not "clubbable," as the expression runs. These penises are magical, but not most of the time. Most of the time they are "at rest." In the "at rest" position they are small, almost shriveled, and easily concealed in carpenter's aprons, chaps, bathing suits, or ordinary trousers. Actually they are not anything that you would want to show anyone, in this state; they are rather like mushrooms or, possibly, large snails. The magic, at these times, resides in other parts of the father (fingertips, right arm) and not in the penis. Occasionally a child, usually a bold six-year-old daughter, will request permission to see it. This request should be granted, once. Be matter-of-fact, kind, and undramatic. Pretend, for the moment, that it is as mundane as a big toe. About sons you must use your own judgment. It is injudicious (as well as unnecessary) to terrify them; you have many other ways of accomplishing that. Chancre is a good reason for not doing any of this. When the penises of fathers are semi-erect, titillated by some stray erotic observation, such as a glimpse of an attractive female hoof, bereft of its slipper, knowing smiles should be exchanged with the other fathers present (better: half smiles) and the matter let drop. Semierectness is a half measure, as Aristotle knew; that is why most of the penises in museums have been knocked off with a mallet. The original artificers could not bear the idea of Aristotle's disapproval, and multilated their work rather than merit the scorn of the great Peripatetic. The notion that this mutilation was carried out by later (Christian) "cleanup squads" is untrue, pure legend. The matter is as I have presented it. Many other things can be done with the penises of fathers, but these have already been adequately described by other people. The penises of fathers are in every respect superior to the penises of nonfathers, not because of size or weight or any consideration of that sort but because of a metaphysical "responsibility." This is true even of poor, bad, or insane fathers. African artifacts reflect this special situation. Pre-Columbian artifacts, for the most part, do not.

•

I knew a father named Yamos who was landlord of the bear gardens at Southwark. Yamos was known to be a principled man and never, never, never ate any of his children no matter how dire the state of his purse. Yet the children, one by one, disappeared.

•

We have seen that the key idea, in fatherhood, is "responsibility." First, that heavy chunks of blue or gray sky do not fall down and crush our bodies, or that the solid earth does not turn into a yielding pit beneath us (although the tunneling father is sometimes responsible, in the wrong sense, for the latter). The responsibility of the father is chiefly that his child not die, that enough food is pushed into its face to sustain it, and that heavy blankets protect it from the chill, cutting air. The father almost always meets this responsibility with valor and steadfastness (except in the case of child abusers or thieves of children or managers of child labor or sick, unholy sexual ghouls). The child lives, mostly, lives and grows into a healthy, normal adult. Good! The father has been successful in his burdensome, very often thankless task, that of keeping the child breathing. Good work, Sam, your child has taken his place in the tribe, has a good job selling thermocouples, has married a nice girl whom you like, and has impregnated her to the point that she will doubtless have a new child, soon. And is not in jail. But have you noticed the slight curl at the end of Sam II's mouth, when he looks at you? It means that he didn't want you to name him Sam II, for one thing, and for two other things it means that he has a sawed-off in his left pant leg, and a baling hook in his right pant leg, and is ready to kill you with either one of them, given the opportunity. The father is taken aback. What he usually says, in such a confrontation, is "I changed your diapers for you, little snot." This is not the right thing to say. First, it is not true (mothers change nine diapers out of ten), and secondly, it instantly reminds Sam II of what he is mad about. He is mad about being small when you were big, but no, that's not it, he is mad about being helpless when you were powerful, but no, not that either, he is mad about being contingent when you were necessary, not quite it, he is insane because when he loved you, you didn't notice.

•

The death of fathers: When a father dies, his fatherhood is returned to the All-Father, who is the sum of all dead fathers taken together. (This is not a definition of the Dead Father, only an aspect of his being.) The fatherhood is returned to the All-Father, first because that is where it belongs and secondly in order that it may be denied to you. Transfers of power of this kind are marked with appropriate ceremonies; top hats are burned. Fatherless now, you must deal with the memory of a father. Often that memory is more potent than the living presence of a father, is an inner voice commanding, haranguing, yes-ing and no-ing—a binary code, yes no yes no yes no yes no, governing your every, your slightest movement, mental or physical. At what point do you become yourself? Never, wholly, you are always partly him. That privileged position in your inner ear is his last "perk" and no father has ever passed it by.

Similarly, jealousy is a useless passion because it is directed mostly at one's peers, and that is the wrong direction. There is only one jealousy that is useful and important, the original jealousy.

•

Patricide: Patricide is a bad idea, first because it is contrary to law and custom and secondly because it proves, beyond a doubt, that the father's every fluted accusation against you was correct: You are a thoroughly bad individual, a patricide!—member of a class of persons universally ill-regarded. It is all right to feel this hot emotion, but not to act upon it. And it is not necessary. It is not necessary to slay your father, time will slay him, that is a virtual certainty. Your true task lies elsewhere.

Your true task, as a son, is to reproduce every one of the enormities touched upon in this manual, but in attenuated form. You must become your father, but a paler, weaker version of him. The enormities go with the job, but close study will allow you to perform the job less well than it has previously been done, thus moving toward a golden age of decency, quiet, and calmed fevers. Your contribution will not be a small one, but "small" is one of the concepts that you should shoot for. If your father was a captain in Battery D, then content yourself with a corporalship in the same battery. Do not attend the annual reunions. Do not drink beer or sing songs at the reunions. Begin by whispering, in front of a mirror, for thirty minutes a day. Then tie your hands behind your back for thirty minutes a day, or get someone else to do this for you. Then, choose one of your most deeply held beliefs, such as the belief that your honors and awards have something to do with you, and abjure it. Friends will help you abjure it, and can be telephoned if you begin to backslide. You see the pattern, put it into practice. *Fatherhood can be, if not conquered, at least "turned down" in this generation*—by the combined efforts of all of us together. Rejoice.

At the End of the Mechanical Age

I went to the grocery store to buy some soap. I stood for a long time before the soaps in their attractive boxes, RUB and FAB and TUB and suchlike, I couldn't decide so I closed my eyes and reached out blindly and when I opened my eyes I found her hand in mine.

Her name was Mrs. Davis, she said, and TUB was best for important cleaning experiences, in her opinion. So we went to lunch at a Mexican restaurant which as it happened she owned, she took me into the kitchen and showed me her stacks of handsome beige tortillas and the steam tables which were shiny-brite. I told her I wasn't very good with women and she said it didn't matter, few men were, and that nothing mattered, now that Jake was gone, but I would do as an interim project and sit down and have a Carta Blanca. So I sat down and had a cool Carta Blanca, God was standing in the basement reading the meters to see how much grace had been used up in the month of June. Grace is electricity, science has found, it is not *like* electricity, it *is* electricity and God was down in the basement reading the meters in His blue jump suit with the flashlight stuck in the back pocket.

"The mechanical age is drawing to a close," I said to her.

"Or has already done so," she replied.

"It was a good age," I said. "I was comfortable in it, relatively. Probably I will not enjoy the age to come quite so much. I don't like its look."

"One must be fair. We don't know yet what kind of an age the next one will be. Although I feel in my bones that it will be an age inimical to personal well-being and comfort, and that is what I like, personal well-being and comfort."

"Do you suppose there is something to be done?" I asked her.

"Huddle and cling," said Mrs. Davis. "We can huddle and cling. It will pall, of course, everything palls, in time . . ."

Then we went back to my house to huddle and cling, most women are two different colors when they remove their clothes especially in summer but Mrs. Davis was all one color, an ocher. She seemed to like huddling and clinging, she stayed for many days. From time to time she checked the restaurant keeping everything shiny-brite and distributing sums of money to the staff, returning with tortillas in sacks, cases of Carta Blanca, buckets of guacamole, but I paid her for it because I didn't want to feel obligated.

There was a song I sang her, a song of great expectations.

"*Ralph is coming,*" I sang, "*Ralph is striding in his suit of lights over moons and mountains, over parking lots and fountains, toward your silky side. Ralph is coming, he has a coat of many colors and all major credit cards and he is striding to meet you and culminate your foggy dreams in an explosion of blood and soil, at the end of the mechanical age. Ralph is coming preceded by fifty running men with spears and fifty dancing ladies who are throwing leaf spinach out of little baskets, in his path. Ralph is perfect,*" I sang, "*but he is also full of interesting tragic flaws, and he can drink fifty running men under the table without breaking his stride, and he can have congress with fifty dancing ladies without breaking his stride, even his socks are ironed, so natty is Ralph, but he is also right down in the mud with the rest of us, he markets the mud at high prices for specialized industrial uses and he is striding, striding, striding, toward your waiting heart. Of course you may not like him, some people are awfully picky . . . Ralph is coming,*" I sang to her, "*he is striding over dappled plains and crazy rivers and he will change your life for the better, probably, you will be fainting with glee at the simple touch of his grave gentle grizzled hand although I am aware that some people can't stand prosperity, Ralph is com-*

ing, I hear his hoofsteps on the drumbead of history, he is striding as he has been all his life toward you, you, you."

"Yes," Mrs. Davis said, when I had finished singing, "that is what I deserve, all right. But probably I will not get it. And in the meantime, there is you."

God then rained for forty days and forty nights, when the water tore away the front of the house we got into the boat. Mrs. Davis liked the way I maneuvered the boat off the trailer and out of the garage, she was provoked into a memoir of Jake.

"Jake was a straight-ahead kind of man," she said, "he was simpleminded and that helped him to be the kind of man that he was." She was staring into her Scotch-and-floodwater rather moodily I thought, debris bouncing on the waves all around us but she paid no attention. "That is the type of man I like," she said, "a strong and simpleminded man. The case-study method was not Jake's method, he went right through the middle of the line and never failed to gain yardage, no matter what the game was. He had a lust for life, and life had a lust for him. I was inconsolable when Jake passed away." Mrs. Davis was drinking the Scotch for her nerves, she had no nerves of course, she was nerveless and possibly heartless also but that is another question, gutless she was not, she had a gut and a very pretty one ocher in color but that was another matter. God was standing up to His neck in the raging waters with a smile of incredible beauty on His visage, He seemed to be enjoying His creation, the disaster, the waters all around us were raging louder now, raging like a mighty tractor-trailer tailgating you on the highway.

Then Mrs. Davis sang to me, a song of great expectations.

"Maude is waiting for you," Mrs. Davis sang to me, *"Maude is waiting for you in all her seriousness and splendor, under her gilded onion dome, in that city which I cannot name at this time, Maude waits. Maude is what you lack, the profoundest of your lacks. Your every yearn since the first yearn has been a yearn for Maude, only you did not know it*

until I, your dear friend, pointed it out. She is going to heal your scrappy and generally unsatisfactory life with the balm of her Maudeness, luckiest of dogs, she waits only for you. Let me give you just one instance of Maude's inhuman sagacity. Maude named the tools. It was Maude who thought of calling the rattail file a rattail file. It was Maude who christened the needle-nose pliers. Maude named the rasp. Think of it. What else could a rasp be but a rasp? Maude in her wisdom went right to the point, and called it rasp. *It was Maude who named the maul. Similarly the sledge, the wedge, the ball-peen hammer, the adz, the shim, the bone, the strop. The bandsaw, the hacksaw, the bucksaw, and the fretsaw were named by Maude, peering into each saw and intuiting at once its specialness. The scratch awl, the scuffle hoe, the prick punch and the countersink—I could go on and on. The tools came to Maude, tool by tool in a long respectful line, she gave them their names. The vise. The gimlet. The cold chisel. The reamer, the router, the gouge. The plumb bob. How could she have thought up the rough justice of these wonderful cognomens? Looking languidly at a pair of tin snips, and then deciding to call them* tin snips*—what a burst of glory! And I haven't even cited the bush hook, the grass snath, or the plumber's snake, or the C-clamp, or the nippers, or the scythe. What a tall achievement, naming the tools! And this is just one of Maude's contributions to our worldly estate, there are others. What delights will come crowding,"* Mrs. Davis sang to me, *"delight upon delight, when the epithalamium is ground out by the hundred organ grinders who are Maude's constant attendants, on that good-quality day of her own choosing, which you have desperately desired all your lean life, only you weren't aware of it until I, your dear friend, pointed it out. And Maude is young but not too young,"* Mrs. Davis sang to me, *"she is not too old either, she is* just right *and she is waiting for you with her tawny limbs and horse sense, when you receive Maude's nod your future and your past will begin."*

There was a pause, or pall.

"Is that true," I asked, "that song?"

"It is a metaphor," said Mrs. Davis, "it has metaphorical truth."

"And the end of the mechanical age," I said, "is that a metaphor?"

"The end of the mechanical age," said Mrs. Davis, "is in my judgment an actuality straining to become a metaphor. One must wish it luck, I suppose. One must cheer it on. Intellectual rigor demands that we give these damned metaphors every chance, even if they are inimical to personal well-being and comfort. We have a duty to understand everything, whether we like it or not—a duty I would scant if I could." At that moment the water jumped into the boat and sank us.

At the wedding Mrs. Davis spoke to me kindly.

"Tom," she said, "you are not Ralph, but you are all that is around at the moment. I have taken in the whole horizon with a single sweep of my practiced eye, no giant figure looms there and that is why I have decided to marry you, temporarily, with Jake gone and an age ending. It will be a marriage of convenience all right, and when Ralph comes, or Maude nods, then our arrangement will automatically self-destruct, like the tinted bubble that it is. You were very kind and considerate, when we were drying out, in the tree, and I appreciated that. That counted for something. Of course kindness and consideration are not what the great songs, the Ralph-song and the Maude-song, promise. They are merely flaky substitutes for the terminal experience. I realize that and want you to realize it. I want to be straight with you. That is one of the most admirable things about me, that I am always straight with people, from the sweet beginning to the bitter end. Now I will return to the big house where my handmaidens will proceed with the robing of the bride."

It was cool in the meadow by the river, the meadow Mrs. Davis had selected for the travesty, I walked over to the tree under which my friend Blackie was standing, he was the best man, in a sense.

"This disgusts me," Blackie said, "this hollow pretense and

empty sham and I had to come all the way from Chicago."

God came to the wedding and stood behind a tree with just part of His effulgence showing, I wondered whether He was planning to bless this makeshift construct with His grace, or not. It's hard to imagine what He was thinking of in the beginning when He planned everything that was ever going to happen, planned everything exquisitely right down to the tiniest detail such as what I was thinking at this very moment, my thought about His thought, planned the end of the mechanical age and detailed the new age to follow, and then the bride emerged from the house with her train, all ocher in color and very lovely.

"And do you, Anne," the minister said, "promise to make whatever mutually satisfactory accommodations necessary to reduce tensions and arrive at whatever previously agreed-upon goals both parties have harmoniously set in the appropriate planning sessions?"

"I do," said Mrs. Davis.

"And do you, Thomas, promise to explore all differences thoroughly with patience and inner honesty ignoring no fruitful avenues of discussion and seeking at all times to achieve rapprochement while eschewing advantage in conflict situtions?"

"Yes," I said.

"Well, now we are married," said Mrs. Davis, "I think I will retain my present name if you don't mind, I have always been Mrs. Davis and your name is a shade graceless, no offense, dear."

"OK," I said.

Then we received the congratulations and good wishes of the guests, who were mostly employees of the Mexican restaurant, Raul was there and Consuelo, Pedro and Pepe came crowding around with outstretched hands and Blackie came crowding around with outstretched hands, God was standing behind the caterer's tables looking at the enchiladas and chalupas and chile con queso and chicken mole as if He had never seen such things before but that was hard to believe.

I started to speak to Him as all of the world's great religions with a few exceptions urge, from the heart, I started to say

"Lord, Little Father of the Poor, and all that, I was just wondering now that an age, the mechanical age, is ending and a new age beginning or so they say, I was just wondering if You could give me a hint, sort of, not a Sign, I'm not asking for a Sign, but just the barest hint as to whether what we have been told about Your nature and our nature is, forgive me and I know how You feel about doubt or rather what we have been told you feel about it, but if You could just let drop the slightest indication as to whether what we have been told is authentic or just a bunch of apocryphal heterodoxy—"

But He had gone away with an insanely beautiful smile on His lighted countenance, gone away to read the meters and get a line on the efficacy of grace in that area, I surmised, I couldn't blame Him, my question had not been so very elegantly put, had I been able to express it mathematically He would have been more interested, maybe, but I have never been able to express anything mathematically.

After the marriage Mrs. Davis explained marriage to me.

Marriage, she said, an institution deeply enmeshed with the mechanical age.

Pairings smiled upon by law were but reifications of the laws of mechanics, inspired by unions of a technical nature, such as nut with bolt, wood with wood screw, aircraft with Plane-Mate.

Permanence or impermanence of the bond a function of (1) materials and (2) technique.

Growth of literacy a factor, she said.

Growth of illiteracy also.

The center will not hold if it has been spot-welded by an operator whose deepest concern is not with the weld but with his lottery ticket.

God interested only in grace—keeping things humming.

Blackouts, brownouts, temporary dimmings of household illumination all portents not of Divine displeasure but of Divine indifference to executive-development programs at middle-management levels.

He likes to get out into the field Himself, she said. With His flashlight. He is doing the best He can.

We two, she and I, no exception to general ebb/flow of world juice and its concomitant psychological effects, she said.

Bitter with the sweet, she said.

After the explanation came the divorce.

"Will you be wanting to contest the divorce?" I asked Mrs. Davis.

"I think not," she said calmly, "although I suppose one of us should, for the fun of the thing. An uncontested divorce always seems to me contrary to the spirit of divorce."

"That is true," I said, "I have had the same feeling myself, not infrequently."

After the divorce the child was born. We named him A. F. of L. Davis and sent him to that part of Russia where people live to be one hundred and ten years old. He is living there still, probably, growing in wisdom and beauty. Then we shook hands, Mrs. Davis and I, and she set out Ralphward, and I, Maudeward, the glow of hope not yet extinguished, the fear of pall not yet triumphant, standby generators ensuring the flow of grace to all of God's creatures at the end of the mechanical age.

Rebecca

Rebecca Lizard was trying to change her ugly, reptilian, thoroughly unacceptable last name.

"Lizard," said the judge. "Lizard, Lizard, Lizard. Lizard. There's nothing wrong with it if you say it enough times. You can't clutter up the court's calendar with trivial little minor irritations. And there have been far too many people changing their names lately. Changing your name countervails the best interests of the telephone company, the electric company, and the United States government. Motion denied."

Lizard in tears.

Lizard led from the courtroom. A chrysanthemum of Kleenex held under her nose.

"Shaky lady," said a man, "are you a schoolteacher?"

Of course she's a schoolteacher, you idiot. Can't you see the poor woman's all upset? Why don't you leave her alone?

"Are you a homosexual lesbian? Is that why you never married?"

Christ, yes, she's a homosexual lesbian, as you put it. *Would you please shut your face?*

Rebecca went to the damned dermatologist (a new damned dermatologist), but he said the same thing the others had said. "Greenish," he said, "slight greenishness, genetic anomaly, nothing to be done, I'm afraid, Mrs. Lizard."

"Miss Lizard."

"Nothing to be done, Miss Lizard."

"Thank you, Doctor. Can I give you a little something for your trouble?"

"Fifty dollars."

When Rebecca got home the retroactive rent increase was waiting for her, coiled in her mailbox like a pupil about to strike.

Must get some more Kleenex. Or a Ph.D. No other way.

She thought about sticking her head in the oven. But it was an electric oven.

Rebecca's lover, Hilda, came home late.

"How'd it go?" Hilda asked, referring to the day.

"Lousy."

"Hmmm," Hilda said, and quietly mixed strong drinks of busthead for the two of them.

Hilda is a very good-looking woman. So is Rebecca. They love each other—an incredibly dangerous and delicate business, as we know. Hilda has long blond hair and is perhaps a shade the more beautiful. Of course Rebecca has a classic and sexual figure which attracts huge admiration from every beholder.

"You're late," Rebecca said. "Where were you?"

"I had a drink with Stephanie."

"Why did you have a drink with Stephanie?"

"She stopped by my office and said let's have a drink."

"Where did you go?"

"The Barclay."

"How is Stephanie?"

"She's fine."

"Why did you have to have a drink with Stephanie?"

"I was ready for a drink."

"Stephanie doesn't have a slight greenishness, is that it? Nice, pink Stephanie."

Hilda rose and put an excellent C & W album on the record player. It was David Rogers's "Farewell to the Ryman," Atlantic SD 7283. It contains such favorites as "Blue Moon of Kentucky," "Great Speckled Bird," "I'm Movin' On," and "Walking the Floor Over You." Many great Nashville personnel appear on this record.

"Pinkness is not everything," Hilda said. "And Stephanie is a little bit boring. You know that."

"Not so boring that you don't go out for drinks with her."

"I am not interested in Stephanie."

"As I was leaving the courthouse," Rebecca said, "a man unzipped my zipper."

David Rogers was singing "Oh please release me, let me go."

"What were you wearing?"

"What I'm wearing now."

"So he had good taste," Hilda said, "for a creep." She hugged Rebecca, on the sofa. "I love you," she said.

"Screw that," Rebecca said plainly, and pushed Hilda away. "Go hang out with Stephanie Sasser."

"I am not interested in Stephanie Sasser," Hilda said for the second time.

Very often one "pushes away" the very thing that one most wants to grab, like a lover. This is a common, although distressing, psychological mechanism, having to do (in my opinion) with the fact that what is presented is not presented "purely," that there is a tiny little canker or grim place in it somewhere. However, worse things can happen.

"Rebecca," said Hilda, "I really don't like your slight greenishness."

The term "lizard" also includes geckos, iguanas, chameleons, slowworms, and monitors. Twenty existing families make up the order, according to the *Larousse Encyclopedia of Animal Life*, and four others are known only from fossils. There are about twenty-five hundred species, and they display adaptations for walking, running, climbing, creeping, or burrowing. Many have interesting names, such as the Bearded Lizard, the Collared Lizard, the Flap-Footed Lizard, the Frilled Lizard, the Girdle-Tailed Lizard, and the Wall Lizard.

"I have been overlooking it for these several years, because I love you, but I really don't like it so much," Hilda said. "It's slightly—"

"Knew it," said Rebecca.

Rebecca went into the bedroom. The color television set was turned on, for some reason. In a greenish glow, a film called *Green Hell* was unfolding.

I'm ill, I'm ill.

I will become a farmer.

Our love, our sexual love, our ordinary love!

Hilda entered the bedroom and said, "Supper is ready."

"What is it?"

"Pork with red cabbage."

"I'm drunk," Rebecca said.

Too many of our citizens are drunk at times when they should be sober—suppertime, for example. Drunkenness leads to forgetting where you have put your watch, keys, or money clip, and to a decreased sensitivity to the needs and desires and calm good health of others. The causes of overuse of alcohol are not as clear as the results. Psychiatrists feel in general that alcoholism is a serious problem but treatable, in some cases. AA is said to be both popular and effective. At base, the question is one of willpower.

"Get up," Hilda said. "I'm sorry I said that."

"You told the truth," said Rebecca.

"Yes, it was the truth," Hilda admitted.

"You didn't tell me the truth in the beginning. In the beginning, you said it was beautiful."

"I was telling you the truth, in the beginning. I did think it was beautiful. Then."

This "then," the ultimate word in Hilda's series of three brief sentences, is one of the most pain-inducing words in the human vocabulary, when used in this sense. Departed time! And the former conditions that went with it! How is human pain to be measured? But remember that Hilda, too . . . It is correct to feel for Rebecca in this situation, but, reader, neither can Hilda's position be considered an enviable one, for truth, as Bergson knew, is a hard apple, whether one is throwing it or catching it.

"What remains?" Rebecca said stonily.

"I can love you *in spite of*—"

Do *I* want to be loved *in spite of?* Do you? Does anyone? But aren't we all, to some degree? Aren't there important parts of all of us which must be, so to say, gazed past? I turn a blind eye to that aspect of you, and you turn a blind eye to that aspect of me, and with these blind eyes eyeball-to-eyeball, to use an expression from the early 1960s, we continue our starched and fragrant lives. Of course it's also called "making the best of things," which I have always considered a rather soggy idea for an American ideal. But my criticisms of this idea must be tested against those of others—the late President McKinley, for example, who maintained that maintaining a good, if not necessarily sunny, disposition was the one valuable and proper course.

Hilda placed her hands on Rebecca's head.

"The snow is coming," she said. "Soon it will be snow time. Together then as in other snow times. Drinking busthead 'round the fire. Truth is a locked room that we knock the lock off from time to time, and then board up again. Tomorrow you will hurt me, and I will inform you that you have done so, and so on and so on. To hell with it. Come, viridian friend, come and sup with me."

They sit down together. The pork with red cabbage steams before them. They speak quietly about the McKinley Administration, which is being revised by revisionist historians. The story ends. It was written for several reasons. Nine of them are secrets. The tenth is that one should never cease considering human love, which remains as grisly and golden as ever, no matter what is tattoed upon the warm tympanic page.

The Captured Woman

The captured woman asks if I will take her picture.

I shoot four rolls of 35 mm. and then go off very happily to the darkroom . . .

I bring back the contacts and we go over them together. She circles half a dozen with a grease pencil—pictures of herself staring. She does not circle pictures of herself smiling, although there are several very good ones. When I bring her back prints (still wet) she says they are not big enough.

"Not big enough?"

"Can you make enlargements?"

"How big?"

"How big can you make them?"

"The largest paper I have is twenty-four by thirty-six."

"Good!"

The very large prints are hung around her room with pushpins.

"Make more."

"For what?"

"I want them in the other rooms too."

"The staring ones?"

"Whichever ones you wish."

I make more prints using the smiling negatives. (I also shoot another half dozen rolls.) Soon the house is full of her portraits, she is everywhere.

•

M. calls to tell me that he has captured a woman too.

"What kind?"

"Thai. From Thailand."

"Can she speak English?"

"Beautifully. She's an English teacher back home, she says."

"How tall?"

"As tall as yours. Maybe a little taller."

"What is she doing?"

"Right now?"

"Yes."

"She's polishing her rings. I gave her a lot of rings. Five rings."

"Was she pleased?"

"I think so. She's polishing like a house afire. Do you think that means she's tidy?"

"Have to wait and see. Mine is throwing her football."

"What?"

"I gave her a football. She's sports-minded. She's throwing passes into a garbage can."

"Doesn't that get the football dirty?"

"Not the regular garbage can. I got her a special garbage can."

"Is she good at it?"

"She's good at *everything*."

There was a pause.

"Mine plays the flute," M. says. "She's asked for a flute."

"Mine probably plays the flute too but I haven't asked her. The subject hasn't come up."

"Poor Q.," M. says.

"Oh, come now. No use pitying Q."

"Q. hasn't a chance in the world," M. says, and hangs up.

•

I say: "What will you write in the note?"

"You may read it if you wish. I can't stop you. It's you after all who will put it in the mail."

"Do you agree not to tell him where you are?"

"This is going to be almost impossible to explain. You understand that."

"Do you love him?"

"I waited six years to have a baby."

"What does that mean?"

"I wasn't sure, I suppose."

"Now you're sure?"

"I was growing older."

"How old are you now?"

"Thirty-two last August."

"You look younger."

"No I don't."

She is tall and has long dark hair which has, in truth, some gray in it already.

She says: "You were drunk as a lord the first time I saw you."

"Yes, I was."

When I first met her (in a perfectly ordinary social situation, a cocktail party) she clutched my wrists, tapping them then finally grabbing, in the wildest and most agitated way, meanwhile talking calmly about some movie or other.

She's a wonderful woman, I think.

•

She wants to go to church!

"*What!*"

"It's Sunday."

"I haven't been inside a church in twenty years. Except in Europe. Cathedrals."

"I want to go to church."

"What kind?"

"Presbyterian."

"Are you a Presbyterian?"

"I was once."

I find a Presbyterian church in the Yellow Pages.

We sit side by side in the pew for all the world like a married couple. She is wearing a beige linen suit which modulates her body into a nice safe Sunday quietude.

The two ministers have high carved chairs on either side of the lectern. They take turns conducting the service. One is young, one is old. There is a choir behind us and a solo tenor so startlingly good that I turn my head to look at him.

We stand and sit and sing with the others as the little mimeographed order-of-service dictates.

The old minister, fragile, eagle beak, white close-cropped hair, stands at the lectern in a black cassock and white thin lacy surplice.

"Sacrifice," the minister says.

He stares into the choir loft for a moment and then repeats the thought: "Sacrifice."

We are given a quite admirable sermon on Sacrifice which includes quotations from Euripides and A. E. Housman.

After the service we drive home and I tie her up again.

•

It is true that Q. will never get one. His way of proceeding is far too clumsy. He might as well be creeping about carrying a burlap sack.

P. uses tranquilizing darts delivered by a device which resembles the Sunday *New York Times.*

D. uses chess but of course this limits his field of operations somewhat.

S. uses a spell inherited from his great-grandmother.

F. uses his illness.

T. uses a lasso. He can make a twenty-foot loop and keep it spinning while he jumps in and out of it in his handmade hundred-and-fifty-dollar boots—a mesmerizing procedure.

C. has been accused of jacklighting, against the law in this state in regard to deer. The law says nothing about women.

X. uses the Dionysiac frenzy.

L. is the master. He has four now, I believe.

I use Jack Daniel's.

•

I stand beside one of the "staring" portraits and consider whether I should attempt to steam open the note.

Probably it is an entirely conventional appeal for rescue.

I decide that I would rather not know what is inside, and put it in the mail along with the telephone bill and a small ($25) contribution to a lost but worthy cause.

•

Do we sleep together? Yes.

What is to be said about this?

It is the least strange aspect of our temporary life together. It is as ordinary as bread.

She tells me what and how. I am sometimes inspired and in those moments need no instructions. Once I made an X with masking tape at a place on the floor where we'd made love. She laughed when she saw it. That is, I am sometimes able to amuse her.

What does she think? Of course, I don't know. Perhaps she regards this as a parenthesis in her "real" life, like a stay in the hospital or being a member of a jury sequestered in a Holiday Inn during a murder trial. I have criminally abducted her and am thus clearly in the wrong, a circumstance which enables her to regard me very kindly.

She is a wonderful woman and knows herself to be wonderful—she is (justifiably) a little vain.

The rope is forty feet long (that is, she can move freely forty feet in any direction) and is in fact thread—Belding mercerized cotton, shade 1443.

What does she think of me? Yesterday she rushed at me and stabbed me three times viciously in the belly with a book, the Viking *Portable Milton*. Later I visited her in her room and was warmly received. She let me watch her doing her exercises. Each exercise has a name and by now I know all the names: Boomerang, Melon, Hip Bounce, Diamond, Whip, Hug, Headlights, Ups and Downs, Bridge, Flags, Sitting Twist, Swan, Bow and Arrow, Turtle, Pyramid, Bouncing Ball, Accordion. The movements are amazingly erotic. I knelt by her side and touched her lightly. She smiled and said, not now. I went to my room and watched television—*The Wide World of Sports*, a soccer match in São Paulo.

•

The captured woman is smoking her pipe. It has a long graceful curving stem and a white porcelain bowl decorated with little red flowers. For dinner we had shad roe and buttered yellow beans.

"He looks like he has five umbrellas stuck up his ass," she says suddenly.

"Who?"

"My husband. But he's a very decent man. But of course that's not uncommon. A great many people are very decent. Most people, I think. Even you."

The fragrance of her special (ladies' mixture) tobacco hangs about us.

"This is all rather like a movie. That's not a criticism. I like things that are like movies."

I become a little irritated. All this effort and all she can think of is movies?

"This is not a movie."

"It is," she says. "It is it is it is."

•

M. calls in great agitation.

"Mine is sick," he says.

"What's the matter?"

"I don't know. She's listless. Won't eat. Won't polish. Won't play her flute."

M.'s is a no-ass woman of great style and not inconsiderable beauty.

"She's languishing," I say.

"Yes."

"That's not good."

"No."

I pretend to think—M. likes to have his predicaments taken seriously.

"Speak to her. Say this: My soul is soused, imparadised, imprisoned in my lady."

"Where's that from?"

"It's a quotation. Very powerful."

"I'll try it. Soused, imprisoned, imparadised."

"No. Imparadised, imprisoned. It actually sounds better the way you said it, though. Imparadised last."

"OK. I'll say it that way. Thanks. I love mine more than you love yours."

"No you don't."

"Yes I do."

I bit off my thumb, and bade him do as much.

•

The extremely slow mailman brings her an answer to her note.

I watch as she opens the envelope.

"That bastard," she says.

"What does he say?"

"That incredible bastard."

"What?"

"I offer him the chance to rescue me on a white horse—one of the truly great moments this life affords—and he natters on about how well he and the kid are doing together. How she hardly ever cries now. How *calm* the house is."

"The bastard," I say happily.

"I can see him sitting in the kitchen by the microwave oven and reading his *Rolling Stone*."

"Does he read *Rolling Stone?*"

"He thinks *Rolling Stone* is neat."

"Well . . ."

"He's not *supposed* to be reading *Rolling Stone*. It's not aimed at him. He's too old, the dumb fuck."

"You're angry."

"Damn right."

"What are you going to do?"

She thinks for a moment.

"What happened to your hand?" she says, noticing at last.

"Nothing," I say, placing the bandaged hand behind my back. (Obviously I did not bite the thumb clean through but I did give it a very considerable gnaw.)

"Take me to my room and tie me up," she says. "I'm going to hate him for a while."

I return her to her room and go back to my own room and settle down with *The Wide World of Sports*—international fencing trials in Belgrade.

•

This morning, at the breakfast table, a fierce attack from the captured woman.

I am a shit, a vain preener, a watcher of television, a blatherer, a creephead, a monstrous coward who preys upon etc. etc. etc. and is not man enough to etc. etc. etc. Also I drink too much.

This is all absolutely true. I have often thought the same things myself, especially, for some reason, upon awakening.

I have a little more Canadian bacon.

"And a skulker," she says with relish. "One who—"

I fix her in the viewfinder of my Pentax and shoot a whole new series, *Fierce*.

The trouble with capturing one is that the original gesture is almost impossible to equal or improve upon.

•

She says: "He wants to get that kid away from me. He wants to keep that kid for himself. He has captured that kid."

"She'll be there when you get back. Believe me."

"When will that be?"

"It's up to you. You decide."

"Ugh."

Why can't I marry one and live with her uneasily ever after? I've tried that.

"Take my picture again."

"I've taken enough pictures. I don't want to take any more pictures."

"Then I'll go on Tuesday."

"Tuesday. OK. That's tomorrow."

"Tuesday is tomorrow?"

"Right."

"Oh."

She grips the football and pretends to be about to throw it through the window.

"Do you ever capture somebody again after you've captured them once?"

"Almost unheard of."

"Why not?"

"It doesn't happen."

"Why not?"

"It just doesn't."

"Tomorrow. Oh my."

I go into the kitchen and begin washing the dishes—the more scutwork you do, the kindlier the light in which you are regarded, I have learned.

•

I enter her room. L. is standing there.

"What happened to your hand?" he asks.

"Nothing," I say.

Everyone looks at my bandaged hand for a moment—not long enough.

"Have you captured her?" I ask.

L. is the master, the nonpareil, the O. J. Simpson of our aberration.

"I have captured him," she says.

"Wait a minute. That's not how it works."

"I changed the rules," she says. "I will be happy to give you a copy of the new rules which I have written out here on this legal pad."

L. is smirking like a mink, obviously very pleased to have been captured by such a fine woman.

"But wait a minute," I say. "It's not Tuesday yet!"

"I don't care," she says. She is smiling. At L.

I go into the kitchen and begin scrubbing the oven with Easy-Off.

How original of her to change the rules! She is indeed a rare spirit.

"French Russian Roquefort or oil-and-vinegar," she says sometimes, in her sleep—I deduce that she has done some waitressing in her day.

•

The captured woman does a backward somersault from a standing position.

I applaud madly. My thumb hurts.

"Where is L.?"

"I sent him away."

"Why?"

"He had no interesting problems. Also he did a sketch of me which I don't like."

She shows me the charcoal sketch (L.'s facility is famous) and it is true that her beauty suffers just a bit, in this sketch. He must have been spooked a little by my photographs, which he did not surpass.

"Poor L."

The captured woman does another somersault. I applaud again. Is today Tuesday or Wednesday? I can't remember.

"Wednesday," she says. "Wednesday the kid goes to dance after which she usually spends the night with her pal Regina because Regina lives close to dance. So there's really no point in my going back on a Wednesday."

•

A week later she is still with me. She is departing by degrees.

If I tore her hair out, no one but me would love her. But she doesn't want me to tear her hair out.

I wear different shirts for her: red, orange, silver. We hold hands through the night.

I Bought a Little City

So I bought a little city (it was Galveston, Texas) and told everybody that nobody had to move, we were going to do it just gradually, very relaxed, no big changes overnight. They were pleased and suspicious. I walked down to the harbor where there were cotton warehouses and fish markets and all sorts of installations having to do with the spread of petroleum throughout the Free World, and I thought, A few apple trees here might be nice. Then I walked out on this broad boulevard which has all these tall thick palm trees maybe forty feet high in the center and oleanders on both sides, it runs for blocks and blocks and ends up opening up to the broad Gulf of Mexico—stately homes on both sides and a big Catholic church that looks more like a mosque and the Bishop's Palace and a handsome red brick affair where the Shriners meet. I thought, What a nice little city, it suits me fine.

It suited me fine so I started to change it. But softly, softly. I asked some folks to move out of a whole city block on I Street, and then I tore down their houses. I put the people into the Galvez Hotel, which is the nicest hotel in town, right on the seawall, and I made sure that every room had a beautiful view. Those people had wanted to stay at the Galvez Hotel all their lives and never had a chance before because they didn't have the money. They were delighted. I tore down their houses and made that empty block a park. We planted it all to hell and put some nice green iron benches in it and a little fountain—all standard stuff, we didn't try to be imaginative.

I was pleased. All the people who lived in the four blocks

surrounding the empty block had something they hadn't had before, a park. They could sit in it, and like that. I went and watched them sitting in it. There was already a black man there playing bongo drums. I hate bongo drums. I started to tell him to stop playing those goddamn bongo drums but then I said to myself, No, that's not right. You got to let him play his goddamn bongo drums if he feels like it, it's part of the misery of democracy, to which I subscribe. Then I started thinking about new housing for the people I had displaced, they couldn't stay in that fancy hotel forever.

But I didn't have any ideas about new housing, except that it shouldn't be too imaginative. So I got to talking to one of these people, one of the ones we had moved out, guy by the name of Bill Caulfield who worked in a wholesale-tobacco place down on Mechanic Street.

"So what kind of a place would you like to live in?" I asked him.

"Well," he said, "not too big."

"Uh-huh."

"Maybe with a veranda around three sides," he said, "so we could sit on it and look out. A screened porch, maybe."

"Whatcha going to look out at?"

"Maybe some trees and, you know, the lawn."

"So you want some ground around the house."

"That would be nice, yeah."

" 'Bout how much ground are you thinking of?"

"Well, not too much."

"You see, the problem is, there's only *x* amount of ground and everybody's going to want to have it to look at and at the same time they don't want to be staring at the neighbors. Private looking, that's the thing."

"Well, yes," he said. "I'd like it to be kind of private."

"Well," I said, "get a pencil and let's see what we can work out."

We started with what there was going to be to look at, which was damned difficult. Because when you look you don't want to be able to look at just one thing, you want to be able to shift your gaze. You need to be able to look at at least three things, maybe four. Bill Caulfield solved the problem. He showed me a box. I opened it up and inside was a jigsaw puzzle with a picture of the Mona Lisa on it.

"Lookee here," he said. "If each piece of ground was like a piece of this-here puzzle, and the tree line on each piece of property followed the outline of a piece of the puzzle—well, there you have it, QED and that's all she wrote."

"Fine," I said. "Where are the folk going to park their cars?"

"In the vast underground parking facility," he said.

"OK, but how does each householder gain access to his household?"

"The tree lines are double and shade beautifully paved walkways possibly bordered with begonias," he said.

"A lurkway for potential muggists and rapers," I pointed out.

"There won't be any such," Caulfield said, "because you've bought our whole city and won't allow that class of person to hang out here no more."

That was right. I had bought the whole city and could probably do that. I had forgotten.

"Well," I said finally, "let's give 'er a try. The only thing I don't like about it is that it seems a little imaginative."

We did and it didn't work out badly. There was only one complaint. A man named A. G. Bartie came to see me.

"Listen," he said, his eyes either gleaming or burning, I couldn't tell which, it was a cloudy day, "I feel like I'm living in this gigantic jiveass jigsaw puzzle."

He was right. Seen from the air, he was living in the middle of a titanic reproduction of the Mona Lisa, too, but I thought it best not to mention that. We allowed him to square off his property into a standard 60 × 100 foot lot and later some other people did that too—some people just like rectangles, I guess. I must say it improved the concept. You run across an occasional rectangle in Shady Oaks (we didn't want to call the development anything too imaginative) and it surprises you. That's nice.

I said to myself:

Got a little city
Ain't it pretty

By now I had exercised my proprietorship so lightly and if I do say so myself tactfully that I wondered if I was enjoying myself enough (and I had paid a heavy penny too—near to half my fortune). So I went out on the streets then and shot six thousand dogs. This gave me great satisfaction and you have no idea how wonderfully it improved the city for the better. This left us with a dog population of 165,000, as opposed to a human population of something like 89,000. Then I went down to the Galveston *News*, the morning paper, and wrote an editorial denouncing myself as the vilest creature the good God had ever placed upon the earth, and were we, the citizens of this fine community, who were after all free Americans of whatever race or creed, going to sit still while one man, *one man*, if indeed so vile a critter could be so called, etc. etc.? I gave it to the city desk and told them I wanted it on the front page in fourteen-point type, boxed. I did this just in case they might have hesitated to do it themselves, and because I'd seen that Orson Welles picture where the guy writes a nasty notice about his own wife's terrible singing, which I always thought was pretty decent of him, from some points of view.

A man whose dog I'd shot came to see me.

"You shot Butch," he said.

"Butch? Which one was Butch?"

"One brown ear and one white ear," he said. "Very friendly."

"Mister," I said, "I've just shot six thousand dogs, and you expect me to remember Butch?"

"Butch was all Nancy and me had," he said. "We never had no children."

"Well, I'm sorry about that," I said, "but I own this city."

"I know that," he said.

"I am the sole owner and I make all the rules."

"They told me," he said.

"I'm sorry about Butch but he got in the way of the big campaign. You ought to have had him on a leash."

"I don't deny it," he said.

"You ought to have had him inside the house."

"He was just a poor animal that had to go out sometimes."

"And mess up the streets something awful?"

"Well," he said, "it's a problem. I just wanted to tell you how I feel."

"You didn't tell me," I said. "How do you feel?"

"I feel like bustin' your head," he said, and showed me a short length of pipe he had brought along for the purpose.

"But of course if you do that you're going to get your ass in a lot of trouble," I said.

"I realize that."

"It would make you feel better, but then I own the jail and the judge and the po-lice and the local chapter of the American Civil Liberties Union. All mine. I could hit you with a writ of mandamus."

"You wouldn't do that."

"I've been known to do worse."

"You're a black-hearted man," he said. "I guess that's it. You'll roast in Hell in the eternal flames and there will be no mercy or cooling drafts from any quarter."

He went away happy with this explanation. I was happy to be a black-hearted man in his mind if that would satisfy the issue between us because that was a bad-looking piece of pipe he had there and I was still six thousand dogs ahead of the game, in a sense. So I owned this little city which was very, very pretty and I couldn't think of any more new innovations just then or none that wouldn't get me punctuated like the late Huey P. Long, former governor of Louisiana. The thing is, I had fallen in love with Sam Hong's wife. I had wandered into this store on Tremont Street where they sold Oriental novelties, paper lanterns, and cheap china and bamboo birdcages and wicker footstools and all that kind of thing. She was smaller than I was and I thought I had never seen that much goodness in a woman's face before. It was hard to credit. It was the best face I'd ever seen.

"I can't do that," she said, "because I am married to Sam."

"Sam?"

She pointed over to the cash register where there was a Chinese man, young and intelligent-looking and pouring that intelligent look at me with considered unfriendliness.

"Well, that's dismal news," I said. "Tell me, do you love me?"

"A little bit," she said, "but Sam is wise and kind and we have one and one-third lovely children."

She didn't look pregnant but I congratulated her anyhow, and then went out on the street and found a cop and sent him down to H Street to get me a bucket of Colonel Sanders' Kentucky Fried Chicken, extra crispy. I did that just out of meanness. He was humiliated but he had no choice. I thought:

> I own a little city
> Awful pretty
> Can't help people
> Can hurt them though
> Shoot their dogs
> Mess 'em up
> Be imaginative
> Plant trees
> Best to leave 'em alone?
> Who decides?
> Sam's wife is Sam's wife and coveting
> Is not nice.

So I ate the Colonel Sanders' Kentucky Fried Chicken, extra crispy, and sold Galveston, Texas, back to the interests. I took a bath on that deal, there's no denying it, but I learned something—don't play God. A lot of other people already knew that, but I have never doubted for a minute that a lot of other people are smarter than me, and figure things out quicker, and have grace and statistical norms on their side. Probably I went wrong by being too imaginative, although really I was guarding against that. I did very little, I was fairly restrained. God does a lot worse things, every day, in one little family, any family, than I did in that whole city. But He's got a better imagination than I do. For instance, I still covet Sam Hong's wife. That's torment. Still covet Sam Hong's wife, and probably always will. It's like having a tooth pulled. For a year. The same tooth. That's a sample of His imagination. It's powerful.

So what happened? What happened was that I took the other half of my fortune and went to Galena Park, Texas, and lived inconspicuously there, and when they asked me to run for the school board I said No, I don't have any children.

The Sergeant

The orderly looked at the paper and said, There's nothing wrong with this. Take it to room 400.

I said, Wait a minute.

The orderly looked at me. I said, Room 400.

I said something about a lawyer.

He got to his feet. You know what this is? he asked, pointing to an MP in the hall.

I said yes, I remembered.

OK. Room 400. Take this with you.

He handed me the paper.

I thought, They'll figure it out sooner or later. And: The doctor will tell them.

The doctor said, Hello, young trooper.

•

The other sergeant looked at me. How come you made sergeant so quick?

I was always a sergeant, I said. I was a sergeant the last time, too.

I got more time in grade, he said, so I outrank you.

I said not if you figured from my original date-of-rank which was sometime in '53.

Fifty-three, he said, what war was that?

I said the war with the Koreans.

I heard about it, he said. But you been away a long time.

I said that was true.

What we got here is a bunch of re-cruits, he said, they don't love the army much.

I said I thought they were all volunteers.

The e-conomic debacle volunteered 'em, he said, they heard the eagle shits once a month regularly.

I said nothing. His name was Tomgold.

They'll be rolling training grenades under your bunk, he said, just as soon as we teach 'em how to pull the pin.

I said they wouldn't do that to me because I wasn't supposed to be here anyway, that it was all a mistake, that I'd done all this before, that probably my discharge papers would come through any day now.

That's right, he said, you do look kind of old. Can you still screw?

•

I flicked on the barracks lights.

All right you men, I said.

But there was only one. He sat up in his bunk wearing skivvies, blinking in the light.

OK soldier roll out.

What time is it sarge?

It's five-forty-five soldier, get dressed and come with me. Where are the other men?

Probably haven't got back from town, sarge.

They have overnight passes?

Always got passes, sarge. Lots and lots of passes. Look, I got a pass too.

He showed me a piece of paper.

You want me to write you a pass, sarge?

I said I really wasn't supposed to be here at all, that I'd done all this before, that it was all a mistake.

You want me to fix you up with discharge papers, sarge? It'll cost you.

I said that if his section chief found out what he was doing they'd put him way back in the jailhouse.

You want me to cut some orders for you, sarge? You want a nice TDY to Hawaii?

I said I didn't want to get mixed up in anything.

If you're mixed up in this, then you got to get mixed up in that, he said. Would you turn them lights out, as you go?

•

The IG was a bird colonel with a jumper's badge and a general's pistol belt. He said, Well, sergeant, all I know is what's on the paper.

Yes sir, I said, but couldn't you check it out with the records center?

They're going to have the same piece of paper I have, sergeant.

I said that I had been overseas for sixteen months during the Korean War and that I had then been reassigned to Fort Lewis, Washington, where my CO had been a Captain Llewellyn.

None of this is in your 201 file, the IG said.

Maybe there's somebody else with my name.

Your name *and* your serial number?

Colonel, I did all this before. Twenty years ago.

You don't look that old, sergeant.

I'm forty-two.

Not according to this.

But that's wrong.

The colonel giggled. If you were a horse we could look at your teeth.

Yes, sir.

OK sergeant, I'll take it under advisement.

Thank you, sir.

I sat on the edge of my bed and looked at my two pairs of boots beautifully polished for inspection, my row of shirts hanging in my cubicle with all the shoulder patches facing the same way.

I thought: Of course, it's what I deserve. I don't deny that. Not for a minute.

•

Sergeant, he said, I'd be greatly obliged.

I said I wasn't sure I had fifty dollars to lend.

Look in your pocket there, sargie, the lieutenant said. Or maybe you have a bank account?

I said yes but not here.

My momma is sick and I need fifty dollars to take the bus home, he said. You don't want to impede my journey in the direction of my sick momma, do you?

What has she got? I asked.

Who?

Your mother.

I'll let you keep my 'lectric frying pan as security, the lieutenant said, showing it to me.

I'm not supposed to be in the army at all, I said. It's a fuckup of some kind.

Where are you from, sargie-san? You can cook yourself the dishes of your home region, in this frying pan.

I said the food in the NCO mess was pretty good, considering.

You're not going to lend me the fifty dollars?

I didn't say that, I said.

Sergeant, I can't *order* you to lend me the fifty dollars.

I know that, sir.

It's against regulations to do that, sergeant.

Yes, sir.

I can't read and write, sergeant.

You can't read and write?

If they find out, my ass is in terrible, terrible trouble, sergeant.

Not at all?

You want a golf club? I'll sell you a golf club. Fifty dollars.

I said I didn't play.

What about my poor momma, sergeant?

I said I was sorry.

I ride the blue bus, sergeant. Carries me clear to Gainesville. You ever ride the blue bus, sergeant?

•

I spoke to the chaplain who was playing the pinball machine at the PX. I said I didn't love the army much.

Nonsense, the chaplain said, you do, you do, you do or you wouldn't be here. Each of us is where we are, sergeant, because we want to be where we are and because God wants us to be where we are. Everybody in life is in the right place, believe me, may not seem that way sometimes but take it from me, take it from me, all part of the Divine plan, you got any quarters on you?

I gave him three quarters I had in my pocket.

Thank you, he said, I'm in the right place, you're in the right place, what makes you think you're so different from me? You think God doesn't know what He's doing? I'm right here ministering to the Screaming Falcons of the Thirty-third Division and if God didn't want me to be ministering to the wants and needs of the Screaming Falcons of the Thirty-third Division I wouldn't be here, would I? What makes you think you're so different from me? Works is what counts, boy, forget about anything else and look to your works, your works tell the story, nothing wrong with you, three stripes and two rockers, you're doing very well, now leave me, leave me, don't let me see your face again, you hear, sergeant? Good boy.

I thought: Works?

•

Two MPs stopped me at the main gate.

Where you headed, sergeant?

I said I was going home.

That's nice, said the taller of the two. You got any orders?

I showed them a pass.

How come you takin' off at this hour, sergeant? It's four o'clock in the morning. Where's your car?

I said I didn't have a car, thought I'd walk to town and catch a bus.

The MPs looked at me peculiarly.

In this fog and stuff? they asked.

I said I liked to walk in the early morning.

Where's your gear, sergeant? Where's your AWOL bag? You don't have a bag?

I reached into the pocket of my field jacket and showed them my razor and a fresh T-shirt.

What's your outfit, sergeant?

I told them.

The shorter MP said: But this razor's not clean.

We all crowded closer to look at the razor. It was not clean.

And this-here pass, he said, it's signed by General Zachary Taylor. Didn't he die?

•

I was holding on to a sort of balcony or shelf that had been tacked on to the third floor of the barracks. It was about to fall off the barracks and I couldn't get inside because somebody'd nailed the windows shut.

Hey, slick, came a voice from the parking lot, you gonna fall.

Yes yes, I said, I'm going to fall.

Jump down here, she said, and I'll show you the secrets of what's under my shirt.

Yeah yeah, I said, I've heard that before.

Jump little honey baby, she said, you won't regret it.

It's so far, I said.

Won't do nothin' 'cept break your head, she called, at the very most.

I don't want my head broken, I said, trying to get my fingers into that soft decayed pine.

Come on, GI, she said, you ain't comfortable up there.

I did all this, I said, once, twenty years ago. Why do I have to do it all over again?

You do look kind of old, she said, you an RA or something? Come down, my little viper, come down.

I either jumped or did not jump.

•

I thought: Of course, it's what I deserve. I don't deny it for a minute.

The captain said: Harm that man over there, sergeant.

Yes, sir. Which one?

The one in the red tie.

You want me to harm him?
Yes, with your M-16.
The man in the red tie. Blue suit.
Right. Go ahead. Fire.
Black shoes.
That's the one, sergeant, are you temporizing?
I think he's a civilian, sir.
You're refusing an order, sergeant?
No I'm not refusing sir I just don't think I can do it.
Fire your weapon sergeant.

He's not even in uniform, sir, he's wearing a suit. And he's not doing anything, he's just standing there.

You're refusing a direct order?

I just don't feel up to it, sir. I feel weak.

Well sergeant if you don't want to harm the man in the red tie I'll give you an alternative. You can stuff olives with little onions for the general's martinis.

That's the alternative?

There are eight hundred thousand gallon cans of olives over at the general's mess, sergeant. And four hundred thousand gallon cans of little onions. I think you ought to consider that.

I'm allergic to onions, sir. They make me break out. Terribly.

Well you've a nice little problem there, haven't you, sergeant? I'll give you thirty seconds.

•

The general was wearing a white short-sleeved shirt, blue seersucker skirt, and gold wire-rimmed glasses.

Four olives this time, sergeant.

I said: Penelope!

The School

Well, we had all these children out planting trees, see, because we figured that . . . that was part of their education, to see how, you know, the root systems . . . and also the sense of responsibility, taking care of things, being individually responsible. You know what I mean. And the trees all died. They were orange trees. I don't know why they died, they just died. Something wrong with the soil possibly or maybe the stuff we got from the nursery wasn't the best. We complained about it. So we've got thirty kids there, each kid had his or her own little tree to plant, and we've got these thirty dead trees. All these kids looking at these little brown sticks, it was depressing.

It wouldn't have been so bad except that just a couple of weeks before the thing with the trees, the snakes all died. But I think that the snakes—well, the reason that the snakes kicked off was that . . . you remember, the boiler was shut off for four days because of the strike, and that was explicable. It was something you could explain to the kids because of the strike. I mean, none of their parents would let them cross the picket line and they knew there was a strike going on and what it meant. So when things got started up again and we found the snakes they weren't too disturbed.

With the herb gardens it was probably a case of overwatering, and at least now they know not to overwater. The children were very conscientious with the herb gardens and some of them probably . . . you know, slipped them a little extra water when we weren't looking. Or maybe . . . well, I don't like to think about sabotage, although it did occur to us. I mean, it was something that crossed our minds. We were thinking that way probably because before that the gerbils had died, and the white mice had died, and the salamander . . . well, now they know not to carry them around in plastic bags.

Of course we *expected* the tropical fish to die, that was no surprise. Those numbers, you look at them crooked and they're belly-up on the surface. But the lesson plan called for a tropical-fish input at that point, there was nothing we could do, it happens every year, you just have to hurry past it.

We weren't even supposed to have a puppy.

We weren't even supposed to have one, it was just a puppy the Murdoch girl found under a Gristede's truck one day and she was afraid the truck would run over it when the driver had finished making his delivery, so she stuck it in her knapsack and brought it to school with her. So we had this puppy. As soon as I saw the puppy I thought, Oh Christ, I bet it will live for about two weeks and then . . . And that's what it did. It wasn't supposed to be in the classroom at all, there's some kind of regulation about it, but you can't tell them they can't have a puppy when the puppy is already there, right in front of them, running around on the floor and yap yap yapping. They named it Edgar—that is, they named it after me. They had a lot of fun running after it and yelling, "Here, Edgar! Nice Edgar!" Then they'd laugh like hell. They enjoyed the ambiguity. I enjoyed it myself. I don't mind being kidded. They made a little house for it in the supply closet and all that. I don't know what it died of. Distemper, I guess. It probably hadn't had any shots. I got it out of there before the kids got to school. I checked the supply closet each morning, routinely, because I knew what was going to happen. I gave it to the custodian.

And then there was this Korean orphan that the class adopted through the Help the Children program, all the kids brought in a quarter a month, that was the idea. It was an unfortunate thing, the kid's name was Kim and maybe we adopted him too late or something. The cause of death was not stated in the letter we got, they suggested we adopt another child instead and sent us some interesting case histories, but we didn't have the heart. The class took it pretty hard, they began (I think; nobody ever said anything to me directly) to feel that maybe there was something wrong with the school. But I don't think there's anything wrong with the school, particularly, I've seen better and I've seen worse. It was just a run of bad luck. We had an extraordinary number of parents passing away, for instance. There were I think two heart attacks and two suicides, one drowning, and four killed together in a car accident. One stroke. And we had the usual heavy mortality rate among the grandparents, or maybe it was heavier this year, it seemed so. And finally the tragedy.

The tragedy occurred when Matthew Wein and Tony Mavrogordo were playing over where they're excavating for the new federal office building. There were all these big wooden beams stacked, you know, at the edge of the excavation. There's a court case coming out of that, the parents are claiming that the beams were poorly stacked. I don't know what's true and what's not. It's been a strange year.

I forgot to mention Billy Brandt's father, who was knifed fatally when he grappled with a masked intruder in his home.

One day, we had a discussion in class. They asked me, where did they go? The trees, the salamander, the tropical fish, Edgar, the poppas and mommas, Matthew and Tony, where did they go? And I said, I don't know, I don't know. And they said, who knows? and I said, nobody knows. And they said, is death that which gives meaning to life? And I said, no, life is that which gives meaning to life. Then they said, but isn't death, considered as a fundamental datum, the means by which the taken-for-granted mundanity of the everyday may be transcended in the direction of—

I said, yes, maybe.

They said, we don't like it.

I said, that's sound.

They said, it's a bloody shame!

I said, it is.

They said, will you make love now with Helen (our teaching assistant) so that we can see how it is done? We know you like Helen.

I do like Helen but I said that I would not.

We've heard so much about it, they said, but we've never seen it.

I said I would be fired and that it was never, or almost never, done as a demonstration. Helen looked out of the window.

They said, please, please make love with Helen, we require an assertion of value, we are frightened.

I said that they shouldn't be frightened (although I am often frightened) and that there was value everywhere. Helen came and embraced me. I kissed her a few times on the brow. We held each other. The children were excited. Then there was a knock on the door, I opened the door, and the new gerbil walked in. The children cheered wildly.

The Great Hug

At the last breakfast after I told her, we had steak and eggs. Bloody Marys. Three pieces of toast. She couldn't cry, she tried. Balloon Man came. He photographed the event. He created the Balloon of the Last Breakfast After I Told Her—a butter-colored balloon. "This is the kind of thing I do so well," he said. Balloon Man is not modest. No one has ever suggested that. "This balloon is going to be extra-famous and acceptable, a documentation of raw human riches, the plain canvas flag of the thing. The Pin Lady will never be able to bust this balloon, never, not even if she hugs me for a hundred years." We were happy to have pleased him, to have contributed to his career.

The Balloon Man won't sell to kids.

Kids will come up to the Balloon Man and say, "Give us a blue balloon Man," and the Balloon Man will say, "Get outa here kids, these balloons are adults-only." And the kids will say, "C'mon, Balloon Man, give us a red balloon and a green balloon and a white balloon, we got the money." "Don't want any kid-money," the Balloon Man will say, "kid-money is wet and nasty and makes your hands wet and nasty and then you wipe 'em on your pants and your pants get all wet and nasty and you sit down to eat and the *chair* gets all wet and nasty, let that man in the brown hat draw near, he wants a balloon." And the kids will say, "Oh please Balloon Man, we want five yellow balloons that never pop, we want to make us a smithereen." "Ain't gonna make no smithereen outa my fine yellow balloons," says the Balloon Man, "your red balloon will pop sooner and your green balloon will pop later but your yellow balloon will never pop no matter how you stomp on it or stick it and besides the Balloon Man don't sell to kids, it's against his principles."

The Balloon Man won't let you take his picture. He has something to hide. He's superheavy Balloon Man, doesn't want the others to steal his moves. It's all in the gesture—the precise, reunpremeditated right move.

Balloon Man sells the Balloon of Fatigue and the Balloon of Ora Pro Nobis and the Rune Balloon and the Balloon of the Last Thing to Do at Night; these are saffron-, cinnamon-, salt-, and celery-colored, respectively. He sells the Balloon of Not Yet and the Balloon of Sometimes. He works the circus, every circus. Some people don't go to the circus and so don't meet the Balloon Man and don't get to buy a balloon. That's sad. Near to most people in any given city at any given time won't be at the circus. That's unfortunate. They don't get to buy a brown, whole-life-long cherishable Sir Isaiah Berlin Balloon. "I don't sell the Balloon Jejune," the Balloon Man will say, "let them other people sell it, let them other people have all that wet and nasty kid-money mitosising in their sock. That a camera you got there mister? Get away." Balloon Man sells the Balloon of Those Things I Should Have Done I Did Not Do, a beige balloon. And the Balloon of the Ballade of the Crazy Junta, crimson of course. Balloon Man stands in a light rain near the popcorn pushing the Balloon of Wish I Was, the Balloon of Busoni Thinking, the Balloon of the Perforated Septum, the Balloon of Not Nice. Which one is my balloon, Balloon Man? Is it the Balloon of the Cartel of Noose Makers? Is it the Balloon of God Knows I Tried?

One day the Balloon Man will meet the Pin Lady. It's in the cards, in the stars, in the entrails of sacred animals. Pin Lady is a woman with pins stuck in her couture, rows of pins and pins not in rows but placed irregularly here a pin there a pin, maybe eight thousand pins stuck in her couture or maybe ten thousand pins or twelve thousand pins. Pin Lady tells the truth. The embrace of Balloon Man and Pin Lady will be something to see. They'll roll down the hill together, someday. Balloon Man's arms will be wrapped around Pin Lady's pins and Pin Lady's embrangle will be wrapped about Balloon Man's balloons. They'll roll down the hill together. Pin Lady has the Pin of I Violently Desire. She has the Pin of Crossed Fingers Behind My Back, she has the Pin of Soft Talk, she has the Pin of No More and she is rumored to have the Pin of the Dazed Sachem's Last Request. She's into puncture. When puncture becomes widely accepted and praised, it will be the women who will have the sole license to perform it, Pin Lady says.

Pin Lady has the Pin of Tomorrow Night—a wicked pin, those who have seen it say. That great hug, when Balloon Man and Pin Lady roll down the hill together, will be frightening. The horses will run away in all directions. Ordinary people will cover their heads with shopping bags. I don't want to think about it. You blow up all them balloons yourself, Balloon Man? Or did you have help? Pin Lady, how come you're so aprickledededee? Was it something in your childhood?

Balloon Man will lead off with the Balloon of Grace Under Pressure, Do Not Pierce or Incinerate.

Pin Lady will counter with the Pin of Oh My, I Forgot.

Balloon Man will produce the Balloon of Almost Wonderful. Pin Lady will come back with the Pin of They Didn't Like Me Much. Balloon Man will sneak in there with the Balloon of the Last Exit Before the Toll is Taken. Pin Lady will reply with the Pin of One Never Knows for Sure. Balloon Man will propose the Balloon of Better Days. Pin Lady, the Pin of Whiter Wine.

It's gonna be *bad,* I don't want to think about it.

Pin Lady tells the truth. Balloon Man doesn't lie, exactly. How can the Quibbling Balloon be called a lie? Pin Lady is more straightforward. Balloon Man is less straightforward. Their stances are semiantireprophetical. They're falling down the hill together, two falls out of three. Pin him, Pin Lady. Expand, Balloon Man. When he created our butter-colored balloon, we felt better. A little better. The event that had happened to us went floating out into the world, was made useful to others. Balloon Man says, "I got here the Balloon of the Last Concert. It's not a bad balloon. Some people won't like it. Some people *will* like it. I got the Balloon of Too Terrible. Not every balloon can make you happy. Not every balloon can trigger glee. *But I insist that these balloons have a right to be heard!* Let that man in the black cloak step closer, he wants a balloon.

"The Balloon of Perhaps. My best balloon."

Our Work and Why We Do It

As admirable volume after admirable volume tumbled from the sweating presses . . .

The pressmen wiped their black hands on their pants and adjusted the web, giving it just a little more impression on the right side, where little specks of white had started to appear in the crisp, carefully justified black prose.

I picked up the hammer and said into the telephone, "Well, if he comes around here he's going to get a face full of hammer

"A four-pound hammer can mess up a boy's face pretty bad

"A four-pound hammer can make a bloody rubbish of a boy's face."

I hung up and went into the ink room to see if we had enough ink for the rest of the night's runs.

"Yes, those were weary days," the old printer said with a sigh. "Follow copy even if it flies out the window, we used to say, and oft—"

Just then the Wells Fargo man came in, holding a .38 loosely in his left hand as the manual instructs

It was pointed at the floor, as if he wished to

But then our treasurer, old Claiborne McManus

The knobs of the safe

Sweet were the visions inside.

He handed over the bundle of Alice Cooper T-shirts we had just printed up, and the Wells Fargo man grabbed them with his free hand, gray with experience, and saluted loosely with his elbow, and hurried the precious product out to the glittering fans.

And coming to work today I saw a brown Mercedes with a

weeping woman inside, her head was in her hands, a pretty blond back-of-the-neck, the man driving the Mercedes was paying no attention and

But today we are running the Moxxon Travel Guide in six colors

The problems of makeready, registration, show-through, and feed

Will the grippers grip the sheet correctly?

And I saw the figure 5 writ in gold

"Down time" was a big factor in the recent negotiations, just as "wash-up time" is expected to complicate the negotiations to come. Percy handed the two-pound can of yellow ink to William.

William was sitting naked in the bed wearing the black hat. Rowena was in the bed too, wearing the red blanket. We have to let them do everything they want to do, because they own the business. Often they scandalize the proofreaders, and then errors don't get corrected and things have to be reset, or additional errors are *inserted* by a proofreader with his mind on the shining thing he has just seen. Atlases are William's special field of interest. There are many places he has never been.

"Yesterday," William began

You have your way of life and we ours

A rush order for matchbook covers for Le Foie de Veau restaurant

The tiny matchbook-cover press is readied, the packing applied, the "Le Foie de Veau" form locked into place. We all stand around a small table watching the matchbook press at work. It is exactly like a toy steam engine. Everyone is very fond of it, although we also have a press big as a destroyer escort—that one has a crew of thirty-five, its own galley, its own sick bay, its own band. We print the currency of Colombia, and the Acts of the Apostles, and the laws of the land, and the fingerprints

"My dancing shoes have rusted," said Rowena, "because I have remained for so long in this bed."

Of criminals, and Grand Canyon calendars, and gummed labels, some things that don't make any sense, but that isn't our job, to make sense of things—our job is to kiss the paper with the form or plate, as the case may be, and make sure it's not getting too much ink, and worry about the dot structure of the engravings, or whether a tiny shim is going to work up during the run and split a fountain.

William began slambanging Rowena's dancing shoes with steel wool. "Yesterday," he said

Salesmen were bursting into the room with new orders, each salesman's person bulging with new orders

And old Lucien Frank was pushing great rolls of Luxus Semi-Fine No. 2 through the room with a donkey engine

"Yesterday," William said, "I saw six Sabrett hot-dog stands on wheels marching in single file down the middle of Jane Street followed at a slow trot by a police cruiser. They had yellow-and-blue umbrellas and each hot-dog stand was powered by an elderly man who looked ill. The elderly men not only looked ill but were physically small—not more than five-six, any of them. They were heading I judged for the Sixth Precinct. Had I had the black hat with me, and sufficient men and horses and lariats and .30–30s, and popular support from the masses and a workable revolutionary ideology and/or a viable myth pattern, I would have rescued them. Removed them to the hills where we would have feasted all night around the fires on tasty Sabrett hot dogs and maybe steaming butts of Ballantine ale, and had bun-splitting contests, sauerkraut-hurling"

He opened the two-pound can of yellow ink with his teeth.

"You are totally wired," Rowena said tenderly

"A boy *likes* to be"

We turned away from this scene, because of what they were about to do, and had some more vodka. Because although we, too, are wired most of the time, it is not the vodka. It is, rather . . . What I mean is, if you have ink in your blood it's hard to get it out of your hands, or to keep your hands off the beautiful typefaces carefully distributed in the huge typecases

Annonce Grotesque
Compacta

Cooper Black
Helvetica Light
Melior
Microgramma Bold
Profil
Ringlet

And one of our volumes has just received a scathing notice in *Le Figaro*, which we also print . . . Should we smash the form? But it's *our* form . . .

Old Kermit Dash has just hurt his finger in the papercutter. "It's not so bad, Kermit," I said, binding up the wound. "I'm scared of the papercutter myself. Always have been. Don't worry about it. Think instead of the extra pay you will be drawing for that first joint, for the rest of your life. Now get back in there and cut paper." I whacked him on the rump, although he is eighty, almost rumpless

We do the *Oxford Book of American Grub*

Rowena handed Bill another joint—I myself could be interested in her, if she were not part of Management and thus "off limits" to us fiercely loyal artisans. And now, the problem of where to hide the damning statistics in the Doe Airframe Annual Report. Hank Witteborn, our chief designer, suggests that they just be "accidentally left out." The idea has merit, but

Crash! Someone has just thrown something through our biggest window. It is a note with a brick wrapped around it:

Sirs:
If you continue to live and breathe
If you persist in walking the path of
Coating the façade of exploitation with
the stucco of good printing

Faithfully

What are they talking about? Was it not we who had the contract for the entire Tanberian Revolution, from the original manifestos hand-set in specially nicked and scarred Blood Gothic to the letterheads of the Office of Permanent Change

& Price Control (18 pt. Ultima on a 20-lb. laid stock)? But William held up a hand, and because he was the boss, we let him speak.

"It is good to be a member of the bourgeoisie," he said. "A boy *likes* being a member of the bourgeoisie. Being a member of the bourgeoisie is *good* for a boy. It makes him feel *warm* and *happy*. He can worry about his *plants*. His green plants. His plants and his quiches. His property taxes. The productivity of his workers. His plants/quiches/property taxes/workers/ Land Rover. His *sword hilt*. His"

William is sometimes filled with self-hatred, but we are not. We have our exhilarating work, and our motto, "Grow or Die," and our fringe benefits, and our love for William (if only he would take his hands off Rowena's hip bones during business hours, if only he would take off the black hat and put on a pair of pants, a vest, a shirt, socks, and)

I was watching over the imposition of the Detroit telephone book. Someone had just dropped all the H's—a thing that happens sometimes.

"Don't anybody move! Now, everybody bend over and pick up the five slugs nearest him. Now, the next five. Easy does it. Somebody call Damage Control and have them send up extra vodka, lean meat, and bandages. Now, the next five. Anybody that steps on a slug gets the hammer in the mouth. Now, the next"

If only we could confine ourselves to matchbook covers!

But matchbook covers are not our destiny. Our destiny is to accomplish 1.5 million impressions per day. In the next quarter, that figure will be upped by twelve percent, unless

"Leather," William says.

"Leather?"

"*Leather,*" he says with added emphasis. "Like they cover cows with."

William's next great idea will be in the area of leather. I am glad to know this. His other great ideas have made the company great.

The new machine for printing underground telephone poles
The new machine for printing smoke on smoked hams

The new machine for writing the figure 5 in gold

All of this weakens the heart. I have the hammer, I will smash anybody who threatens, however remotely, the company way of life. We know what we're doing. The vodka ration is generous. Our reputation for excellence is unexcelled, in every part of the world. And will be maintained until the destruction of our art by some other art which is just as good but which, I am happy to say, has not yet been invented.

The Crisis

—On the dedication page of the rebellion, we see the words "To Clementine." A fine sentiment, miscellaneous organ music next, and, turning several pages, massed orange flags at the head of the column. This will not be easy, but neither will it be hard. Good will is everywhere, and the lighthearted song of the gondoliers is heard in the distance.

—Yes, success is everything. Morally important as well as useful in a practical way.

—What have the rebels captured thus far? One zoo, not our best zoo, and a cemetery. The rebels have entered the cages of the tamer animals and are playing with them, gently.

—Things can get better, and in my opinion will.

—Their Graves Registration procedures are scrupulous—accurate and fair.

—There's more to it than playing guitars and clapping along. Although that frequently gets people in the mood.

—Their methods are direct, not subtle. Dissolution, leaching, sandblasting, cracking and melting of fireproof doors, condemnation, water damage, slide presentations, clamps and buckles.

—And skepticism, although absolutely necessary, leads to not very much.

—The rebels have eaten all the grass on the spacious lawns surrounding the President's heart. That vast organ, the President's heart, beats now on a bald plain.

—It depends on what you want to do. Sometimes people don't know. I mean, don't know even that.

—Clementine is thought to be one of the great rebel leaders of the half-century. Her hat has four cockades.

—I loved her for a while. Then, it stopped.

—Rebel T-shirts, camouflaged as ordinary T-shirts by an intense whiteness no eye can pierce, are worn everywhere.

—I don't know why it stopped, it just stopped. That's happened several times. Is something wrong with me?

—Closely supervised voting in the other cantons produced results clearly favorable to neither faction, but rather a sort of generalized approbation which could be appropriated by anyone who had need of it.

—A greater concentration on one person than you normally find. Then, zip.

—Three or four photographs of the rebel generals, tinted glasses, blond locks blowing in the wind, have been released to the world press, in billboard size.

—Whenever I go there, on the Metroliner, I begin quietly thinking about how to help: better planning, more careful management, a more equal distribution of income, education. Or something new.

—There have been mistakes. No attempt was made to seize Broadcasting House—a fundamental error. The Household Cavalry was not subverted, discontented junior officers of the regular forces were not sought out and offered promotions, or money . . .

—Yes, an afternoon on the links! I'd never been out there before—so green and full of holes and flags. I'm afraid we got in the way, people were shouting at us to get out of the way. We had thought they'd let us just stand there and look or walk around and look, but apparently that's not done. So we went to the pro shop and rented some clubs and bags, and put the bags on our shoulders, and that got us by for a while. We walked around with our clubs and bags, enjoying the cool green and the bright, attractive sportswear of the other participants. That helped some, but we were still under some mysterious system of rules we didn't understand, always in the wrong place at the wrong time, it seemed, yelled at and bumping into people. So finally we said to hell with it and left the links; we didn't want to spoil anybody's fun, so we took the bus back to town, first returning the clubs and bags to the pro shop. Next, we will try the jai-alai courts and soccer fields, of which we have heard the most encouraging things.

—Blocking forces were not provided to isolate the Palace. Diversions were not created to draw off key units. The airports were not invested nor were the security services neutralized. Important civilians were not cultivated and won over, and propaganda was neglected. Photographs of the rebel leaders were distributed but these "leaders" were actors, selected for their red brick foreheads and chins and blond, flowing locks.

—Yes, they pulled some pretty cute tricks. I had to laugh, sometimes, wondering: What has this to do with you and me? Our frontiers are the marble lobbies of these buildings. True, mortar pits ring the elevator banks but these must be seen as friendly, helpful gestures toward certification of the crisis.

—The present goal of the individual in group enterprises is to avoid dominance; leadership is felt to be a character disorder. Clementine has not heard this news, and thus invariably falls forward, into the thickets of closure.

—Well, maybe so. When I knew her she was just an ordinary woman—wonderful, of course, but not transfigured.

—The black population has steered clear of taking sides, sits home and plays, over and over, the sexy part of *Tristan und Isolde*.

—We feel only twenty-five percent of what we ought to feel, according to recent findings. I know that "ought" is a loaded word, in this context.

—Are the great bells of the cathedrals an impoverishment of the folk (on one level) or an enrichment of the folk (on another level), and how are these values to be weighted, how reconciled?

—They won't do anything for the poor people, no matter who gets in, and that's a fact. I wonder if they can.

—The raid on the okra fields was not a success; the rebel answering service just hisses.

—There's such a thing as a flash point. But sometimes you can't find it, even when you know how.

—Our pride in having a rebellion of our own, even a faint,

rather ill-organized one, has turned us once again toward the kinds of questions that deserve serious attention.

—Is something wrong with me? I'm not complaining, just asking. We all have our work, it's the small scale that disturbs. Maybe twenty-five percent is high. They say he's one of the best, but most people don't need his specialty very often. Of course, I admit that when they need it they need it. Cattle too dream of death, and are afraid of it. I don't mean that as an excuse. I did love her for a while, I remember. His strategy is to be cheerful without being optimistic; I'll go along with that. Maybe we ought to have another election. The police are never happier than on Election Day, when their relation to the citizens assumes a calm, even jokey tone. They are allowed to take off their hats. Fetching coffee in paper cups for the poll watchers, or being fetched coffee by them, they stand chest out not too close to the voting machines in fresh-pressed uniforms, spit-polished boots. Bold sergeants arrive and depart in patrol cars, or dash about making arrangements, and only the plainclothesmen are lonely.

—As a magician works with the unique compressibility of doves, finding some, losing others in the same silk foulard, so the rebels fold scratchy, relaxed meanings into their smallest actions.

—I don't quarrel with their right to do it. It's the means I'm worried about.

—Self-criticism sessions were held, but these produced more criticism than could usefully be absorbed or accommodated.

—I decided that something is not wrong with me.

—The rebels have failed to make promises. Promises are, perhaps, the nut of the matter. Had they promised everyone free groceries, for example, or one night of love, then their efforts might have—

—Yes, success is everything. Failure is more common. Most achieve a sort of middling thing, but fortunately one's situation is always blurred, you never know absolutely quite where you are. This allows, if not peace of mind, ongoing attention to other aspects of existence.

—But even a poor rebellion has its glorious moments. Let me list some of them. When the flag fell over, and Clem picked it up. When the high priest smeared himself all over with bacon fat and was attacked by red dogs, and Clem scared them off with her bomb. When it was discovered that all of the drumsticks had been left back at the base, and Clem fashioned new ones from ordinary dowels, bought at the hardware store. When gluttons made the line break and waver, and Clem stopped it by stamping her foot, again and again and again.

—When she gets back from the hills, I intend to call her up. It's worth a try.

—Distant fingers from the rebel forces are raised in fond salute.

—The rebel brigades are reading Leskov's *Why Are Books Expensive in Kiev?*

—Three rebellions ago, the air was fresher. The soft pasting noises of the rebel billposters remind us of Oklahoma, where everything is still the same.

Cortés and Montezuma

Because Cortés lands on a day specified in the ancient writings, because he is dressed in black, because his armor is silver in color, a certain *ugliness* of the strangers taken as a group—for these reasons, Montezuma considers Cortés to be Quetzalcoatl, the great god who left Mexico many years before, on a raft of snakes, vowing to return.

Montezuma gives Cortés a carved jade drinking cup.

Cortés places around Montezuma's neck a necklace of glass beads strung on a cord scented with musk.

Montezuma offers Cortés an earthenware platter containing small pieces of meat lightly breaded and browned which Cortés declines because he knows the small pieces of meat are human fingers.

Cortés sends Montezuma a huge basket of that Spanish bread of which Montezuma's messengers had said, on first encountering the Spaniards, "As to their food, it is like human food, it is white and not heavy, and slightly sweet . . ."

Cortés and Montezuma are walking, down by the docks. Little green flies fill the air. Cortés and Montezuma are holding hands; from time to time one of them disengages a hand to brush away a fly.

Montezuma receives new messages, in picture writing, from the hills. These he burns, so that Cortés will not learn their contents. Cortés is trimming his black beard.

Doña Marina, the Indian translator, is sleeping with Cortés in the palace given him by Montezuma. Cortés awakens; they share a cup of chocolate. *She looks tired,* Cortés thinks.

Down by the docks, Cortés and Montezuma walk, holding hands. "Are you acquainted with a Father Sanchez?" Montezuma asks. "Sanchez, yes, what's he been up to?" says Cortés. "Overturning idols," says Montezuma. "Yes," Cortés says vaguely, "yes, he does that, everywhere we go."

At a concert later that evening, Cortés is bitten on the ankle by a green insect. The bug crawls into his velvet slipper. Cortés removes the slipper, feels around inside, finds the bug and removes it. "Is this poisonous?" he asks Doña Marina. "Perfectly," she says.

Montezuma himself performs the operation upon Cortés's swollen ankle. He lances the bitten place with a sharp knife, then sucks the poison from the wound, spits. Soon they are walking again, down by the docks.

Montezuma writes, in a letter to his mother: "The new forwardness of the nobility has come as a welcome relief. Whereas formerly members of the nobility took pains to hide among the general population, to pretend that they were ordinary people, they are now flaunting themselves and their position in the most disgusting ways. Once again they wear scarlet sashes from shoulder to hip, even on the boulevards; once again they prance about in their great powdered wigs; once again they employ lackeys to stand in pairs on little shelves at the rear of their limousines. The din raised by their incessant visiting of one another is with us from noon until early in the morning . . .

"This flagrant behavior is, as I say, welcome. For we are all tired of having to deal with their manifold deceptions, of uncovering their places of concealment, of keeping track of their movements—in short, of having to think about them, of having to *remember* them. Their new assertiveness, however much it reminds us of the excesses of former times, is easier. The interesting question is, what has emboldened the nobility to emerge from obscurity at this time? Why now?

"Many people here are of the opinion that it is a direct consequence of the plague of devils we have had recently. It is easily seen that, against a horizon of devils, the reappearance of the nobility can only be considered a more or less tolerable circumstance—they themselves must have realized this. Not since the late years of the last Bundle have we had so many spitting, farting, hair-shedding devils abroad. Along with the devils there have been roaches, roaches big as ironing boards. Then, too, we have the Spaniards . . ."

A group of great lords hostile to Montezuma holds a secret meeting in Vera Cruz, under the special protection of the god Smoking Mirror. Debate is fierce; a heavy rain is falling; new arrivals crowd the room.

Doña Marina, although she is the mistress of Cortés, has an Indian lover of high rank as well. Making her confession to Father Sanchez, she touches upon this. "His name is Cuitlahuac? This may be useful politically. I cannot give you absolution, but I will remember you in my prayers."

In the gardens of Tenochtitlán, whisperers exchange strange new words: *guillotine, white pepper, sincerity, temperament.*

Cortés's men break through many more walls but behind these walls they find, invariably, only the mummified carcasses of dogs, cats, and sacred birds.

Down by the docks, Cortés and Montezuma walk, holding hands. Cortés has employed a detective to follow Montezuma; Montezuma has employed a detective to follow Father Sanchez. "There are only five detectives of talent in Tenochtitlán," says Montezuma. "There are others, but I don't use them. Visions are best—better than the best detective."

Atop the great Cue, or pyramid, Cortés strikes an effigy of the god Blue Hummingbird and knocks off its golden mask; an image of the Virgin is installed in its place.

"The heads of the Spaniards," says Doña Marina, "Juan de Escalante and the five others, were arranged in a row on a pike. The heads of their horses were arranged in another row on another pike, set beneath the first."

Cortés screams.

The guards run in, first Cristóbal de Olid, and following him Pedro de Alvarado and then de Ordás and de Tapia.

Cortés is raving. He runs from the palace into the plaza where he meets and is greeted by Montezuma. Two great lords stand on either side of Montezuma supporting his arms, which are spread wide in greeting. They fold Montezuma's arms around Cortés. Cortés speaks urgently into Montezuma's ear.

Montezuma removes from his bosom a long cactus thorn and pricks his ear with it repeatedly, until the blood flows.

Doña Marina is walking, down by the docks, with her lover Cuitlahuac, Lord of the Place of the Dunged Water. "When I was young," says Cuitlahuac, "I was at school with Montezuma. He was, in contrast to the rest of us, remarkably chaste. A very religious man, a great student—I'll wager that's what they talk about, Montezuma and Cortés. Theology." Doña Marina tucks a hand inside his belt, at the back.

Bernal Diaz del Castillo, who will one day write *The True History of the Conquest of New Spain*, stands in a square whittling upon a piece of mesquite. The Proclamation of Vera Cruz is read, in which the friendship of Cortés and Montezuma is denounced as contrary to the best interests of the people of Mexico, born and yet unborn.

Cortés and Montezuma are walking, down by the docks. "I especially like the Holy Ghost. Qua idea," says Montezuma. "The other God, the Father, is also—" "One God, three Persons," Cortés corrects gently. "That the Son should be sacrificed," Montezuma continues, "seems to me wrong. It seems to me He should be sacrificed *to*. Furthermore," Montezuma stops and taps Cortés meaningfully on the chest with a brown forefinger, "where is the Mother?"

Bernal asks Montezuma, as a great favor, for a young pretty woman; Montezuma sends him a young woman of good family, together with a featherwork mantle, some crickets in cages, and a quantity of freshly made soap. Montezuma observes, of Bernal, that "he seems to be a gentleman."

"The ruler prepares dramas for the people," Montezuma says.

Cortés, sitting in an armchair, nods.

"Because the cultivation of maize requires on the average only fifty days' labor per person per year, the people's energies may be invested in these dramas—for example the eternal struggle to win, to retain, the good will of Smoking Mirror, Blue Hummingbird, Quetzalcoatl . . ."

Cortés smiles and bows.

"Easing the psychological strain on the ruler who would otherwise be forced to face alone the prospect of world collapse, the prospect of the world folding in on itself . . ."

Cortés blinks.

"If the drama is not of my authorship, if events are not controllable by me—"

Cortés has no reply.

"Therefore it is incumbent upon you, dear brother, to disclose to me the ending or at least what you know of the drama's probable course so that I may attempt to manipulate it in a favorable direction with the application of what magic is left to me."

Cortés has no reply.

Breaking through a new wall, Cortés's men discover, on the floor of a chamber behind the wall, a tiny puddle of gold. The Proclamation is circulated throughout the city; is sent to other cities.

Bernal builds a stout hen coop for Doña Marina. The sky over Tenochtitlán darkens; flashes of lightning; then rain sweeping off the lake.

Down by the docks, Cortés and Montezuma take shelter in a doorway. "Doña Marina translated it; I have a copy," says Cortés.

"When you smashed Blue Hummingbird with the crowbar—"

"I was rash. I admit it."

"You may take the gold with you. All of it. My gift."

"Your Highness is most kind."

"Your ships are ready. My messengers say their sails are as many as the clouds over the water."

"I cannot leave until all of the gold in Mexico, past, present and future, is stacked in the holds."

"Impossible on the face of it."

"I agree. Let us talk of something else."

Montezuma notices that a certain amount of white lint has accumulated on his friend's black velvet doublet. He thinks: *She should take better care of him.*

In bed with Cortés, Doña Marina displays for his eyes her beautiful golden buttocks, which he strokes reverently. A tiny green fly is buzzing about the room; Cortés brushes it away with a fly whisk made of golden wire. She tells him about a vision. In the vision Montezuma is struck in the forehead by a large stone, and falls. His enraged subjects hurl more stones.

"Don't worry," says Cortés. "Trust me."

Father Sanchez confronts Cortés with the report of the detective he has hired to follow Doña Marina, together with other reports, documents, photographs. Cortés orders that all of the detectives in the city be arrested, that the profession of detective be abolished forever in Tenochtitlán, and that Father Sanchez be sent back to Cuba in chains.

In the marketplaces and theaters of the city, new words are passed about: *tranquillity, vinegar, entitlement, schnell.*

On another day Montezuma and Cortés and Doña Marina and the guard of Cortés and certain great lords of Tenochtitlán leave their palaces and are carried in palanquins to the part of the city called Cotaxtla.

There, they halt before a great house and dismount.

"What is this place?" Cortés asks, for he has never seen it before.

Montezuma replies that it is the meeting place of the Aztec council or legislature which formulates the laws of his people.

Cortés expresses surprise and states that it had been his understanding that Montezuma is an absolute ruler answerable to no one—a statement Doña Marina tactfully neglects to translate lest Montezuma be given offense by it.

Cortés, with his guard at his back and Montezuma at his right hand, enters the building.

At the end of a long hallway he sees a group of functionaries each of whom wears in his ears long white goose quills filled with powdered gold. Here Cortés and his men are fumigated with incense from large pottery braziers, but Montezuma is not, the major-domos fix their eyes on the ground and do not look at him but greet him with great reverence saying, "Lord, my Lord, my Great Lord."

The party is ushered through a pair of tall doors of fragrant cedar into a vast chamber hung with red and yellow banners. There, on low wooden benches divided by a broad aisle, sit the members of the council, facing a dais. There are perhaps three hundred of them, each wearing affixed to his buttocks a pair of mirrors as is appropriate to his rank. On the dais are three figures of considerable majesty, the one in the center raised somewhat above his fellows; behind them, on the wall, hangs a great wheel of gold with much intricate featherwork depicting a whirlpool with the features of the goddess Chalchihuitlicue in the center. The council members sit in attitudes of rigid attention, arms held at their sides, chins lifted, eyes fixed on the dais. Cortés lays a hand on the shoulder of one of them, then recoils. He raps with his knuckles on that shoulder which gives forth a hollow sound. "They are pottery," he says to Montezuma. Montezuma winks. Cortés begins to laugh. Montezuma begins to laugh. Cortés is choking, hysterical. Cortés and Montezuma run around the great hall, dodging in and out of the rows of benches, jumping into the laps of one or another of the clay figures, overturning some, turning others backwards in their seats. "I am the State!" shouts Montezuma, and Cortés shouts, "Mother of God, forgive this poor fool who doesn't know what he is saying!"

In the kindest possible way, Cortés places Montezuma under house arrest.

"Best you come to stay with me a while."

"Thank you but I'd rather not."

"We'll have games and in the evenings, home movies."

"The people wouldn't understand."

"We've got Pitalpitoque shackled to the great chain."

"I thought it was Quintalbor."

"Pitalpitoque, Quintalbor, Tendile."

"I'll send them chocolate."

"Come away, come away, come away with me."

"The people will be frightened."

"What do the omens say?"

"I don't know I can't read them anymore."

"Cutting people's hearts out, forty, fifty, sixty at a crack."

"It's the custom around here."

"The people of the South say you take too much tribute."

"Can't run an empire without tribute."

"Our Lord Jesus Christ loves you."

"I'll send Him chocolate."

"Come away, come away, come away with me."

Down by the docks, Cortés and Montezuma are walking with Charles V, Emperor of Spain. Doña Marina follows at a respectful distance carrying two picnic baskets containing many delicacies: caviar, white wine, stuffed thrushes, gumbo.

Charles V bends to hear what Montezuma is saying; Cortés brushes from the person of the Emperor little green flies, using a fly whisk made of golden wire. "Was there no alternative?" Charles asks. "I did what I thought best," says Cortés, "proceeding with gaiety and conscience." "I am murdered," says Montezuma.

The sky over Tenochtitlán darkens; flashes of lightning; then rain sweeping off the lake.

The pair walking down by the docks, hand in hand, the ghost of Montezuma rebukes the ghost of Cortés. "Why did you not throw up your hand, and catch the stone?"

The New Music

—What did you do today?

—Went to the grocery store and Xeroxed a box of English muffins, two pounds of ground veal and an apple. In flagrant violation of the Copyright Act.

—You had your nap, I remember that—

—I had my nap.

—Lunch, I remember that, there was lunch, slept with Susie after lunch, then your nap, woke up, right?, went Xeroxing, right?, read a book not a whole book but part of a book—

—Talked to Happy on the telephone saw the seven o'clock news did not wash the dishes want to clean up some of this mess?

—If one does nothing but listen to the new music, everything else drifts, goes away, frays. Did Odysseus feel this way when he and Diomedes decided to steal Athene's statue from the Trojans, so that they would become dejected and lose the war? I don't think so, but who is to know what effect the new music of that remote time had on its hearers?

—Or how it compares to the new music of this time?

—One can only conjecture.

—Ah well. I was talking to a girl, talking to her mother actually but the daughter was very much present, on the street. The daughter was absolutely someone you'd like to take to bed and hug and kiss, if you weren't too old. If she weren't too young. She was a wonderful-looking young woman and she was looking at me quite seductively, very seductively, *smoldering* a bit, and I was thinking quite well of myself, very well indeed, thinking myself quite the— Until I realized she was just practicing.

—Yes, I still think of myself as a young man.

—Yes.

—A slightly old young man.

—That's not unusual.

—A slightly old young man still advertising in the trees and rivers for a mate.

—Yes.

—Being clean.

—You're very clean.

—Cleaner than most.

—It's not escaped me. Your cleanness.

—Some of these people aren't clean. People you meet.

—What can you do?

—Set an example. Be clean.

—Dig it, dig it.

—I got three different shower heads. Different degrees of sting.

—Dynamite.

—I got one of these Finnish pads that slip over the hand.

—*Numero uno.*

—Pedicare. That's another thing.

—Think you're the mule's eyebrows don't you?

—No. I feel like Insufficient Funds.

—Feel like a busted-up car by the side of the road stripped of value.

—Feel like *I don't like this!*

—You're just a little down, man, down, that's what they call it, down.

—Well how come they didn't bring us no ring of roses with a purple silk sash with gold lettering on that mother? How come that?

—Dunno baby. Maybe we lost?

—How could we lose? How could we? We!

—We were standing tall. Ready to hand them their asses, clean their clocks. Yet maybe—

—I remember the old days when we almost automatically—

—Yes. Almost without effort—

—Right. Come in, Commander. Put it right there, anywhere will do, let me move that for you. Just put that sucker down right there. An eleven-foot-high silver cup!

—Beautifully engraved, with dates.

—Beautifully engraved, with dates. That was then.

—Well. Is there help coming?

—I called the number for help and they said there was no more help.

—I'm taking you to Pool.

—I've been there.

—I'm taking you to Pool, city of new life.

—Maybe tomorrow or another day.

—Pool, the revivifier.

—Oh man I'm not up for it.

—Where one can taste the essences, get swindled into health.

—I got things to do.

—That lonesome road. It ends in Pool.

—Got to chop a little cotton, go by the drugstore.

—Ever been to Pool?

—Yes I've been there.

—Pool, city of new hope.

—Get my ocarina tuned, sew a button on my shirt.

—Have you traveled much? Have you traveled enough?

—I've traveled a bit.

—Got to go away 'fore you can get back, that's fundamental.

—The joy of return is my joy. Satisfied by a walk around the block.

—Pool. Have you seen the new barracks? For the State Police? They used that red rock they have around there, quite a handsome structure, dim and red.

—Do the cops like it?

—No one has asked them. But they could hardly . . . I mean it's new.

—Got to air my sleeping bag, scrub up my canteen.

—Have you seen the new amphitheater? Made out of red rock. They play all the tragedies.

—Yeah I've seen it that's over by the train station right?

—No it's closer to the Great Lyceum. The Great Lyceum glowing like an ember against the hubris of the city.

—I could certainly use some home fries 'long about now. Home fries and ketchup.

—Pool. The idea was that it be one of those new towns. Where everyone would be happier. The regulations are quite strict. They don't let people have cars.

—Yes, I was in on the beginning. I remember the charette, I was asked to prepare a paper. But I couldn't think of anything. I stood there wearing this blue smock stenciled with the Pool emblem, looked rather like a maternity gown. I couldn't think of anything to say. Finally I said I would go along with the group.

—The only thing old there is the monastery, dates from 1720 or thereabouts. Has the Dark Virgin, the Virgin is black, as is the Child. Dates from 1720 or around in there.

—I've seen it. Rich fare, extraordinarily rich, makes you want to cry.

—And in the fall the circus comes. Plays the red rock gardens where the carved red asters, carved red phlox, are set off by borders of yellow beryl.

—I've seen it. Extraordinarily rich.

—So it's settled, we'll go to Pool, there'll be routs and revels, maybe a sock hop, maybe a nuzzle or two on the terrace with one of the dazzling Pool beauties—

—Not much for nuzzling, now. I mostly kneel at their feet, knit for them or parse for them—

—And the Pool buffalo herd. Six thousand beasts. All still alive.

—Each house has its grand lawns and grounds, brass candlesticks, thrice-daily mail delivery. Elegant widowed women living alone in large houses, watering lawns with whirling yellow sprinklers, studying the patterns of the grass, searching out brown patches to be sprinkled. Sometimes there is a grown child in the house, or an almost-grown one, working for a school or hospital in a teaching or counseling position. Frequently there are family photographs on the walls of the house, about which you are encouraged to ask questions. At dusk medals are awarded those who have made it through the day, the Cross of St. Jaime, the Cross of St. Em.

—Meant to be one of those new towns where everyone would be happier, much happier, that was the idea.

—Serenity. Peace. The dead are shown in art galleries, framed. Or sometimes, put on pedestals. Not much different from the practice elsewhere except that in Pool they display the actual—

—Person.

—Yes.

—And they play a tape of the guy or woman talking, right next to his or her—

—Frame or pedestal.

—Prerecorded.

—Naturally.

—Shocked white faces talking.

—Killed a few flowers and put them in pots under the faces, everybody does that.

—Something keeps drawing you back like a magnet.

—Watching the buffalo graze. It can't be this that I've waited for, I've waited too long. I find it intolerable, all this putter. Yet in the end, wouldn't mind doing a little grazing myself, it would look a little funny.

—Is there bluegrass in heaven? Make inquiries. I saw the streets of Pool, a few curs broiling on spits.

—And on another corner, a man spinning a goat into gold.

—Pool projects positive images of itself through the great medium of film.

—Cinemas filled with industrious product.

—Real films. Sent everywhere.

—Film is the great medium of this century—hearty, giggling film.

—So even if one does not go there, one may assimilate the meaning of Pool.

—I'd just like to rest and laze around.

—Soundtracks in Burmese, Italian, Twi, and other tongues.

—One film is worth a thousand words. At least a thousand.

—There's a film about the new barracks, and a film about the new amphitheater.

—Good. Excellent.

—In the one about the new barracks we see Squadron A at morning roll call, tense and efficient. "Mattingly!" calls the sergeant. "Yo!" says Mattingly. "Morgan!" calls the sergeant. "Yo!" says Morgan.

—A fine bunch of men. Nervous, but fine.

—In the one about the amphitheater, an eight-day dramatization of Eckermann's *Conversations with Goethe.*

—What does Goethe say?

—Goethe says: "I have devoted my whole life to the people and their improvement."

—Goethe said that?

—And is quoted in the very superior Pool production which is enlustering the perception of Pool worldwide.

—Rich, very rich.

—And there is a film chronicling the fabulous Pool garage sales, where one finds solid-silver plates in neglected bags.

—People sighing and leaning against each other, holding their silver plates. Think I'll just whittle a bit, whittle and spit.

—Lots of accomodations in Pool, all of the hotels are empty.

—See if I have any benefits left under the GI Bill.

—Pool is new, can make you new too.

—I have not the heart.

—I can get us a plane or a train, they've cut all the fares.

—People sighing and leaning against one another, holding their silver plates.

—So you just want to stay here? Stay here and be yourself?

—Drop by the shoe store, pick up a pair of shoes.

—Blackberries, buttercups, and wild red clover. I find the latest music terrific, although I don't generally speaking care much for the new, qua new. But this new music! It has won from our group the steadiest attention.

—Momma didn't 'low no clarinet played in here. Unfortunately.

—Momma.

—Momma didn't 'low no clarinet played in here. Made me sad.

—Momma was outside.

—Momma was *very* outside.

—Sitting there 'lowing and not-'lowing. In her old rocking chair.

—'Lowing this, not-'lowing that.

—Didn't 'low oboe.

—Didn't 'low gitfiddle. Vibes.

—Rock over your damn foot and bust it, you didn't pop to when she was 'lowing and not-'lowing.

—Right. 'Course, she had all the grease.

—True.

—You wanted a little grease, like to buy a damn comic book or something, you had to go to Momma.

—Sometimes yes, sometimes no. Her variously colored moods.

—Mauve. Warm gold. Citizen's blue.

—Mauve mood that got her thrown in the jug that time.

—Concealed weapons. Well, what can you do?

—Carried a .357 daytimes and a .22 for evenings. Well, what can you do?

—Momma didn't let nobody work her over, nobody.

—She just didn't give a hang. She didn't care.

—I thought she cared. There were moments.

—She never cared. Didn't give pig shit.

—You could even cry, she wouldn't come.

—I tried that, I remember. Cried and cried. Didn't do a damn bit of good.

—Lost as she was in the Eleusinian mysteries and the art of love.

—Cried my little eyes out. The sheet was sopping.

—Momma was not to be swayed. Unswayable.

—Staring into the thermostat.

—She had a lot on her mind. The chants. And Daddy, of course.

—Let's not do Daddy today.

—Yes, I remember Momma, jerking the old nervous system about with her electric *diktats*.

—Could Christ have performed the work of the Redemption had He come into the world in the shape of a pea? That was one she'd drop on you.

—Then she'd grade your paper.

—I got a C, once.

—She dyed my beard blue, on the eve of my seventh marriage. I was sleeping on the sun porch.

—Not one to withhold comment, Momma.

—Got pretty damned tired of that old woman, pretty damned tired of that old woman. Gangs of ecstatics hanging about beating on pots and pans, trash-can lids—

—Trying for a ticket to the mysteries.

—You wanted a little grease, like to go to the brothel or something, you had to say, Momma can I have a little grease to go to the brothel?

—She was often underly generous.

—Give you eight when she knew it was ten.

—She had her up days and her down days. Like most.

—Out for a long walk one early evening I noticed in the bare brown cut fields to the right of me and to the left of me the following items of interest: in the fields to the right of me, couple copulating in the shade of a car, tan Studebaker as I remember, a thing I had seen previously only in old sepia-toned photographs taken from the air by playful barnstormers capable of flying with their knees, I don't know if that's difficult or not—

—And in the field to your left?

—Momma. Rocking.

—She'd lugged the old rocking chair all that way. In a mauve mood.

—I tipped my hat. She did not return the greeting.

—She was pondering. "The goddess Demeter's anguish for all her children's mortality."

—Said my discourse was sickening. That was the word she used. Said it repeatedly.

—I asked myself: Do I give a bag of beans?

—This bird that fell into the back yard?

—The south lawn.

—The back yard. I wanted to give it a Frito?

—Yeah?

—Thought it might be hungry. Sumbitch couldn't fly you understand. It had crashed. Couldn't fly. So I went into the house to get it a Frito. So I was trying to get it to eat the Frito. I had the damn bird in one hand, and in the other, the Frito.

—She saw you and whopped you.

—She did.

—She gave you that "the bird is our friend and we never touch the bird because it hurts the bird" number.

—She did.

—Then she threw the bird away.

—Into the gutter.

—Anticipating no doubt handling of the matter by the proper authorities.

—Momma. You'd ask her how she was and she'd say, "Fine." Like a little kid.

—That's what they say. "Fine."

—That's all you can get out of 'em. "Fine."

—Boy or girl, don't make a penny's worth of difference. "Fine."

—Fending you off. Similarly, Momma.

—Momma 'lowed lute.

—Yes. She had a thing for lute.

—I remember the hours we spent. Banging away at our lutes.

—Momma sitting there rocking away. Dosing herself with strange intoxicants.

—Lime Rickeys.

—Orange Blossoms.

—Rob Roys.

—Cuba Libres.

—Brandy Alexanders and Bronxes. How could she drink that stuff?

—An iron gut. And divinity, of course.

—Well. Want to clean up some of this mess?

—Some monster with claws, maybe velvet-covered claws or Teflon-covered claws, inhabits my dreams. Whistling, whistling. I say, Monster, how goes it with you? And he says, Quite happily, dreammate, there are certain criticisms, the Curator of Archetypes thinks I don't quite cut it, thinks I'm shuckin' and jivin' when what I should be doing is attacking, attacking, attacking—

—Ah, my bawcock, what a fine fellow thou art.

—*But on the whole,* the monster says, I feel fine. Then he says, Gimme that corn flake back. I say, What? He says, Gimme that corn flake back. I say, You gave me that corn flake it's my corn flake. He says, Gimme that corn flake back or I'll claw you to thread. I say, I can't man you gave it to me I already ate it. He says, C'mon man gimme the corn flake back did you butter it first? I say, C'mon man be reasonable, you don't butter a corn flake—

—How does it end?

—It doesn't end.

—Is there help coming?

—I called that number and they said whom the Lord loveth He chasteneth.

—Where is succor?

—In the new music.

—Yes, it isn't often you hear a polka version of *Un Coup de Dés.* It's strengthening.

—The new music is drumless, which is brave. To make up for the absence of drums the musicians pray nightly to the Virgin, kneeling in their suits of lights in damp chapels provided for the purpose off the corridors of the great arenas—

—Momma wouldn't have 'lowed it.

—As with much else. Momma didn't 'low Patrice.

—I remember. You still see her?

—Once in a way. Saw her Saturday. I hugged her and her body leaped. That was odd.

—How did that feel?

—Odd. Wonderful.

—The body knows.
—The body is perspicacious.
—The body ain't dumb.
—Words can't say what the body knows.
—Sometimes I hear them howling from the hospital.
—The detox ward.
—Tied to the bed with beige cloths.
—We've avoided it.
—So far.
—Knock wood.
—I did.
—Well, it's a bitch.
—Like when she played Scrabble. She played to kill. Used the filthiest words insisting on their legitimacy. I was shocked.
—In her robes of deep purple.
—Seeking the ecstatic vision. That which would lift people four feet off the floor.
—Six feet.
—Four feet or six feet off the floor. Persephone herself appearing.
—The chanting in the darkened telesterion.
—Persephone herself appearing, hovering. Accepting offerings, balls of salt, solid gold serpents, fig branches, figs.
—Hallucinatory dancing. All the women drunk.
—Dancing with jugs on their heads, mixtures of barley, water, mint—
—Knowledge of things unspeakable—
—Still, all I wanted to do was a little krummhorn. A little krummhorn once in a while.
—Can open graves, properly played.
—I was never good. Never really good.
—Who could practice?
—And your clavier.
—Momma didn't 'low clavier.
—Thought it would unleash in her impulses better leashed? I don't know.
—Her dark side. They all have them, mommas.

—I mean they've seen it all, felt it all. Spilled their damn blood and then spooned out buckets of mushy squash meanwhile telling the old husband that he wasn't number three on the scale of all husbands . . .

—Tossed him a little bombita now and then just to keep him on his toes.

—He was always on his toes, spent his whole life on his toes, the poor fuck. Piling up the grease.

—We said we weren't going to do Daddy.

—I forgot.

—Old Momma.

—Well, it's not easy, conducting the mysteries. It's not easy, making the corn grow.

—Asparagus too.

—I couldn't do it.

—*I* couldn't do it.

—Momma could do it.

—Momma.

—Luckily we have the new music now. To give us aid and comfort.

—And Susie.

—Our Susie.

—Our darling.

—Our pride.

—Our passion.

—I have to tell you something. Susie's been reading the Hite Report. She says other women have more orgasms than she does. Wanted to know why.

—Where does one go to complain? Where does one go to complain, when fiends have worsened your life?

—I told her about the Great Septuagesimal Orgasm, implying she could have one, if she was good. But it is growing late, very late indeed, for such as we.

—But perhaps one ought *not* to complain, when fiends have worsened your life. But rather, emulating the great Stoics, Epictetus and so on, just zip into a bar and lift a few, whilst listening to the new, incorrigible, great-white-shark, knife, music.

—I handed the tall cool Shirley Temple to the silent priest. The new music, I said, is not specifically anticlerical. Only in its deepest effects.

—I know the guy who plays washboard. Wears thimbles on all his fingers.

—The new music burns things together, like a welder. The new music says, life becomes more and more exciting as there is less and less time.

—Momma wouldn't have 'lowed it. But Momma's gone.

—To the curious: A man who was a Communist heard the new music, and now is not. Fernando the fish-seller was taught to read and write by the new music, and is now a leper, white as snow. William Friend was caught trying to sneak into the new music with a set of bongos concealed under his cloak, but was garroted with his own bicycle chain, just in time. Propp the philosopher, having dinner with the Holy Ghost, was told of the coming of the new music but also informed that he would not live to hear it.

—The new, down-to-earth, think-I'm-gonna-kill-myself music, which unwraps the sky.

—Succeed! It has been done, and with a stupidity that can astound the most experienced.

—The rest of the trip presents no real difficulties.

—The rest of the trip presents no real difficulties. The thing to keep your eye on is less time, more exciting. Remember that.

—As if it were late, late, and we were ready to pull on our red-and-gold-striped nightshirts.

—Cup of tea before retiring.

—Cup of tea before retiring.

—Dreams next.

—We can deal with that.

—Remembering that the new music will be there tomorrow and tomorrow and tomorrow.

—There is always a new music.

—Thank God.

—Pull a few hairs out of your nose poised before the mirror.

—Routine maintenance, nothing to write home about.

The Zombies

In a high wind the leaves fall from the trees. The zombies are standing about talking. "Beautiful day!" "Certainly is!" The zombies have come to buy wives from the people of this village, the only village for miles around that will sell wives to zombies. "Beautiful day!" "Certainly is!" The zombies have brought many cattle. The bride-price to a zombie is exactly twice that asked of an ordinary man. The cattle are also zombies and the zombies are in terror lest the people of the village understand this.

These are good zombies. Gris Grue said so. They are painted white all over. Bad zombies are unpainted and weep with their noses, their nostrils spewing tears. The village chief calls the attention of the zombies to the fine brick buildings of the village, some of them one thousand bricks high—daughters peering from the windows, green plants in some windows and, in others, daughters. "You must promise not to tell the Bishop," say the zombies, "promise not to tell the Bishop, beautiful day, certainly is."

The white-painted zombies chatter madly, in the village square, in an impersonation of gaiety. "Bought a new coat!" "You did!" "Yes, bought a new coat, this coat I'm wearing, I think it's very fine!" "Oh it is, it is, yes, I think so!" The cattle kick at the chain-link fence of the corral. The kiss of a dying animal, a dying horse or dog, transforms an ordinary man into a zombie. The owner of the ice-cream shop has two daughters. The crayfish farmer has five daughters, and the captain of the soccer team, whose parents are dead, has a sister. Gris Grue is not here. He is away in another country, seeking a specific for deadly nightshade. A zombie with a rectal thermometer is creeping around in the corral, under the bellies of the large, bluish-brown animals. Someone says the Bishop has been seen riding in his car at full speed toward the village.

If a bad zombie gets you, he will weep on you, or take away your whiskey, or hurt your daughter's bones. There are too many daughters in the square, in the windows of the buildings, and not enough husbands. If a bad zombie gets you, he will scratch your white paint with awls and scarifiers. The good zombies skitter and dance. "Did you see that lady? Would that lady marry me? I don't know! Oh what a pretty lady! Would that lady marry me? I don't know!" The beer distributor has set up a keg of beer in the square. The local singing teacher is singing. The zombies say: "Wonderful time! Beautiful day! Marvelous singing! Excellent beer! Would that lady marry me? I don't know!" In a high wind the leaves fall from the trees, from the trees.

The zombie hero Gris Grue said: "There are good zombies and bad zombies, as there are good and bad ordinary men." Gris Grue said that many of the zombies known to him were clearly zombies of the former kind and thus eminently fit, in his judgment, to engage in trade, lead important enterprises, hold posts in the government, and participate in the mysteries of Baptism, Confirmation, Ordination, Marriage, Penance, the Eucharist, and Extreme Unction. The Bishop said no. The zombies sent many head of cattle to the Bishop. The Bishop said, everything but Ordination. If a bad zombie gets you, he will create insult in your bladder. The bad zombies banged the Bishop's car with a dead cow, at night. In the morning the Bishop had to pull the dead zombie cow from the windshield of his car, and cut his hand. Gris Grue decides who is a good zombie and who is a bad zombie; when he is away, his wife's mother decides. A zombie advances toward a group of thin blooming daughters and describes, with many motions of his hands and arms, the breakfasts they may expect in a zombie home.

"Monday!" he says. "Sliced oranges boiled grits fried croakers potato croquettes radishes watercress broiled spring chicken batter cakes butter syrup and café au lait! Tuesday! Grapes hominy broiled tenderloin of trout steak French-fried potatoes celery fresh rolls butter and café au lait! Wednesday! Iced figs Wheatena porgies with sauce tartare potato chips broiled ham scrambled eggs French toast and café au lait! Thursday! Bananas with cream oatmeal broiled patassas fried liver with bacon poached eggs on toast waffles with syrup and café au lait! Friday! Strawberries with cream broiled oysters on toast celery fried perch lyonnaise potatoes cornbread with syrup and café au lait! Saturday! Musk-melon on ice grits stewed tripe herb omelette olives snipe on toast flannel cakes with syrup and café au lait!" The zombie draws a long breath. "Sunday!" he says. "Peaches with cream cracked wheat with milk broiled Spanish mackerel with sauce maître d'hôtel creamed chicken beaten biscuits broiled woodcock on English muffin rice cakes potatoes à la duchesse eggs Benedict oysters on the half shell broiled lamb chops pound cake with syrup and café au lait! And imported champagne!" The zombies look anxiously at the women to see if this prospect is pleasing.

A houngan (zombie-maker) grasps a man by the hair and forces his lips close to those of a dying cat. If you do heavy labor for a houngan for ten years, then you are free, but still a zombie. The Bishop's car is working well. No daughter of this village has had in human memory a true husband, or anything like it. The daughters are tired of kissing each other, although some are not. The fathers of the village are tired of paying for their daughters' sewing machines, lowboys, and towels. A bald zombie says, "Oh what a pretty lady! I would be nice to her! Yes I would! I think so!" Bad zombies are leaning against the walls of the buildings, watching. Bad zombies are allowed, by law, to mate only with sheep ticks. The women do not want the zombies, but zombies are their portion. A woman says to another woman: "These guys are zombies!" "Yes," says the second woman, "I saw a handsome man, he had his picture in the paper, but he is not here." The zombie in the corral finds a temperature of one hundred and ten degrees.

The villagers are beating upon huge drums with mops. The Bishop arrives in his great car with white episcopal flags flying from the right and left fenders. "Forbidden, forbidden, forbidden!" he cries. Gris Grue appears on a silver sled and places his hands over the Bishop's eyes. At the moment of sunset the couples, two by two, are wed. The corral shudders as the cattle collapse. The new wives turn to their new husbands and say: "No matter. This is what we must do. We will paste photographs of the handsome man in the photograph on your faces, when it is time to go to bed. Now let us cut the cake." The good zombies say, "You're welcome! You're very welcome! I think so! Undoubtedly!" The bad zombies place sheep ticks in the Bishop's car. If a bad zombie gets you, he will scarify your hide with chisels and rakes. If a bad zombie gets you, he will make you walk past a beautiful breast without even noticing.

The King of Jazz

Well I'm the king of jazz now, thought Hokie Mokie to himself as he oiled the slide on his trombone. Hasn't been a 'bone man been king of jazz for many years. But now that Spicy MacLammermoor, the old king, is dead, I guess I'm it. Maybe I better play a few notes out of this window here, to reassure myself.

"Wow!" said somebody standing on the sidewalk. "Did you hear that?"

"I did," said his companion.

"Can you distinguish our great homemade American jazz performers, each from the other?"

"Used to could."

"Then who was that playing?"

"Sounds like Hokie Mokie to me. Those few but perfectly selected notes have the real epiphanic glow."

"The what?"

"The real epiphanic glow, such as is obtained only by artists of the caliber of Hokie Mokie, who's from Pass Christian, Mississippi. He's the king of jazz, now that Spicy MacLammermoor is gone."

Hokie Mokie put his trombone in its trombone case and went to a gig. At the gig everyone fell back before him, bowing.

"Hi Bucky! Hi Zoot! Hi Freddie! Hi George! Hi Thad! Hi Roy! Hi Dexter! Hi Jo! Hi Willie! Hi Greens!"

"What we gonna play, Hokie? You the king of jazz now, you gotta decide."

"How 'bout 'Smoke'?"

"Wow!" everybody said. "Did you hear that? Hokie Mokie

can just knock a fella out, just the way he pronounces a word. What a intonation on that boy! God Almighty!"

"I don't want to play 'Smoke,' " somebody said.

"Would you repeat that, stranger?"

"I don't want to play 'Smoke.' 'Smoke' is dull. I don't like the changes. I refuse to play 'Smoke.' "

"He refuses to play 'Smoke'! But Hokie Mokie is the king of jazz and he says 'Smoke'!"

"Man, you from outa town or something? What do you mean you refuse to play 'Smoke'? How'd you get on this gig anyhow? Who hired you?"

"I am Hideo Yamaguchi, from Tokyo, Japan."

"Oh, you're one of those Japanese cats, eh?"

"Yes I'm the top trombone man in all of Japan."

"Well you're welcome here until we hear you play. Tell me, is the Tennessee Tea Room still the top jazz place in Tokyo?"

"No, the top jazz place in Tokyo is the Square Box now."

"That's nice. OK, now we gonna play 'Smoke' just like Hokie said. You ready, Hokie? OK, give you four for nothin'. One! Two! Three! Four!"

The two men who had been standing under Hokie's window had followed him into the club. Now they said:

"Good God!"

"Yes, that's Hokie's famous 'English sunrise' way of playing. Playing with lots of rays coming out of it, some red rays, some blue rays, some green rays, some green stemming from a violet center, some olive stemming from a tan center—"

"That young Japanese fellow is pretty good, too."

"Yes, he is pretty good. And he holds his horn in a peculiar way. That's frequently the mark of a superior player."

"Bent over like that with his head between his knees—good God, he's sensational!"

He's sensational, Hokie thought. Maybe I ought to kill him.

But at that moment somebody came in the door pushing in front of him a four-and-one-half-octave marimba. Yes, it was Fat Man Jones, and he began to play even before he was fully in the door.

"What're we playing?"

" 'Billie's Bounce.' "

"That's what I thought it was. What're we in?"

"F."

"That's what I thought we were in. Didn't you use to play with Maynard?"

"Yeah I was on that band for a while until I was in the hospital."

"What for?"

"I was tired."

"What can we add to Hokie's fantastic playing?"

"How 'bout some rain or stars?"

"Maybe that's presumptuous?"

"Ask him if he'd mind."

"You ask him, I'm scared. You don't fool around with the king of jazz. That young Japanese guy's pretty good, too."

"He's sensational."

"You think he's playing in Japanese?"

"Well I don't think it's English."

This trombone's been makin' my neck green for thirty-five years, Hokie thought. How come I got to stand up to yet another challenge, this late in life?

"Well, Hideo—"

"Yes, Mr. Mokie?"

"You did well on both 'Smoke' and 'Billie's Bounce.' You're just about as good as me, I regret to say. In fact, I've decided you're *better* than me. It's a hideous thing to contemplate, but there it is. I have only been the king of jazz for twenty-four hours, but the unforgiving logic of this art demands we bow to Truth, when we hear it."

"Maybe you're mistaken?"

"No, I got ears. I'm not mistaken. Hideo Yamaguchi is the new king of jazz."

"You want to be king emeritus?"

"No, I'm just going to fold up my horn and steal away. This gig is yours, Hideo. You can pick the next tune."

"How 'bout 'Cream'?"

"OK, you heard what Hideo said, it's 'Cream.' You ready, Hideo?"

"Hokie, you don't have to leave. You can play too. Just move a little over to the side there—"

"Thank you, Hideo, that's very gracious of you. I guess I will play a little, since I'm still here. Sotto voce, of course."

"Hideo is wonderful on 'Cream'!"

"Yes, I imagine it's his best tune."

"What's that sound coming in from the side there?"

"Which side?"

"The left."

"You mean that sound that sounds like the cutting edge of life? That sounds like polar bears crossing Arctic ice pans? That sounds like a herd of musk ox in full flight? That sounds like male walruses diving to the bottom of the sea? That sounds like fumaroles smoking on the slopes of Mt. Katmai? That sounds like the wild turkey walking through the deep, soft forest? That sounds like beavers chewing trees in an Appalachian marsh? That sounds like an oyster fungus growing on an aspen trunk? That sounds like a mule deer wandering a montane of the Sierra Nevada? That sounds like prairie dogs kissing? That sounds like witchgrass tumbling or a river meandering? That sounds like manatees munching seaweed at Cape Sable? That sounds like coatimundis moving in packs across the face of Arkansas? That sounds like—"

"Good God, it's Hokie! Even with a cup mute on, he's blowing Hideo right off the stand!"

"Hideo's playing on his knees now! Good God, he's reaching into his belt for a large steel sword— Stop him!"

"Wow! That was the most exciting 'Cream' ever played! Is Hideo all right?"

"Yes, somebody is getting him a glass of water."

"You're my man, Hokie! That was the dadblangedest thing I ever saw!"

"You're the king of jazz once again!"

"Hokie Mokie is the most happening thing there is!"

"Yes, Mr. Hokie sir, I have to admit it, you blew me right off the stand. I see I have many years of work and study before me still."

"That's OK, son. Don't think a thing about it. It happens to the best of us. Or it almost happens to the best of us. Now I want everybody to have a good time because we're gonna play 'Flats.' 'Flats' is next."

"With your permission, sir, I will return to my hotel and pack. I am most grateful for everything I have learned here."

"That's OK, Hideo. Have a nice day. He-he. Now, 'Flats.' "

Morning

—Say you're frightened. Admit it.

—In Colorado, by the mountains. In California, by the sea. Everywhere, by breaking glass.

—Say you're frightened. Confess.

—Timid as a stag. They've got a meter wired to my sheet, I don't know what it measures. I get a dollar a night. When I wake suddenly, I notice it's there. I watch my hand aging, sing a little song.

—Were you invited to the party?

—Yes, I was. Stood there smiling. I thought, Those are tight pants, how kind of her. Wondered if she was orange underneath. What shall we do? Call up Mowgli? Ask him over? Do you like tongue? Sliced? With mushrooms? Is it a private matter? Is Scriabin as smart as he looks? This man's a fool—why are you talking to him? Yes, his clothes are interesting, but inside are dull bones.

—This gray light, I don't see how you stand it.

—A firestorm of porn all around—orange images, dunes and deserts. Bursts of quarreling through the walls. I wonder who the people are? I tried that Cuisine Minceur, didn't like it. Oh, it looks pretty—

—Say you're frightened.

—I'm frightened. By flutes and flower girls and sirens. We get a lot of sirens because of the hospital. By coffee, dead hanging plants, people who think too fast, vestments and bells.

—Get some Vitamin E. I take eight hundred units.

—The sound of glass breaking. I thought, Oh Christ, not again. The last time they got a bicycle, fancy Japanese bicycle somebody'd left in the hall. We changed the lock. Guy left his crowbar. Actually it wasn't a crowbar it was a jack handle.

—I'm not afraid of crime, there's got to be crime, it's the manner or mode that— I mean if they could just take it out of your bank account, by punching a few buttons or something . . .

—I'm not afraid of snakes. There was a snake-handling bunch where we spent the summers. I used to go to their meetings now and again, do a little handling.

—Not afraid of the mail, not so much as I used to be, all those threatening letters, I just say sticks and stones, sticks and stones, see the triage nurse.

—It's only when you stop to think about it. I don't stop.

—Not afraid of hurricanes because we used to have them, where I lived, not afraid of tarantulas, used to have them too, they jump, have to chop them up with a hoe, long-handled hoe as opposed to the stoop hoe, by preference.

—Nature in general not seen as antipathetic. Nor are other people, except for those who want to slap your ears back without first presenting their carefully reasoned, red-white-and-blue threats.

—Behavior in general a wonderful sea, in which we can swim, or leap, or stumble.

—She got out of bed and, doing a cute little walk, walked to the bathroom. I dreaded the day I would see her real walk.

—There's the sunset gun. That means we can loosen up and get friendly. Think we can get any of that government money?

—I sent for the forms. Merrily merrily merrily merrily.

—Think we can get us some of that good per diem?

—If you decide to run for it a bus is better. No one's seated facing you. They've got bigger windows now, and the drivers are usually reliable.

—Well that's one thing I want to stay away from. Flight, I mean. Too much like defeat.

—But when I get to all these strange places they seem empty. Nobody on the streets and I'm not used to that. Their restaurants all have the same things: filet, surf 'n' turf, prime rib. Spend a few days in a hotel and then check out, leaving a dollar or two for the maids.

—Turkeying around trying to get situated.

—Searching the room for someone to go to bed with. What if she agrees?

—That's happened to me several times. You just have to be honest.

—The love of gain is insatiable. This is true.

—What are you afraid of? Mornings, noons, or nights?

—Mornings. I send out a lot of postcards.

—Take a picture of this exceptionally dirty window. Its grays. I think I can get you a knighthood, I know a guy. What about the Eternal Return?

—Distant, distant, distant. Thanks for calling Jim it was good to talk to you.

—They played "One O'Clock Jump," "Two O'Clock Jump," "Three O'Clock Jump," and "Four O'Clock Jump." They were very good. I saw them on television. They're all dead now.

—That scare you?

—Naw that doesn't scare me.

—That scare you?

—Naw that doesn't scare me.

—What scares you?

—My hand scares me. It's not well.

—Hear that? That's wolf talk. Not bad is it?

—Scarcely had I reloaded when a black rhinoceros, a female as it proved, stood drinking at the water.

—Let me give you a hint: *Find me one animal that is capable of personal friendship*.

—So I decided it was about time we got gay. I changed the record, that helped, and fiddled with the lights—

—Call up Bomba the Jungle Boy? Get his input?

—Fixed up the punch with some stuff I had with me. Complicated the decor with carefully placed items of lawn furniture, birdbaths, sundials, mirrored globes on stands . . .

—That set toes to tapping, did it?

—They were pleased. We danced Inventions & Sinfonias. It wasn't bad. It was a success.

—It is this that the new portraits are intended to celebrate.

—Then, out of another chute, the bride appeared, caracoling and sunfishing across the arena.

—I knew her. I was very fond of her. I am very fond of her. I wish them well.

—As do I. She's brave.

—Think we can get some of that fine grant money?

—If we can make ourselves understood. If I applaud, the actors understand that I am pleased. If I take a needle and singe it with a match, you understand that I have picked up a splinter in my foot. If I say "Have any of the English residents been murdered?", you understand that I am cognizant of native unrest. If I hand you two copies of a thesis bound in black cloth, you understand that I am trying to improve myself. Appeals to patriotism, small-boat warnings up.

—Say you're frightened.

—I'm frightened. But maybe not tomorrow.

—Well that's one thing I want to stay away from. You can get mad instead. I got mad, really got mad.

—Put-on anger. A technique of managers.

—Got so mad I coulda bit a chisel in two.

—And very graciously. Skin of dreams, paint marks, red scratches, grass stains. We watched *60 Minutes*. Fed on ixias, wild garlic, the core of aloes, gum of acacias. She's gone now, took an early plane. How do I feel? OK.

—Another bright glorious day. How do you feel? Have you tried to get a drink on one of these new trains? It's as easy as pie. Have you got anything we could put over the windows? Tarpaper or maybe some boards? Do you want to hear "The Battle Hymn of the Republic"? Is there any more of this red?

—Jugs and jugs. Two weeks would do it, two weeks in a VW Rabbit.

—Going home.

—No, thank you.

—You're afraid of it?

—Indeed, do I still live?

—What are you afraid of?

—One old man alone in a room. Two old men alone in a room. Three old men alone in a room.

—Well maybe you could talk to them or something.

—And say: Howdy, have you heard about pleasure, have you heard about fun? Let's go out and bust up a bar, it's been a long time. What are you up to, what are your plans? Still lifting weights? I've been screwing all night, how 'bout you? "You please me, happiness!"

—Well I don't think about this stuff a lot of the time.

—Humility is barefoot, Lewdness is physically attractive and holds a sprig of colewort, the Hour is a wheel, and Courage is strangling a lion, by shoving a mailed fist down its throat.

—How did the party end?

—I wasn't there. Got to scat, I said, got to get away, got to creep, it's that time of night. Matthew, Mark, Luke, and John, bless the bed that I lie on.

—Say you're frightened.

—Less and less. I have a smoke detector and tickets to everywhere. I have a guardian angel blind from birth and a packet of Purple-top White Globe turnip seeds, for the roof.

—Want to see my collection of bass clarinets? Want to see my collection of painters' ears? This gray light, I don't see how you stand it.

—I grayed it up myself. Sets off the orange.

—A fine person. Took the Fire Department exam and passed it. That's just one example.

—All women are mortal, she explained to me, and Caius is a woman.

—Say you're not frightened. Inspire me.

—After a while, darkness, and they give up the search.

The Death of Edward Lear

The death of Edward Lear took place on a Sunday morning in May 1888. Invitations were sent out well in advance. The invitations read:

Mr. Edward LEAR
Nonsense Writer and Landscape Painter
Requests the Honor of Your Presence
On the Occasion of his DEMISE.
San Remo 2:20 A.M.
The 29th of May *Please reply*

One can imagine the feelings of the recipients. Our dear friend! is preparing to depart! and such-like. Mr. Lear! who has given us so much pleasure! and such-like. On the other hand, his years were considered. Mr. Lear! who must be, now let me see . . . And there was a good deal of, I remember the first time I (dipped into) (was seized by) . . . But on the whole, Mr. Lear's acquaintances approached the occasion with a mixture of solemnity and practicalness, perhaps remembering the words of Lear's great friend, Tennyson:

Old men must die,
or the world would grow mouldy

and:

For men may come and men may go,
But I go on forever.

People prepared to attend the death of Edward Lear as they might have for a day in the country. Picnic baskets were packed (for it would be wrong to expect too much of Mr. Lear's hospitality, under the circumstances); bottles of wine were wrapped in white napkins. Toys were chosen for the children. There were debates as to whether the dog ought to be taken or left behind. (Some of the dogs actually present at the death of Edward Lear could not restrain themselves; they frolicked about the dying man's chamber, tugged at the bedclothes, and made such nuisances of themselves that they had to be removed from the room.)

Most of Mr. Lear's friends decided that the appropriate time to arrive at the Villa would be midnight, or in that neighborhood, in order to allow the old gentleman time to make whatever remarks he might have in mind, or do whatever he wanted to do, before the event. Everyone understood what the time specified in the invitation meant. And so, the visitors found themselves being handed down from their carriages (by Lear's servant Giuseppe Orsini) in almost total darkness. Pausing to greet people they knew, or to corral straying children, they were at length ushered into a large room on the first floor, where the artist had been accustomed to exhibit his watercolors, and thence by a comfortably wide staircase to a similar room on the second floor, where Mr. Lear himself waited, in bed, wearing an old velvet smoking jacket and his familiar silver spectacles with tiny oval lenses. Several dozen straight-backed chairs had been arranged in a rough semicircle around the bed; these were soon filled, and later arrivals stood along the walls.

Mr. Lear's first words were: "I've no money!" As each new group of guests entered the room, he repeated, "I've no money! No money!" He looked extremely tired, yet calm. His ample beard, gray yet retaining patches of black, had evidently not been trimmed in some days. He seemed nervous and immediately began to discourse, as if to prevent anyone else from doing so.

He began by thanking all those present for attending and expressing the hope that he had not put them to too great an inconvenience, acknowledging that the hour was "an unusual one for visits!" He said that he could not find words sufficient to disclose his pleasure in seeing so many of his friends gathered together at his side. He then delivered a pretty little lecture, of some twelve minutes' duration, on the production of his various writings, of which no one has been able to recall the substance, although everyone agreed that it was charming, graceful, and wise.

He then startled his guests with a question, uttered in a kind of shriek: "Should I get married? Get married? Should I marry?"

Mr. Lear next offered a short homily on the subject of Friendship. Friendship, he said, is the most golden of the affections. It is also, he said, often the *strongest* of human ties, surviving strains and tempests fatal to less sublime relations. He noted that his own many friendships constituted the richest memory of a long life.

A disquisition on Cats followed.

When Mr. Lear reached the topic Children, a certain restlessness was observed among his guests. (He had not ceased to shout at intervals, "Should I get married?" and "I've no money!") He then displayed copies of his books, but as everybody had already read them, not more than a polite interest was generated. Next he held up, one by one, a selection of his watercolors, views of various antiquities and picturesque spots. These, too, were familiar; they were the same watercolors the old gentleman had been offering for sale, at £5 and £10, for the past forty years.

Mr. Lear now sang a text of Tennyson's in a setting of his own, accompanying himself on a mandolin. Although his voice was thin and cracked frequently, the song excited vigorous applause.

Finally he caused to be hauled into the room by servants an enormous oil, at least seven feet by ten, depicting Mount Athos. There was a murmur of appreciation, but it did not seem to satisfy the painter, for he assumed a very black look.

At 2:15 Mr. Lear performed a series of actions the meaning of which was obscure to the spectators.

At 2:20 he reached over to the bedside table, picked up an old-fashioned pen which lay there, and died. A death mask was immediately taken. The guests, weeping unaffectedly, moved in a long line back to the carriages.

People who attended the death of Edward Lear agreed that, all in all, it had been a somewhat tedious performance. Why had he seen fit to read the same old verses, sing again the familiar songs, show the well-known pictures, run through his repertoire once more? Why invitations? Then something was understood: that Mr. Lear had been doing what he had always done and therefore, not doing anything extraordinary. Mr. Lear had transformed the extraordinary into its opposite. He had, in point of fact, created a gentle, genial misunderstanding.

Thus the guests began, as time passed, to regard the affair in an historical light. They told their friends about it, reenacted parts of it for their children and grandchildren. They would reproduce the way the old man had piped "I've no money!" in a comical voice, and quote his odd remarks about marrying. The death of Edward Lear became so popular, as time passed, that revivals were staged in every part of the country, with considerable success. The death of Edward Lear can still be seen, in the smaller cities, in versions enriched by learned interpretation, textual emendation, and changing fashion. One modification is curious; no one knows how it came about. The supporting company plays in the traditional way, but Lear himself appears shouting, shaking, vibrant with rage.

The Abduction from the Seraglio

I was sitting in my brand-new Butler building, surrounded by steel of high quality folded at ninety-degree angles. The only thing prettier than ladies is an I-beam painted bright yellow. I told 'em I wanted a big door. A big door in front where a girl could hide her car if she wanted to evade the gaze of her husband the rat-poison salesman. You ever been out with a rat-poison salesman? They are fine fellows with little red eyes.

I was playing with my forty-three-foot overhead traveling crane which is painted bright yellow. I was practicing knocking over the stepladder with the hook. I was at a low point, I'd been thinking about bread, colored steel bread, all kinds of colors of steel bread—red yellow purple green brown steel bread—then I thought no, that's not it. And I'd already made all the welded-steel four-thousand-pound artichokes the world could accommodate that week, and they wouldn't let me drink no more, only a little Lone Star beer now and then which I don't much care for. And my new Waylon Jennings record had a scratch on it, went crack crack crack across the whole width of Side One. It was the kind of impasse us creative people reach every Thursday, some prefer other days. So I figured that in order not to waste this valuable time of my life, I had better get on the stick and bust Constanze out of the seraglio

Chorus:
Oh Constanze oh Constanze
What you doin' in that se-rag-li-o?
I been poppin' Darvon and mothballs

Poppin' Darvon and mothballs
Ever since I let you go.

Well, I motored out to the seraglio, got blindsided on the Freeway by two hundred thousand guys trying to get home from their work at the rat-poison factories, all two hundred thousand tape decks playin' the same thing, some kind of roll-on-down-the-road song

rollin'
rollin'
rollin'
rollin'

but there wasn't just a hell of a lot of actual forward motion despite this hymn to possibility. The seraglio turned out to be a Butler building too, much like mine only vaster of course, that son of a bitch. I spent a little while admiring that fine red-painted steel that you can put the pieces together of out of a catalogue and set her down on your slab and be barbecuing your flank steak from the A&P by five o'clock on the same day. The Pasha didn't have any great big doors in his, just one little tee-ninesy door with a picture of an unfed-recently Doberman pasted on it, I took that as a hint and I thought Constanze, Constanze, how could you be so dumb?

The thing is, and I hate to admit it, Constanze's a little dumb. She's not so dumb as a lady I once knew who thought the Mark of Zorro was an N, but she's not perfect. You tell her you heard via the jungle drums that there's a vacancy in Willie Jake Johnson's bed and her eyes will cut to the side just for a moment, which means she's thinking. She's not conservative. I'm some kind of an artist, but I'm conservative. Mine is the art of the possible, plus two. She, on the contrary, spent many years as a talented and elegant country-music groupie. She knows things I do not know. Happy dust is $1,900 an ounce now, I hear tell—she's tasted it, I haven't. It's a small thing, but irritating. She's dumb in what she knows, if you follow me.

Chorus:
Oh Constanze oh Constanze
What you doin' in that se-rag-li-o?
I been sleepin' on paper towels
Sleepin' on paper towels and
Drinkin' Sea & Ski
Ever since I let you go.

The Pasha is a Plymouth dealer, actually. He has this mysterious power over people and events which is called ten million dollars a year, gross. About the only thing we share in the way of common humanity is four welded-steel artichokes, which he bought right from the studio, which is where he saw Constanze. The artichoke is a beautiful form, maybe too mannerly, I roughen mine up some, that's where the interest is. I don't even mind the damn Plymouth, as a form, but what I can't stand is a dealer. In anything. I know that this is a small picky-minded dumb-ass prejudice, but it's been earned. Anyhow the Pasha, as we call him, noticed that Constanze was some beautiful, in fact semi-incredible looking, with black hair. He turned her head, as used to be said. He'd got to the left of flank steak, and he employed that. If we're having Neiman-Marcus time, I can't compete. (In all honesty I have to concede that he is fairly handsome, for a Pasha, and excels in a number of expensive sports.) He put her in a Butler building just to mock me and because she's not so dumb she'd be caught dead in a big fancy layout in River Oaks or somewhere. She's got values. What I'm trying to suggest is, she's in a delicate relation to the real.

I can't understand this. She is so great. When we go partying she always takes care to dance with Bill Cray's four-year-old girl, who's a fool for dancing. She made me read *War and Peace*, which struck me at first glance as terrible thick. She renews my subscription to the *Texas Observer* every year. She contributes regularly to the United Way and got gassed in great cities a time or two while expressing her opinion of the recent war. She's kind to rat-poison salesmen. She's afraid of the dark. She took care of me that time I had my little psychotic episode.

She is so great. Once I saw her slug a guy in a supermarket who was whacking his kid, his legal right, with undue enthusiasm. The really dreadful thought, to me, is that her real might be the real one.

Well, I opened the door. The Doberman came at me raging and snarling and generally carrying on in the way he felt was expected of him. I threw him a fifty-five-pound reinforced-concrete pork chop which knocked him silly. I spoke to Constanze. We used to walk down the street together bumping our hipbones together in joy, before God and everybody. I wanted to float in the air again some feeling of that. It didn't work. I'm sorry. But I guess, as the architects say, there's no use crying over split marble. She will undoubtedly move on and up and down and around in the world, New York, Chicago, and Temple, Texas, making everything considerably better than it was, for short periods of time. We adventured. That's not bad.

Chorus:
Oh Constanze oh Constanze
What you doin' in that se-rag-li-o?
How I miss you
How I miss you

On the Steps of the Conservatory

—C'mon Hilda don't fret.

—Well Maggie it's a blow.

—Don't let it bother you, don't let it get you down.

—Once I thought they were going to admit me to the Conservatory but now I know they will never admit me to the Conservatory.

—Yes they are very particular about who they admit to the Conservatory. They will never admit you to the Conservatory.

—They will never admit me to the Conservatory, I know that now.

—You are not Conservatory material I'm afraid. That's the plain truth of it.

—You're not important, they told me, just remember that, you're not important, what's so important about you? What?

—C'mon Hilda don't fret.

—Well Maggie it's a blow.

—When are you going to change yourself, change yourself into a loaf or a fish?

—Christian imagery is taught at the Conservatory, also Islamic imagery and the imagery of Public Safety.

—Red, yellow, and green circles.

—When they told me I got between the poles of my rickshaw and trotted heavily away.

—The great black ironwork doors of the Conservatory barred to you forever.

—Trotted heavily away in the direction of my house. My small, poor house.

—C'mon Hilda don't fret.

—Yes, I am still trying to get into the Conservatory, although my chances are probably worse than ever.

—They don't want pregnant women in the Conservatory.

—I didn't tell them, I lied about it.

—Didn't they ask you?

—No they forgot to ask me and I didn't tell them.

—Well then it's hardly on that account that—

—I felt they knew.

—The Conservatory is hostile to the new spirit, the new spirit is not liked there.

—Well Maggie it's a blow nevertheless. I had to go back to my house.

—Where although you entertain the foremost artists and intellectuals of your time you grow progressively more despondent and depressed.

—Yes he was a frightful lawyer.

—Lover?

—That too, frightful. He said he could not get me into the Conservatory because of my unimportance.

—Was there a fee?

—There's always a fee. Pounds and pounds.

—I stood on the terrace at the rear of the Conservatory and studied the flagstones reddened with the lifebloods of generations of Conservatory students. Standing there I reflected: Hilda will never be admitted to the Conservatory.

—I read the Conservatory Circular and my name was not among those listed.

—Well I suppose it was in part your espousal of the new spirit that counted against you.

—I will never abjure the new spirit.

—And you're a veteran too, I should have thought that would have weighed in your favor.

—Well Maggie it's a disappointment, I must admit that frankly.

—C'mon Hilda don't weep and tear your hair here where they can see you.

—Are they looking out of the windows?

—Probably they're looking out of the windows.

—It's said that they import a cook, on feast days.

—They have naked models too.

—Do you really think so? I'm not surprised.

—The best students get their dinners sent up on trays.

—Do you really think so? I'm not surprised.

—Grain salads and large portions of choice meats.

—Oh it hurts, it hurts, it hurts.

—Bread with drippings, and on feast days cake.

—I'm as gifted as they are, I'm as gifted as some of them.

—Decisions made by a committee of ghosts. They drop black beans or white beans into a pot.

—Once I thought I was to be admitted. There were encouraging letters.

—You're not Conservatory material I'm afraid. Only the best material is Conservatory material.

—I'm as good as some of those who rest now in the soft Conservatory beds.

—Merit is always considered closely.

—I could smile back at the smiling faces of the swift, dangerous teachers.

—Yes, we have naked models. No, the naked models are not emotionally meaningful to us.

—I could work with clay or paste things together.

—Yes, sometimes we paste things on the naked models—clothes, mostly. Yes, sometimes we play our Conservatory violins, cellos, trumpets for the naked models, or sing to them, or correct their speech, as our deft fingers fly over the sketch pads . . .

—I could I suppose fill out another application, or several.

—Yes, you have considerable of a belly on you now. I remember when it was flat, flat as a book.

—I will die if I don't get into the Conservatory, die.

—Naw you won't you're just saying that.

—I will completely croak if I don't get into the Conservatory, I promise you.

—Things are not so bad, you can always do something else, I don't know what, c'mon Hilda be reasonable.

—My whole life depends on it.

—Oh God I remember when it was flat. Didn't we tear things up, though? I remember running around that town, and hiding in dark places, that was a great town and I'm sorry we left it.

—Now we are grown, grown and proper.

—Well, I misled you. The naked models are emotionally meaningful to us.

—They are?

—We love them and sleep with them all the time—before breakfast, after breakfast, during breakfast.

—Why that's all right!

—Why that's rather neat!

—I like that!

—That's not so bad!

—I wish you hadn't told me that.

—C'mon Hilda don't be so single-minded, there are lots of other things you can do if you want.

—I guess they operate on some kind of principle of exclusivity. Keeping some people out while letting other people in.

—We got a Coushatta Indian in there, real full-blooded Coushatta Indian.

—In there?

—Yes. He does hanging walls out of scraps of fabric and twigs, very beautiful, and he does sand paintings and plays on whistles of various kinds, sometimes he chants, and he bangs on a drum, works in silver, and he's also a weaver, and he translates things from Coushatta into English and from English into Coushatta and he's also a crack shot and can bulldog steers and catch catfish on trotlines and ride bareback and make medicine out of common ingredients, aspirin mostly, and he sings and he's also an actor. He's very talented.

—My whole life depends on it.

—Listen Hilda maybe you could be an Associate. We have this deal whereby you pay twelve bucks a year and that makes you an Associate. You get the Circular and have all the privileges of an Associate.

—What are they?

—You get the Circular.

—That's all?

—Well I guess you're right.

—I'm just going to sit here I'm not going to go away.

—Your distress is poignant to me.

—I'll have the baby right here right on these steps.

—Well maybe there'll be good news one of these days.

—I feel like a dead person sitting in a chair.

—You're still pretty and attractive.

—That's good to hear I'm pleased you think that.

—And warm you're warm you're very warm.

—Yes I have a warm nature very warm.

—Weren't you in the Peace Corps also years ago?

—I was and drove ambulances too down in Nicaragua.

—The Conservatory life is just as halcyon as you imagine it—precisely so.

—I guess I'll just have to go back to my house and clean up, take out the papers and the trash.

—I guess that kid'll be born one of these days, right?

—Continue working on my études no matter what they say.

—That's admirable I think.

—The thing is not to let your spirit be conquered.

—I guess that kid'll be born after a while, right?

—I guess so. Those boogers are really gonna keep me out of there, you know that?

—Their minds are inflexible and rigid.

—Probably because I'm a poor pregnant woman don't you think?

—You said you didn't tell them.

—But maybe they're very shrewd psychologists and they could just look at my face and tell.

—No it doesn't show yet how many months are you?

—Two and a half just about you can tell when I take my clothes off.

—You didn't take your clothes off did you?

—No I was wearing you know what the students wear. Jeans and a serape. I carried a green book bag.

—Jam-packed with études.

—Yes. He asked where I had gotten my previous training and I told him.

—Oh boy I remember when it was flat, flat as the deck of something, a boat or a ship.

—You're not important, they told me.

—Oh sweetie I am so sorry for you.

—We parted then I walking through the gorgeous Conservatory light into the foyer and then through the great black ironwork Conservatory doors.

—I was a face on the other side of the glass.

—My aspect as I departed most dignified and serene.

—Time heals everything.

—No it doesn't.

—Cut lip fat lip puffed lip split lip.

—Haw! haw! haw! haw!

—Well Hilda there are other things in life.

—Yes Maggie I suppose there are. None that I want.

—Non-Conservatory people have their own lives. We Conservatory people don't have much to do with them but we are told they have their own lives.

—I suppose I could file an appeal if there's anywhere to file an appeal to. If there's anywhere.

—That's an idea we get stacks of appeals, stacks and stacks.

—I can wait all night. Here on the steps.

—I'll sit with you. I'll help you formulate the words.

—Are they looking out of the windows?

—Yes I think so. What do you want to say?

—I want to say my whole life depends on it. Something like that.

—It's against the rules for Conservatory people to help non-Conservatory people you know that.

—Well goddamnit I thought you were going to help me.

—Okay. I'll help you. What do you want to say?

—I want to say my whole life depends on it. Something like that.

—We got man naked models and woman naked models, harps, giant potted plants, and drapes. There are hierarchies, some people higher up and others lower down. These mingle, in the gorgeous light. We have lots of fun. There's lots of green furniture you know with paint on it. Worn green paint. Gilt lines one-quarter inch from the edges. Worn gilt lines.

—And probably flambeaux in little niches in the walls, right?

—Yeah we got flambeaux. Who's the father?

—Guy named Robert.

—Did you have a good time?

—The affair ran the usual course. Fever, boredom, trapped.

—Hot, rinse, spin dry.

—Is it wonderful in there Maggie?

—I have to say it is. Yes. It is.

—Do you feel great, being there? Do you feel wonderful?

—Yes, it feels pretty good. Very often there is, upon the tray, a rose.

—I will never be admitted to the Conservatory.

—You will never be admitted to the Conservatory.

—How do I look?

—Okay. Not bad. Fine.

—I will never get there. How do I look?

—Fine. Great. Time heals everything Hilda.

—No it doesn't.

—Time heals everything.

—No it doesn't. How do I look?

—Moot.

The Leap

—Today we make the leap to faith. Today.

—Today?

—Today.

—We're really going to do it? At last?

—Spent too much time fooling around. Today we do it.

—I don't know. Maybe we're not ready?

—I am cheered by the wine of possibility and the growing popularity of light. Today's the day.

—You're serious.

—Intensely. First, we examine our consciences.

—I am a double-minded man. Have always been a double-minded man.

—Each examining his own conscience, rooting out, naming, remembering and re-experiencing every last little cank and wrinkle. Root and branch.

—Smiting each conscience hip and thigh.

—Thigh and hip. Smite! Smite!

—God is good and we are but poor wretches who—

—Wait.

—Poor slovening wretches who but for the goodness of God would—

—Wait. This will be painful, you know. A bit.

—Oh my God.

—What?

—I just had a thought.

—A prick of conscience.

—Yes. Item 34.

—What's Item 34?

—An unkindness. One of a series. Series long as your arm.

—You list them separately.

—Yes.

—You don't just throw them all together in a great big trash bag labeled—

—No. I sweat each one.

—I said it would be painful.

—Might we postpone it?

—Meditate instead on His works? Their magnificence.

—Not that we could in a hundred million years exhaust—

—It's a sort of if-a-bird-took-one-grain-of-sand-and-flew-all-his-life-and-then-another-bird-took-another-grain-of-sand-and-flew-all-his-life situation.

—Contemplate only the animals. Restrict the field. 'Course we got over a million species, so far. New ones being identified every day. Insects, mostly.

—I like plants better than animals.

—Animals give you a lot of warmth. A dog would be an example.

—I like people better than plants, plants better than animals, paintings better than animals, and music better than animals.

—Praising the animals, then, would not be your first impulse.

—I *respect* the animals. I *admire* the animals. But could we contemplate something else?

—Take a glass of water, for example. A glass of water is a miraculous thing.

—The blue of the sky, against which we find the shocking green of the leaves of the trees.

—The trees. "I think that I shall never see slash A poem lovely as a tree."

—"A tree whose hungry mouth is prest slash Against the earth's sweet flowing breast."

—Why "mouth"?

—Why "breast"?

—The working of the creative mind.

—An unfathomable mystery.

—Never to be fathomed.

—I wouldn't even want to fathom it. If one fathomed it, who can say what frightful things might thereupon be fathomed?

—Fathoming such is beyond the powers of poor ravening noodles like ourselves, who but for the—

—And another thing. The human voice.

—My God you're right. The human voice.

—Bessie Smith.

—Alice Babs.

—Joan Armatrading.

—Aretha Franklin.

—Each voice testifying to the greater honor and glory of God, each in its own way.

—Damn straight.

—Sweet Emma Barrett the Bell Gal.

—Got you.

—*Das Lied von der Erde.*

—I couldn't agree more.

—Then there are the bad things. Cancer.

—An unfathomable mystery, at this point. But one which must inevitably succumb to the inexorable forward march of scientific progress.

—Economic inequality.

—In my view, this will be ameliorated in the near future by the pressure of population growth. Pressure of population growth being such that economic inequality simply cannot endure.

—What about ZPG?

—An ideal rather than a social slash political reality.

—So God's creatures, in your opinion, multiplying and multiplying and multiplying as per instruction, will—

—Propagate fiercely until the sum total of what has been propagated yields a pressure so intense that every feature great or small of every life great or small is instantly scrutinized weighed judged decided upon and disposed of by the sum total of one's peers in doubtless electronic ongoing all-seeing everlasting congress assembled. Thus if one guy has a little advantage, a little edge, it is instantly taken away from him and similarly if another guy has a little lack, some little lack, this little lack is instantly supplied, by the arbiters. Things cannot be otherwise. Because there's not going to be any room to fucking *move*, man, do you follow me? there's not going to be any room to fucking *sneeze*, without you're sneezing *on* somebody . . .

—This is the Divine plan?

—Who can know the subtle workings of His mind? But it seems to be the way events are—

—That's another thing. The human mind.

—Good God yes. The human mind.

—The human mind which is in my judgment the finest of our human achievements.

—Much the finest. I can think of nothing remotely comparable.

—Is a flower, however beautiful and interesting, comparable to the human mind? I think not.

—Matter of higher and lower levels of complexity.

—I concur. This is not to knock the flower.

—This is not to say that the beautiful, interesting flower is not, in its own terms, entirely fantastic.

—The toast of the earth. Did I ever tell you about that time when I was in Saigon and Cardinal Spellman came to see us at Christmas and his plane was preceded by another plane broadcasting sacred music over the terrain? Spraying the terrain as it were with sacred music?

—So that those on earth could hear and be edified.

—"O Little Town of Bethlehem."

—Yes, the human mind deserves the greatest respect. Not so good of course as the Divine mind, but not bad.

—Leibniz. William of Ockham. Maimonides. The Vienna Circle. The Frankfurt School. Manichaeus. Peirce. Occasionalism. A pretty array. I believe Occasionalism's been discredited. But let it stand. It was a nice try, and philosophy, as my dear teacher taught me so long long ago, is not to be regarded as a graveyard of dead systems.

—The question of suicide. Self-slaughter. Maybe we ought to think about it?

—What's to think about?

—Look at this.
—What is it?
—The bill.
—For what is it the bill?
—A try.
—Whose?
—An acquaintance.
—Good God.
—Yes.
—Ought two slash twenty-four electrocardiogram ought two ought ought ought ought one, thirty-five bucks.
—Ought two slash twenty-four cardiopulmonary two ought ought ought ought ought one, forty bucks.
—Ought two slash twenty-four inhalation therapy one four ought ought ought ought one, sixty bucks.
—Ought two slash twenty-four room four nine one five, a neat one-eighty.
—It goes on for miles.
—What's the total?
—Shade under two thousand. Nineteen hundred and two dollars and ninety cents.
—You'd think they'd give you the ninety cents.
—You'd think they would.
—And the acquaintance?
—She's well.
—This being an example of the leap away from faith.
—Exactly. You can jump either way.
—Shall we examine our consciences now?
—You are mad with hurry.
—We are but poor lapsarian futiles whose preen glands are all out of kilter and who but for the grace of God's goodness would—
—Do you think He wants us to grovel quite so much?
—I don't think He gives a rap. But it's traditional.
—We hang by a slender thread.
—The fire boils below us.
—The pit. Crawling with roaches and other things.

—Tortures unimaginable, but the worst the torture of knowing it could have been otherwise, had we shaped up.

—Purity of heart is to will one thing.

—No. Here I differ with Kierkegaard. Purity of heart is, rather, to will several things, and not know which is the better, truer thing, and to worry about this, forever.

—A continuing itch of the mind.

—Sometimes assuagable by timely masturbation.

—I forgot. Love.

—Oh my God, yes. Love. Both human and divine.

—Love, the highest form of human endeavor.

—Coming or going, the absolute zenith.

—Is it *permitted* to differ with Kierkegaard?

—Not only permitted but necessary. If you love him.

—Love, which is a kind of permission to come closer than ordinary norms of good behavior might usually sanction.

—Back rubs.

—Which enables us to see each other without clothes on, for example, in lust and shame.

—Examining perfections, imperfections.

—Which allows us to say wounding things to each other which would not be kosher under the ordinary rules of civilized discourse.

—Walkin' my baby back home.

—Love which allows us to live together male and female in small grubby apartments that would only hold one sane person, normally.

—Misting the plants together—the handsome, talented plants.

—He who hath not love is a sad cookie.

—This is the way, walk ye in it. Isaiah 30:21.

—Can't make it, man.

—What?

—I can't make it.

—The leap.

—Can't make it. I am a double-minded man.

—Well.

—An incorrigibly double-minded man.

—What then?

—Keep on trying?

—Yes. We must.

—Try again another day?

—Yes. Another day when the plaid cactus is watered, when the hare's-foot fern is watered.

—Seeds tingling in the barrens and veldts.

—Garden peas yellow or green wrinkling or rounding.

—Another day when locust wings are baled for shipment to Singapore, where folks like their little hit of locust-wing tea.

—A jug of wine. Then another jug.

—The Brie-with-pepper meeting the toasty loaf.

—Another day when some eighty-four-year-old guy complains that his wife no longer gives him presents.

—Small boys bumping into small girls, purposefully.

—Cute little babies cracking people up.

—Another day when somebody finds a new bone that proves we are even ancienter than we thought we were.

—Gravediggers working in the cool early morning.

—A walk in the park.

—Another day when the singing sunlight turns you every way but loose.

—When you accidentally notice the sublime.

—Somersaults and duels.

—Another day when you see a woman with really red hair. I mean really red hair.

—A wedding day.

—A plain day.

—So we'll try again? Okay?

—Okay.

—Okay?

—Okay.

Aria

Do they lie? Fervently. Do they steal? Only silver and gold. Do they remember? I am in constant touch. Hardly a day passes. The children. Some can't spell, still. Took a walk in the light-manufacturing district, where everything's been converted. Lots of little shops, wine bars. Saw some strange things. Saw a group of square steel plates arranged on a floor. Very interesting. Saw a Man Mountain Dean dressed in heavenly blue. Wild, chewing children. They were small. Petite. Out of scale. They came and went. Doors banging. They were of different sexes but wore similar clothes. Wandered away, then they wandered back. They're vague, you know, they tell you things in a vague way. Asked me to leave, said they'd had enough. Enough what? I asked. Enough of my lip, they said. Although the truth was that I had visited upon them only the palest of apothegms—the one about the salt losing its savor, the one about the fowls of the air. Went for a walk, whistling. Saw a throne in a window. I said: What chair is this? Is it the one great Ferdinand sat in, when he sent the ships to find the Indies? The seat is frayed. Hardly a day passes without an announcement of some kind, a marriage, a pregnancy, a cancer, a rebirth. Sometimes they drift in from the Yukon and other far places, come in and sit down at the kitchen table, want a glass of milk and a peanut-butter-and-jelly, I oblige, for old times' sake. Sent me the schedule for the Little League soccer teams, they're all named after cars, the Mustangs vs. the Mavericks, the Chargers vs. the Impalas. Something funny about that. My son. Slept with What's-Her-Name, they said, while she was asleep, I don't think that's fair. Prone and helpless in the glare of the headlights. They went away, then they came back, at Christmas and Eastertide, had quite a full table, maybe a dozen in all including all the little . . . partners they'd picked up on their travels . . . Snatch them baldheaded, slap their teeth out. Little starved faces four feet from the screen, you'd speak to them in a loud, commanding voice, get not even a twitch. Use of the preemptive splint, not everyone knows about it. The world reminds us of its power, again and again and again. Going along minding your own business, and suddenly an act of God, right there in front of you. Great falls of snow and bursting birds. Getting guilty, letting it all slide. Sown here and there like little . . . petunias, one planted in Old Lyme, one in Fairbanks, one in Tempe. Alleged that he slept with her while she was asleep, I can see it, under certain circumstances. You may wink, but not at another person. You may wink only at pigeons. You may pound in your tent pegs, pitch your tent, gather wood for the fire, form the hush puppies. They seek to return? Back to the nest? The warm arms? The ineffable smells? Not on your tintype. Well, I think that's a little harsh. Think that's a little harsh do you? Yes I think that's a little harsh. Think that's a little harsh do you? Yes, harsh. Harsh. Well that's a sketch, that is, that's a tin-plated sketch—They write and telephone. Short of cash? Give us a call, all inquiries handled with the utmost confidentiality. They call constantly, they're calling still, saying *williwaw, williwaw*—

I walked to the end of my rope, discovered I was tied, tethered. I never stopped to think about it, just went ahead and did it, it was a process, had one and then took care of that one and had another and then took care of the two, the others followed, and now these in turn make more and more and more. . . . Little yowls yonder kept you hopping. They came to me and said goodbye. Goodbye? I said. Goodbye, they said. You're not ridin' with me anymore, is that it? I said. That's it, they said. You're pullin' your blanket, is that it? I said. They said, that's the story Morning Glory. I saw a fish big as a house, and a tea set of Sunderland pink. Ran through the rooms ululating, pulling the tails of the curly curators, came in to say goodnight sometimes, curtsies and bows, these occasions were rare. Things they needed for their lives: hockey sticks, lobster pots, Mazdas. Simultaneously courting and shunning. This is a test of the system, this is only a test. Throw their wet and stinking parkas on the floor as per usual. Turn on the music and turn it off again. Clean your room, please clean your room, I beg of you, clean your room. There's a long tall Sally, polish her shoes. Polish your own shoes, black for black and brown for brown, do you see anything in my palm? just a little sheep-dip, complete your education, he's right and you're wrong, the inside track is thought to be the best, attain it, better to appear at ease, in clothes not conspicuously new, thou shalt not a, b, c, d, e, turn a little to the right, now a little to the left, *hold it!* Naked girls with the heads of Marx and Malraux prone and helpless in the glare of the headlights, tried to give them a little joie de vivre but maybe it didn't take, their constant bickering and smallness, it's like a stroke of lightning, the world reminds you of its power, tracheotomies right and left, I am spinning, my pretty child, don't scratch, pick up your feet, the long nights, spent most of my time listening, this is a test of the system, this is only a test.

The Emerald

Hey buddy what's your name?

My name is Tope. What's your name?

My name is Sallywag. You after the emerald?

Yeah I'm after the emerald you after the emerald too?

I am. What are you going to do with it if you get it?

Cut it up into little emeralds. What are you going to do with it?

I was thinking of solid emerald armchairs. For the rich.

That's an idea. What's your name, you?

Wide Boy.

You after the emerald?

Sure as shootin'.

How you going to get in?

Blast.

That's going to make a lot of noise isn't it?

You think it's a bad idea?

Well . . . What's your name, you there?

Taptoe.

You after the emerald?

Right as rain. What's more, I got a plan.

Can we see it?

No it's my plan I can't be showing it to every—

Okay okay. What's that guy's name behind you?

My name is Sometimes.

You here about the emerald, Sometimes?

I surely am.

Have you got an approach?

Tunneling. I've took some test borings. Looks like a stone cinch.

If this is the right place.

You think this may not be the right place?

The last three places haven't been the right place.

You tryin' to bring me down?

Why would I want to do that? What's that guy's name, the one with the shades?

My name is Brother. Who are all these people?

Businessmen. What do you think of the general situation, Brother?

I think it's crowded. This is my pal, Wednesday.

What say, Wednesday. After the emerald, I presume?

Thought we'd have a go.

Two heads better than one, that the idea?

Yep.

What are you going to do with the emerald, if you get it?

Facet. Facet and facet and facet.

Moll talking to a member of the news media.

Tell me, as a member of the news media, what do you do?

Well we sort of figure out what the news is, then we go out and talk to people, the newsmakers, those who have made the news—

These having been identified by certain people very high up in your organization.

The editors. The editors are the ones who say this is news, this is not news, maybe this is news, damned if I know whether this is news or not—

And then you go out and talk to people and they tell you everything.

They tell you a surprising number of things, if you are a member of the news media. Even if they have something to hide, questionable behavior or one thing and another, or having killed their wife, that sort of thing, still they tell you the most amazing things. Generally.

About themselves. The newsworthy.

Yes. Then we have our experts in the various fields. They are experts in who is a smart cookie and who is a dumb cookie. They write pieces saying which kind of cookie these various cookies are, so that the reader can make informed choices. About things.

Fascinating work I should think.

Your basic glamour job.

I suppose you would have to be very well-educated to get that kind of job.

Extremely well-educated. Typing, everything.

Admirable.

Yes. Well, back to the pregnancy. You say it was a seven-year pregnancy.

Yes. When the agency was made clear to me—

The agency was, you contend, extraterrestrial.

It's a fact. Some people can't handle it.

The father was—

He sat in that chair you're sitting in. The red chair. Naked and wearing a morion.

That's all?

Yes he sat naked in the chair wearing only a morion, and engaged me in conversation.

The burden of which was—

Passion.

What was your reaction?

I was surprised. My reaction was surprise.

Did you declare your unworthiness?

Several times. He was unmoved.

Well I don't know, all this sounds a little unreal, like I mean unreal, if you know what I mean.

Oui, je sais.

What role were you playing?

Well obviously I was playing myself. Mad Moll.

What's a morion?

Steel helmet with a crest.

You considered his offer.

More in the nature of a command.

Then, the impregnation. He approached your white or pink as yet undistended belly with his hideously engorged member—

It was more fun than that.

I find it hard to believe, if you'll forgive me, that you, although quite beautiful in your own way, quite lush of figure and fair of face, still the beard on your chin and that black mark like a furry caterpillar crawling in the middle of your forehead—

It's only a small beard after all.

That's true.

And he seemed to like the black mark on my forehead. He caressed it.

So you did in fact enjoy the . . . event. You understand I wouldn't ask these questions, some of which I admit verge on the personal, were I not a duly credentialed member of the press. Custodian as it were of the public's right to know. Everything. Every last little slippy-dippy thing.

Well okay yes I guess that's true strictly speaking. I suppose that's true. Strictly speaking. I could I suppose tell you to buzz off but I respect the public's right to know. I think. An informed public is, I suppose, one of the basic bulwarks of—

Yes I agree but of course I would wouldn't I, being I mean in my professional capacity my professional role—

Yes I see what you mean.

But of course I exist aside from that role, as a person I mean, as a woman like you—

You're not like me.

Well no in the sense that I'm not a witch.

You must forgive me if I insist on this point. You're not like me.

Well, yes, I don't disagree, I'm not arguing, I have not after all produced after a pregnancy of seven years a gigantic emerald weighing seven thousand and thirty-five carats—Can I, could I, by the way, see the emerald?

No not right now it's sleeping.

The emerald is sleeping?

Yes it's sleeping right now. It sleeps.

It sleeps?

Yes didn't you hear me it's sleeping right now it sleeps just like any other—

What do you mean the emerald is sleeping?

Just what I said. It's asleep.

Do you talk to it?

Of course, sure I talk to it, it's mine, I mean I *gave birth* to it, I cuddle it and polish it and talk to it, what's so strange about that?

Does it talk to you?

Well I mean it's only one month old. How could it talk?

Hello?

Yes?

Is this Mad Moll?

Yes this is Mad Moll who are you?

You the one who advertised for somebody to stand outside the door and knock down anybody tries to come in?

Yes that's me are you applying for the position?

Yes I think so what does it pay?

Two hundred a week and found.

Well that sounds pretty good but tell me lady who is it I have to knock down for example?

Various parties. Some of them not yet known to me. I mean I have an inkling but no more than that. Are you big?

Six eight.

How many pounds?

Two forty-nine.

IQ?

One forty-six.

What's your best move?

I got a pretty good shove. A not-bad bust in the mouth. I can trip. I can fall on 'em. I can gouge. I have a good sense of where the ears are. I know thumbs and kneecaps.

Where did you get your training?

Just around. High school, mostly.

What's your name?

Soapbox.

That's not a very tough name if you'll forgive me.

You want me to change it? I've been called different things in different places.

No I don't want you to change it. It's all right. It'll do.

Okay do you want to see me or do I have the job?

You sound okay to me Soapbox. You can start tomorrow.

What time?

Dawn?

Understand, ye sons of the wise, what this exceedingly precious Stone crieth out to you! Seven years, close to tears. Slept for the first two, dreaming under four blankets, black, blue, brown, brown. Slept and pissed, when I wasn't dreaming I was pissing, I was a fountain. After the first year I knew something irregular was in progress, but not what. I thought, moonstrous! Salivated like a mad dog, four quarts or more a day, when I wasn't pissing I was spitting. Chawed moose steak, moose steak and morels, and fluttered with new men—the butcher, baker, candlestick maker, especially the butcher, one Shatterhand, he was neat. Gobbled a lot of iron, liver and rust from the bottoms of boats, I had serial nosebleeds every day of the seventeenth trimester. Mood swings of course, heigh-de-ho, instances of false labor in years six and seven, palpating the abdominal wall I felt edges and thought, edges? Then on a cold February night the denouement, at six sixty-six in the evening, or a bit past seven, they sent a Miss Leek to do the delivery, one of us but not the famous one, she gave me scopolamine and a little swan-sweat, that helped, she turned not a hair when the emerald presented itself but placed it in my arms with a kiss or two and a pat or two and drove away, in a coach pulled by a golden pig.

Vandermaster has the Foot.

Yes.

The Foot is very threatening to you.

Indeed.

He is a mage and goes around accompanied by a black bloodhound.

Yes. Tarbut. Said to have been raised on human milk.

Could you give me a little more about the Foot. Who owns it?

Monks. Some monks in a monastery in Merano or outside of Merano. That's in Italy. It's their Foot.

How did Vandermaster get it?

Stole it.

Do you by any chance know what order that is?

Let me see if I can remember—Carthusian.

Can you spell that for me?

C-a-r-t-h-u-s-i-a-n. I think.

Thank you. How did Vandermaster get into the monastery?

They hold retreats, you know, for pious laymen or people who just want to come to the monastery and think about their sins or be edified, for a week or a few days . . .

Can you describe the Foot? Physically?

The Foot proper is encased in silver. It's about the size of a foot, maybe slightly larger. It's cut off just above the ankle. The toe part is rather flat, it's as if people in those days had very flat toes. The whole is quite graceful. The Foot proper sits on top of this rather elaborate base, three levels, gold, little claw feet . . .

And you are convinced that this, uh, reliquary contains the true Foot of Mary Magdalene.

Mary Magdalene's Foot. Yes.

He's threatening you with it.

It has a history of being used against witches, throughout history, to kill them or mar them—

He wants the emerald.

My emerald. Yes.

You won't reveal its parentage. Who the father was.

Oh well hell. It was the man in the moon. Deus Lunus.

The man in the moon ha-ha.

No I mean it, it was the man in the moon. Deus Lunus as he's called, the moon god. Deus Lunus. Him.

You mean you want me to believe—

Look woman I don't give dandelions what you believe you asked me who the father was. I told you. I don't give a zipper whether you believe me or don't believe me.

You're actually asking me to—

Sat in that chair, that chair right there. The red chair.

Oh for heaven's sake all right that's it I'm going to blow this pop stand I know I'm just a dumb ignorant media person but if you think for one minute that . . . I respect your uh conviction but this has got to be a delusionary belief. The man in the moon. A delusionary belief.

Well I agree it sounds funny but there it is. Where else would I get an emerald that big, seven thousand and thirty-five carats? A poor woman like me?

Maybe it's not a real emerald?

If it's not a real emerald why is Vandermaster after me?

You going to the hog wrassle?

No I'm after the emerald.

What's your name?

My name is Cold Cuts. What's that machine?

That's an emerald cutter.

How's it work?

Laser beam. You after the emerald too?

Yes I am.

What's your name?

My name is Pro Tem.

That a dowsing rod you got there?

No it's a giant wishbone.

Looks like a dowsing rod.

Well it dowses like a dowsing rod but you also get the wish.

Oh. What's his name?

His name is Plug.

Can't he speak for himself?

He's deaf and dumb.

After the emerald?

Yes. He has special skills.

What are they?

He knows how to diddle certain systems.

Playing it close to the vest is that it?

That's it.

Who's that guy there?

I don't know, all I know about him is he's from Antwerp.
The Emerald Exchange?
That's what I think.
What are all those little envelopes he's holding?
Sealed bids?

Look here, Soapbox, look here.
What's your name, man?
My name is Dietrich von Dietersdorf.
I don't believe it.
You don't believe my name is my name?
Pretty fancy name for such a pissant-looking fellow as you.
I will not be balked. Look here.
What you got?
Silver thalers, my friend, thalers big as onion rings.
That's money, right?
Right.
What do I have to do?
Fall asleep.
Fall asleep at my post here in front of the door?
Right. Will you do it?
I could. But should I?
Where does this "should" come from?
My mind. I have a mind, stewing and sizzling.
Well deal with it, man, deal with it. Will you do it?
Will I? Will I? *I don't know!*

Where is my daddy? asked the emerald. My da?
Moll dropped a glass, which shattered.
Your father.
Yes, said the emerald, amn't I supposed to have one?
He's not here.
Noticed that, said the emerald.
I'm never sure what you know and what you don't know. I ask in true perplexity.
He was Deus Lunus. The moon god. Sometimes thought of as the man in the moon.
Bosh! said the emerald. I don't believe it.

Do you believe I'm your mother?

I do.

Do you believe you're an emerald?

I am an emerald.

Used to be, said Moll, women wouldn't drink from a glass into which the moon had shone. For fear of getting knocked up.

Surely this is superstition?

Hoo, hoo, said Moll. I like superstition.

I thought the moon was female.

Don't be culture-bound. It's been female in some cultures at some times, and in others, not.

What did it feel like? The experience.

Not a proper subject for discussion with a child.

The emerald sulking. Green looks here and there.

Well it wasn't the worst. Wasn't the worst. I had an orgasm that lasted for three hours. I judge that not the worst.

What's an orgasm?

Feeling that shoots through one's electrical system giving you little jolts, *spam spam*, many little jolts, *spam spam spam spam* . . .

Teach me something. Teach me something, mother of mine, about this gray world of yours.

What have I to teach? The odd pitiful spell. Most of them won't even put a shine on a pair of shoes.

Teach me one.

"To achieve your heart's desire, burn in water, wash in fire."

What does that do?

French-fries. Anything you want French-fried.

That's all?

Well.

I have buggered up your tranquillity.

No no no no no.

I'm valuable, said the emerald. I am a thing of value. Over and above my personhood, if I may use the term.

You are a thing of value. A value extrinsic to what I value.

How much?

Equivalent I would say to a third of a sea.

Is that much?

Not inconsiderable.

People want to cut me up and put little chips of me into rings and bangles.

Yes. I'm sorry to say.

Vandermaster is not of this ilk.

Vandermaster is an ilk unto himself.

The more threatening for so being.

Yes.

What are you going to do?

Make me some money. Whatever else is afoot, this delight is constant.

Now the Molljourney the Molltrip into the ferocious Out with a wire shopping cart what's that sucker there doing? tips his hat bends his middle shuffles his feet why he's doing courtly not seen courtly for many a month he does a quite decent courtly I'll smile, briefly, out of my way there citizen sirens shrieking on this swarm summer's day here an idiot there an idiot that one's eyeing me eyed me on the corner and eyed me round the corner as the Mad Moll song has it and that one standing with his cheek crushed against the warehouse wall and that one browsing in a trash basket and that one picking that one's pocket and that one with the gotch eye and his hands on his I'll twoad 'ee bastard I'll—

Hey there woman come and stand beside me.

Buzz off buster I'm on the King's business and have no time to trifle.

You don't even want to stop a moment and look at this thing I have here?

What sort of thing is it?

Oh it's a rare thing, a beautiful thing, a jim-dandy of a thing, a thing any woman would give her eyeteeth to look upon.

Well yes okay but what is it?

Well I can't tell you. I have to show you. Come stand over here in the entrance to this dark alley.

Naw man I'm not gonna go into no alley with you what do you think I am a nitwit?

I think you're a beautiful woman even if you do have that bit of beard there on your chin like a piece of burnt toast or something, most becoming. And that mark like a dead insect on your forehead gives you a certain—

Cut the crap daddy and show me what you got. Standing right here. Else I'm on my way.

No it's too rich and strange for the full light of day we have to have some shadow, it's too—

If this turns out to be an ordinary—

No no no nothing like that. You mean you think I might be a what-do-you-call-'em, one of those guys who—

Your discourse sir strongly suggests it.

And your name?

Moll. Mad Moll. Sometimes Moll the Poor Girl.

Beautiful name. Your mother's name or the name of some favorite auntie?

Moll totals him with a bang in the balls.

Jesus Christ these creeps what can you do?

She stops at a store and buys a can of gem polish.

Polish my emerald so bloody bright it will bloody blind you.

Sitting on the street with a basket of dirty faces for sale. The dirty faces are all colors, white black yellow tan rosy-red.

Buy a dirty face! Slap it on your wife! Buy a dirty face! Complicate your life!

But no one buys.

A boy appears pushing a busted bicycle.

Hey lady what are those things there they look like faces.

That's what they are, faces.

Lady, Halloween is not until—

Okay kid move along you don't want to buy a face move along.

But those are actual faces lady Christ I mean they're *actual faces*—

Fourteen ninety-five kid you got any money on you?

I don't even want to *touch* one, look like they came off dead people.

Would you feel better if I said they were plastic?

Well I hope to God they're not—

Okay they're plastic. What's the matter with your bike?

Chain's shot.

Give it here.

The boy hands over the bicycle chain.

Moll puts the broken ends in her mouth and chews for a moment.

Okay here you go.

The boy takes it in his hands and yanks on it. It's fixed.

Shit how'd you do that, lady?

Moll spits and wipes her mouth on her sleeve.

Run along now kid beat it I'm tired of you.

Are you magic, lady?

Not enough.

Moll at home playing her oboe.

I love the oboe. The sound of the oboe.

The noble, noble oboe!

Of course it's not to every taste. Not everyone swings with the oboe.

Whoops! Goddamn oboe let me take that again.

Not perhaps the premier instrument of the present age. What would that be? The bullhorn, no doubt.

Why did he interfere with me? Why?

Maybe has to do with the loneliness of the gods. Oh thou great one whom I adore beyond measure, oh thou bastard and fatherer of bastards—

Tucked-away gods whom nobody speaks to anymore. Once so lively.

Polish my emerald so bloody bright it will bloody blind you.

Good God what's that?

Vandermaster used the Foot!

Oh my God look at that hole!

It's awful and tremendous!

What in the name of God?

Vandermaster used the Foot!

The Foot did that? I don't believe it!

You don't believe it? What's your name?

My name is Coddle. I don't believe the Foot could have done that. I one hundred percent don't believe it.

Well it's right there in front of your eyes. Do you think Moll and the emerald are safe?

The house seems structurally sound. Smoke-blackened, but sound.

What happened to Soapbox?

You mean Soapbox who was standing in front of the house poised to bop any mother's son who—

Good Lord Soapbox is nowhere to be seen!

He's not in the hole!

Let me see there. What's your name?

My name is Mixer. No, he's not in the hole. Not a shred of him in the hole.

Good, true Soapbox!

You think Moll is still inside? How do we know this is the right place after all?

Heard it on the radio. What's your name by the way?

My name is Ho Ho. Look at the ground smoking!

The whole thing is tremendous, demonstrating the awful power of the Foot!

I am shaking with awe right now! Poor Soapbox!

Noble, noble Soapbox!

Mr. Vandermaster.

Madam.

You may be seated.

I thank you.

The red chair.

Thank you very much.

May I offer you some refreshment?

Yes I will have a splash of something thank you.

It's Scotch I believe.

Yes Scotch.

And I will join you I think, as the week has been a most fatiguing one.

Care and cleaning I take it.

Yes, care and cleaning and in addition there was a media person here.

How tiresome.

Yes it was tiresome in the extreme her persistence in her peculiar vocation is quite remarkable.

Wanted to know about the emerald I expect.

She was most curious about the emerald.

Disbelieving.

Yes disbelieving but perhaps that is an attribute of the profession?

So they say. Did she see it?

No it was sleeping and I did not wish to—

Of course. How did this person discover that you had as it were made yourself an object of interest to the larger public?

Indiscretion on the part of the midwitch I suppose, some people cannot maintain even minimal discretion.

Yes that's the damned thing about some people. Their discretion is out to lunch.

Blabbing things about would be an example.

Popping off to all and sundry about matters.

Ah well.

Ah well. Could we, do you think, proceed?

If we must.

I have the Foot.

Right.

You have the emerald.

Correct.

The Foot has certain properties of special interest to witches.

So I have been told.

There is a distaste, a bad taste in the brain, when one is forced to put the boots to someone.

Must be terrible for you, terrible. Where is my man Soapbox by the way?

That thug you had in front of the door?

Yes, Soapbox.

He is probably reintegrating himself with the basic matter of the universe, right now. Fascinating experience I should think.

Good to know.

I intend only the best for the emerald, however.

What is the best?

There are as you are aware others not so scrupulous in the field. Chislers, in every sense.

And you? What do you intend for it?

I have been thinking of emerald dust. Emerald dust with soda, emerald dust with tomato juice, emerald dust with a dash of bitters, emerald dust with Ovaltine.

I beg your pardon?

I want to live twice.

Twice?

In addition to my present life, I wish another, future life.

A second life. Incremental to the one you are presently enjoying.

As a boy, I was very poor. Poor as pine.

And you have discovered a formula.

Yes.

Plucked from the arcanum.

Yes. Requires a certain amount of emerald. Powdered emerald.

Ugh!

Carat's weight a day for seven thousand thirty-five days.

Coincidence.

Not at all. Only *this* emerald will do. A moon's emerald born of human witch.

No.

I have been thinking about bouillon. Emerald dust and bouillon with a little Tabasco.

No.

No?

No.

My mother is eighty-one, said Vandermaster. I went to my mother and said, Mother, I want to be in love.

And she replied?

She said, me too.

Lily the media person standing in the hall.

I came back to see if you were ready to confess. The hoax.

It's talking now. It talks.
It what?
Lovely complete sentences. Maxims and truisms.
I don't want to hear this. I absolutely—
Look kid this is going to cost you. Sixty dollars.
Sixty dollars for what?
For the interview.
That's checkbook journalism!
Sho' nuff.
It's against the highest traditions of the profession!
You get paid, your boss gets paid, the stockholders get their slice, why not us members of the raw material? Why shouldn't the raw material get paid?
It talks?
Most assuredly it talks.
Will you take a check?
If I must.
You're really a witch.
How many times do I have to tell you?
You do tricks or anything?
Consulting, you might say.
You have clients? People who come to see you regularly on a regular basis?
People with problems, yes.
What kind of problems, for instance?
Some of them very simple, really, things that just need a specific, bit of womandrake for example—
What's womandrake?
Black bryony. Called the herb of beaten wives. Takes away black-and-blue marks.
You get beaten wives?
Stick a little of that number into the old man's pork and beans, he retches. For seven days and seven nights. It near to kills him.
I have a problem.
What's the problem?
The editor, or editor-king, as he's called around the shop.
What about him?

He takes my stuff and throws it on the floor. When he doesn't like it.

On the floor?

I know it's nothing to you but it *hurts me.* I cry. I know I shouldn't cry but I cry. When I see my stuff on the floor. Pages and pages of it, so carefully typed, *every word spelled right—*

Don't you kids have a union?

Yes but he won't speak to it.

That's this man Lather, right?

Mr. Lather. Editor-imperator.

Okay I'll look into it that'll be another sixty you want to pay now or you want to be billed?

I'll give you another check. *Can* Vandermaster live twice?

There are two theories, the General Theory and the Special Theory. I take it he is relying on the latter. Requires ingestion of a certain amount of emerald. Powdered emerald.

Can you defend yourself?

I have a few things in mind. A few little things.

Can I see the emerald now?

You may. Come this way.

Thank you. Thank you at last. My that's impressive what's that?

That's the thumb of a thief. Enlarged thirty times. Bronze. I use it in my work.

Impressive if one believed in that sort of thing ha-ha I don't mean to—

What care I? What care I? In here. Little emerald, this is Lily. Lily, this is the emerald.

Enchanté, said the emerald. What a pretty young woman you are!

This emerald is young, said Lily. Young, but good. I do not believe what I am seeing with my very eyes!

But perhaps that is a sepsis of the profession? said the emerald.

Vandermaster wants to live twice!

Oh, most foul, most foul!

He was very poor, as a boy! Poor as pine!

Hideous presumption! Cheeky hubris!

He wants to be in love! In love! Presumably with another person!

Unthinkable insouciance!

We'll have his buttons for dinner!

We'll clean the gutters with his hair!

What's your name, buddy?

My name is Tree and I'm smokin' mad!

My name is Bump and I'm just about ready to bust!

I think we should break out the naked-bladed pikes!

I think we should lay hand to torches and tar!

To live again! From the beginning! *Ab ovo!* This concept riles the very marrow of our minds!

We'll flake the white meat from his bones!

And that goes for his damned dog, too!

Hello is this Mad Moll?

Yes who is this?

My name is Lather.

The editor?

Editor-king, actually.

Yes Mr. Lather what is the name of your publication I don't know that Lily ever—

World. I put it together. When *World* is various and beautiful, it's because I am various and beautiful. When *World* is sad and dreary, it's because I am sad and dreary. When *World* is not thy friend, it's because *I* am not thy friend. And if I am not thy friend, baby—

I get the drift.

Listen, Moll, I am not satisfied with what Lily's been giving me. She's not giving me potato chips. I have decided that I am going to handle this story personally, from now on.

She's been insufficiently insightful and comprehensive?

Gore, that's what we need, actual or psychological gore, and this twitter she's been filing—anyhow, I have sent her to Detroit.

Not Detroit!

She's going to be second night-relief paper clipper in the Detroit bureau. She's standing here right now with her bags packed and ashes in her hair and her ticket in her mouth.

Why in her mouth?

Because she needs her hands to rend her garments with.

All right Mr. Lather send her back around. There is new bad news. Bad, bad, new bad news.

That's wonderful!

Moll hangs up the phone and weeps every tear she's capable of weeping, one, two, three.

Takes up a lump of clay, beats it flat with a Bible.

Let me see what do I have here?

I have Ya Ya Oil, that might do it.

I have Anger Oil, Lost & Away Oil, Confusion Oil, Weed of Misfortune, and War Water.

I have graveyard chips, salt, and coriander—enough coriander to freight a ship. Tasty coriander. Magical, magical coriander!

I'll eye-bite the son of a bitch. Have him in worm's hall by teatime.

Understand, ye sons of the wise, what this exceedingly precious Stone crieth out to you!

I'll fold that sucker's tent for him. If my stuff works. One never knows for sure, dammit. And where is Papa?

Throw in a little dwale now, a little orris . . .

Moll shapes the clay into the figure of a man.

So mote it be!

What happened was that they backed a big van up to the back door.

Yes.

There were four of them or eight of them.

Yes.

It was two in the morning or three in the morning or four in the morning—I'm not sure.

Yes.

They were great big hairy men with cudgels and ropes and pads like movers have and a dolly and come-alongs made of barbed wire—that's a loop of barbed wire big enough to slip over somebody's head, with a handle—

Yes.

They wrapped the emerald in the pads and placed it on the dolly and tied ropes around it and got it down the stairs through the door and into the van.

Did they use the Foot?

No they didn't use the Foot they had four witches with them.

Which witches?

The witches Aldrin, Endrin, Lindane, and Dieldrin. Bad-ass witches.

You knew them.

Only by repute. And Vandermaster was standing there with clouds of 1, 1, 2, 2-tetrachloroethylene seething from his nostrils.

That's toxic.

Extremely. I was staggering around bumping into things, tried to hold on to the walls but the walls fell away from me and I fell after them trying to hold on.

These other witches, they do anything to you?

Kicked me in the ribs when I was on the floor. With their pointed shoes. I woke up emeraldless.

Right. Well I guess we'd better get the vast resources of our organization behind this. *World.* From sea to shining sea to shining sea. I'll alert all the bureaus in every direction.

What good will that do?

It will harry them. When a free press is on the case, you can't get away with anything really terrible.

But look at this.

What is it?

A solid silver louse. They left it.

What's it mean?

Means that the devil himself has taken an interest.

A free press, madam, is not afraid of the devil himself.

Who cares what's in a witch's head? Pretty pins for sticking pishtoshio redthread for sewing names to shrouds gallant clankers I'll twoad 'ee and the gollywobbles to give away and the trinkum-trankums to give away with a generous hand pricksticks for the eye damned if I do and damned if I don't what's that upon her forehead? said my father it's a mark said my mother black mark like a furry caterpillar I'll scrub it away with the Ajax and what's that upon her chin? said my father it's a bit of a beard said my mother I'll pluck it away with the tweezers and what's that upon her mouth? said my father it must be a smirk said my mother I'll wipe it away with the heel of my hand she's got hair down there already said my father is that natural? I'll shave it said my mother no one will ever know and those said my father pointing *those?* just what they look like said my mother I'll make a bandeau with this nice clean dish towel she'll be flat as a jack of diamonds in no time and where's the belly button? said my father flipping me about I don't see one anywhere must be coming along later said my mother I'll just pencil one in here with the Magic Marker this child is a bit of a mutt said my father recall to me if you will the circumstances of her conception it was a dark and stormy night said my mother . . . But who cares what's in a witch's head caskets of cankers shelves of twoads for twoading paxwax scalpel polish people with scares sticking to their faces memories of God who held me up and sustained me until I fell from His hands into the world . . .

Twice? Twice? Twice? Twice?

Hey Moll.

Who's that?

It's me.

Me who?

Soapbox.

Soapbox!

I got it!

Got what?

The Foot! I got it right here!

I thought you were blown up!

Naw I pretended to be bought so I was out of the way. Went with them back to their headquarters, or den. Then when they put the Foot back in the refrigerator I grabbed it and beat it back here.

They kept it in the refrigerator?

It needs a constant temperature or else it gets restless. It's hot-tempered. They said.

It's elegant. Weighs a ton though.

Be careful you might—

Soapbox, I am not totally without—it's warm to the hand.

Yes it is warm I noticed that, look what else I got.

What are those?

Thalers. Thalers big as onion rings. Forty-two grand worth.

What are you going to do with them?

Conglomerate!

It is wrong to want to live twice, said the emerald. If I may venture an opinion.

I was very poor, as a boy, said Vandermaster. Nothing to eat but gruel. It was gruel, gruel, gruel. I was fifteen before I ever saw an onion.

These are matters upon which I hesitate to pronounce, being a new thing in the world, said the emerald. A latecomer to the welter. But it seems to me that, having weltered, the wish to *re*-welter might be thought greedy.

Gruel today, gruel yesterday, gruel tomorrow. Sometimes gruel substitutes. I burn to recoup.

Something was said I believe about love.

The ghostfish of love has eluded me these forty-five years.

That Lily person is a pleasant person I think. And pretty too. Very pretty. Good-looking.

Yes she is.

I particularly like the way she is dedicated. She's extremely dedicated. Very dedicated. To her work.

Yes I do not disagree. Admirable. A free press is, I believe, an essential component of—

She is true-blue. Probably it would be great fun to talk to her and get to know her and kiss her and sleep with her and everything of that nature.

What are you suggesting?

Well, there's then, said the emerald, that is to say, your splendid second life.

Yes?

And then there's now. Now is sooner than then.

You have a wonderfully clear head, said Vandermaster, for a rock.

Okay, said Lily. I want you to tap once for yes and twice for no. Do you understand that?

Tap.

You are the true Foot of Mary Magdalene?

Tap.

Vandermaster stole you from a monastery in Italy?

Tap.

A Carthusian monastery in Merano or outside Merano?

Tap.

Are you uncomfortable in that reliquary?

Tap tap.

Have you killed any witches lately? In the last year or so?

Tap tap.

Are you morally neutral or do you have opinions?

Tap.

You have opinions?

Tap.

In the conflict we are now witnessing between Moll and Vandermaster, which of the parties seems to you to have right and justice on her side?

Tap tap tap tap.

That mean Moll? One tap for each letter?

Tap.

Is it warm in there?

Tap.

Too warm?

Tap tap.

So you have been, in a sense, an unwilling partner in Vandermaster's machinations.

Tap.

And you would not be averse probably to using your considerable powers on Moll's behalf.

Tap.

Do you know where Vandermaster is right now?

Tap tap.

Have you any idea what his next move will be?

Tap tap.

What is your opinion of the women's movement?

Tap tap tap tap tap tap tap tap tap tap tap tap tap tap.

I'm sorry I didn't get that. Do you have a favorite color what do you think of cosmetic surgery should children be allowed to watch television after ten P.M. how do you feel about aging is nuclear energy in your opinion a viable alternative to fossil fuels how do you deal with stress are you afraid to fly and do you have a chili recipe you'd care to share with the folks?

Tap tap.

The first interview in the world with the true Foot of Mary Magdalene and no chili recipe!

Mrs. Vandermaster.

Yes.

Please be seated.

Thank you.

The red chair.

You're most kind.

Can I get you something, some iced tea or a little hit of Sanka?

A Ghost Dance is what I wouldn't mind if you can do it.

What's a Ghost Dance?

That's one part vodka to one part tequila with half an onion. Half a regular onion.

Wow wow wow wow wow.

Well when you're eighty-one, you know, there's not so much. Couple of Ghost Dances, I begin to take an interest.

I believe I can accommodate you.

Couple of Ghost Dances, I begin to look up and take notice.

Mrs. Vandermaster, you are aware are you not that your vile son has, with the aid of various parties, abducted my emerald? My own true emerald?

I mighta heard about it.

Well have you or haven't you?

'Course I don't pay much attention to that boy myself. He's bent.

Bent?

Him and his dog. He goes off in a corner and talks to the dog. Looking over his shoulder to see if I'm listening. As if I'd care.

The dog doesn't—

Just listens. *Intently*.

That's Tarbut.

Now I don't mind somebody who just addresses an occasional remark to the dog, like "Attaboy, dog," or something like that, or "Get the ball, dog," or something like that, but he *confides* in the dog. Bent.

You know what Vandermaster's profession is.

Yes, he's a mage. Think that's a little bent.

Is there anything you can do, or would do, to help me get my child back? My sweet emerald?

Well I don't have that much say-so.

You don't.

I don't know too much about what-all he's up to. He comes and goes.

I see.

The thing is, he's bent.

You told me.

Wants to live twice.

I know.

I think it's a sin and a shame.

You do.

And your poor little child.

Yes.

A damned scandal.

Yes.

I'd witch his eyes out if I were you.

The thought's appealing.

His eyes like onions . . .

A black bloodhound who looks as if he might have been fed on human milk. Bloodhounding down the center of the street, nose to the ground.

You think this will work?

Soapbox, do you have a better idea?

Where did you find him?

I found him on the doorstep. Sitting there. In the moonlight.

In the moonlight?

Aureoled all around with moonglow.

You think that's significant?

Well I don't think it's happenstance.

What's his name?

Tarbut.

There's something I have to tell you.

What?

I went to the refrigerator for a beer?

Yes?

The Foot's walked.

Dead! Kicked in the heart by the Foot!

That's incredible!

Deep footprint right over the breastbone!

That's ghastly and awful!

After Lily turned him down he went after the emerald with a sledge!

Was the emerald hurt?

Chipped! The Foot got there in the nick!

And Moll?

She's gluing the chips back with grume!

What's grume?

Clotted blood!

And was the corpse claimed?

Three devils showed up! Lily's interviewing them right now!

A free press is not afraid of a thousand devils!

There are only three!

What do they look like?

Like Lather, the editor!

And the Foot?

Soapbox is taking it back to Italy! He's starting a security-guard business! Hired Sallywag, Wide Boy, Taptoe, and Sometimes!

What's your name by the way?

My name is Knucks. What's your name?

I'm Pebble. And the dog?

The dog's going to work for Soapbox too!

Curious, the dog showing up on Moll's doorstep that way!

Deus Lunus works in mysterious ways!

Deus Lunus never lets down a pal!

Well how 'bout a drink!

Don't mind if I do! What'll we drink to?

We'll drink to living once!

Hurrah for the here and now!

Tell me, said the emerald, what are diamonds like?

I know little of diamonds, said Moll.

Is a diamond better than an emerald?

Apples and oranges I would say.

Would you have *preferred* a diamond?

Nope.

Diamond-hard, said the emerald, that's an expression I've encountered.

Diamonds are a little ordinary. Decent, yes. Quiet, yes. But *gray*. Give me step-cut zircons, square-cut spodumenes, jasper, sardonyx, bloodstones, Baltic amber, cursed opals, peridots of your own hue, the padparadscha sapphire, yellow chrysoberyls, the shifty tourmaline, cabochons . . . But best of all, an emerald.

But what is the *meaning* of the emerald? asked Lily. I mean overall? If you can say.

I have some notions, said Moll. You may credit them or not.

Try me.

It means, one, that the gods are not yet done with us.

Gods not yet done with us.

The gods are still trafficking with us and making interventions of this kind and that kind and are not dormant or dead as has often been proclaimed by dummies.

Still trafficking. Not dead.

Just as in former times a demon might enter a nun on a piece of lettuce she was eating so even in these times a simple Mailgram might be the thin edge of the wedge

Thin edge of the wedge.

Two, the world may congratulate itself that desire can still be raised in the dulled hearts of the citizens by the rumor of an emerald.

Desire or cupidity?

I do not distinguish qualitatively among the desires, we have referees for that, but he who covets not at all is a lump and I do not wish to have him to dinner.

Positive attitude toward desire.

Yes. Three, I do not know what this Stone portends, whether it portends for the better or portends for the worse or merely portends a bubbling of the in-between but you are in any case rescued from the sickliness of same and a small offering in the hat on the hall table would not be ill regarded.

And what now? said the emerald. What now, beautiful mother?

We resume the scrabble for existence, said Moll. We resume the scrabble for existence, in the sweet of the here and now.

How I Write My Songs

Some of the methods I use to write my songs will be found in the following examples. Everyone has a song in him or her. Writing songs is a basic human trait. I am not saying that it is easy; like everything else worthwhile in this world it requires concentration and hard work. The methods I will outline are a good way to begin and have worked for me but they are by no means the only methods that can be used. There is no one set way of writing your songs, every way is just as good as the other as Kipling said. (I am talking now about the lyrics; we will talk about the melodies in a little bit.) The important thing is to put true life into your songs, things that people know and can recognize and truly feel. You have to be open to experience, to what is going on around you, the things of daily life. Often little things that you don't even think about at the time can be the basis of a song.

A knowledge of all the different types of songs that are commonly accepted is helpful. To give you an idea of the various types of songs there are I am going to tell you how I wrote various of my own, including "Rudelle," "Last Night," "Sad Dog Blues," and others—how I came to write these songs and where I got the idea and what the circumstances were, more or less, so that you will be able to do the same thing. Just remember, *there is no substitute for sticking to it* and listening to the work of others who have been down this road before you and have mastered their craft over many years.

In the case of "Rudelle" I was sitting at my desk one day with my pencil and yellow legal pad and I had two things that were irritating me. One was a letter from the electric company that said "The check for $75.60 sent us in payment of your bill has been returned to us by the bank unhonored etc. etc." Most of you who have received this type of letter from time to time know how irritating this kind of communication can be as well as embarrassing. The other thing that was irritating me was that I had a piece of white thread tied tight around my middle at navel height as a reminder to keep my stomach pulled in to strengthen the abdominals while sitting—this is the price you pay for slopping down too much beer when your occupation is essentially a sit-down one! Anyhow I had these two things itching me, so I decided to write a lost-my-mind song.

I wrote down on my legal pad the words:

When I lost my baby
I almost lost my mine

This is more or less a traditional opening for this type of song. Maybe it was written by somebody originally way long ago and who wrote it is forgotten. It often helps to begin with a traditional or well-known line or lines to set a pattern for yourself. You can then write the rest of the song and, if you wish, cut off the top part, giving you an original song. *Songs are always composed of both traditional and new elements.* This means that you can rely on the tradition to give your song "legs" while also putting in your own experience or particular way of looking at things for the new.

Incidentally the lines I have quoted may look pretty bare to you but remember you are looking at just one element, the words, and there is also the melody and the special way various artists will have of singing it which gives flavor and freshness. For example, an artist who is primarily a blues singer would probably give the "when" a lot of squeeze, that is to say, draw it out, and he might also sing "baby" as three notes, "bay-ee-bee," although it is only two syllables. Various artists have their own unique ways of doing a song and what may appear to be rather plain or dull on paper becomes quite different when it is a song.

I then wrote:

When I lost my baby
I almost lost my mine
When I lost my baby
I almost lost my mine
When I found my baby
The sun began to shine.

You will notice I retained the traditional opening because it was so traditional I did not see any need to delete it. With the addition of various material about Rudelle and what kind of woman she was, it became gold in 1976.

Incidentally while we are talking about use of traditional materials here is a little tip: you can often make good use of colorful expressions in common use such as "If the good Lord's willin' and the creek don't rise" (to give you just one example) which I used in "Goin' to Get Together" as follows:

Goin' to get to-geth-er
Goin' to get to-geth-er
If the good Lord's willin' and the creek don't rise.

These common expressions are expressive of the pungent ways in which most people often think—they are the salt of your song, so to say. Try it!

It is also possible to give a song a funny or humorous "twist":

Show'd my soul to the woman at
the bank
She said put that thing away boy,
put that thing away
Show'd my soul to the woman at
the liquor store
She said put that thing away boy,
'fore it turns the wine

Show'd my soul to the woman at
    the 7-Eleven
She said: Is that all?

You will notice that the meter here is various and the artist is given great liberties.

Another type of song which is a dear favorite of almost everyone is the song that has a message, some kind of thought that people can carry away with them and think about. Many songs of this type are written and gain great acceptance every day. Here is one of my own that I put to a melody which has a kind of martial flavor:

How do you spell truth? L-o-v-e is
    how you spell truth
How do you spell love? T-r-u-t-h
    is how you spell love
Where were you last night?
Where were you last night?

When "Last Night" was first recorded, the engineer said "That's a keeper" on the first take and it was subsequently covered by sixteen artists including Walls.

The I-ain't-nothin'-but-a-man song is a good one to write when you are having a dry spell. These occur in songwriting as in any other profession and if you are in one it is often helpful to try your hand at this type of song which is particularly good with a heavy rhythm emphasis in the following pattern

Da da da da *da*
Whomp, whomp

where some of your instruments are playing da da da da *da*, hitting that last note hard, and the others answer whomp, whomp. Here is one of my own:

I'm just an ordinary mane
Da da da da *da*
Whomp, whomp
Just an ordinary mane
Da da da da *da*
Whomp, whomp
Ain't nothin' but a mane
Da da da da *da*
Whomp, whomp
I'm a grizzly mane
Da da da da *da*
Whomp, whomp
I'm a hello-goodbye mane
Da da da da *da*
Whomp, whomp
I'm a ramblin'-gamblin' mane
Da da da da *da*
Whomp, whomp
I'm a *mane's* mane
Da da da da *da*
Whomp, whomp
I'm a woeman's mane
Da da da da *da*
Whomp, whomp
I'm an upstairs-downstairs mane
Da da da da *da*
Whomp, whomp
I'm a today-and-tomorrow mane
Da da da da *da*
Whomp, whomp
I'm a Freeway mane
Da da da da *da*
Whomp, whomp

Well, you see how it is done. It is my hope that these few words will get you started. Remember that although this business may seem closed and standoffish to you, looking at it from the outside, inside it has some very warm people in it, some of the finest people I have run into in the course of a varied life. The main thing is to persevere and to believe in yourself, no matter what the attitude of others may be or appear to be. I could never have written my songs had I failed to believe in Bill B. White, not as a matter of conceit or false pride but as a human being. I will continue to write my songs, for the nation as a whole and for the world.

The Farewell

—Well Maggie I have finally been admitted to the damn Conservatory. Finally.

—Yes Hilda I was astonished when I heard the news, astonished.

—A glorious messenger came riding. Said I was to be admitted. At last.

—Well Hilda I suppose they must have changed the standards or something.

—He was clothed all in silver, and his hat held a pure white plume. He doffed his hat and waved it in the air, and bowed.

—The Admissions Committee's been making some pretty strange calls lately, lots of talk about it.

—A Presidential appointment, he said. Direct from the President himself.

—Yes those are for disadvantaged people who would not otherwise be considered. Who would not otherwise be considered in a million years.

—Well Maggie now that we are both members of the Conservatory maybe you won't be so snotty.

—Snotty?

—Maybe you won't be lording it over me quite so much, all those little vicious digs.

—Me?

—All those innocent remarks with little curly hooks in them.

—Hilda this can't be me you're talking about. Me, your dear friend.

—Well it doesn't matter now anyway because we are both on the same plane at last. Both members of the Conservatory.

—Hilda I have to tell you something.

—What?

—A lot of people are leaving. The Conservatory. Leaving the Conservatory and transferring to the Institution.

—What's that?

—A new place. Very rigorous.

—You mean people are leaving the Conservatory?

—Yes. Switching to the Institution.

—It's called the Institution?

—Yes. It's a new place.

—What's so good about it?

—It's new. Very rigorous.

—You mean after I've killed myself to get into the Conservatory there's a new place that's better?

—Yes they have new methods. New, superior methods. I would say that the cream of the Conservatory is transferring to the institution or will transfer to the Institution.

—But you're still at the Conservatory aren't you?

—Thinking of transferring. To the Institution.

—But I *sweated blood* to get into the Conservatory you know that. You know it!

—At the Institution they have not only improved methodologies but also a finer quality of teacher. The teachers are more dedicated, twice as dedicated or three times as dedicated. The design of the Institution buildings has been carefully studied, and is new. Each student has his or her own personal wickiup wherein he or she may spend hours one-on-one with his or her own personal, supremely dedicated teacher.

—I cannot believe this!

—Savory meals are left in steaming baskets outside each wickiup door. All meals are lobster, unless the student has indicated a preference for beautifully marbled beef. There are four Olympic-sized pool tables for every one student.

—It's just unfair, hideously unfair.

—The Institution song was composed by Tammy and the Rayettes and the Institution T-shirt is by Hedwig McMary. And of course they have the improved methodologies.

—Of course.

—Yes.

—Maggie?

—What?

—I guess this joint is tough to get into, right?

—Impossible.

—Then how can you—

—There's this guy I know he's the Chancellor. Boss of the whole shebang. He likes me.

—I see.

—He is devoted to me and always has been. Me and my potential. He is wonderful on the subject of my potential.

—I already had a babysitter hired. For those hours I would have spent at the Conservatory.

—Well don't be downhearted Hilda, the Conservatory is a very fine place too. Within its limits.

—I already had a babysitter laid on. For those days on which I would have been wending my way up the hill through the gum trees to the Conservatory. Once the zenith of my aspirations.

—Yes how is that kid you're a mother now must make you feel different.

—What can I tell you? It eats.

—I guess the father what's-his-name never showed up again did he?

—Sent some Q-tips in the mail.

—The beast.

—Maggie you've got to help me.

—Help you what?

—I must get into the Institution.

—You?

—I must get into the Institution.

—Oh my.

—If I don't get into the Institution I will shrink into a little shrunken mummy, self-esteem-wise.

—O my dear one your plight is painful to me.

—My plight?

—Wouldn't you call it a plight?

—I guess so. Good of you to find the *mot juste*.

—Hilda I will do everything in my power to help you achieve your mete measure of personal growth. Everything.

—Thank you Maggie. I believe you.

—But we have to be realistic.

—What does that mean?

—There are some kinds of places for some kinds of people and other kinds of places for other kinds of people.

—What does that mean?

—Did I tell you I got a grant?

—What kind of a grant?

—There are these excellence grants they give to people who are excellent. I got one.

—Oh. I thought you already had a grant.

—That was my old grant. That was for enrichment. This is new. It's for excellence.

—I could I suppose just sink down into the gutter. The gutter of plain life. Life without excellence.

—Hilda it's not like you to give up like this. It's sensible, but not like you.

—Maggie I am floating away from you. Floating away. Like a brown leaf in the gutter.

—Where will you go?

—I have decided. There'll be a night-long, block-long farewell party. Everyone will be invited. All those who have mocked me will not be invited but all those who have loved me will be invited. There will be crystal, silver, Persian lilies, torches, garlic bread, and jugs of rare jug wine.

—When do you figure this will be?

—Maybe Thursday. All my friends smiling faithfully up at me from their assigned places at the block-long table. Spaced carefully here and there, interesting-looking men who look like ads. Smiling up at me from their places where they have been put as interesting stuffing between all my friends.

—All your friends.

—Yes. All my glorious shining friends.

—Who?

—All my friends.

—Yes but who? Who specifically?

—All my friends. I see what you mean.

—I can't believe I said that Hilda. Did I say that?

—Yes you did.

—I didn't mean it. It was the truth, but I didn't mean it. I'm sorry.

—OK.

—It just slipped out.

—Doesn't matter.

—Can you forgive me?

—Of course. I'll have the party anyhow. Maybe ask a lot of answering services or something.

—I will come. If I'm invited.

—Who if not you?

—You'll make it Hilda I'm sure you will. One of these days.

—That's good to hear Maggie I'm glad I have your support.

—You will not only endure, you will prevail.

—Well thanks a lot Maggie. Thanks. Over what?

—Over everything. It's in the cards Hilda I know it.

—Well thanks a lot. Do you really think so?

—I really think so. I really do.

—All my friends smiling faithfully up at me. Well, fuck it.

The Emperor

Each morning the Emperor weighs the documents brought to him, each evening he weighs them again; he will not rest until a certain weight has passed through his hands; he has declared six to be the paramount number of his reign, black the paramount color; he hurries from palace to palace, along the underground corridors, ignoring gorgeous wall hangings, bells, drums, beautiful ladies; how many more responsible officials must be strangled before his will prevails, absolutely?

The Emperor sleeps in a different palace each night, to defeat assassins; of the two hundred and seventy palaces, some are congenial to him, some not; the three worms inspiring disease, old age and death have yet to find him; his presents this morning included a most dazzling parcel-gilt bronze wine warmer, gift of the grateful people of Peiho, and a sumptuous set of nine bronze bells tuned in scale, gift of the worshipful citizens of Yuchang; he has decided that all officers in these places will be promoted one rank, and that the village well in Peiho will be given the title of Minister of the Fifth Rank . . .

The First Emperor has decreed that the people of his realm will be called the Blackheaded People; in the ocean there are three fairy islands, Penglai, Fangchang and Ingchou, where immortals live, and he has sent the scholar Hsu Fu, with several thousand young boys and girls, to find them; he dictates a memorial which begins, *"The Throne appreciates . . .";* the famous assassin Ching K'o has purchased, for a hundred pieces of gold, a bronze dagger said to be the sharpest in the kingdom.

Hats are six inches wide, carriages six feet wide, the Empire has been divided into thirty-six provinces; a jade cicada is placed upon the tongues of ministers of the Sixth through the First Rank, upon interment; as he hurries through the corridors he is beseeched by wives, so many that he no longer attempts to remember their names, but addresses each as "Wife!" and flees their fatiguing excellences; he sends armies hither and thither as others send messengers; the model of all China he has decreed must be inspected, its rivers of quicksilver and cities of celadon must be approved; if you have artisans strangled for poor work there remain their families, consistently large, whispering against you in the squares and taverns . . .

The Emperor Ch'in Shih Huang Ti has decreed that six thousand archers, lancers, charioteers and musicians be buried alive, along with two thousand horses, in military formation on the four sides of his tomb; responsible officials attempt to reason with him, stating that this will enflame the people against him; but his tomb must be defended by precisely six thousand archers, lancers, charioteers and musicians, lest it suffer the fate of other tombs in other times; the enfeoffed Marquis of Chienchang has wrongly seized territory in that area, stranglers are summoned; generals on the frontier must be regularly and thoroughly frightened, so that they do not misremember where their true allegiance rests . . .

His gifts this morning include two white-jade tigers, at full scale, carved by the artist Lieh Yi, and the Emperor himself takes brush in hand to paint their eyes with dark lacquer; responsible officials have suggested that six thousand terra-cotta soldiers and two thousand terra-cotta horses, at full scale, be buried, for the defense of his tomb; the Emperor in his rage orders that three thousand convicts cut down all the trees on Mount Hsiang, leaving it bare, bald, so that responsible officials may understand what is possible; the Emperor commands the court poets to write poems about immortals, pure beings, and noble spirits who by their own labors change night to day, and has these sung to him; everyone knows that executions should not be carried out in the spring, even a child knows it, but in certain cases . . .

The deft and subtle assassin Ching K'o is beheaded, and his botched attempt recorded in the annals, and his botched last words excised from the annals; the Emperor hurries through the corridors of his plethora of palaces accepting petitions which he thrusts into the sleeves of his robe; seventy thousand convicts are at work on the construction of his tomb, which has been in progress since his thirteenth year and measures 2173 meters north-south and 974 meters east-west; the ceiling of the inmost chamber has a sky in which pearls of ungodly size represent the stars, the constellations; the Emperor Ch'in Shih Huang Ti pauses, drinks warm wine, and considers whether sufficient chairs have been provided, in his tomb, for the suites of wives, generals and responsible officials who will be buried with him; the scholar Hsu Fu, and the youths and maidens who embarked with him, have not been heard from, have most certainly been devoured by monsters . . .

For a thousand piculs of grain a commoner can now purchase noble rank, a scandal; the Emperor has had a building stone too large to be moved through the Kirin Gate given sixty lashes, to punish it; there is a woman who excites him, the Lady Yao (with the long scar on the right leg) but to find his way back to the pavilion that contains her is an almost impossible task; a blasphemer has described him as a dog, a hen, and a snake, and he rejoices in the poverty of mind displayed; he will cause Mount Hsiang to be planted in squared-off stakes, so that certain officials may achieve a more sophisticated comprehension of the Imperial will . . .

No. He will permit the six thousand clay soldiers to be buried, and with them, one real soldier, a prince, a secret happiness; he will prepare with his own hands for this prince a potion to put him softly to sleep, a fatherly happiness; he will whisper into this prince's ear, before administering the potion, a lifetime of secrets, a delirious happiness; he will have the buriers of the prince themselves buried, a geometric happiness; those who perform the second burial will be sent away to a war, which he will contrive through transcendent military skill to lose, a sad, remote, and professional happiness; he will walk through the streets of the capital barefoot and carrying a thorn bush with which to flagellate his naked shoulders for having lost this war, a hidden and painful happiness; these happinesses taken together may be the equal of the herbs of immortality growing like weeds on the magic island of Penglai; like weeds.

Thailand

Yes, said the old soldier, I remember a time. It was during the Krian War.

Bless you and keep you, said his hearer, silently.

It was during the Krian War, said the old soldier. We were up there on the 38th parallel, my division, round about the Chorwon Valley. This was in '52.

Oh God, said the listener to himself. Enchiladas in green sauce. Dos Equis. Maybe a burrito or two.

We had this battalion of Thais attached to us, said the old sergeant. Nicest people you'd ever want to meet. We used to call their area Thailand, like it was a whole country. They are small of stature. We used to party with them a lot. What they drink is Mekong, it'll curl your teeth. In Kria we weren't too particular.

Enchiladas in green sauce and Gilda. Gilda in her sizzling blouse.

This time I'm talking about, we were partying at Thailand, there was this Thai second john who was a personal friend of mine, named Sutchai. Tall fellow, thin, he was an exception to the rule. We were right tight, even went on R&R together, you're too young to know what that is, it's Rest and Recreation where you zip off to Tokyo and sample the delights of that great city for a week.

I am young, thought the listener, young, young, praise the Lord I am young.

This time I am talking about, said the old sarge, we were on the side of a hill, they held this hill which sort of anchored the MLR—that's Main Line of Resistance—at that point, pretty good-sized hill I forget what the designation was, and it was a feast day, some Thai feast, a big holiday, and the skies were sunny, sunny. They had set out thirty-seven washtubs full of curry I never saw anything like it. Thirty-seven washtubs full of curry and a different curry in every one. They even had eel curry.

I cannot believe I am sitting here listening to this demento carry on about eel curry.

It was a golden revel, said the sergeant, if you liked curry and I did and do. Beef curry, chicken curry, the delicate Thai worm curry, all your various fish curries and vegetable curries. The Thai cooks were number one, even in the sergeant's mess which I was the treasurer of for a year and a half we didn't eat like that. Well, you're too young to know what a quad-fifty is but it's four fifty-caliber machine guns mounted on a half-track and they had quad-fifties dug in on various parts of their hill as well as tanks which was just about all you could do with a tank in that terrain, and toward evening they were firing off tracer bursts from the quad-fifties to make fireworks and it was just very festive, very festive. They had fighting with wooden swords at which the Thais excel, it's like a ballet dance, and the whole battalion was putting away the Mekong and beer pretty good as were the invited guests such as me and my buddy Nick Pirelli who was my good buddy in the motor pool, anytime I wanted a vehicle of any type for any purpose all I had to do was call Nick and he'd redline that vehicle and send it over to me with a driver—

I too have a life, thought the listener, but it is motes of dust in the air.

They had this pretty interesting, actually highly interesting, ceremony, said the sargie-san, as part of the feast, on that night on that hill in Kria, where everybody lined up and their colonel, that was Colonel Parti, I knew him, a wise and handsome man, stripped to the waist and the men, one by one, passed before him and poured water on his head, half a cupful per man. The Colonel sat there and they poured water on his head, it had some kind of religious significance—they're Buddhists—the whole battalion, that's six hundred men more or less, passed in front of him and poured water on his head, it was a blessing or something, it was spring. Colonel Parti always used to say to me, his English wasn't too good but it was a hell of a lot better than my Thai which didn't exist, he always used to say "Sergeant, after the war I come to Big PX"—that's what they called America, the Big PX—"I come to Big PX and we play golf." I didn't even know they had golf in Thailand but he was supposed to be some kind of hot-shot golf player, I heard he'd been on their Olympic golf team at one time, funny to think of them having one but they were surprising and beautiful people, our houseboy Kim, we had these Krian houseboys who kept the tent policed up and cleaned your rifle and did the laundry, pretty near everybody in Kria is named Kim by the way, Kim had been with the division from the beginning and had gone to the Yalu with the division in '50 when the Chinese came in and kicked our asses all the way back to Seoul and Kim had been in a six-by-six firing some guy's M-1 all the way through the retreat which was a nightmare and therefore everybody was always very respectful of him even though he was only a houseboy . . . Anyhow, Kim had told me Colonel Parti was a high-ranked champion golfer. That's how I knew it.

He reminds me of poor people, thought the young man, poor people whom I hate.

The Chinese pulled all these night attacks, said the sergeant.

The babble of God-given senility, said the listener to his inner ear.

It was terrifying. There'd be these terrifying bugles, you'd sit up in your sleeping bag hearing the bugles which sounded like they were coming from every which way, all around you, everybody grabbing his weapon and running around like a chicken with his head cut off, DivArty would be putting down a barrage you could hear it but God knows what they thought they were firing at, your communications trenches would be full of insane Chinese, flares popping in the sky—

I consign you to history, said his hearer. I close, forever, the book.

Once, they wanted to send me to cooks-and-bakers school, said the sergeant who was wearing a dull-red bathrobe, but I told them no, I couldn't feature myself a cook, that's why I was in heavy weapons. This party at Thailand was the high point of that tour. I never before or since saw thirty-seven washtubs full of curry and I would like to go to that country someday and talk to those people some more, they were great people. Sutchai wanted to be Prime Minister of Thailand, that was his ambition, never made it to my knowledge but I keep looking for him in the newspaper, you never know. I was on this plane going from Atlanta to Brooke Medical Center in San Antonio, I had to have some scans, there were all these young troopers on the plane, they were all little girls. Looked to be about sixteen. They all had these OD turtlenecks with Class A uniforms if you can imagine, they were the sloppiest soldiers I ever did see, the all-volunteer Army I suppose I know I shouldn't criticize.

Go to cooks-and-bakers school, bake there, thought the young man. Bake a bathrobe of bread.

Thirty-seven damn washtubs, said the sergeant. If you can imagine.

Requiescat in pace.

They don't really have worm curry, said the sergeant. I just made that up to fool you.

Heroes

These guys, you know, if they don't know what's the story how can they . . .

—Exactly.

—So I inform myself. *U.S. News & World Report. Business Week. Scientific American.* I make it a point to steep myself in information.

—Yes.

—Otherwise your decisions have little meaning.

—Right.

—I mean they have *meaning*, because no decisions are meaningless in and of themselves, but they don't have *informed* meaning.

—Every citizen has a right.

—To what?

—To act. According to his lights.

—That's right.

—But his lights are not going to be that great. If he doesn't take the trouble. To find out what's the story.

—Take a candidate for something.

—Absolutely.

—There are all these candidates.

—More all the time. Hundreds.

—Now how does the ordinary man—

—The man in the street—

—*Really know.* Anything. About these birds.

—The media.

—Right. The media. That's how we know.

—Façades.

—One of these birds, maybe he calls you on the telephone.

—Right.

—You're flattered out of your skull, right?

—Right.

—You say, Oh my God, I'm talking to a goddamn *senator* or something.

—You're covered with awe.

—Or whoever it is. He's got your name on a little card, right? He's holding the card in his hand.

—Right.

—Say your name is George. He says, Well, George, very good to talk to you, what do you think about the economy? Or whatever it is.

—What do you say?

—You say, Well, Senator, it looks to me like it's a little shaky, the economy.

—You've informed yourself about the economy.

—Wait a minute, wait a minute, that's not the point. I mean it's *part* of the point but it's not the *whole* point.

—Right.

—So you tell him your opinion, it's a little shaky. And he agrees with you and everybody hangs up feeling good.

—Absolutely.

—But this is the point. Does he *act* on your opinion?

—No.

—Does he even remember your opinion?

—He reaches for the next card.

—He's got just a hell of a lot of cards there.

—Maybe two hundred or three hundred.

—And this is just one session on the phone.

—He must get tired of it.

—Bored out of his skull. But that's not the point. The point is, the whole thing is meaningless. You don't know one damn thing more about him than before.

—Well, sometimes you can tell something. From the voice.

—Or say you meet him in person.

—The candidate. He comes to where you work.

—He's out there in the parking lot slapping skin.

—He shakes your hand.

—Then he shakes the next guy's hand. What do you know after he's shook your hand?

—Zero. Zip.

—Let me give you a third situation.

—What?

—You're standing on the sidewalk and he passes in his motorcade. Waving and smiling. What do you learn? That he's got a suntan.

—What is the reality? What is the man behind the mask? You don't learn.

—Therefore we rely on the media. We are *forced* to rely on the media. The print media and the electronic media.

—Thank God we got the media.

—That's what we have. Those are our tools. To inform ourselves.

—Correct. One hundred percent.

—*But.* And this is the point. There are distortions in the media.

—They're only human, right?

—The media are not a clear glass through which we can see a thing clearly.

—We see it darkly.

—I'm not saying these are intentional. The ripples in the clear glass. But we have to take them into consideration.

—We are prone to error.

—Now, you take a press conference.

—The candidate. Or the President.

—*Sometimes they ask them the questions that they want to be asked.*

—Pre-prepared questions.

—I'm not saying all of them. I'm not even saying most of them. But it happens.

—I figured.

—Or he doesn't pick the one to answer that he knows is going to shoot him a toughie.

—He picks the guy behind him.

—I mean he's been in this business a long time. He knows

that one guy is going to ask him about the economy and one guy is going to ask him about nuclear holocaust and one guy is going to ask him about China. So he can predict—

—What type of question a particular guy is going to pop on him.

—That's right. Of course some of these babies, they're as smart as he is. In their own particular areas of expertise.

—They can throw him a curve.

—He's got egg on his face.

—Or maybe he just decides to tough it out and *answer* the damned question.

—But what we get, what the public gets—

—The tip of the iceberg.

—There's a lot more under the surface that we don't get.

—The whole iceberg.

—We're like blind men feeling the iceberg.

—So you have to have *many, many* sources. To get a picture.

—Both print and electronic.

—When we see a press conference on the tube, *it's not even the whole press conference.*

—It's the highlights.

—Just the highlights. Most of the time.

—Maybe there was something that you wanted to know that got cut out.

—Five will get you ten there's something touching your vital personal interests that got cut out.

—Absolutely.

—They don't do it on purpose. They're human beings.

—I know that. And without them we would have nothing.

—But sometimes bias creeps in.

—Very subtle bias that colors their objectivity.

—Maybe they're not even aware of it but it creeps in. The back door.

—Like you're looking at the newspaper and they have pictures of all the candidates. They're all out campaigning, different places. And maybe they run one guy's picture twice as big as another guy's picture.

—Why do they do that?

—Maybe it's more humanly interesting, the first guy's picture. But it's still bias.

—Maybe they ought to measure them, the pictures.

—Maybe they *like* the guy. Maybe they just like him as a human being. He's more likable. That creeps in.

—One-on-one, the guy's more likable.

—But to be fair you should print the guy's picture you don't like as big as this guy's.

—Or maybe the guy they don't like, they give him more scrutiny. His personal life. His campaign contributions.

—Or maybe you want a job if he gets elected. It's human.

—That's a low thought. That's a *terrible* thought.

—Well, be realistic.

—I don't think that happens. There aren't that many jobs that they would want.

—In the damn *government* there aren't that many jobs?

—That were better than their present jobs. I mean which would you rather be, some government flunky or a powerful figure in the media?

—The latter. Any day in the week.

—I mean what if you're the goddamn *Wall Street Journal*, for instance? A powerful voice. A Cassandra crying in the wilderness. They're scared of what you might reveal or might not reveal. You can hold your head up. You bow to no man, not even presidents or kings—

—You have to stand up if he comes into the room, that's the rule.

—Well, standing up is not bowing.

—The thing is to study their faces, these guys, these guys that are running, on the tube. *With the sound turned off.* So you can see.

—You can read their souls.

—You can't read their souls, you can get an idea, a glimpse. The human face is a dark pool with dark things swimming in it, under the surface. You look for a long time, using your whole experience of life. To discern what's with this guy.

—I mean he's trying to look good, the poor bastard, busting his ass to look good in every nook and cranny of America.

—What do we really know about him? What do we know?

—He wants the job.

—Enormous forces have pressured him into wanting the job. Destiny. Some people are bigger than you or I. A bigger destiny. It's tearing him apart, not to have the job, he sees some other guy's got the job and he says to himself, My destiny is as big as that guy's destiny—If I can just get these mothers to elect me.

—The rank and file. Us.

—If I can just get them to rally to my banner, the dummies.

—You think he thinks that?

—What's he going to think? It's tearing him apart, not to be elected.

—We're mere pawns. Clowns. Garbage.

—No. Without us, they can't realize their destinies. Can't even begin. No way.

—We make the judgments. Shrewd, informed judgments. Because we have informed ourselves.

—Taking into account the manifold distractions of a busy fruitful life.

—If it is fruitful.

—It's mostly going to be fruitful. If the individual makes the effort, knows what's the story—

—How did they know before they had the media?

—Vast crowds would assemble, from every hearth in the land. You had to be able to make a speech, just a dilly of a speech. "You shall not crucify mankind upon a cross of gold"—William Jennings Bryan. You had to be larger than life.

—The hearer of the speech knew—

—They were noble figures.

—They had to have a voice like an organ.

—The vast crowd swept by a fervor, as if by a wind.

—They were heroes and the individual loved them.

—Maybe misled. History sorts it out.

—Giant figures with voices like a whole church choir, plus the organ—

—A strange light coming from behind them, maybe it was only the sun . . .

Bishop

Bishop's standing outside his apartment building.

An oil truck double-parked, its hose coupled with the sidewalk, the green-uniformed driver reading a paperback called *Name Your Baby.*

Bishop's waiting for Cara.

The martini rule is not before quarter to twelve.

Eyes go out of focus. He blinks them back again.

He had a beer for breakfast, as usual, a Pilsner Urquell. Imported beer is now ninety-nine cents a bottle at his market.

The oil truck's pump shuts off with a click. The driver tosses his book into the cab and begins uncoupling.

Cara's not coming.

The painter John Frederick Peto made a living playing cornet in a camp meeting for the last twenty years of his life, according to Alfred Frankenstein.

Bishop goes back inside the building and climbs one flight of stairs to his apartment.

His bank has lost the alimony payment he cables twice a month to his second wife, in London. He switches on the FM, dialing past two classical stations to reach Fleetwood Mac.

Bishop's writing a biography of the nineteenth-century American painter William Michael Harnett. But today he can't make himself work.

Cara's been divorced, once.

At twenty minutes to twelve he makes himself a martini.

Hideous bouts of black anger in the evening. Then a word or a sentence in the tone she can't bear. The next morning he remembers nothing about it.

The artist Peto was discovered when, after his death, his pictures were exhibited with the faked signatures of William Michael Harnett, according to Alfred Frankenstein.

His second wife, working in London, recently fainted at her desk. The company doctor sent her home with something written on a slip of paper—a diagnosis. For two days she stared at the piece of paper, then called Bishop and read him the word: *lipothymia*. Bishop checked with the public library, called her again in London. "It means fainting," he said.

On the FM, a program called *How to Protect Against Radiation Through Good Nutrition*. He switches it off.

In the morning he remembers nothing of what had been said the previous night. But, coming into the kitchen and seeing her harsh, set face, he knows there's been a quarrel.

His eyes ache.

He's not fat.

She calls.

"I can't make it."

"I noticed."

"I'm sorry."

"How about tonight?"

"I'll have to see. I'll let you know."

"When?"

"As soon as I can."

"Can you give me a rough idea?"

"Before six."

Bishop types a letter to a university declining a speaking engagement.

He's been in the apartment for seventeen years.

His rent has just been raised forty-nine dollars a month.

Bishop is not in love with Cara, and she is certainly not in love with him. Still, they see each other rather often, sleep together rather often.

When he's given up on Cara, on a particular evening, he'll make a Scotch to take to bed with him. He lies on one elbow in the dark, smoking and sipping the Scotch.

He has a birthday in July, he'll be forty-nine.

Waking in the middle of the night he notices, again and

again and again, that he sleeps with one fist jammed against his jaw—forearm, upper arm, and jaw making a rigid defensive triangle.

Cara says: "Everyone's got good taste, it just doesn't mean that much."

She's in textiles, a designer.

He rarely goes to lunch with anyone now.

On the street, he greets a neighbor he's never even nodded to before, a young man who is, he's heard, a lawyer. Bishop remembers the young man as a tall thin child with evasive eyes.

He buys flowers, daffodils.

In front of his liquor store there are six midday drunks in a bunch, youngish men, perhaps late thirties. They're lurching about and harassing passersby, a couple of open half pints visible (but this liquor store, Bishop knows, doesn't sell half pints). One of them, a particularly clumsy man with a red face under red stubble, makes a grab for his paper-wrapped flowers, Bishop sidesteps him easily, so early in the day, where do they get the money?

He thinks of correspondences between himself and the drunks.

He's not in love with Cara but he admires her, especially her ability to survive the various men she takes up with from time to time, all of whom (he does not include himself) seem intent on tearing her down (she confides to him), on tearing her to pieces. . . .

When Bishop puts out a grease fire in the oven by slapping at it with a dish towel she criticizes his performance, even though he's burned his arm.

"You let too much oxygen in."

He's convinced that his grandfather and grandmother, who are dead, will come back to life one day.

Bishop's telephone bill is a nightmare of long-distance charges: Charleston, Beverly Hills, New Orleans, Charleston, Charleston, London, Norfolk, Boston, Beverly Hills, London—

When they make love in the darkness of his very small bedroom, with a bottle of indifferent California wine on the night table, she locks her hands in the small of his back, exerting astonishing pressure.

Gray in his beard, three wavy lines across his forehead.

"He would frequently paint one picture over another and occasionally a third picture over the second." Frankenstein, on Peto.

The flowers remain in their paper wrapping in the kitchen, on the butcher-block bar.

He watches the four o'clock movie, a film he's seen possibly forty times, Henry Fonda as Colonel Thursday dancing with Sergeant Major Ward Bond's wife at the Fort Apache noncommissioned officers' ball. . . .

Cara calls. Something's come up.

"Have a good evening."

"You too."

Bishop makes himself a Scotch, although it's only four-thirty and the rule about Scotch is not before five.

Robert Young says: "Sanka brand coffee *is* real coffee."

He remembers driving to his grandparents' ranch, the stack of saddles in a corner of the ranch house's big inner room, the rifles on pegs over the doors, sitting on the veranda at night and watching the headlights of cars coming down the steep hill across the river.

During a commercial he gets out the television schedule to see what he can expect of the evening.

6:00 (2, 4, 7, 31) News
(5) I Love Lucy
(9) Joker's Wild
(11) Sanford and Son
(13) As We See It
(21) Once Upon a Classic
(25) Mister Rogers

A good movie, *Edison*, with Spencer Tracy, at eight.

He could call his brother in Charleston.

He could call a friend in Beverly Hills.

He could make a couple of quarts of chili, freeze some of it.

Bishop stands in front of a mirror, wondering why his eyes hurt.

He could read some proofs that have been sitting on his desk for two weeks.

Another Scotch. *Fort Apache* is over.

He walks from the front of the apartment to the back, approving of the furniture, the rugs, the peeling paint.

Bishop puts on his down jacket and goes out to the market. At the meat counter a child in a stroller points at him and screams: *"Old man!"*

The child's mother giggles and says: "Don't take it personally, it's the beard."

What's easiest? Steak, outrageously priced, what he doesn't eat will be there for breakfast.

He picks out two bunches of scallions to chop up for his baked potato.

He looks around for something foolish to buy, to persuade himself he's on top of things.

His right arm still has three ugly red blotches from the episode of the grease fire.

Caviar is sixty-seven dollars for four ounces. But he doesn't like caviar.

Bishop once bought records, Poulenc to Bob Wills, but now does not.

Also, he formerly bought prints. He has a Jim Dine and a de Chirico and a Bellmer and a Richard Hamilton. It's been years since he's bought a print.

(Although he reads the art magazines religiously.)

A shrink once said to him: "Big Daddy, is that it?"

He's had wives, thick in emotional texture, with many lovely problems, his advice is generally good.

Diluted by caution perhaps.

When his grandfather and grandmother come back to life, Bishop sits with them on the veranda of the ranch house looking down to the river, they seem just the same and talk about the things they've always talked about. He walks with his grandfather over the terrain studded with caliche like half-buried skulls, a dirty white, past a salt lick and the windmill and then another salt lick, and his grandfather points out the place where his aunt had been knocked off her horse by a low-lying tree branch. His grandmother is busy burning toast and then scraping it (the way they like it), and is at the same time reading the newspaper, crying aloud "Ben!" and then reading him something about the Stewart girl, you remember who she is, getting married to that fellow who, you remember, got in all the trouble. . . .

With his Scotch in bed, Bishop summons up an image of felicity: walking in the water, the shallow river, at the edge of the ranch, looking for minnows in the water under the overhanging trees, skipping rocks across the river, intent . . .

Grandmother's House

—Grandmother's house? What? Landmark status? What? She's been eating? What? Strangers? She's been eating strangers? Sitting up in bed eating strangers? Hey? Pale, pink strangers? Zut! Lithium? What? They're giving her lithium? Hey? She's a what? Wolf? She's a wolf? Gad! Second opinion? Hey? She's a wolf. Well. Well, then. And Grandfather? What? Living with a stranger? Hey? A pale, pink stranger? Abominable! What's her name? What? What? Belle? Tush. BelleBelleBelleBelleBelle no I don't like it. Well if Grandmother's house has landmark status that means we can't build the brothel, right? Can't build the brothel, right? No brothel, right? Damn and damn and damn.

—Right.

—Well if we can't build the brothel we'd better go out and look for nymphs, right? Do a little nymphing? Get us to the glade?

—Right.

—Or we could steal a kid. A child. A kid. Steal one. Grab it and keep it. Raise it for our very own. Tickle it, light judicious tickling, swab it with rubbing alcohol against the itch, bundle it up and make it warm where previously it had been cold, right? Wham it when it is bad, right? Teach it to be afraid of the dark, the vast, unplumbed dark, the wet, glowing dark . . .

—Right.

—Shoulder the so-called real parents off the stage, those lunks. The former parents, those lunks, standing there uttering dull threats. Get off my case! and the like. Their connubial bliss in tatters, at this juncture. The bonds of gamomania but a spider-work, at this juncture. Send them notes from time to time, progress reports, little Luke has produced a tooth. Hey? Little Luke showing every sign of that sweetness of soul characteristic of breech presentations. Hey? Hey? Hey? Sing to it and pinch it, "Greensleeves" and "I'm an Old Cowhand." Teach it to figger and bottom-deal, get it a job cleaning telephone booths for the Telephone Company. And in our dotage—

—Our what?

—And in our senescence, it will take us by the hand, take you by your hand and me by my hand, and lead us gently over the hill to the poorhouse. Luke. Our kid.

—There's a naked woman in the next room.

—There's a what?

—Naked woman in the next room. On a couch. Blue velvet couch. Reclining. Flowers in her hair.

—I've seen one. In a magazine.

—Well they're all different, jackass. You can't just say *I've seen one.*

—Well I've got jury duty had an interesting case on Thursday guy'd got his car crushed in an elevator in a parking garage we gave him the Blue Book price, twenty-three hundred something Right?

—I mean you can't just say *I've seen one*. That's not enough.

—Well I'm tired, man, tired, I've been tired ever since I heard the truly dreadful news about Grandmother's house, a thing like that brings you down, man, brings you down and makes you tired, know what I mean?

—They're all different. That's what makes them so . . . luminous.

—But she's a stranger.

—But after you sleep with them they're less strange. Get downright familiar, laugh at you and pull your beard.

—I remember.

—Demystify themselves with repeated actions of a repetitive kind.

—Their moves. Their cold moves and their cozy moves.

—Want to go to the flicks, the flicks, the flicks—

—I saw one once, about this guy who jumped from place to

place swinging on a vine, and yodeled, yodeled and jumped from place to place swinging on a vine, ran around with an ape a small ape, wore these leather flaps with a knife stuck in the back flap—It was a good flick. I enjoyed it.

—I've seen a bunch. Six or seven thousand.

—Of course this is not to say that what has been demystified cannot be *re*mystified.

—How?

—Well you can take them on a trip or something. To a far place. Bergen.

—And then what?

—Seen with tall cool drinks in fetching costumes against the hot white sands or whatever they are partially remystified.

—No hot white sands in Bergen, man.

—Seen against the deep cool fjords with penguins in their hands they are partially remystified.

—No penguins in Bergen, man.

—Or some kind of new erotic behavior you can start biting them some people like that. People who've never been bitten much.

—How do you know how hard to bite?

—It's a skill.

—It is?

—As a matter of fact I saw another movie, movie about this guy who meets this woman and then they fall in love and then she leaves him and then he meets another woman.

—So what happens?

—He begins living with the second one. She's very nice.

—And then what?

—She leaves him.

—That's all?

—He is seen in a crowded street. Walking away from the camera. The figure becoming smaller and smaller and smaller until it's lost in the crowd. It was a very good movie. I liked it. I liked the one about the guy swinging on the vine a little better, maybe. Well. Want to steal a kid?

—I don't know.

—We could tickle the little sumbitch for a while and then, wham it.

—Feed it brownies and bubble gum.

—Tell it stories and great flaming lies.

—Gypsies steal kids.

—Right.

—Gypsies steal kids every day.

—It's well known.

—Hardly ever prosecuted.

—The wily gypsy. Hard to catch.

—What do they do with the kids I wonder?

—The wily, terrible gypsy. Gone today and gone tomorrow.

—What do they do with the kids I wonder?

—Train them in the gypsy arts. Wine-watering, horse-dyeing, the barbering of dreams.

—Gypsy airs scratched into the gypsy firelight.

—Deconstructing dreams like nobody's business. You want to know, go see the gypsy.

—Ever interfere with a gypsy?

—Well not an official gypsy. They only interfere with other gypsies. Now if you're talking about gypsy-*like*—

—Under the caravan. In the rank, sweet grass.

—Now if you're talking about a gypsy-*like* individual, wild and free and snarling and biting—

—I meant a real one.

—No.

—I'm sorry.

—But when I saw the great Gaudí church in Barcelona, the great Sagrada Familia, the great ghost of a cathedral or rather great skeleton of a cathedral, then did I realize especially after seeing also the plans and models in the basement for those portions of the great cathedral not yet built and perhaps never to be built, the plans under plastic on the walls of the basement and the models on sawhorses on the floor of the basement, the artisans in smocks still working on the beautifully inked plans and the white plaster models, and the workmen on the extant towers of the Templo Expiatorio de la Sagrada Familia in Barcelona, the workmen on and between the extant towers and walls of the Templo Expiatorio de la Sagrada Familia in Barcelona, the amazingly few workmen still working and still *to be* working for God knows how many decades hence, if the money can be got together, we left our contribution in a plastic box, the amazingly few but truly dedicated workmen still working under the burning inspiration of the sainted Catalan architect Antonio Gaudí, having seen all this I then realized what I had not realized before, what had escaped my notice these many years, that not only is less more but that *more is more too.* I swooned, under the impact of the ethical corollary.

—What is the ethical corollary?

—More.

—When you swooned, did you fall?

—I swooned *upward.* While staring from the ground at the great extant towers of the Sagrada Familia. Reverse vertigo.

—Gaudí however was laboring *in nomine Domini.* I do not see that the ethical corollary as you put it applies, privately.

—Puts an idea under greed.

—My life is a poor one. Relative to—

—I know that.

—*Your* life is a poor one. Not bad, but not replete.

—Well I can think can't I? I thought of the brothel, didn't I?

—Poorly that was a very poor idea this one guy thinks of a cathedral and you think of a brothel? Congratulations. You see what I mean?

—I say we steal one, a kid. Find a good-looking one and steal it, it's not the worst idea I ever heard.

—Not the worst idea.

—And when it grew to the age of sexual availability, we could tell it to wait.

—That's what I told her.

—That's what I told mine too. Told her to wait.

—You told her to wait?

—That's what I told her.

—How did she take it?

—She sat silently listening to me telling her to wait.

—I told mine to wait too.

—How did she react?
—She just sat there.
—You think she's waiting?
—How do I know?
—Some people think sixteen.
—Biologically of course it's a bitch. For them.
—I never understood why things were so . . . out of phase. The biological with the cultural.
—Cultural-psychological.
—Odd to be in that position. Telling someone to wait.
—Has she got someone in mind?
—There's this guy he has a Honda.
—You don't let her . . . Those things can be, like *dangerous*, man.
—He gave her a helmet.
—You mean she's running around town on the back of this guy's Honda clutching him tightly around the stomach and her chest rubbing into his back muscles? At fourteen?
—Well what can I do?
—Tell her to wait?
—Well at least it's not a Harley.
—What's his name?
—Juan.
—Oh.
—How 'bout yours?
—Mine's seeing various candidates. Various candidates have presented themselves. The leader of the pack, you might say, is this Claude.
—His name is Claude?
—Well that's not his fault.
—There is one thing, one small point, on which I think we may congratulate ourselves. We gave them plain names.
—Plain, but beautiful.
—What did I see the other day? Jahne. J-a-h-n-e.
—You're kidding.
—Nope. J-a-h-n-e.
—Amazing.
—Yes. So what's with this Claude?

—He's seventeen.
—He's seventeen?
—Yep.
—Little old for fourteen don't you think?
—What can I do?
—Seventeen is a wild age.
—Seventeen is anarchy.
—I was atrocious when I was seventeen. Absolutely atrocious.
—Likewise.
—Drunk driving was the least of it.
—When you think about it now you turn pale.
—And *I* wasn't crazy, some of those guys they were flat crazy.
—I knew a few.
—I mean they thought blood on the saddle was the *plan,* man.
—Don't remind me.
—Talk about behavior.
—Yes.
—Boy this was behavior.
—Yes.
—You can tell them to wait but what do you tell them after you tell them to wait?
—Tell them to keep their ass the hell out of Grandmother's house.
—Not very likely.
—Not very likely.
—Well at least we gave them plain names.
—Plain, but beautiful.
—Steal a kid. Begin all over again.
—Tear it up, tear it up, tear it up.
—Or get us to the glade.
—The heat of the glade.
—The damned nymphs have to be somewhere.
—Beautiful necks for biting.
—Soft anthropological bites.

—Bosomed nymphs, nymphs with a stripe of hair . . .

—Polka nymphs, red-eyed nymphs, drudge nymphs, bombous nymphs . . .

—Nymphs in warmup suits, Mohawks, clown nymphs . . .

—The splendid language of their hair . . .